AN *UN*WILLING SPY

AN *UN*WILLING SPY

A COLD WAR NOVEL SET AT **THE UNITED NATIONS**

LORAINE SIEVERS

Allardt Press

An UNwilling Spy. Copyright © 2022 by Loraine Sievers. All rights reserved. Printed in the United States of America. No part of this book may be used or reproduced in any manner whatsoever without written permission except in the case of brief quotations embodied in critical articles and reviews. For information address Allardt Press, 222 Good Hill Road, Weston, CT 06883.

FIRST EDITION

Designed by Spiro Books

Library of Congress Cataloging-in-Publications Data has been applied for.

ISBN 979-8-9855719-0-5 (hardcover)
ISBN 979-8-9855719-1-2 (international edition)
ISBN 979-8-9855719-2-9 (paperback)
ISBN 979-8-9855719-3-6 (ebook)

First published in 2022

For Magda,
who through her courage won our respect,
and through her sweetness won our love

PREFACE AND ACKNOWLEDGEMENTS

I joined the United Nations in 1974, the year in which I have set this novel. Compared to today, the organization was rougher around the edges and, to be honest, a much more fun place to work. My early years there were full of colorful characters and dramatic events. And while the plot of this book is entirely fictional, I have woven in some real occurrences – such as the staff strike or the plane circling the UN premises – and tried to recreate the atmosphere of the Cold War within the organization at that time. The United Nations, for its staff, has always been a place of great rewards and great frustrations. I know it has had a profound effect on me, as I think it has had on everyone who has worked there.

Some readers have felt that the young women in this book too readily accept an inferior status at work. So here I would wish to clarify that the 1970s were far more constraining for women and minorities than today. For example, it was not until 1974 that women were granted the right to obtain credit cards separately from their husbands. And it took until 1977 for US courts to recognize sexual harassment in the workplace.

I wish to extend my heartfelt appreciation to two groups of people – those who made my time at the UN during the 1970s so noteworthy, and those who helped with the preparation of this manuscript.

Among the former, I must mention with deep affection Vivian Bernstein, Dulcie Bull, Hector Fernandez, Audrey Gottlieb, Spyridon Granitsas, Gerhard Haensel, Margaret Logan, Jennifer Love, Ozdinç Mustafa, Carmen Ozomyk, Gloria Perez, Hubert Pinçon, Paula Refolo, Margaret Riddle, Joyce Rosenblum, Hugo Rocha, Samir Sanbar, Donna Sliby, Ann Terry, Petr Vokn, George Yacoub and Angela Zubrzycki.

I wish also to warmly thank those who gave me some key ideas for scenes in the book, including Takeshi Akahori, Matt Alkaitis, Sam Alkaitis, Linda Hooper, Jun Husabe, Hilding Lundkvist, Mahesh Reddy and my friends at the Weston Post Office.

It's fair to say that my early drafts of this manuscript were awful. That it has become vastly improved (though still not perfect) is owing to Jessica Speart, my highly gifted, inspiring, patient and much loved instructor at the Westport Writers Workshop, and my fellow classmates: Jo Bolles, Judy Fisher, Johanna Garvey, Ellen Grogan, Eric Kurzenberger, Tom Plummer and Judi Robins. I can't thank them enough for their insightful comments, brainstorming and encouragement. I am also indebted to Suzanne Hoover, who rightly has been called "a master teacher of fiction writing craft", for her perceptive review of the manuscript.

In addition, I very much want to thank my special friends who read earlier versions of the manuscript and offered invaluable, and sometimes humorous, feedback: Takeshi Akahori, Marilyn Alfred, Angel Angelov, Nan Bauroth, Deniz Dalay, Clara Dinkelbach, Ilia Du Buisson, Judye Dubelman, Carla Foster, Aida Hodžić, Paul Hoeffel, Bridget Holmes, Cheryl Ridderhoff, Gail Roussey, Debbie Solomon, Joanne Szamreta and Dolores Tufariello.

My gratitude also goes to the inimitable Richard Gowan, whose generous (and witty) inclusion of this book in his "Summer Reading List for Exhausted Multilateralists" (*World Politics Review*, July 12, 2022) engendered more interest than I ever could have hoped.

For bringing the book to life, I truly worked with an "A Team". I can't adequately express my gratitude to Deena So'Oteh for her beautiful and evocative cover illustrations and to Christina Rycz for her compelling cover design, as well as to Jess Erickson of Spiro Books for his masterly design of the book interior, and Diane Wortman for her comprehensive proofreading.

Loraine Sievers

CONTENTS

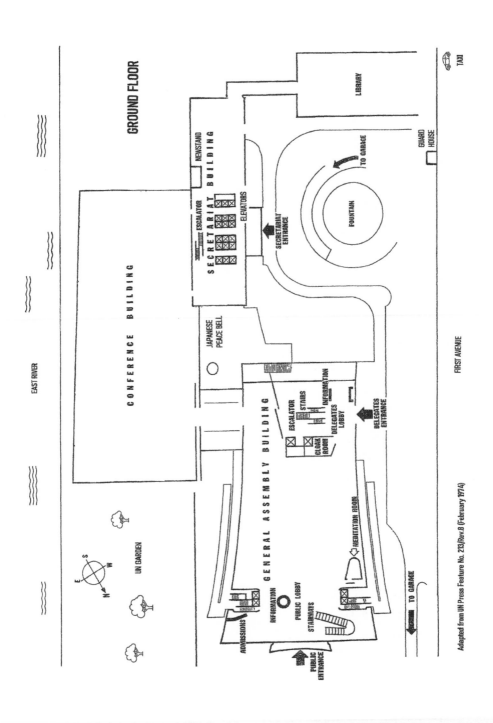

GROUND FLOOR

EAST RIVER

CONFERENCE BUILDING

SECRETARIAT BUILDING

GENERAL ASSEMBLY BUILDING

NEWSSTAND

ESCALATOR

ELEVATORS

SECRETARIAT ENTRANCE

JAPANESE PEACE BELL

ESCALATOR

STAIRS

INFORMATION

CLOAK ROOM

DELEGATES LOBBY

DELEGATES ENTRANCE

FOUNTAIN

TO GARAGE

GUARD HOUSE

LIBRARY

TAXI

FIRST AVENUE

UN GARDEN

N E S W

ADMISSIONS

INFORMATION

PUBLIC LOBBY

STAIRWAYS

MEDITATION ROOM

PUBLIC ENTRANCE

TO GARAGE

Adapted from UN Press Feature No. 213/Rev.8 (February 1974)

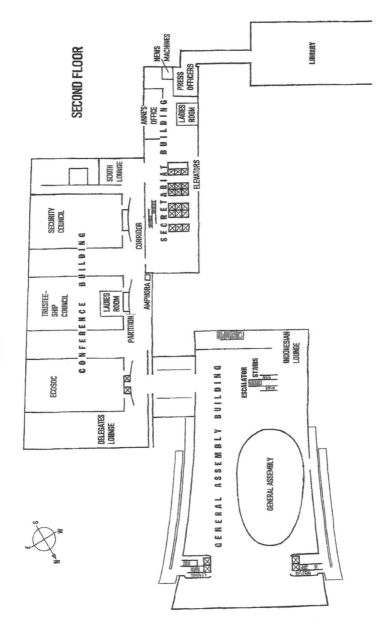

SECOND FLOOR

EAST RIVER

SECRETARIAT BUILDING

CONFERENCE BUILDING

GENERAL ASSEMBLY BUILDING

ECOSOC

DELEGATES LOUNGE

TRUSTEE-SHIP COUNCIL

LADIES ROOM

PARTITION

SECURITY COUNCIL

CORRIDOR

AMPHORA

SOUTH LOUNGE

ANNE'S OFFICE

NEWS MACHINES

PRESS OFFICERS

LADIES ROOM

ELEVATORS

LIBRARY

GENERAL ASSEMBLY

ESCALATOR

STAIRS

INDONESIAN LOUNGE

N E S W

FIRST AVENUE

Adapted from UN Press Feature No. 213/Rev.8 (February 1974)

AN *UN*WILLING SPY

OUT OF NOWHERE

Anne stepped gingerly down the escalator, frozen in place at that late hour. On the ground floor, she strode across the checkered black and white terrazzo of the United Nations lobby, her heels echoing loudly through the vast, empty space.

As she approached the security guard, she tried to ignore the way he was looking her up and down. She picked up a pen at the podium to sign out in the logbook.

"You worked late again tonight," he said, lifting an eyebrow. "Not good for a girl's social life."

Anne gave him her best eye roll.

The guard lifted his hands and grinned. "Just trying to be friendly. I'll get you a cab."

New York in 1974 was so crime-ridden that some UN staff felt safer serving in war zones than at Headquarters. With no shops or restaurants on that stretch of First Avenue, the neighborhood after hours was deserted and bleak. More than one knifing had occurred in the vicinity. Anne was glad the UN had responded to its employees' fears by installing a blinking "Taxi" sign at the street to flag down cabs driving uptown at night.

As she exited the building through the revolving door, Anne was hit by the mugginess of a late New York summer evening. The hot, humid air was too heavy to be lifted by the strong wind blowing off the East River. Still, it was a relief to be outside after a long day in the office.

Traversing the traffic circle, Anne edged closer to the circular pool to catch refreshing drops of water scattering from its fountain. She walked a few more steps, and then turned to take in the grandeur of the massive glass building rising behind her against the dark sky. After working for the UN for almost a year, she still felt a rush of excitement at being part of this preeminent world organization.

Passing through the street gate, Anne waved goodnight to the security officer in the guard house. With the "Taxi" sign blinking overhead, she saw a cab was already approaching. She stepped off the curb to meet it.

Anne was gazing absentmindedly across the street when she heard the security officer shout. Looking back at the guard house, she saw him wave frantically as he yelled, "Watch out, watch out!"

Whirling back around to find out what was alarming him, Anne saw the taxi accelerating toward her.

She jumped back toward the sidewalk, but the taxi kept heading straight at her. Out of the corner of her eye, she saw the guard slam aside the glass door of his booth and start running in her direction. The taxi was now so close its motor drowned out his shouts.

She tried to move further back but stumbled in her panic. Still the taxi hurtled toward her. Then everything went black.

JUST A FEW QUESTIONS

"Detective James Royce, New York Police Department."

"Bob Patterson, FBI. We have just a few questions to ask you."

Anne's head throbbed and all sound seemed amplified. The light over her closed eyes felt harsh. Her eyelids were swollen and she didn't even attempt to open them. As one-by-one she became aware of her bones, she felt waves of pain.

"Later," she managed in a slur. "Come back … later."

"We wish we could," the first voice said, "but I'm afraid some of our questions can't wait."

She heard a woman say, "I'll help you sit up."

"No-oh," Anne protested. But strong arms were already pulling her gently, yet firmly, to a sitting position.

The man resumed, "Miss Thomas, you're an American. We know you joined the UN last year. Can you tell us a little about what you do there?"

She tried to slip back down, but the nurse's hands restrained her. "Go away," she murmured.

"Miss Thomas, these questions are necessary," said the other man.

Anne sighed. If she answered, maybe they'd finish quickly and she could go back to sleep. Being awake was too painful.

"I'm a 'Tri-lingual Clerk-Typist'," she began, enunciating each word carefully. "I type. I file. I xerox. My boss puts his dull pencils in his outbox for me to sharpen." It wasn't the kind of job Anne had aspired to do when she was in college. But, it was almost the only type of position available to women at the UN who weren't placed there by their governments.

"Miss Thomas, we know you're enrolled in the UN's staff language program, taking Russian. Tell us about that."

Anne struggled to open her eyes. Slowly focusing, she saw that hers was the only bed in the room. The lights, reflecting off the white walls, were too bright. She closed her eyes. "The classes are free for UN staff. I worked as a secretary for a Russian psychiatrist when I did a year of law school. I heard her speak the language and I liked how it sounded, and the strange alphabet. And I wanted to read Pushkin in the original. Now please go away."

"Miss Thomas, does your boss handle any sensitive dossiers that might be of interest to either side in the Cold War? Has he, or anyone else, confided in you?"

The questions were making less and less sense. Anne forced herself to open her eyes again. After blinking several times, her blurred vision slowly began to clear. The shapes of two men, sitting closer to her bed than she'd realized, began to emerge into view like two ships breaking through seaside fog.

One man, with light blond hair, appeared to Anne to be in his thirties. He had well-defined features, a strong jaw and erect posture. What most captured Anne's attention were his alert cobalt blue eyes, which locked onto hers and remained there.

Uncomfortable under his penetrating stare, Anne shifted her gaze to the other man. The appearance of the two couldn't have been more different. While the first wore an impeccably pressed blue shirt, the man sitting to his right was dressed in rumpled clothes that looked as though they'd been scavenged from a thrift shop. He sat in a slouch which emphasized his slight paunch, and it was likely he'd cut his disorderly brown hair himself. His features were ordinary and indistinct. A day's stubble cradled his chin and made it hard to determine his age, but Anne guessed he was in his late forties.

But the eyes of the two men most told Anne how unlike they were. The second man's eyes were weary and focused inward, as though he'd seen too much of the world and no longer wanted to look at anything in it.

The first man said gently, "Miss Thomas, we're trying to help you." Then he repeated his question. "Does your boss handle any sensitive dossiers?"

Turning toward him, Anne was surprised to see an NYPD badge on his shirt pocket. He really was a policeman. And she hadn't been cooperating.

Despite the discomfort it caused her, she sat up a little straighter and tried to concentrate on his question. "Our Section distributes materials to the worldwide UN Information Centres and receives information back from them, but all of it's public. If my boss handles other documents, I wouldn't know about it."

The older man roused himself and brought his jaded eyes to rest on Anne's face. "Are you aware of any policy disagreements in your department, or any factions?"

Anne's forehead compressed as she tried to focus her thoughts. While she did, the pain at the back of her head became even more intense and her vision blurred again. The image of the taxi hurtling toward her flashed back and she flinched. "I had an accident," she said softly, and started to cry.

The two men exchanged a glance and then shrugged. "Okay, Miss Thomas," the detective said. "We'll let you rest now."

She slid back down onto the bed, and this time no one stopped her. The nurse said, "I'll give her something to help her go back to sleep."

Anne felt the prick of a needle in her arm. At the same time, she heard the men push back in their chairs and start walking to the door.

Just as the drug was beginning to make her drowsy, Anne lifted her head slightly off the pillow. She whispered, "I forgot…to tell you…"

The men paused in the doorway.

"For ten months…I was in Cyprus…with the UN Peacekeeping Force…I got back last month."

They turned toward the bed, but Anne's head had already dropped onto the pillow and her breath had deepened. "I'm sorry," the nurse told them. "She'll be out now for at least six hours."

EVENTS OF THE DAY

Despite the medication, Anne slept fitfully that night. The day's events leading up to the taxi accident played groggily through her mind. She saw herself back in the office late that evening, when finally she'd cleared her desk of all the work that couldn't wait until the next day. She had tugged the grey plastic cover over her typewriter, pushed back in her rolling chair, and gathered up her things. She moved to the door, took one last look around the grey office to see that everything was in order, and turned out the lights.

The darkened hallway was completely still – an extreme contrast to the commotion earlier in the day, when throngs of people, speaking a babble of languages, had streamed through the area.

One of the responsibilities of Anne's office was to tend the bulky, cacophonous teletype machines which ceaselessly printed out, on long strips of chemicalized paper, news from all over the world. There was one machine each for *Reuters*, *Agence France-Presse*, *Deutsche Presse-Agentur* and *UPI*. Diplomats, UN staff and representatives of liberation movements crowded the hallway outside the small room housing the machines. Throughout the day, they waited for Anne, or one of her officemates, to hang the paper strips from hooks high on the wall. Then they jostled with each other to read the breaking news, essential to staying well-informed, before rushing off to tell their colleagues and friends.

That evening, as Anne shut the office door, she couldn't help smiling at the little girl in the photo taped there. Anne had cut it from a *National Geographic* magazine because she'd gotten such a lift from the girl's beaming face and the Russian words printed at the top: *Dobro pozhalovat* – Welcome.

This was the second picture of the little girl that Anne had taped to the door. When she arrived at work one morning, she found the first photo torn to shreds and left in her otherwise empty wastebasket, clearly the sign of someone's displeasure. Who would do such a thing? The Polish refugee women who cleaned the area at night? Having escaped from a life under communism, maybe they'd expressed their resentment over Soviet domination of their homeland by tearing down a sign written in Russian. But couldn't Anne post a cheerful greeting of "Welcome" without straying into the division of the world into two antagonistic blocs?

She knew the answer to that question. The Cold War was nowhere more present than at the United Nations, as Anne had quickly discovered upon joining it in 1973. She did her work, rode the elevators, ate in the staff cafeteria, attended official meetings, walked in the UN Garden, and even used the restrooms under the Cold War's constant shadow.

Having studied international relations, Anne was well aware there was an intense rivalry between the United States and the Soviet Union. But after watching the untruths told over the war in Vietnam, she'd come to believe her government was exaggerating the seriousness of the Cold War so as to foster loyalty among Americans.

That's not what she thought now. During her first weeks at the UN, Anne couldn't help noticing the furtive glances, the whispered conversations, the seemingly innocent questions which had to be answered cautiously, and the doubts of some UN staff about the true loyalties of other colleagues.

Anne was coming to understand the basis for her government's fears. East Europeans had poured into New York City to work for the UN. How many of them were communist spies who might take advantage of being there to cultivate contacts among Westerners? It would be all too easy to casually exchange sensitive information during a normal workday without arousing suspicion. But she was also pretty sure the NATO countries had their own agents within the organization, to gather intelligence and try to recruit informants.

Anne had seen enough to put her on edge. But she'd also begun to recognize that Cold War tensions at the UN didn't seem to press in on everyone equally. Among staff members from regions outside the East or West, some seemed almost surreally oblivious to the intrigues around them. That included Anne's new coworkers, Juanita and Benedetta.

The evening of the accident, Anne had been reflecting on all this as she stepped outside into the muggy night air. Thinking of the Cold War always made her uneasy, and she'd been more eager than usual to get into a cab instead of walking alone in the dark up First Avenue. But that evening she'd approached the sidewalk unaware that this time, calling a taxi would not keep her safe.

A BILLBOARD WARNING

Several days later, Anne was drifting off to sleep when she heard the door open slightly and felt cool air enter her room from the corridor. A fussy middle-aged woman's voice said, "Sir, wait here while I see if she's awake. And presentable."

Anne was certain she wasn't presentable. Not after being in the hospital for an indeterminate amount of time. Days? Weeks? She had no idea. She knew she had a head wound, internal bleeding, and quite a few stitches, but she didn't know if the doctors were telling her everything. What she was sure of was that she must look pretty bad, because the whole time the nurses had kept the mirror covered.

Her head still throbbed, and the slightest movement on the uncomfortable hospital mattress made every bone in her body ache. The last thing she wanted was a visitor.

At the sound of the approach of soft-soled shoes, Anne's eyelids fluttered open. She smelled Prell shampoo as the nurse bent over her and said, "Hon, that nice policeman is back to see you."

What nice policeman? Anne must have looked blank because the nurse added, "You know, the tall young man who came the first night, with the older fellow."

Anne shook her head as much as the pain would allow. "I don't remember either of them."

"Well, anyway, he's here to see you. Before I have him come in, let's get you sitting up. And why don't you smooth your hair a bit. We don't want him thinking our patients aren't well cared for, now do we?"

Anne gritted her teeth as the tilting mattress painfully brought her upright. She grudgingly ran her fingers through her hair while the nurse walked back to the door and opened it wide. An attractive man, probably in his early thirties, walked into the room.

"Hello, Miss Thomas. I don't know if you remember me. Detective Royce, NYPD." His voice was masculine and confident. "I'm glad to see you looking on the mend."

Anne took in his light blond hair, symmetrical features, and intense cobalt blue eyes. He did seem vaguely familiar.

Pointing to the metal chair the nurse had placed beside Anne's bed, he asked, "May I?"

"Sure."

"You were very groggy the evening Agent Patterson and I came to interview you, so we cut our visit short. That's why I've come back today." He moved the chair closer to the bed.

"What did I tell you last time?"

His laugh was pleasant. "Not much."

"What would you like to know?"

He took a small green notebook out of his shirt pocket. For a moment he fingered the two pens there and then pulled out the thinner one. "What do you recall of the taxi accident?"

"It all happened so fast. While the cab was approaching, I stepped off the curb to meet it. Then the guard behind me shouted. I turned to find out why. He was pointing beyond me. I spun back around, and that's when I saw the taxi heading straight for me." She shuddered. "That's all I remember."

"How far away was the taxi when you realized it was likely to hit you?"

"I really don't know. Like I said, it happened so fast."

"Did you get a look at the cabby's face? See anything that would help you recognize him, or the taxi?"

"It was just a big yellow blur, bearing down on me. At night, it's very dark outside the UN."

"True. Well, was anyone else waiting for a cab then?"

"No, just me." He was definitely handsome, but something about him was perplexing Anne, something she couldn't quite read.

Royce made a note and then asked, "How well do you know the guard who was on duty that evening?"

There was a perfunctory knock at the door and a thin woman entered with a plate under a stainless cover. She pulled out Anne's tray table and set down the plate. "Here's your lunch, sweetheart. And you should eat a little more than you did yesterday."

As soon as the woman left, Anne gingerly lifted the cover, releasing the odor of overcooked string beans and tired meat loaf. She made a face and quickly put back the cover.

Wrinkling his nose, Royce said, "No wonder you didn't eat much yesterday. Where were we? Oh yeah, I was asking about the guard."

"I've seen him off and on since I got back from Cyprus about a month ago."

Royce made another note. "Was it unusual for you to be leaving work that late?"

Maybe it was partly because of the pain Anne was in, but Royce's probing was starting to rattle her. She tried to keep the uneasiness out of her voice as she answered. "Every third day I work the evening shift in my office, and we usually finish around 9:00."

Royce scribbled something and then looked at her attentively. "So, Miss Thomas, why are you there?"

"In the Department of Public Information? That's where there was an opening when I applied."

"No, why are you at the UN? What drew you there?"

Anne's discomfort was growing. This felt like a re-run of when the FBI originally was interviewing her for clearance to work at the UN. They made it sound like just the idea of getting a job there was suspicious.

Royce seemed to sense her hesitancy. His tone became friendlier. "Well, do you remember how you first heard about the United Nations?"

Anne smiled despite her unease. "My introduction to the UN wasn't very favorable. I was a kid in the back seat of my grandma's car when we passed a billboard saying 'U.S. OUT OF U.N.' I asked her what it meant. She said the United Nations was an international government trying to take over the world and deprive the United States of its power."

Royce grinned. "If that's how you first heard about the organization, I'm surprised you ever set foot in the building. What does your grandma think of you working there now?"

A shadow came over Anne's face. "She died while I was in college."

"I'm sorry to hear that." He paused. "What does the rest of your family think?"

Anne covered her eyes with her palms. "You know, I'm starting to feel really tired. Could we finish up another day?"

Royce closed his notebook. "This will be sufficient, Miss Thomas. What I was looking for was a general picture. I think I got what I needed."

Anne's shoulders softened with relief. Maybe it wasn't his questions that had been disconcerting. Maybe it was having an attractive man sit close to her bed and look at her so intently, with no clue as to what he was thinking.

Royce carefully returned the pen and notebook to his shirt pocket and stood up. When he reached the doorway, he turned and said, "I hope you'll continue to recover quickly."

Those eyes. Those unsettling cobalt blue eyes.

5

A NEW WORRY

Anne was sitting, with her knees up, on the hospital bed trying to do the *New York Times* crossword puzzle. That's how bored she was. But she was getting nowhere. "Absurdly exaggerated – five letters." No idea. "Unobtrusive invader – 11 letters." Even worse.

She was relieved to hear a knock at the door. "Come in."

Detective Royce stood in the doorway, holding a white plastic shopping bag. "Hi there. I was visiting someone in this wing, and thought I'd drop by to see how you're doing. Am I intruding?"

He was the last person Anne expected to see. Startled, she tried to compose herself. She tossed aside the *Times* and said, "You're not disturbing me. On the contrary, you've just saved me from crossword puzzle meltdown."

Royce laughed and crossed the room. "May I sit down?"

"Of course." Anne's voice was cordial, but she was looking at him warily. Maybe he was dissatisfied with some of her earlier answers. She couldn't help asking, "Did I leave something out when you were here last week?"

"No, no, nothing like that. As I said, I was visiting a friend and passed by your door." He lifted the plastic bag. "I brought him some Tandoori takeout, but he wasn't hungry. I remember the awful meal they gave you when I was here. Would you prefer this?"

Anne took the bag and opened it. Inhaling deeply, she said, "Mmmm, it smells delicious. I'm definitely not turning down this offer. Thank you." She carefully placed the bag on her tray table.

Royce asked, "So how are you feeling? You're looking much better."

"Thank you, that's encouraging to hear. I'm doing okay." As she spoke, she self-consciously smoothed her hair.

"Good." He tilted back casually in the chair. "Last time, I got enough information about the accident. But afterwards, I started thinking about your having been in Cyprus. For my own curiosity, wasn't that kind of an unusual assignment?"

It was flattering that he'd been thinking about her. She answered, "Yes, it was unusual. I'd been hired by the UN to work in New York, but after only a few days on the job, my boss was reassigned to be Spokesman for the Peacekeeping Force in Cyprus. He knew from my resume that I'd written a college thesis about UN mediation there. With that background, he thought I could be very helpful to him as his secretary. So off I went."

"I'm impressed. And envious. I'd love to spend time on a Mediterranean island. I'll bet you really enjoyed it."

"I did. The work was fascinating. But I was especially happy there because of all the history and art." New enthusiasm came into her voice. "Most people know Greeks and Turks live on Cyprus now, but before, there were many other civilizations that left ruins and art there."

"So you like art. Do you go to the museums here?"

"Yes, a lot. I love everything here in the city – Broadway, off-Broadway, Lincoln Center, concerts in Central Park, the used bookstores. All of it! But especially the museums, and ballet."

"Then we have something in common. That list just about describes my favorite things to do in New York." Royce grinned. "Except the ballet."

Her eyebrows lifted. "Really?"

"Are you thinking a cop should spend his free time in bars or at Knicks games? We weren't rich growing up, but our parents made sure we listened to good music at home and took full advantage of live performances and museums. That was smart of them. It kept my brothers and me out of trouble when we were teenagers." He smiled and then asked, "What draws you to ballet?

"I dance myself," she answered shyly. "That is, I take classes once a week upstairs at the UN, and some evenings at a studio near Lincoln Center. And I go to American Ballet Theatre a lot."

They were interrupted by a knock at the door. It opened to a young woman, whose face quickly broke into a broad smile. "Anne, you're looking better and better every day."

Anne smiled back and said, "Juanita, let me introduce you to Detective Royce. Detective, Juanita is my colleague from work."

Juanita, Anne's fellow secretary, was Guatemalan. At 23, she was a year younger than Anne, yet she'd directed the work of their Section for several months until a new boss was appointed. Her dark wavy hair, which she wore short, softly framed her even features. Her chocolate eyes were lively, and Anne had rarely seen her without a smile, often a slightly mischievous one.

Royce rose and walked over to Juanita, extending his hand. "Pleased to meet you."

Juanita looked from him to Anne, and back at him. "I can come another day," she said.

"No, it's fine," Royce responded. "I've taken up enough of Anne's time." He put his hand on the doorknob. "Enjoy your time together, girls. But Juanita, don't stay too long. I'm sure Anne still needs rest."

As he was leaving, he said to Anne, "I'll look for you the next time I'm at Lincoln Center."

Juanita's dark eyes shone with delight. As soon as Royce was gone, she said breathlessly, "Oh, Anne, I think he likes you."

Anne felt color come to her cheeks. "I doubt that. I'm sure my face still looks awful."

Juanita only smiled knowingly. Then shaking her head, she added, "But *querida*, it's a true miracle you came through this accident as well as you did, with no broken bones. You must thank God and be more grateful."

Anne nodded. "You're right, Juanita. The nurse told me that after the doctors saw the accident report, they also called it a miracle."

"And don't worry, you'll be back with us before you know it. In the meantime, everyone is thinking of you. Here." Juanita pulled a red plaid box out of her tote bag.

"Walkers shortbread cookies!" Anne exclaimed.

"They're from Benedetta. She's still on vacation, but she asked me to give them to you as a get-well gift. She knows how much you like them." Benedetta, an Italian brunette with a madonna's luminous face, was the third member of their secretarial trio.

"That's so nice of her," Anne said. "Please tell her a big thank-you from me."

"I will. But I won't stay any longer today, since you've already had a visit. I'll come back tomorrow." Juanita was just standing up when she sat down again. "Oh, I almost forgot. We have a new Professional working in our office." She leaned forward to emphasize her next words. "He's a German. An *East* German."

Anne was instantly alert. "There haven't been any East Germans in the UN Secretariat up to now. I wonder why they decided to place him in our Section."

"His name is Jürgen Bieler and he's very courtly. He arrived with lovely presents for us secretaries, including you. And he says how much he's looking forward to meeting you when you return."

Anne felt her body tense. Her friend Peggy, from Russian class, had told her that out of all the East European communists, East German spies worked most closely with the Soviet KGB. If that was true, it wouldn't be a problem for Juanita or Benedetta. Guatemala and Italy weren't players in the Cold War. But Anne feared it would be uncomfortable, even risky, for her as an American. As far as she knew, no East Europeans came to the UN without a commitment to work for their government's secret service. Cautiously she asked, "What's he like?"

"It's too soon to tell, but I think our boss is wary of him. Señor Duarte isn't giving him any real work to do."

A nurse stepped to the door. "I'm sorry, visiting hours are over."

Juanita gave Anne a warm but careful hug. Then with a teasing smile, she said, "I want you to know all the men are asking when you'll be back."

Anne looked at Juanita with mock exasperation and then waved as she slipped out of the room.

After the door closed, Anne frowned. An East German spy. In her office. How closely would he watch her? Would he try to recruit her? If she inadvertently witnessed him doing something out of line, what might he do to silence her?

Up to now, she'd been eager to get back to work. Juanita's news had put an abrupt end to that. Now she was full of misgivings about what awaited her there.

To distract herself, she reached for the crossword puzzle and looked again at the word she'd been stuck at when Royce walked in. "Unobtrusive invader – 11 letters."

Then the word came to her. With a sense of foreboding, she wrote, "I-N-F-I-L-T-R-A-T-O-R".

6

WHAT'S TO BE DONE?

Anne was sitting across from Detective Royce and Agent Patterson at a formica table in the hospital cafeteria. Royce's crisp blue shirt highlighted the color of his eyes. Anne found herself hoping she looked prettier now that she was wearing a forest green blouse instead of the washed-out hospital gowns he'd seen her in before.

As if reading her thoughts, he said, "You're a completely different girl from the one I first saw, swollen and pale, three weeks ago. Pink cheeks, bright eyes, lovely smile. Have they said when they're going to discharge you?"

Anne tried not to blush at his compliment. "I think today is sort of a test run. This is the first time they've let me leave my room and eat in the cafeteria. I'm hoping that if you gentlemen give the doctors a good report, they'll let me go home tomorrow."

Patterson's face clouded. "That might be a little soon. First we want to be sure that everything will be fine before you go back to your apartment, especially since you live alone."

The tone of his voice made Anne look at him quizzically. She asked hesitantly, "Is there something you and Detective Royce haven't told me?" Then she became very still. "You don't think it was an accident," she breathed out slowly.

How could she have been so obtuse? Distracted by Royce's presence during his bedside visits, she'd never considered why he was asking so many questions about what happened that night.

Royce said gently, "Anne, we have no concrete evidence. But to be completely honest, we can't exclude that the taxi struck you deliberately."

"But why?"

"That's what we've been trying to find out," Patterson answered. "There could be any number of connections. It could be because someone you work with has something to hide, or because of your tour of duty in Cyprus. You're studying Russian. Maybe someone's afraid you overheard something. Or perhaps you were mistaken for someone else." He looked off in the distance. "At this point, we simply don't know."

Anne stared down at her half-finished soup. She felt lost and frightened. She didn't want to ask the next question. "Do you think I'm in danger now?"

Royce put a hand gently on her arm. "We're not going to allow you to get into any situation where we feel your life would be at risk."

"But will I be safe in my apartment? I live on the top floor, and it's a four-story walk-up, with dark landings and no doorman."

"We know that," Patterson said. "That's why we'd like you to stay in the hospital a little longer, until we're sure your building will be completely secure for you."

"Thank you," Anne said softly. To her, the light in the room now seemed to be undulating, and the ordinary cafeteria noises sounded miles away.

"But Anne," Patterson continued, "we'll be better able to help you if you're fully honest with us."

"What do you mean by that?" Anne asked. "I'm not holding anything back."

Patterson tilted his head to one side, looking unconvinced.

"Really I'm not," Anne stammered. Her face went pale. What was he alluding to? After an uncomfortable pause, she pushed back from the table and stood up unsteadily. "If you'll excuse me, I'll go back to my room now. I still get very tired sometimes."

The men followed Anne with their eyes until she disappeared through the cafeteria door. Then they pushed their empty plates to one side. Royce offered Patterson a Marlboro. They smoked in silence, each following his own thoughts.

Finally, Royce spoke. "So what do you make of it?"

Patterson's tired eyes watched the smoke from his cigarette wander toward the ceiling. "It's a mixed picture. I reread the routine FBI profile we do for Americans who land a job at the UN. The agent running the check had some doubts about her, but he couldn't pin them down. She marched in some demonstrations against the Vietnam War, but so did just about every college kid. She had a friend in a radical campus group, but she herself didn't join." Patterson shifted in his chair and looked at Royce. "But now she's living in Manhattan's Czech neighborhood, in a building where all the other tenants are East European refugees. And she's studying Russian. Why Russian?"

Royce asked, "Anything she could be blackmailed for? Debt? Promiscuity? Homosexuality? Drugs?"

"No hard drugs, from what we could find out. While she was in Cyprus she had a boyfriend, a Swede, but she doesn't seem to be dating here in New York."

"That surprises me," Royce replied. "She's attractive." He slowly tapped his cigarette on the edge of the ashtray. "What about her relatives? What's her home town, by the way?"

"Lincoln City, on the Oregon coast. She doesn't have relatives, at least not close ones. There's no father's name on her birth certificate. After Anne was born, her teenaged mom parked her with her mother and left town. Granma died during Anne's last year at Wellesley, but it doesn't sound like they had much of a relationship anyway."

Royce shook his head. "So that's why she clammed up when I asked about her family. Poor kid. She has no one to go home to."

"That's her problem, not ours. What worries me is with that childhood, she could be prey for anyone who pretends to care about her. Someone from the other side who'd try to enlist her." He absent-mindedly ran his fingers through his scruffy brown hair. "When you talked with her, did you find out how she spends her free time?"

"Mostly ballet."

Patterson snorted, sending a heavy stream of smoke through his nose.

"You may have the wrong idea," Royce countered. "Ballet takes strength and discipline, like martial arts. She takes classes every week and sees a lot of ballet performances. She seems hungry for culture." He paused until two doctors carrying empty trays toward the trash bins were out of earshot before asking, "What bothers you about the Russian lessons?"

"Just a feeling," Patterson answered. "Clerical staff get a pay increment if they pass a competency exam in any of the UN's six languages. Her French was already good, so why not Russian." He leaned forward. "But I don't buy what she told us that first night, about liking the alphabet. Those UN classes are taught by wives of Soviet diplomats, and the textbooks are full of indoctrination about the noble Soviet system." He looked as though he were about to say more, but checked himself. Instead, he asked Royce, "And on your end?"

Royce pulled out his small notebook and flipped it open. "It's clear the taxi was speeding, but that's not unusual for First Avenue at night. For a few blocks south, it's only empty factory buildings and the Con Edison plant on the riverfront. Cabbies don't expect to see fares there, so they accelerate until they cross 42nd Street." Royce appraised a young nurse as she walked past their table before continuing. "It looks like the taxi started heading for the curb about 50 feet back, instead of last-minute. But the driver could have been drowsy or fiddling with the radio. That kind of thing happens when it's late."

Patterson said, "Two of our men are looking for cabs that show signs of impact. At that speed, there must be a good-sized dent on the hood. But from what you're saying, it's still possible it was an accident."

Royce nodded and then added, "The one thing that points to its being intentional is what the security guard says."

"Which is…?"

"That he's sure the cabby headed straight for Anne on purpose. He's cursing himself now that he didn't get the license plate number, but all he was thinking of was running to help her." Royce carefully returned his notebook to his pocket. "So, do we have a case or not? And if we do, is it yours or ours?"

Patterson fingered the stubble on his chin. "I don't think we have enough info yet to know if we have a case or not. If the cabby hitting her was a simple crime, of course it'll go to you guys at NYPD. But my FBI team's going to want it if it turns out that national security is involved. You know, that it has something to do with America's enemies. The UN is crawling with them." He slowly blew smoke through his nostrils. "But either way, something about this – about her – doesn't add up."

Royce said, "Maybe things will be clearer after your men find the taxi."

"Yeah, mebbe. Anyway, while we're waiting, we do need to get her apartment secured."

Royce nodded. "Any roommates?"

"She lives by herself, in a cheap four-floor walk-up on First Avenue, between 73rd and 74th. Her apartment's in the back, overlooking a small courtyard."

Royce had been leaning back casually in his chair, but now he straightened up and an alert look came into his eyes. "NYPD can handle the surveillance. It'll be easy for us to set it up."

After Patterson didn't reply, Royce added, "She's a sweet girl. I wouldn't want to see anything happen to her."

Patterson studied Royce carefully. For a moment, his eyes revealed a shrewdness they hadn't shown before. Royce, stubbing out his cigarette, missed it.

Patterson said matter-of-factly, "The FBI will handle the surveillance and keep NYPD informed." He scraped his chair back from the table and hefted his stocky frame. The conversation was over.

Royce also rose. "At least I can accompany her home from the hospital."

Patterson shook his head. "Nah. We'll send her home by herself. In a limo, though. We're not going to make her deal again with a cab just yet." He cautioned, "If she drove up with a New York City cop, that could attract attention. You forget, we don't know who else may be watching her building."

1365 FIRST AVENUE

Three days later, Anne stood at the entrance to 1365 First Avenue. The entire limo ride there, she'd clenched the house key tightly in her grip. She wanted it ready so she wouldn't have to linger on the threshold any longer than necessary.

She quickly inserted the key and shouldered open the tall, heavy door. It was reassuring to see that the flimsy lock, which made her so uneasy when she first moved in, had been replaced by a solid Schlage. And she felt comforted knowing that over her shoulder, on the opposite side of the street, one of Patterson's men would be watching the building entrance.

Still, Anne couldn't shake a sense of apprehension. In the hospital, with doctors and nurses making rounds around the clock, she'd felt secure. Now, out of that safe container, she felt exposed and vulnerable. As she reached each landing, she paused to look up the next flight of stairs before stepping out into the full view of anyone who might be above her. Again, though, she took comfort from Patterson's handiwork, this time in the form of brighter lights overhead.

Finally she arrived at the fourth floor. Her apartment key fit into a new lock which, although just as tarnished as the old one, was much sturdier.

A stale, musty odor greeted her as the door swung open. She closed it behind her and quickly threw the deadbolt into place. Leaning against the door, she slowly looked around.

It was good to be back in her apartment. She did, however, have to admit its many flaws. The building was an old-law tenement, after all. The floor sloped so much that when something round dropped on one side of the apartment, it often ended up lying against the opposite wall. But the price was right. The illegal sublet cost her only $75 a month. And, it was a

30-block walk to the UN, convenient for those days when she didn't have enough money for bus fare.

The apartment had one small room, and one smaller room. Against a wall in the main room was a large metal tub, painted white, which sat on high legs and was covered by two side-by-side metal lids. With the lids up, it was her bathtub. With them down, it was her food prep surface.

The small bathroom cubby had only a toilet. The tenant before her had punched a small hole in the wall and stuck in a piece of broomstick to hold toilet paper rolls. It was that kind of building. Gazing at the jagged hole one day, Anne saw it resembled the shape of Australia. So she cut all the continents out of bright red Con–Tact paper and attached them to the cubby wall, turning it into a map of the world, with Australia covering the hole. She always enjoyed the laughter coming through the closed door the first time her friends went inside to use the toilet.

One afternoon soon after she moved in, Anne was washing her hair at the small sink in the main room when a young man crept along the fire escape outside. He stopped at the window nearest her and tried to pry it open. Her heart pounding furiously, Anne shrieked. The young man looked directly at her and then ran off.

Trembling, she called the police. "Throw some metal gates on your windows and you'll be fine," the officer said blandly. "But it sounds like you're new here. Don't do anything stupid, okay? If a man tries to take your handbag on the street, give it to him. And if someone tries to rape you, don't fight. Otherwise you'll end up hurt. Or dead." He hung up.

Was this what life in New York was going to be like? After Anne finally stopped shaking, she walked to the hardware store on her block and got them to install metal accordion gates outside both windows that same afternoon. Not pretty, but necessary.

Yet despite its deficiencies, the apartment had begun to feel like home. She'd laid out a blue-green carpet from Woolworths that reminded her of the Pacific Ocean she knew so well from growing up in Oregon. She painted the walls a clean white. She draped the formica table with a lively red and green patterned tablecloth, and set her cheerful thrift shop dishes on the shelves above it. And all her books fit perfectly in the bookcase over her non-working fireplace.

Now, after taking in the whole apartment, Anne walked over to the mirror above the sink. The face gazing back was that of a stranger. Because the nurses had kept her from seeing her reflection, she hardly remembered what she looked like. She'd also forgotten how to make allowances for the slight distortion of her apartment mirror, since she hadn't looked into it for almost three weeks. Had it really been that long?

As she studied her image, Anne saw she still had one large bruise on the left side of her face, some stitches under her hairline, and puffiness around her eyes. But all in all, she'd come through the ordeal remarkably well. Relieved, she tidied her wavy brown hair, which rested on her shoulders. Her face was heart-shaped and her features were attractive, although Juanita kept nudging her to use more makeup. The fashion standards at the UN were much higher than she was used to, growing up in a small town.

It was Anne's eyes that drew the most comment, from strangers and friends alike. Intelligent green eyes which, they said, had a soft depth that was unusual. Yet the eyes now looking back at Anne were different. She could read in them an anxiety that wasn't there before the accident.

She was opening her small fridge, to see if there was any unspoiled food, when the phone rang. "Dr. Ruzhinsky, how nice of you to call," Anne said. "I just got back from…from my vacation."

"Yes, your vacation." Anne smiled hearing the older woman's Moscow accent, which she hadn't lost even though she'd lived in New York since World War II.

Dr. Ruzhinsky continued, "It was odd, my dear, that you only phoned to tell me you'd be away after you'd already left. And there was so much noise in the background that I could hardly hear you. Were you at the airport? But my dear…" Her voice tightened. "That's not why I called. Something distressing has happened."

8

A PROBLEMATIC APPLICATION

With a trembling voice, the elderly woman said, "Two different men, both with heavy Russian accents, just telephoned me, one after the other."

During the year Anne was a law student at Columbia, a friend, knowing she was short of money, told her of an opening with an émigré Russian psychiatrist. The day Anne arrived at Dr. Ruzhinsky's Upper East Side apartment, the door was opened by a diminutive woman who studied her face attentively and then welcomed her with a charmingly lopsided smile. As they sat in the apartment's tiny kitchen to get acquainted, Anne immediately took to the psychiatrist whose eyes, set in a deeply lined face, sparkled with undimmed enthusiasm for life.

Dr. Ruzhinsky hired Anne as her private secretary, and they quickly developed a close relationship. It eased the loneliness of an old woman who rarely left her building, and that of a young woman, new to the city, who hadn't yet made close friends her own age. After Anne's money ran out, she'd left law school, her degree unearned, and joined the UN. But even then, she continued to visit the psychiatrist's Old World apartment on weekends and still did as much typing for her as she could fit in.

Dr. Ruzhinsky had hired Anne not to help with her psychiatric paperwork, but with a memoir she was writing about her family. In Russia, her relatives had belonged to the socialist movement working to unseat the Czar and install a new government. However, they were allied not with Lenin's Bolsheviks, but with the more moderate Mensheviks. Only for a while were the Mensheviks able to stand up to the Bolsheviks' quest for absolute power. As Lenin brutally consolidated his authority, Dr. Ruzhinsky's husband was severely beaten and her brother was murdered. That's when she fled first to Paris, and then to the United States.

Now, holding the phone, Anne felt sorry she'd lied about being on vacation, instead of telling the truth about being in the hospital. But she'd been afraid that if the elderly woman heard about the taxi accident, it would aggravate her heart condition.

The psychiatrist continued her story. "The way those men spoke was so very crude. Soviet KGB thugs, unquestionably."

"I don't like the sound of that, Dr. Ruzhinsky. What did they want?"

"Each man asked me to take him on as a patient. I told them I was fully booked and couldn't see anyone new. They insisted that I must help them with their psychological problems, but I remained firm."

"Do you think you should call the police?" Anne asked. But then she mused, "I guess there's really no point to that. They didn't actually do anything illegal. Have you told your son Grigor?" She flinched inwardly. Grigor dismissed his mother's memoir as pointless dwelling on the past, and his aversion expressed itself in noticeable dislike of Anne.

"I'm not going to disturb my son while he's at work, but I'll certainly phone him this evening."

"Please do," Anne said. "I'm sure he'll give you some helpful advice. And you should tell your doormen not to let anyone they don't recognize come up to your apartment."

"But my dear," the elderly woman asked, "why would the KGB trouble me now, after leaving me in peace here for so many years?"

"Well, it could be that..." Anne halted mid-sentence. For the first time since Dr. Ruzhinsky had begun telling her about the phone calls, it came to Anne with a jolt that the Soviets' sudden interest must be her fault. Still holding the phone, she collapsed onto her sofa and held one hand to her head.

How could she have been so naïve? Anne hadn't wanted to admit on her UN application that her work with the psychiatrist was that of a mere private secretary. She worried that if she did so, the Personnel Office would label her as best suited for clerical work, while she was eager to be hired as a writer. So she'd tried to impress them by grandly saying she was helping her boss with "a book on the history of the Russian Revolution".

At the time, it never occurred to Anne that there would be staff from communist countries in virtually every UN office, including Personnel.

Her resume, with its mention of a book on the Russian Revolution, would have jumped out at them. Now Dr. Ruzhinsky's phone calls were showing her the consequences of her carelessness.

After working one year for the UN, Anne more clearly understood Soviet thinking. While the Kremlin didn't mind having Stalin or Khrushchev discredited, Lenin was another matter. He was the father of Russian communism and a powerful symbol, important not only for uniting the Soviet people, but also for inspiring other countries to adopt communism. Everything must be done to protect Lenin's image. The Mensheviks, as the opposition party, had known far more about Lenin's harsh suppression of dissent and mass executions than Moscow would ever want to see brought to light. So Anne was sure Dr. Ruzhinsky was right that the callers were KGB agents. Undoubtedly, they were trying to find out more about the book, and maybe even how to stop it.

She quickly ended the phone call with Dr. Ruzhinsky and then sat immobile. She was devastated by her mistake, especially because she saw no way to undo it. Anne had worried that telling the elderly woman about the taxi accident might aggravate her heart problems. Even more, she didn't dare tell the psychiatrist that it must have been her UN application that stirred up the KGB's interest. And if Anne told Grigor, he was sure to explode in anger, which would be worse for his mother's heart. Anne would have to keep silent, hoping he would keep a close watch after hearing what had happened.

Deep foreboding swept over Anne. She'd barely been out of the hospital for an hour, and already she was being drawn back into the Cold War.

9

RETURNING TO WORK

The morning of Anne's first day back at work, she left her apartment early. She wanted to arrive at the office before the others. That way, she could get resettled before the hallways filled up and the day's commotion began.

Riding the bus for the 30 blocks from her apartment to the UN, Anne glanced at the headlines on the newspapers the other passengers were reading. The day before, China and France had each tested a nuclear bomb in the atmosphere. Palestinians had attacked an Israeli kibbutz, while Israeli commandos had raided three Lebanese ports. Ethiopian troops had seized Addis Ababa, and a terrorist bomb had exploded in the Tower of London. And that was only the front-page news. Anne knew the day would be a full one.

After passing through security at the UN gate, Anne headed for the tall Secretariat Building. Once inside, she took the escalator to the second floor and then walked through double glass doors and down a short hallway to her office. After unlocking the door, she paused in the doorway to reacclimate herself.

The main office was long and had an exit door at each end. Next to the far door was a large table for the many documents their Section handled each day. Arranged across the grey linoleum floor were three bulky metal desks where Benedetta, Juanita and Anne sat. To the left of their desks were the offices of their male professional colleagues, who had stunning views of the East River.

Anne moved to her desk. As she dropped her handbag into her desk drawer, she spotted a box on her blotter. It was wrapped in thick embossed paper. Curious, she quickly opened it. Inside she found a delicate white porcelain vase, artfully decorated with wispy pink blossoms and green tendrils. It was a costly gift. Turning it over, she saw *Dresden* printed on the bottom.

She pulled a notecard out of the box. In flowery script, an equally flowery message had been written:

"Esteemed new colleague Anne, may this modest gift, which brings with it the beauty of my native land, brighten your first day back to this worthy office, and may it also with pleasantness introduce to you someone who hopes to become your valued friend. Most very sincerely yours, Jürgen."

Anne finished reading the note with consternation. She'd completely forgotten about the new East German Juanita had told her about in the hospital. This "modest" gift was far too expensive. And instead of wanting the giver to become her "valued friend", her firm resolve was to keep as much distance between them as possible. Her situation was already unsettling enough without adding another Cold War complication.

Anne was looking at the vase and frowning when the door opened. A man she'd never seen before bounded into the office. A broad, artificial smile instantly spread across his face. His two hands shot out and firmly seized her right hand, even though she hadn't offered it, and shook it emphatically. She tried gingerly to extract her hand, but he continued shaking it.

The stranger immediately launched into a series of compliments. "Ah, dear Anne, you are every bit as pretty as everyone has said. And from what I hear, and from the intelligent look in your eyes, I am well persuaded that you are as wise as you are pretty. What an honour to be privileged to share in the noble work of the United Nations together with a special young woman such as yourself."

As soon as she heard his German accent, Anne's shoulders tensed. This had to be Jürgen Bieler himself. Trying not to make eye contact, she finally managed to retrieve her hand.

When at last Jürgen stopped talking, he stood waiting before her expectantly. Surely he wasn't thinking she would return his compliments in kind. She knew East Germans were isolated, but did he really think he would endear himself to Western women by addressing them in such an overly flattering way?

She tried to take in a little of his appearance while still avoiding his eyes. He was probably in his mid-thirties, with white blond hair and an average build. His face was square and oddly lined for a man his age. He didn't strike Anne as looking "German", although her time at the UN had already taught her that there was not a typical look for any nationality. What most stood out to her was the contrast between his unflagging smile and his sharply focused eyes.

She limited herself to a few perfunctory words of reply. "Thank you for your gift, and let me welcome you to our office. I'm sure you'll make a helpful contribution to our work." Then she added, "And now you must excuse me. I came early to the office because I have some important things to do."

She began shuffling through the papers on her desk, while trying to disregard Jürgen's presence. But instead of taking the hint, he lingered there, still smiling.

Just when Anne thought she couldn't bear his intrusiveness any longer, a sound at the door caused both of them to turn toward it.

A young woman, about Anne's age, with beautiful olive skin and flowing brown hair, entered the office. Her dark almond eyes opened in pleased surprise as she caught sight of Anne. "Anne, you're back! I thought you wouldn't be here until next week."

As Anne rose from her chair, Jürgen stepped aside to give her room to approach the newcomer. She said, "Benedetta, I'm so happy to see you."

Shyly, the two gave each other a hug. Once they stepped back, Benedetta observed Anne's face. "Oh, you look so much better than I was expecting. I see one bruise, but otherwise you look quite well." Benedetta turned toward Jürgen and her smile grew brighter. "She does, doesn't she, Jürgen?"

"Indeed she does," he replied, a little too heartily to Anne's ear.

Ignoring him, Anne told Benedetta, "I'm feeling much better, thank you. And you yourself look very well, and your skirt is beautiful." As Anne spoke, she reached out and gently fingered the diaphanous purple fabric, subtly interwoven with gold threads. "Did you get this in Italy? When did you get back?"

"Only last Monday." Benedetta's voice caught. "My parents begged me not to return to New York. You see, we're a close-knit family and no one has ever left Italy before. So to reassure them that they're still very dear to me, I added another week to my vacation."

Just then, the door opened again. It was Juanita. She hurried to Anne and threw her arms around her. Then she said, "Look, Benedetta, look. Now we are three again." To Jürgen, Juanita said, "You'll have to excuse us, but we must go straight to the cafeteria and treat Anne to a plum Danish to celebrate her return."

Laughing and chatting, the three young women were heading for the door when it opened yet again. A short, stocky man, with thick grey hair and alert eyes strode in. "Anne, here you are," he said as he extended his hand. "You have been very much missed, right, girls?"

As Anne returned his handshake, he told her, "We've been extremely busy, and you should know that Juanita and Benedetta worked very hard in your absence. You haven't returned a moment too soon." Then looking with narrowed eyes at the three of them, he added, "I hope you weren't planning to go off for coffee. We have a lot of deadlines to meet today."

The three secretaries exchanged disappointed glances and silently went to their desks.

Jürgen bowed and said, "How nice that our office family is complete once again. And, young ladies, what a beautiful tableau you make together. But," he added officiously, "now that Señor Duarte has reminded us of our responsibilities, let us all get on with today's work."

With a bow, he turned and walked to his office at the far end.

Juanita and Benedetta quickly brought Anne up to date on the most important work they'd done while she was away. Then Juanita suggested to her, "Why don't you start with the filing. Looking at the different letters, reports and memos will help you catch up."

"That's a great idea," Anne replied.

She was standing in front of a tall file cabinet studying a memo when Duarte's door opened. As he was walking through it, he stopped abruptly and whirled around. A muffled crash followed.

"What was that?" asked Juanita.

"Something dropped down outside my window," Duarte answered. "Come, let's have a look."

Juanita, Benedetta and Anne followed their boss into his office. He went to one of his large windows and with effort, heaved it upward. "Careful now, girls," he advised.

The window frame was broad enough that he, Benedetta and Juanita could all lean out at the same time. Anne, as the newest secretary, waited patiently for her turn. There was a brief pause, and then all three exclaimed in unison, "It's a typewriter!"

"What?" Anne said.

"Yes, yes, see for yourself," said Juanita, making space for her at the window.

Anne braced herself on the ledge and leaned out. The cool breeze blowing off the East River tousled strands of hair around her face as she looked down. Sure enough, there on the walkway, one story below, was a battered typewriter. Long metal strips – typewriter keys – lay scattered in every direction.

"What on earth could have happened?" Anne wondered.

"Well, girls," said Duarte, shaking his head, "the story will come out eventually. Let's all get to work."

Laughing, the young women filed back to their desks.

Juanita's phone was ringing. She picked it up and after listening for a few moments, exclaimed, "¡*No me digas!* Don't tell me!" Putting her hand over the receiver, she whispered to Benedetta and Anne, "A secretary on the eighth floor got so mad at her boss that she threw her typewriter out the window. Now she's going to be fired."

As Juanita returned to her phone call, Anne asked Benedetta, "Does Juanita get all the news that fast?"

Benedetta nodded, smiling. "You're lucky they assigned you to this office. Juanita's a key member of the Latin American grapevine. If something's happening in the building, she knows about it."

Juanita's friend was probably right, Anne mused. But didn't each typewriter leave distinguishing marks on a page that could identify the exact machine? Could it be instead that someone wanted to get rid of a typewriter that might be incriminating?

10

DELEGATES LOUNGE ENCOUNTER

The office clock read 3:20.

"Come! Come!" Juanita called out.

Anne abandoned mid-sentence the memo she was typing and jumped up from her chair. She grabbed her handbag and followed Juanita out the office door.

The first few times Juanita had called "Come! Come!" Anne had asked why. Now she no longer bothered. From experience, she knew it meant that Juanita, through her extensive grapevine, had found out that something exciting was about to take place.

The day before, Juanita had propelled Anne quickly to the double glass doors at the end of their hallway. From there, they could see anyone entering or exiting the elevators to the Secretary-General's floor. That day, they arrived just in time to watch an erect Fidel Castro emerge and stride purposefully toward the steps which led to the corridor connecting the main Council Chambers. In his signature battle fatigues and exuding self-confidence, the Cuban President made a striking contrast to the deferential diplomats in expensive suits who tried to keep pace with him. Juanita and Anne had found it hard to suppress their smiles.

Today, Juanita headed briskly down those same steps, followed by Anne. They turned left onto the carpeted corridor, which runs the length of the low middle building of the UN complex. Although Anne was taller than Juanita, she had to exert herself to match Juanita's rapid pace.

It wasn't until they were approaching the Delegates Lounge, situated at the far north end of the corridor, that Juanita slowed down. Taking a cue from her, Anne did the same. As they passed in front of the desk for the receptionists, Anne heard two of them speaking French and Russian as they fielded telephone calls. Another receptionist, using Spanish, was paging the Uruguayan ambassador.

Late afternoon sun streamed through the double-height windows, spreading soft light throughout the spacious Lounge. Potted palms and three-stemmed metal floor lamps gave the Lounge a 1950s ambience. Around low tables, small clusters of well-dressed men sat comfortably in the Mies van der Rohe and Knoll chairs. They were conversing in the muted voices which exemplified the diplomatic skill of speaking just loudly enough to be heard only by an intended listener.

The two secretaries walked leisurely to the polished wood bar at the far end of the Lounge and each ordered a cappuccino. They needn't have bothered. The attendant there had already thrown his machine into operation as soon as he saw them approaching.

Cappuccino in hand, Juanita led the way to a table near the back. It wasn't where they normally sat. That added to Anne's anticipation that something unusual was about to happen.

They'd barely settled into their chairs when four diplomats in dark suits, with meticulously trimmed black hair, strode into the Lounge. Walking to a seating arrangement off to one side, the most prominent among them sat down. The other men took places around the small table in front of him. None of them went to get coffee. Instead, they opened slim briefcases and began arranging documents on the table.

Juanita said nothing, but the attention in her eyes told Anne this was the reason they'd come.

Five minutes later, a second group of diplomats, similar in appearance, entered the Lounge. Without glancing around, they walked directly to a table next to the first group. Once seated, these men, too, quietly removed papers from their briefcases.

As Anne glanced over, she realized that the two apparent leaders were sitting back-to-back, their heads inches away from each other. For the next 20 minutes, while she and Juanita made small talk, Anne watched covertly as the two men carried on a quiet conversation over their shoulders. Not once did either of them turn his head to look at his interlocutor. None of the others at the tables said anything, but occasionally one would hand over a document.

Anne was careful to keep any sign of her rising curiosity from show-ing on her face. She'd been at the UN long enough to understand that the more surprising an occurrence, the more important it was to appear disinterested.

Finally, the first group returned their papers to their briefcases. They shut the cases with an almost simultaneous snap and stood up as if they were one. Without looking at the other men, they walked out of the Lounge.

Five minutes later, the second group silently left.

As soon as the last man had disappeared around the corner, Anne turned expectantly to Juanita for an explanation. "What did I just see?"

"That was the Israelis and the Palestinians."

"Amazing," Anne said. She knew the Israeli Government and the Palestinians had no official relations and avoided all public contact, except when they harangued each other in front of TV cameras at UN meetings. Yet it made sense that with so much happening on the ground, they needed some kind of back channel. Otherwise, even a small incident could escalate into a crisis that neither side wanted.

Anne was about to ask Juanita how often these encounters took place, when something made her look across the room. Two men in dark suits were sitting at a table along the wall. With a start, Anne realized they were staring fixedly at her.

Seeing Anne's face turned in his direction, one of them nodded to her, while his lips formed an ingratiating smile. It was Yevgeni Zimov. Again.

Had the men been there all along, or did they only come later? Anne recalled that as she and Juanita entered the Lounge, one of the reception-ists was speaking on the phone in Russian. Was Anne being paranoid, or might the receptionist have alerted Yevgeni to her arrival?

Juanita's puzzled voice sounded far away. "Anne, is something wrong?"

She answered softly, "Don't look now, but there's a man sitting at the other end of the Lounge who bothered me in the cafeteria a little while ago, before the accident."

"What do you mean, 'bothered'?"

"Well, he's a Soviet," Anne answered. "He came up to me and started chatting. He asked a lot of questions and seemed too friendly. I've run into him twice since then, and each time he started probing about…" Anne's voice trailed off as she saw a skeptical look come over Juanita's face.

Juanita said, "Maybe he just wants to be sociable and isn't very good at making conversation."

Anne replied, "You may be right. It's probably nothing." But her voice sounded strained when she added, "I think we should go back to the office now. I still have to finish typing that report for Señor Duarte."

"Yes, of course."

When Anne set her unfinished cappuccino down on the table, her hand shook slightly. As they walked out of the Lounge, Juanita was chatting cheerfully, but Anne wasn't really listening. From the way the two men had been staring at her, she was sure their eyes were on her back now. She tried to convince herself that Juanita was probably right about Yevgeni, but she couldn't shake the sense that these were not chance encounters. He wanted something from her.

11

AN UNSETTLING INTRODUCTION

Anne had met Yevgeni a few weeks before the taxi accident. One morning she'd looked up at the wall clock over Juanita's desk. 11:30! No wonder her eyes kept closing. It was almost lunch time and she hadn't yet had any caffeine. She stood up from her desk. "I'm going up for a coffee. Would you like to come along?"

Juanita and Benedetta shook their heads. "I've got to finish this memo," Juanita said. "But could you bring one for me?"

"Me, too?" asked Benedetta.

"Sure."

Anne grabbed her handbag and took the escalator to the fourth floor. As she walked into the staff cafeteria, bright sunlight was shining through the expanse of tall windows overlooking the East River. It threw cheerful beams across the large open space filled with pleasant groupings of small tables.

Anne always enjoyed coming to the cafeteria. In one enormous room, she could see a whole array of staff members conversing with friends, often of nationalities other than their own. Some dressed in the unique clothing of their home countries. That day Anne spotted several African men in flowing robes of vibrant colors, as well as staff wearing batik shirts, saris, and colorfully embroidered skirts and blouses.

While Anne filled three paper cups from the bulbous urns off to one side, she listened with pleasure to the soft murmur of many different languages. She felt proud to belong to this multicultural revolution. But then, out of the corner of her eye, Anne perceived a young man with Slavic features hovering to her right. She didn't want to look directly at him, but she sensed he was studying her.

Then he was at her side. "Let me help you. You have one cup too many to carry." As he spoke, he picked up two of her coffees. "You must be a very nice person to be getting coffee for other people as well."

Anne registered his thick Russian accent and was instantly alert. She doubted it was accidental that this Soviet was approaching her. She tried to take back the two cups. "Thank you, but I can manage."

Undaunted, the man held tightly to the coffees and said, "Let me introduce myself. Yevgeni Voronovich Zimov, from the Department of Political and Security Council Affairs. And you?"

Mustering a neutral tone, Anne replied, "Department of Public Information."

Looking steadily at her, Yevgeni said, "That must be a fascinating place to work. And very important, too."

Anne cringed inwardly at his patronizing tone. His square head and pasty complexion added to her distaste. She was now convinced this was no chance encounter. She was sure he'd been told to try to find out more about her.

"And what did you say your name was?" Yevgeni asked.

Anne wanted to retort, "I didn't say, and I don't intend to." But if this Soviet had started the conversation on purpose, he must have a reason. And so she worried that if she mishandled her replies, it might have repercussions for her.

"Anne," she answered.

"Anne," he repeated. "That's lovely. And your last name?"

She stifled her rising impatience. "Thomas."

"Well, Anne Thomas, while we're waiting in line to pay, I'll tell you a funny story. Yesterday in the Security Council, the Soviet ambassador wanted to make a point and he used an idiomatic expression. Russian happens to be a language full of colorful idioms. By chance do you know any Russian?"

She nodded minimally. Could the man be any clumsier in trying to lead the conversation where he wanted it to go?

"Ah, you do. So you'll enjoy this story even more. Anyway, the Soviet ambassador said, 'The mulberry bush grows in my backyard and my uncle lives in Kiev.' Now how can a poor interpreter translate that!"

In spite of herself, Anne became interested. "What did the interpreter do?"

"That saying is like your expression *comparing apples with oranges*, but the English interpreter guessed that it meant *something's not quite right here*. And since it had been spoken as an idiom in Russian, he thought he should express the meaning as an idiom, too. Off the top of his head, he said, 'Something is rotten in Denmark'."

"From *Hamlet*," Anne said. "Considering the pressure he was under, that was pretty good."

Yevgeni smirked. That didn't seem to be the end of the story. "What the poor man forgot was that this year Denmark is also a member of the Security Council. When the Danish ambassador heard what the interpreter said, he took the floor and demanded to know why the Soviet representative had insulted his country."

Although Anne hadn't wanted to offer Yevgeni any encouragement, she couldn't help laughing.

He continued, "Of course, the Soviet representative had no idea why the Danish ambassador was angry. The Dane requested an immediate apology, while the Soviet continued to deny he'd said anything wrong. Things got very heated. Finally, the embarrassed interpreter asked for the floor so he could explain."

By then, Anne and Yevgeni had reached the checkout. He placed a dollar in the cashier's hand. "Oh no, no," Anne protested, "I can't let you pay for these coffees."

"I insist," Yevgeni said. "And this has been such an enjoyable chat that we must meet sometime soon for coffee. I would like to get to know you better."

Right, Anne thought to herself. So that afterwards you can report everything I say, or your version of it, to your KGB bosses? No thank you.

Out loud she replied, "That's a kind offer, but my workdays are very busy. As you see, I'm taking coffee back to the office instead of staying here to drink it."

Yevgeni replied, "I'm sure you can find some time for us to further our acquaintance." His look became firm. "I'll call you next week."

He made a gesture as if tipping his hat to her and walked rapidly out of the cafeteria.

12

PEGGY

The students were still laughing as they filed out of the Russian classroom in the UN's First Basement. "You're not upset with us, are you, Ounaïda?" Anne asked with some concern. "We're not making fun of you. It's just that your answers were such an amusing coincidence."

Ounaïda was wearing a brightly colored, fitted dress from her home country, Barbados. She seemed mystified by the hilarity surrounding her, but accepted it with good grace.

Anne's friend Peggy chimed in with her strong Irish accent. "Ounaïda, you know we meant no harm. Those are the kinds of mistakes all of us make, all the time."

All of us but you, Anne was thinking. Peggy had surprised Anne the first day of Russian class earlier that summer. Professor Bulgakova had asked each student to name something they were fond of. With the limited vocabulary of third-term students, the answers were pretty mundane. That is, until the Russian instructor got to Peggy, who replied, "*morskaya rakushka*".

"*Shto?*" several of the students asked. *What?*

Bulgakova had smiled approvingly at Peggy and then drew a seashell on the blackboard. When their instructor repeated the words, Anne noticed how excellent Peggy's pronunciation had been. In fact, all the students were impressed.

As they left the classroom that day, Anne had asked Peggy, "How on earth did you know the word for *seashell*?"

"I studied Russian a little in Ireland," Peggy explained. "That's why I jumped in at Level 3 with all of you, instead of starting at Level 1."

Anne was puzzled. "I don't think of Ireland as a place where many people would be interested in learning Russian."

Peggy laughed. "You forget the Irish love poetry. And who, besides the Irish themselves, writes impassioned verse as well as the Russians? Think of Pushkin, Lermontov, Mayakovsky, Akhmatova."

Peggy was about ten years older than Anne. She had light red, shoulder-length hair and lively blue-grey eyes that were often flirtatious. Although she'd never studied ballet, she had a dancer's lithe body, all too evident in the tight tops and miniskirts she insisted on wearing, long after those fads had dissipated. Her movements were quick and energetic, as was her mind.

Anne soon discovered that besides Russian, she and Peggy shared a love of nature. And they had a similar sense of humor. Today it had taken a mighty effort to avoid each other's eyes when Bulgakova asked Ounaïda what she did in the evening. Ounaïda, who evidently hadn't done her homework, answered slowly, "*Ya gotovlyu knigu.*"

Anne whispered to Ounaïda, "You said that in the evening, you *cook* a book."

"Oh no," exclaimed Ounaïda with embarrassment.

"*Ya* chitayu *knigu,*" Bulgakova corrected her. "I *read* a book. And what do you do after that?"

Ounaïda hesitantly replied, "*Ya* chitayu *uzhin?*"

Anne and Peggy burst out laughing. "Makes perfect sense," said Peggy. "If first you cook the *book*, the next logical thing is to *read* dinner."

Bulgakova's eyes flashed a warning at Anne and Peggy, but by then, all the students were laughing. Mercifully for poor Ounaïda, the wall clock showed the end of the period.

Outside the classroom, Anne glanced at her watch. "Peggy," she said, "I have time to take a quick walk in the UN Garden before I go back to my office. Can you join me?"

"I'd love to, if you wouldn't mind swinging by the staff import shop first. I'm completely out of Irish Breakfast Tea, and that's the only place where I can get my favorite mark."

The shop was also in the First Basement. Once inside, Peggy headed to the display of tea tins in the rear, while Anne scanned the shelves at the front. Any homesick UN staff member was likely to find in the shop a favorite food or handicraft to reconnect with their national culture. In colorful packages were Vietnamese grass jelly, Finnish reindeer meat, Chinese bird's nest drink, Mexican huitlacoche and Swedish pickled herring. Other shelves displayed South African chicken feet, Vegemite from New Zealand, and Japanese rice crackers. Small bins contained items like tea strainers, chopsticks and woven napkins, as well as an array of handicrafts.

After Peggy paid for her tea, the two friends walked across the open area of the First Basement. Skirting the escalator, which terminated there, they continued out through the double glass doors into the UN Garden.

"Tell me more about your job, Peggy," Anne asked. "I don't really understand what your office does."

"When I tell people I work in Outer Space, it always gets a laugh," Peggy answered. "Our official name is 'Office for Peaceful Uses of Outer Space'. Since Sputnik was launched in 1957, both sides in the Cold War have worried about the weaponization of space. Our office has a mandate to try to diminish that risk, and supposedly that's what we work on."

"Why do you say *supposedly*?"

"Almost all our professionals are either from Soviet bloc countries or the United States and its allies. I think the office is here mainly for the East and West to keep an eye on each other.

"Sounds like it could get tense," Anne mused. "What exactly do you do day-to-day?"

"Mainly we organize committee meetings, and sometimes conferences. The delegates decide on a topic – let's say, using space technology for development. Then we prepare all the documents, set up the conference room, and help during the proceedings."

"Do you enjoy the work?"

"I do. There's always something happening. And when we girls assist with the meetings, we get to flirt with the diplomats. That's why today I'm wearing a skirt with a slit up the side." Peggy winked at Anne.

Anne frowned. She liked Peggy, but didn't think she was creating the right image for UN staff with such blatant ploys to catch the eye of a delegate.

Peggy saw Anne's look and nudged her with her elbow. "Oh, don't be so self-righteous. We girls work hard in the office. We deserve to have a little fun." The amusement suddenly left Peggy's eyes. "But something happened yesterday that was upsetting."

"What was that?"

"I had pages of a report spread out on my desk so I could collate the copies. A call came in for my boss, Mr. Ipatov. He's a Soviet. I stepped to his doorway and told him. He said he wanted to take the call in private, so I closed his door and returned to my desk to finish collating. The trouble is, I forgot to put my receiver back after he picked up."

"And…?"

"At first I didn't realize it was still off the hook. But when the girl at the next desk stopped typing, I heard voices coming from my phone. Then of course I quickly hung up. A little while later, Mr. Ipatov came out of his office. He leaned against the wall and asked, very casually, 'So Peggy, why were you listening to my phone conversation?'"

"Uh-oh. What did you say?"

"I tried to keep it light. I told him he was such a hard taskmaster, all I could think of was getting the report ready for his meeting, and that's why I'd forgotten about the phone."

"Do you think he believed you?"

"I don't know. He had a strange grin, like we two had a secret. He stood there a bit longer, just looking at me, before he went back into his office."

"You'll have to be very careful from now on not to give him any reason to doubt you," Anne cautioned.

"You're probably right, although I can assure you I didn't hear anything. That is, except for a moment I thought I heard your name. But then I realized that couldn't be." Peggy paused. "I mean, after all, we're only secretaries, so why would the Russians be talking about you?" Peggy laughed at the idea.

She didn't notice the troubled look in Anne's eyes.

13

MORE THAN SHOES

The warped wooden door shuddered as Anne pushed it open from the street. Tinkling from a small bell announced her entry.

The high-pitched whir of a machine stopped. The man standing in front of it put down the black shoe he'd been buffing. Wiping his hands on his smudged apron, he walked up to the counter. "Yes?"

Silently, Anne handed him a small shoe repair ticket. He took it and started toward the shelves on the side, where rows of brown paper bags with stapled tags were arrayed. But when he checked the red numbers on the ticket, he stopped. Returning, he lifted a hinged section of the counter and nodded in the direction of a thick green curtain at the back.

Being careful not to brush against the stained counter, Anne passed through the opening and pushed aside the curtain. She let it fall shut behind her and then paused for her eyes to get used to the dim light in the small, airless room.

"You're only 20 minutes late," Agent Patterson said as he stood up.

Anne wasn't going to let herself be browbeaten over something as minor as not being on time. She countered, "I didn't have you pegged as the punctual type."

Patterson pulled out a chair on the other side of the little table and motioned for her to sit down. Although the whir from the machine had started up again, the heavy curtain muffled the sound surprisingly well. It was an odd place to meet, but certainly no one would overhear them.

"So you've been back at work for a couple of weeks now," Patterson said. "Anything out of the ordinary?"

"Not really," she answered. "The new East German, Jürgen Bieler, is about what you'd expect. Nosy. I'm keeping my distance as much as I can. Otherwise, everything seems pretty much the same. That Soviet nuisance Yevgeni has been hovering around, but he hasn't spoken to me since my return."

Patterson pulled out a pack of Winstons. "Do you mind?" he asked.

Anne would have replied that she did, but she'd already guessed he'd be easier to deal with when he had a cigarette. "Go ahead," she said.

Patterson struck a match. After taking a long draw on the Winston, he asked, "Have you kept an eye out for any work in your office that might be sensitive?"

"I've been watching, but I haven't seen anything."

"Watching closely, or just watching?"

Anne's voice tightened. "Look, I'm the one who most needs to know if the taxi hit me on purpose. But I'm not going to poke around looking for the other Cold War things you FBI guys are interested in. That's not why I took this job at the UN."

"What if they're the same thing?"

"What do you mean?"

"What if those 'other Cold War things' the FBI is interested in relate to the accident?"

The idea unsettled Anne. "I wouldn't like that," she said softly. "I wouldn't like that at all."

"Well, maybe that will give you an incentive to be less passive." Patterson blew a stream of smoke up to the ceiling. "But so far, since your return, you've seen no reason why someone might want you out of the way?"

She shook her head.

Patterson ruminated for several minutes. Then he said, "I keep having a hunch that your taxi 'accident' is connected with something you did or saw not long before that. Did anything unusual happen that week?"

Anne's brow furrowed as she tried to recall. "Well, the day of the accident itself started out especially busy. I was chained to my desk all morning and didn't even stop for lunch. But things lightened up in the afternoon, enough for Juanita, Benedetta and me to slip out for cappuccinos in the Delegates Lounge."

"How did you get admitted to the Lounge? When the General Assembly is in session, I thought only diplomats and high-level UN officials could access that part of the building."

"You've been doing your homework. I'll make a confession, if you won't report me." She grinned. "I forged All-Area Passes for us."

His eyebrows lifted. "How the hell did you do that?"

"I noticed Señor Duarte's pass was printed on the same green paper as the forms we use for sending cables. So I cut cable paper to the right size, traced the UN emblem, and used our date stamp to add random identification numbers. When I put my passes in plastic nametag holders, you couldn't tell them from the real thing."

Patterson chuckled, then returned to his previous train of thought. "What happened after the cappuccinos?"

"We didn't stay long, since there was still a lot of work waiting for us. As we walked back down the corridor from the Lounge, we were laughing and talking like we always do, but…" Her face clouded over.

"But what?"

"I was feeling discouraged. Señor Duarte is usually kind, but that morning, when I suggested adding a sentence to the report I was typing, he really cut me down. 'Anne, my dear,' he said, 'writing the report is my job. Typing it is yours.'"

"And?"

"That made me feel like a complete nobody. When I was working with the peacekeeping force in Cyprus, things weren't so rigid. They even let me draft some official memos." She bit her lip. "I felt much more competent and respected there than I do here at Headquarters."

"But what does this have to do with that afternoon?"

"Remembering what Señor Duarte said, I didn't feel ready to go back to the office just then. So I told Juanita and Benedetta to continue without me, and that I'd be there shortly. While they went ahead, I walked over to the Cypriot amphora."

"What is that, and where is it?"

"It's a kind of thick clay vase. It's in a case close to the windows of the long corridor that leads from the south end of the building to the Lounge. The amphora is from around 600 B.C., and it's massive – maybe two feet high." Her eyes shone as she described it. "It has graceful curved handles, and its black paint trim has survived the centuries surprisingly intact. Do you know, when the Cyprus government donated it, an art historian said it was 'one of the most beautiful objects of art ever offered to the UN' and..."

"Whoa, whoa, whoa," Patterson said, raising his hands. "I get the picture. Just tell me what happened."

"Sorry. I was walking slowly around the case, recalling how much happier I'd been in Cyprus, with my boyfriend Lars and everything..." Her voice caught and there was a pause before she continued. "Anyway, by then I was standing behind the amphora. This may sound silly, but I realized that because of what I'd been thinking, I was frowning. At the UN, everyone wears a poker face. You never want to let on what you're really feeling. I quickly looked up, hoping no one had noticed me."

Patterson's face was skeptical.

"This *is* going somewhere," she assured him. "Of all people, Yevgeni was heading straight for me."

"I thought you said he hadn't spoken to you."

"I meant he hasn't spoken to me since I got back from the hospital," Anne said. "What I'm telling you about now happened the day of the accident."

"Well, what did he want?"

14

WHY HERE, WHY NOW?

As Anne began to recount to Patterson her conversation with Yevgeni that afternoon, the whole sequence came vividly back to her. Yevgeni had stood looking at her attentively. "I saw you in the Lounge a little while ago. Were those your officemates, the ones you were getting coffee for the day I met you in the cafeteria?'

"Yes."

He continued, "And they've returned to the office?"

She nodded.

"But you, on the other hand, have not. Instead, quite curiously, you've stationed yourself in this out-of-the way place."

She was just about to respond when she became aware of a commotion. António Gavrez was striding down the corridor toward the Security Council Chamber. As always, he was surrounded by a fawning entourage. Two officials keeping pace beside him were talking animatedly, seemingly trying to impress him. But Gavrez was not looking at them. His eyes were fixed on Anne.

She hadn't seen the tall, strikingly handsome Ecuadorian since he left Cyprus to take up his new duties in New York. She started to greet him, but his icy expression instead made her look away. On the island, her relations with Gavrez had been strained. Now that they were both back at Headquarters, she saw he was no more inclined to be cordial to her than before. And with his elevation to Under-Secretary-General, the gap between them in the UN hierarchy was now even more pronounced.

Yevgeni appeared annoyed that Anne's attention had shifted to Gavrez. He repeated his comment with an edge to his voice. "As I was saying, for some reason you've stationed yourself here."

Anne refocused on Yevgeni. She explained, "Last year I served with UNFICYP and got to know a lot about Cypriot antiquities. So I came over to admire the amphora before going back to work."

"And that's really why you're here?" he asked. To Anne, he seemed nervous. His words were controlled, but at his temple, small beads of sweat were forming and a vein was visibly pulsing.

"Yes," she replied, "that's really why."

Yevgeni wouldn't let the subject drop. "But standing here, you could observe people passing by, maybe even overhear their conversations, without them noticing you. Isn't that true?"

She muttered, "Oh, for heaven's sake. I can assure you I have better things to do with my time."

"Such as?"

Anne had had enough. Curtly she said, "You'll have to excuse me now. I've been away from the office long enough."

Without waiting for him to respond, she had turned quickly and left.

"And that," Anne told Patterson, "was the last time I spoke with Yevgeni."

"Well," Patterson replied, "that conversation doesn't tell us much except that he's watching you, and you've told me that already."

"But what strikes me is how agitated he was. Can you think why?"

"From everything you've said about Yevgeni, it sounds like the KGB assigned a bottom-of-the-barrel agent to check you out. I'd guess his nervousness had less to do with you, and more to do with the fact that he's not coming up with anything worthwhile for his superiors."

"That could be," she acknowledged.

"And you can't think of anything else out of the ordinary?"

"No, not a thing."

"Anne," Patterson said, "I'm going to repeat this. We'll be better able to help you if you try to get more information for us."

"And just where should I be looking?"

"Only you would know that," he said evenly.

She sighed with exasperation. "I'll pay attention to what's happening around me, but I'm not going to go around snooping and eavesdropping.

If the Soviets already have questions about me, that would only make things worse."

"Look, whenever you have more to say to me, you know how to get in touch."

Patterson rose from his chair, signaling that their meeting was over.

15

RED-STRIPED AWNING

Anne drew the collar of her beige trench coat closer around her neck. The wind rushing down Fifth Avenue made the day surprisingly chilly for late summer. It was a good thing she was out shopping for a new wool coat. It seemed winter this year would be coming early.

So far, though, the day had been disappointing. She'd tried on at least thirty coats in her price range and hadn't liked any of them.

Near 38th Street, she stopped to peer into the Lord & Taylor display windows. Without even going inside, she knew this grand department store had nothing for sale that she could afford. Still, she could spend a wistful moment picturing herself in those beautiful dresses.

"You're looking pensive, Anne," said a voice above her shoulder. Turning, she was surprised to see James Royce. Self-consciously, she smoothed her wind-blown hair and hoped she didn't look as tired as she felt after several hours of fruitless shopping.

"Detective Royce," she said in a higher pitch than usual. "What are you doing here?"

"I could ask you the same thing," he replied, giving Anne the warm smile that had lightened her mood in the hospital.

"I'm shopping for a winter coat," she answered, "but I'm not having any luck."

"That surprises me. A girl as pretty as you should look good in any coat she tries on."

Anne blushed at the compliment. Trying to keep her voice casual, she said, "It's harder for women to find a nice coat than you men might think."

"Well, since it's lunchtime and you probably haven't eaten yet, why don't we duck into Woolworth's and you can educate me over a couple of burgers."

A confused look came over Anne's face. "But … aren't we supposed to avoid being seen together in public? Isn't that why you didn't accompany me home from the hospital?"

As she spoke, she looked around nervously at the people jostling past them on the sidewalk.

He smiled reassuringly. "Those were very different circumstances. You were pulling up in front of a building that might be under observation. Now we're submerged in a crowd of shoppers who, judging by their intense faces, are single-mindedly pursuing bargains. They won't pay any attention to two friends ducking under that red-striped awning. Come on, it'll do you good to get off those tired feet."

Before Anne could respond, Royce placed his arm gently against the small of her back and guided her across the street. She trembled at his touch. She hoped he wouldn't notice, or would just think she was shivering in the wind.

They passed under the gold letters spelling out *F. W. WOOLWORTH CO.* and entered the lunchroom. After the chill outside, it felt overly warm and stuffy. Cutlery clinked loudly against heavy china and meat sizzled noisily on the grill. The smell of frying onions clung tenaciously to the air and made Anne realize she was in fact very hungry. "Let's take a window seat," she suggested.

"All right." Putting his hand to her elbow, Royce led her over to the red upholstered stools at the formica counter looking out onto Fifth Avenue. "And here you can enjoy moments of *schadenfreude* watching other discouraged shoppers who haven't yet found what they're looking for."

She smiled at Royce, grateful that because of his cheerful patter, she hadn't yet had to say very much. Now that they were away from the street noise of Fifth Avenue, she didn't want him to hear her voice quaver. What was it about him that was so disarming?

A middle-aged waitress in a starched white cap and frilly apron came over to them, her pencil poised over a small stained notepad. Royce waved away the laminated menus and ordered for them both. "Two burgers and two coffees, one black, one with milk."

He remembers how I like my coffee, Anne thought to herself. She felt oddly flattered.

As the waitress headed back to the kitchen, Royce asked Anne, "Have you seen any good plays recently?"

His question brought her back to their enjoyable bedside chat in the hospital about the arts. "No, but since I last saw you, I've been to the opera."

"Which one?" asked Royce, leaning closer.

"*La Bohème* with Pavarotti. He was spectacular. And during intermission, while I was in the standing room section, a woman leaving early handed me her ticket. In Row J!"

"Excellent," Royce said. "So what's it like to be back at work?"

"It's been fine," she answered. "I missed everyone in my office and so I've been happy to be with them again. And you met Juanita in the hospital, so you know how wonderful she is."

Royce nodded and then asked, "And nothing's happened to alarm you in any way?"

Her brow furrowed. "I do feel a little jumpy, especially when I leave at the end of the day. I haven't worked the evening shift yet, and I hope I won't have to for a while. My officemates have kindly been covering it for me."

"And Patterson has been taking good care of you?"

"Actually, I've only seen him once since the hospital."

For some reason, that reply seemed to please Royce. Continuing, he asked, "And no one's been acting strangely toward you in a way that makes you suspicious?" His cobalt eyes seemed particularly intense.

She was on the verge of telling him about Yevgeni when something stopped her. Much as she found Royce fascinating, there was an edge to his queries that was making her uncomfortable. She tried to evade his question with a joke. "It's the UN after all," she said. "Everyone acts suspicious."

Although Royce smiled, the rest of his face seemed stiff. He remained silent for a moment and then changed the subject. "Can I give you a suggestion for your next outing? Last Saturday I went to the Frick Museum, and something tells me you especially would appreciate the Corots there."

She felt relieved that they were back on more comfortable ground. "I like Corot," she replied. "Did you see paintings from the regular collection or some that are on loan?

"Both," Royce said, as he made space on the counter for the plates the waitress was ready to set down. "But now let's enjoy these burgers while they're hot."

The meat tasted greasy to Anne and the fries could have been crisper. Still, her plate, and Royce's, were soon completely clean.

As the waitress cleared away their plates, Royce tapped his watch. "Much as I'm enjoying your company, Anne, I'm afraid I have to go." Looking into her eyes, he added, "And you've probably given me more time than you should have, while your quest for the perfect coat remains unfulfilled. I guess we both need to be on our way."

After laying some dollar bills on the counter, Royce helped Anne down off the stool. He held her coat while she slipped her arms through its sleeves. Turning her toward him, he gently fastened the top button under her chin. "It's cold outside."

After they emerged back onto Fifth Avenue, they stood facing each other on the bustling sidewalk. Anne felt Royce was carefully studying her face as though looking for something. But all he said was, "It was great to run into you like this."

Not trusting her voice, Anne only nodded.

Looking satisfied, he gave her a cheerful wave and then turned and started walking briskly uptown.

Anne's feelings were in complete disarray. That morning, as she headed out, she never dreamed the day would include lunch with Royce. Instead of immediately resuming her shopping, she rested against the building's granite facade and started to replay in her mind their whole conversation.

As she stared off in the distance recalling the attention Royce had shown her, something caught her eye. It was a man, about thirty feet away, dodging rapidly in and out of the crowd. The shape of the back of his head was unusually square, and his hair was dark and cut extremely short. Like Yevgeni's.

16

ARE APPEARANCES DECEIVING?

Standing up from her desk, Juanita said to Anne, "Come on, I want to show you some other parts of the building. You've been doing great with our main jobs, like the meeting summaries and the *Press Analysis* for the Secretary-General. Now it's time to get you involved in our other work."

Anne followed her to the doorway. "Where are we going?"

Juanita held the door open for her. "I want to introduce you to the men on the twelfth floor who log in our mailings for the diplomatic pouches. When we're sending a batch of envelopes to the UN Information Centres, that's where we take them."

"Okay. And where else?"

"If we have a rush mailing, then it's better for us to take it directly to the Pouch Unit in the Third Basement. It's dark and dingy down there, with corridors going in all directions. You need to know your way around."

Anne nodded.

"But first," Juanita said, "let's start up on the third floor. That's where the journalists have their offices, and the Secretary-General's Spokesman, too. When we need copies of press releases for the Information Centres, that's where we pick them up."

As they exited the escalator at the third floor, Anne whispered to Juanita, "They could try a little harder to disguise themselves."

"Who?"

"Those two men talking together over there. The ones with the military 'buzz' haircuts and the very erect postures." To Anne, they looked just like the undercover agents pretending to be students at campus demonstrations against the Vietnam War.

"Oh," Juanita responded, "That's Rick Hunter and Stewart Dunn. They manage the documents for the Spokesman's Office."

"I think they do a little more than that."

Juanita's eyebrows lifted. "What do you mean?"

"Oh, Juanita, with those haircuts and that military bearing? They're definitely FBI agents."

Juanita gave her a doubtful look. "I don't think that having short hair means they're not regular UN staff. And why would the FBI be interested in the Department of Public Information? We don't have any secrets."

Anne should have kept her thoughts to herself. This wasn't the first time she'd realized that Juanita wasn't particularly attuned to the Cold War undercurrents at the UN. And why should she be? As a Guatemalan, she didn't have to worry that her nationality would create problems for her. And she wasn't studying Russian.

The next day, Anne was back on the third floor pulling press release pages out of the grey metal shelving when she heard a voice to her right. "Hi there. You're the new American in the Information Support Section."

She looked up and saw Rick and Stewart. "Yes, I am," she answered, holding out her hand. "Anne Thomas."

"Twenty-four years old, from Oregon, graduated from Wellesley, one year of law school, and posted to Cyprus for ten months," Stewart said.

"And now studying *Russian*," Rick added, giving the last word extra emphasis.

Anne was taken aback. They weren't even trying to pretend. She would take the opposite tack. Feigning not to know anything about them, she asked, "And you are…?"

"Stewart Dunn."

"And Rick Hunter. But my guess is that when you pointed us out to Juanita yesterday, she told you our names."

This is not going well, Anne thought to herself. Before things got worse, she'd better end the conversation. She tried to keep her voice casual. "Well, nice to formally meet you. I should finish collecting these press releases now, but I'm sure I'll see you around."

"I'm sure you will," replied Stewart. "We Americans need to stay on good terms with each other." His tone was not friendly.

17

OLD MASTERS

Sitting at her kitchen table, Anne lingered over a cup of tea. Through the metal security gate on her window, she gazed at the sole tree in the courtyard behind her apartment. Seeing that the leaves of the ailanthus were starting to turn yellow, she felt wistful, knowing that the cold, grey days of winter lay ahead.

Her thoughts wandered back to her conversation with Patterson some days before at the shoe repair shop. She'd taken seriously his hunch that there might be a connection between the accident and something that had happened around the same time. That made it all the more frustrating that she hadn't been able to come up with a viable lead.

Maybe she had quit too soon. Once again, she started going back over the week of the accident, hoping some detail would catch her attention.

She finally got to the encounter with Yevgeni. Patterson had dismissed his nervousness as insignificant, but the memory of the tension in Yevgeni's face had stayed with her. In her other conversations with him, he'd been annoyingly tenacious, but she'd never before seen him that agitated.

Then it came to her. While he was grilling her as to why she was standing there, he had darted a glance at the amphora case. In fact, as she now recalled, he'd done that several times.

The back of her neck tingled. She felt certain she was onto something.

She wanted to rush immediately to the UN and look closely at the glass case. But she thought she'd better discuss it with Patterson first.

She grabbed a sheet of stationery and started a letter to a girlfriend named Cheryl. She wrote a little about what she'd been doing lately, and then suggested they get together at the Museum of Modern Art that coming Saturday at 3:00 p.m. She slid the letter into the blue patterned envelope Patterson had given her and carefully wrote the address she'd memorized.

The next morning as she walked to work, Anne dropped the letter into the designated mailbox at First Avenue and 64th Street. She felt hopeful that once Patterson heard about the amphora case, he'd see it as a lead worth following up.

That Saturday afternoon, Anne strolled into a large gallery. Dominating the room was an imposing Richard Diebenkorn canvas with large, unevenly painted blocks of strong color. Why anyone thought he was a gifted artist was beyond Anne. Yet she herself had chosen MOMA as the meeting place, instead of her beloved Metropolitan Museum. So, she might as well use the opportunity to study the painting and try to become more receptive to Diebenkorn's style.

She moved forward, looking carefully at his bold, confident forms. She was so absorbed that she wasn't aware a museum guard was approaching until he said sharply, "Miss, you need to step back. You can't stand that close to the painting."

She jumped. As she turned to look at him, she saw they were alone, except for two silver-haired women walking through the far doorway into the next gallery. The guard bent his head and murmured close to her ear, "Third floor. The door is marked *Employees Only*."

Then he, too, moved on.

Anne climbed the stairs to the third floor and, without a problem, found the door. After looking around to make sure no one was watching, she slipped inside and found Patterson waiting.

She glanced quickly around the small office, which contained four tidy desks. Two walls were taken up by shelves holding stacks of colorful museum catalogues. The other two walls were decorated with posters.

"Ha!" Anne exclaimed. "They don't like Diebenkorn either."

"What are you talking about?" Patterson asked.

"Look at them all," she said, gesturing at the reproductions.

"Yeah, they're pictures of paintings. I get that."

Anne grinned. "But this is the Museum of Modern Art, and every single one of them is by an Old Master."

He looked at her through narrowed eyes. "How do you know that? You've never been in this room before, have you?"

She thought to herself, I guess not all law enforcement guys know as much about art as Detective Royce. Out loud she explained, "Well, there's a definite style, a kind of brushstroke that ..."

Patterson began to rise from his chair. "Look, if you brought me all this way to give me a class on painting, I'll be going now..."

"No, wait," Anne rushed to say. "I have something to tell you, something I think is important."

Patterson dropped his weary frame back into the chair, which gave out a little "poof" as it took the impact of his weight.

Anne launched into her reason for wanting to see him. "Remember when I told you about Yevgeni approaching me that afternoon?"

"I remember."

"A few days ago, I recalled that while he was questioning me, his eyes kept darting to the amphora case. Now I'm convinced it was something about the case that was making him nervous."

Patterson tilted back in the chair. "That doesn't seem like much to go on."

Her tone was defensive. "You had your hunch and now I have mine. Isn't it something we could at least consider?"

He shrugged. "Well, let's play it out, then. So you're standing next to the amphora. Yevgeni sees you there and walks over." He paused for a moment and then said, "I wonder if there was something on the amphora case he thought you might have noticed, while everyone else was hurrying by and not paying attention. What's in that area?"

"There's a small seating arrangement next to the amphora, but that's about it."

"Can you draw me a sketch?" Patterson held out a notepad.

Anne took it and quickly plotted the corridor, the tall windows overlooking the traffic circle, the amphora stand and, nearby, a small table with four chairs. She handed the notepad back to Patterson.

After studying her drawing, he asked, "Who uses those seats, and for what?"

"I see diplomats there from time to time," she answered. "That seating arrangement is a bit separate from the rest of the corridor, so a conversation there would be more private than one in the Delegates Lounge."

Patterson fingered his chin. "What if a microphone were attached to the case?"

Anne stopped swiveling in her chair and leaned forward. "That's an interesting possibility."

He continued, "Of course, even if there were a mic then, it might not be on the case now. But it's worth checking out. I'll have someone take a look. Anything else?"

Anne stared across at her own sketch while she considered his question. "This is a long shot, but I'm wondering if Yevgeni's nervousness had something to do with the amphora itself."

"Such as?"

"I don't know," she replied. "Maybe it's been damaged in some way? Or maybe it's not quite what the Government says it is?"

"But why would that trouble Yevgeni?"

Anne looked off in the distance. "There's an important link between the Soviet Union and Cyprus, and that's AKEL, the Cypriot communist party. It's the oldest party on the island and very well connected. Maybe AKEL told the Soviets something that relates to the amphora."

"That sounds really far-fetched to me."

She sighed. "I know. It sounds far-fetched to me, too."

"Well, listen. Since we have so few leads, I'll find someone to check out the amphora. I wonder if there's an expert at the Metropolitan Museum who knows…"

"Adriaan van der Waals."

"What?"

"Adriaan van der Waals. He's the Met's curator of Cypriot antiquities. He's Dutch."

"And you know him because…? Oh, I get it. On weekends, you spend endless hours at the Met studying its Cyprus collection. You're there so often that eventually the curator introduces himself, to chat with you about your obvious interest."

"I do other things on weekends besides go to museums," Anne retorted. Then she blushed. "But it was something like that."

"All right. I'll have my office contact your Mr. Van der Waals and see if we can get him over to have a look at the amphora. How do you spell his name?"

Anne gestured for him to hand her his notepad and began writing. "But would you be careful about one thing?" she asked.

"What's that?"

"Van der Waals knows I spent time in Cyprus, but I've never told him I was with the United Nations, or that now I'm working for the UN here in New York."

"Why did you keep that from him?"

She cringed. "Did you hear about that Director of the UN High Commissioner for Refugees? It was in the *New York Times*. When his tour of duty in Cyprus ended, he was caught at the airport trying to fly out several crates of unregistered Cypriot artifacts."

"No wonder you didn't say anything."

She shook her head. "It's so embarrassing for all of us at the UN when our officials do stupid things like that."

"Anything else?" Patterson asked.

Anne cleared her throat. "What's with Rick and Stewart?"

Patterson cocked his head and gave her a penetrating look. "Am I supposed to know who they are?"

"I think so. Hippie days are over, but most men still wear their hair fairly long, even UN diplomats. Rick and Stewart don't blend in very well."

Patterson shrugged. "I will neither affirm nor deny, as they say. But if there are others at the UN checking out the situation in general, they would have nothing to do with your case. That falls to me."

She made a face. "I don't know that I find that reassuring."

"Anne," Patterson said. There was a new note of seriousness in his voice. "In case you're onto something with the amphora or its case, you need to be very careful in that corridor from now on. And if you see Van der Waals in the UN building, don't acknowledge him in any way. If you're in danger, and it possibly relates to the amphora, it could be dangerous for him as well. You realize that, don't you?"

18

NOT WHAT IT SEEMS

The subway car lurched around a curve in the tracks with loudly squealing wheels. The few late evening passengers swayed in their seats.

Patterson was looking straight ahead, but Anne got the feeling he was aware of everything going on around them. Over the racket, he said, "I've got news for you. Your hunch about the amphora wasn't as far-fetched as I thought."

"What do you mean?"

"Before I tell you about that, our man checked out the glass case and there was no microphone…"

Anne sighed with disappointment.

"Wait a minute," Patterson raised a hand. "I said there was no microphone. But along the top edge of the case there was a small speck of putty, the kind our expert says is sometimes used to attach miniature mics."

"Wow," Anne exclaimed, "so that's it!"

"Hold it," Patterson said with exasperation. "That may or may not explain Yevgeni's nervousness. But what I'm trying to tell you is that there's something to your hunch about the amphora itself."

"Like…?"

Patterson's whole focus was now on the graffiti-covered windows across from them. Shifting in his seat, he strained to see through the thick splotches of paint and then said in a loud voice, "This is our station."

Anne grimaced. They'd been changing subway lines non-stop over the last twenty minutes. Now it seemed they had to move again.

She rose and exited after Patterson. She was following him across the platform, when he grabbed her arm and jerked her backward into the neighboring car of the train they'd just left. The doors closed right after them.

As they sat down, Anne rubbed her wrenched shoulder and glared at Patterson.

Unfazed, he continued. "We got Van der Waals temporarily accredited to the Dutch UN delegation, and he strolled with them down the corridor. They stopped at the arrangement of chairs you told me about. As they were sitting down, your curator took his time walking over to his seat and managed to get a good look at the amphora."

"And he saw something?"

"I don't think you know this, but he was consulted in 1964 when the Cyprus government donated the amphora. The UN wanted to find out if it had any special preservation needs, so they asked him. Oh, hang on, this is our next transfer."

Patterson leaped up quickly and Anne did the same. They rushed across the platform and jumped on the express right before the doors shut.

Once seated, Anne commented, "So he knows it quite well."

"Well enough to know that the amphora in the case now is a fake."

"What?!" Anne's handbag tumbled off her lap and onto the filthy floor. "A fake?!"

"Sssh," Patterson hissed in her ear. "Yes, a very professional one, but still a fake."

"Oh my God!" Anne whispered. "What gave it away?"

"According to Van der Waals, the shape and the markings are excellent, but something's not perfect with the ivory paint. He remembered that on the original, there's one spot where the paint is worn away so that the red clay shows through. But there's nothing like that on the reproduction."

"This is so amazing! I'll have to discuss it with Van der Waals right away."

"You'll do no such thing," Patterson said sharply. "You're not to talk about this with anyone. Don't you know what this means?"

"No, I'm afraid I don't."

From the far end of the subway car came the sound of someone retching. Anne screwed up her face and muttered to Patterson, "It's impossible to have a conversation in these conditions."

He laughed softly. "Not yet a city girl, huh?"

She shot him a truly dirty look, but he only laughed again. Then the seriousness returned to his face. "Think about it. If someone went to the trouble to commission such a skilled fake, chances are they unloaded the original on the black market for a very high price."

"You mean it's gone?" Anne was surprised to feel tears forming in her eyes. The amphora meant more to her than she'd realized.

"Well yes, 'gone', if by that you mean that it's now in someone's private collection, and a tidy sum is in someone else's offshore bank account."

Anne fell silent as she absorbed the news. Finally she asked, "What are you going to do?"

Patterson answered, "Our next step will be to make quiet inquiries among some high-end antiquities dealers, here and in Europe. First the legitimate ones, and then the not-so-legitimate ones."

"And will you tell me what you find out?"

The brakes of the subway car screeched as the train pulled into the 59th Street station.

"Come on," Patterson said. "No one's following us. We can have the rest of our conversation on a bus."

They emerged into the brisk evening air and quickly boarded the next M104 going up Broadway. Anne felt relieved to be back above ground. She repeated her question. "Will you tell me what you find out?"

Patterson shook his head. "Right now, I think it's best if you only know what relates directly to your own safety, especially if the amphora has been trafficked. The antiquities market has become very lucrative. Anyone big in the trade is now the equivalent of a drug lord. So if you're going to keep using that UN corridor, you need to stay completely away from the amphora. Don't even look at it from a distance. Understood?" His forehead creased deeply. "There could be people involved in this that you do not want to cross."

19

CAREFUL ATTENTION

When Anne pushed open the office door, Juanita and Benedetta were already at their desks. Both were unwrapping brightly colored packages. Benedetta set aside the foil paper and opened a small box. "Oh," she exclaimed, "it's absolutely beautiful!"

She carefully lifted out a delicate silver necklace with a lustrous dove pendant. She held it up to the light to admire and then immediately clasped it around her neck. "I've never had such an exquisite piece of jewelry."

Juanita was drawing out of her box a similar necklace. "¡Qué lindo!" She looked over at Anne and explained, "Jürgen has returned from Dresden and he's brought us all gifts. Quick, open yours."

"More gifts?" Anne sounded displeased. "Don't you think he's overdoing it?"

Benedetta said, "What do you mean? He's a man with a generous spirit. It gives him great pleasure when he selects gifts that make us happy. It's his way of showing appreciation for how helpful we are. He told me so himself."

Looking resigned, Anne began opening the package he'd left for her. Unlike Juanita's and Benedetta's, hers was long and flat. As soon as she pulled apart enough of the paper to reveal the gift inside, her eyes widened and she gasped.

"What is it?" Juanita and Benedetta hurried to her desk to see.

With a look of amazement, Anne was carefully turning the pages of a book. She reluctantly closed it so they could see the front cover. "It's Wilhelm Waetzoldt's *Dürer und Seine Zeit*."

"But it looks like a used book," Benedetta said, sounding disappointed.

"It is used," Anne replied, "but it's a collector's item. It was published in the 1930s and has superb reproductions of Dürer's finest etchings and paintings. I never dreamed I would have a copy of my own." Then her face clouded over. "I wonder how Jürgen knew."

Juanita responded, "He probably overhears you when you tell us about your museum visits."

Benedetta looked over Anne's shoulder at the pages she was turning. "Well, it does have some nice pictures of Jesus and Mary." Fingering her new necklace, she added, "But I'm glad that I got this lovely jewelry instead of a secondhand book."

Juanita, apparently wanting to smooth over any awkwardness between her officemates, said, "The important thing is that each of us is very happy with what we received."

Juanita and Benedetta returned to their desks and were soon absorbed in the day's typing, but Anne remained transfixed by the book. One by one, she explored its pages, savoring every picture and translating to herself parts of the text.

When Anne noticed Jürgen quietly standing in the doorway, she had the feeling he'd been observing her for several minutes. His boyish face shone with satisfaction. Effusively he said, "Ah, dear Anne, I see I've finally found a gift that pleases you."

Anne regarded him with consternation. She was still deeply distrustful of him and determined to keep him at arm's length. Trying to sound more blasé than she felt, she responded, "Indeed, it's quite a nice book."

Jürgen didn't look fooled. "I realized that the kinds of gifts I was bringing to the office weren't really making you happy. Now I think I better understand you, and what things you appreciate."

"Well, it was most thoughtful of you, but now I must get to work."

She pushed the book aside as though it were insignificant and began taking the cover off her typewriter. It troubled her that in fact he was coming to understand her, as the gift of this special book showed.

Seeing that Jürgen had entered the office, Benedetta and Juanita jumped to their feet. Benedetta said, "Oh Jürgen, I can't thank you enough for this enchanting necklace. It's perfect in every way."

Juanita said, "I love mine, too. Thank you so much."

Jürgen bowed and said, "It is my deepest pleasure to see you two young ladies looking so beautiful wearing my humble gifts."

Then he turned back to Anne and his face sobered. "I'm glad that you, Anne, have been made happy by my modest offering of a book, because I'm afraid I have unsettling news for you."

Anne stopped what she was doing and looked up at him.

"This morning they defused a bundle of dynamite that had been set to go off in the Meditation Room."

Benedetta exclaimed, "The Meditation Room!"

Juanita said, "I heard that from a friend early this morning, but I forgot all about it when I started opening your gift. Why would anyone want to destroy the Meditation Room?"

The UN's revered Secretary-General Dag Hammarskjöld had personally planned every aspect of the Meditation Room. It was located to one side of the UN Public Lobby, behind a grey-green marble wall. Inside, it was graced by a large abstract fresco of interlocking geometric shapes. At the center of the room was a massive slab of iron ore, bathed by an overhead shaft of light. After Hammarskjöld's tragic death in a 1961 plane crash, a dramatic stained glass window, created in his memory by Chagall, was installed at the entrance to the room.

Looking at Anne with concern in his eyes, Jürgen said, "I'm sorry to be the one to bring you such devastating news, but I thought you should know. I'm sure it's alarming for you, because you told me that you often go there to meditate."

"You do?" Juanita asked.

Anne nodded. Her face was pale.

"I didn't know that. Well, don't worry," Juanita said in a reassuring tone. "My friend says the timer wasn't properly activated, so whoever set the dynamite must have been amateurs. Or maybe they didn't really want it to explode, but just to scare people. Anyway, now that this has happened, of course Security will be watching the Meditation Room very carefully. So you should feel safe going back any time you want."

Jürgen nodded in support. "Yes, dear Anne, Juanita is surely right. It will be safe for you to keep going there."

There was no response from Anne.

"Please don't look so upset, Anne," Juanita tried again. "My friend assures me the area will be under constant observation from now on."

Still Anne didn't reply. Her distress didn't stem from fear that someone would try again to bomb the Meditation Room. She was unnerved because she'd never once mentioned to Jürgen that she went there to meditate. Either he, or someone else, had been following her there.

CIRCULAR PATTERNS

Señor Duarte poked his head out of his office. "Anne, stop what you're doing. You're needed upstairs to take dictation."

"In the Director's office?" Anne's eyebrows lifted. How odd. Usually when Mr. Ajiboye had an overflow of work, he asked for Juanita.

"No," Duarte responded, looking puzzled. "It's for Political Affairs. Señor Gavrez."

Anne, who'd been rising from her chair, halted midway. Uncertainly, she repeated, "Señor Gavrez? Are you sure there hasn't been a mistake?"

Both Juanita and Benedetta stopped typing, curious to hear Duarte's answer.

"His secretary called just now and specifically asked for you, Anne. Though I don't understand why he wouldn't get someone from his own department, instead of Public Information."

Juanita said to Anne, "You must know him from when you were in Cyprus. Weren't you both there at the same time?"

"Ye-e-es," Anne said, drawing out the word. "He was in his second year as UN Mediator when I arrived. We overlapped by a few months before he returned to Headquarters."

"Well, that explains it," Juanita responded cheerfully. "Your work there must have impressed him."

Anne sank back down into her chair. That wasn't how she remembered his attitude toward her in Cyprus.

Benedetta said, "He's a rising star. Isn't he the UN's youngest Under-Secretary-General? I don't think he's even 50."

"It's neither here nor there," Duarte interrupted, "why he called for you, Anne. He's an important man. Gather up what you need and go quickly."

She nodded.

As soon as Duarte returned to his office, Peggy emerged from their corner nook, where she'd been reading their copy of *The Economist*. "Lucky you, Anne," she winked. "Gavrez is a dish."

Anne looked nervously at Duarte's closed door. "Peggy," she complained, "I wish you'd keep your thoughts about men to yourself."

"Well, he is," Peggy insisted, with a coy tilt of her head. "He's so macho. And those sensuous lips. If you don't want to go to his office, send me in your place. I'll sit on his lap to take dictation."

Anne reached into a drawer for her stenographer's pad. "You're incorrigible," she muttered.

At the doorway, Anne realized she should tell Juanita and Benedetta how far she'd gotten with her typing. As she turned around, she caught a questioning look pass between them and it added to her own doubts. To be called to do work for another department, let alone for its highest official, was unheard of.

"I've only done half of today's press briefing," she told them. "So if I'm not back by 4:30, you'll probably want to take over for me."

Along with two distinguished-looking men, Anne exited the elevator at the 37th floor. Light beige walls and plush carpeting signaled that she was entering a more rarefied world. It was a far cry from the grey hallways and scuffed linoleum of her part of the UN.

She followed the directional sign on the wall to the very north end of the building. There she entered a sizeable outer office. A striking blonde looked Anne up and down but didn't greet her. Anne noticed that her desk was completely unencumbered by papers, and the cover was still on her typewriter. The secretary sitting across from her was meticulously applying glossy red polish to one of her nails.

The first secretary, after she'd finished scrutinizing Anne, rose leisurely from her chair and sauntered to the half-open door behind her. Condescendingly, she called through the doorway, "She's here."

From the depths of the office, a deep masculine voice, which Anne recognized immediately, responded, "Show her in."

Anne passed through the doorway and stopped a few feet inside. Gavrez's spacious office was arranged with tasteful, expensive-looking furniture which she doubted was UN issue. He was at his desk studying a document and didn't look up.

She remained standing. The wait felt interminable. Had he forgotten she was there? Finally, she summoned the courage to ask, in a barely audible voice, "Sir, where would you like me to sit?"

Gavrez didn't answer right away. Then, without raising his head, he dismissively waved a hand in the direction of a chair several feet from his desk. He kept reading while Anne sat on the edge of the seat, her back stiff, her shoulders tight.

Minutes passed, but Gavrez continued to ignore her presence. With nothing else to do, she began studying what was in his office. A long black cashmere coat and a subtly patterned silk scarf were draped over an upholstered chair in the far corner. High quality etchings and prints decorated the walls. On two side tables were arrayed brightly colored handicrafts which he'd probably brought with him from Ecuador.

The scent of full-bodied hazel smoke drew her eyes to the long cigarette cradled in the marble and bronze ashtray on his desk. She knew it was a Benson & Hedges, the only cigarette he smoked, according to his secretary in Cyprus. "It's the Dom Pérignon of cigarettes, you know," the secretary once told Anne in a patronizing tone, and then ordered her to go into Nicosia to buy him a fresh carton. That secretary had also devoted a fair amount of time to applying nail polish.

Near the ashtray, in a prominent position, was an oceanic snail shell, bigger than Anne's fist. Although muted, its striated colors of grey, rose, and beige were compelling. It was truly beautiful. She could see why, out of all the objects in the room, it was the one he had chosen to have on his desk.

Still not looking at her, Gavrez at last broke the silence. "Take a memo," he commanded.

Anne readied her pen on her steno pad.

"To Hoyer Fenn, Executive Office of the Secretary-General. Since the announcement by Madrid that it is ready to give up the Spanish Sahara, it has come to my attention that the diverging positions of each of the three neighboring countries – dash – Algeria, Mauritania and Morocco – dash – have the potential to…"

Anne struggled to keep up with the fast pace of Gavrez's dictation, but she was afraid to ask him to slow down or repeat any phrases.

After the fifth paragraph, having not once glanced at her, he rose from his chair and walked, with leonine self-assurance, over to the windows. From there, he continued to dictate over his shoulder even more rapidly than before. Anne's pen whirred over the lines. With her left hand, she periodically flipped to the next page as quickly as she could.

Abruptly, the torrent of words stopped.

Gavrez remained at the windows, staring across the East River as the daylight began to fade. Anne didn't want to look in his direction, but her eyes were irresistibly drawn to him. Even seen from behind, his physique gave off an aura of worldliness and unshakable confidence. For one moment, he slightly turned his head, revealing his chiseled profile.

The long wait in silence made Anne increasingly nervous. To control her anxiety, she began quietly looking back at her earlier pages to make sure everything she'd written was clear.

Bent over her steno pad, she sensed, rather than saw, that Gavrez had noiselessly returned to his chair. There he sat, still without speaking, while Anne held her waiting pen upright on her next page.

Finally, she raised her head only enough to be able to see through her eyelashes what Gavrez was doing. With two of his long, tapered fingers, he was methodically tracing the shell's deep spiral, starting at the outer edge and slowly arriving at the dark protruding center point. After pausing there, his fingers followed the spiral back out to the edge. Just when Anne thought he would resume his dictation, he would begin the pattern again.

Dusk deepened, lengthening the shadows that engulfed them, but Anne didn't dare ask if she could turn on the lights. At his desk, Gavrez intently traced and retraced the shell's spiral.

Anne could no longer stand the tense silence. Trying to muster a conversational tone, she asked, "Is that from Cyprus?"

For the first time since she'd entered his office, Gavrez turned his head in her direction. The withering look he gave her stopped what would have been her next sentence. She quickly dropped her eyes.

Again and again Gavrez traced the spiral, seeming now to put more pressure in his fingers, and always ending with finality at the center point before beginning again.

In the strained atmosphere of the darkening office, the shell, for Anne, had transformed from an object of beauty into something unsettling, even ominous.

21

AMERICAN SUSPICIONS

Fouad and Anne held up their passes for the guard at the UN street entrance. He looked from their photos to their faces and then waved them through. As they walked across the traffic circle, Anne admired the luminous crescent moon framed between the tall Secretariat Building and the low-lying Dag Hammarskjöld Library to its right. But she was wincing with each step. She couldn't believe how much her feet hurt.

After she and Fouad rotated through the entry, she went to the podium to sign in.

"I'll wait for you here," Fouad said. "You won't be long, will you?"

The officer on duty gave them a questioning look. "What are you two doing here at this hour? Are you working a night shift?"

Anne pointed down at her brown shoes with gold trim. "I love these shoes, but they're too tight. I've got to change into walking shoes before I even think of getting on a bus."

The guard winked at Fouad. "She got all dressed up for you?"

Anne was emphatic. "We're friends."

Fouad was a Lebanese colleague from her department's front office. He was attractive, with dark curly hair and lively eyes set in a face with pleasant features. A nice guy, and with depth, but not Anne's type.

With a wry smile, Fouad conceded, "The 'friends' part isn't my idea, but I go along with it."

Anne hobbled across the lobby and stepped onto the escalator. Because it was late, the steps were once again locked in place. She painfully climbed each one to the second floor.

Despite her aching feet, she felt content. She hadn't lied to the guard – she and Fouad weren't dating – but there was a nice feeling between them, and she'd thoroughly enjoyed their dinner at the new Lebanese restaurant on Second Avenue.

As she neared the top of the escalator, Anne hesitated. In the half light, the area looked deserted and gloomy. Her whole body tensed and she couldn't go forward. She told herself she was being foolish. Sure, there were situations at work making her nervous. But the only real harm to her had been the taxi accident, and that happened outside the UN building, not in it. And besides, Fouad and the guard knew where she was, so it wasn't like she was coming to the dark area completely alone.

Still, it was a moment before she exited the escalator and headed for the double glass doors. Pushing them aside, she entered the hallway to her office. Two men in blue cleaners' uniforms were swabbing the floor.

"Hold it, Miss," one said, holding up his hand. "You can't walk this way. We're cleaning the linoleum."

"I have to go to my office," Anne said. Seeing the man's deep frown, she added, "I'll be careful not to step where the floor is wet."

The men silently formed a human wall, making clear they weren't going to allow her any further. Why was it that at the UN everyone, even night cleaners, acted like self-important bureaucrats? She sighed with exasperation, but she wasn't going to let wet linoleum decide whether or not she changed into comfortable shoes.

"All right then," she said. She turned away as though to retrace her steps, then spun back around. Catching the cleaners off guard, she rushed past them. Reaching her office door, she flung it open.

She stood speechless. The beam of a flashlight, propped on one of the desks, revealed two men on their knees bending over a large black mat. Wearing latex gloves, they were sorting through a tumble of objects. It didn't take Anne long to recognize that it was the entire contents of her desk drawers.

While she remained in the doorway, immobile, one of the cleaners rushed up behind her and pinned her arms to her sides. As she struggled to free herself, Rick rose to his feet. "Let her go," he said. "Oh, and, by the way, the whole point of you being out there was to keep people away."

Muttering, the "cleaner" released Anne and backed out the doorway.

She rubbed her arms and stared accusingly at Rick and Stewart. "What the hell are you doing?"

Rick answered calmly, "That's the question we should be asking you, Anne."

She walked over to Juanita's chair and slowly sat down. With disdain, she asked, "Did you find anything?"

For a moment, neither Rick nor Stewart replied. Anne felt her composure slip. What if something had been planted in her desk? More politely, she repeated, "Did you find anything?"

This time it was Stewart who spoke. "Anne, you know what's in this desk as well as we do. There's nothing here."

Relief washed over her. Then her irritation returned. Her voice rose in anger. "This is completely out of order. I've done nothing to make you mistrust me."

"Oh, come on, Anne," said Stewart. "Have you forgotten how you handled the FBI phone call?"

Anne cringed. She remembered all too well.

"And there's the question of why you're studying Russian."

"Are those the most damaging things you can come up with? Listen, I've told Patterson and Royce everything I can think of."

Rick and Stewart exchanged a look.

"You don't trust me, do you," Anne said with mounting frustration. "If something's going on, I don't know what it is. I don't know. I don't know!"

"Pull yourself together," Rick said. "Do what you came for, go home, and we'll just forget this evening."

Anne scowled. "Easy for you to say." With resignation, she walked over to the black mat and retrieved a shoebox. She sat down and sullenly exchanged her brown shoes for sneakers. Then she rose and handed the box to Stewart. In a monotone, she said, "Lower right drawer, in the back."

She turned around and walked out the door. The two men in the hallway stepped aside to let her pass.

22

UNWELCOME INVITATION

The bus stopped at 67th Street to take aboard a few more late-night stragglers heading home. Fouad glanced at Anne. "You're awfully quiet. Is anything wrong?"

She hesitated. While they were waiting for the bus, she'd been tempted to tell him about finding Rick and Stewart in her office, but she remembered Patterson's firm instruction not to say anything to her friends. Besides, Fouad had chided her once before about her political naïvete, and she didn't feel like another lecture. Instead, she said, "It's nice of you to take the M15 with me to make sure I get home safely. It's out of your way."

Fouad smiled. "You didn't answer my question."

Anne smiled back but wouldn't meet his eyes. "No, nothing's wrong. I'm just a little tired."

She peered out the smudged windows. "Here's my stop." She was relieved she wouldn't have to parry any more of his queries, however well-intentioned.

They kissed each other's cheeks and then she stood up and tugged on the signal cord. "Thanks again for the lovely dinner."

As she stepped off the bus, Anne was grateful she was now within the safe zone monitored by Patterson's men. Finally she could let her guard down. Once she was sure the bus had carried Fouad beyond where he could see her, her shoulders sagged. Trudging the last two blocks to her building, she mulled over the evening's events. She felt helpless. Somehow the different aspects of her life were combining to make her look suspect not only to the Soviets, but to the Americans, too.

Until Rick mentioned it that evening, she'd managed to exile to a far corner of her mind that embarrassing earlier incident with the FBI. It was just one of several missteps she'd made during her first weeks at the UN. Not willfully. At first she didn't completely get how things worked. She hadn't been cautious enough, suspicious enough.

Prompted by Rick's taunt, now she clearly recalled that evening shortly after she'd joined the UN the previous year, long before the taxi accident. The phone had rung. Hoping it might be someone asking her for a date, she let it ring three times and then picked up.

"Good evening," said a friendly male voice. "May I please speak to Anne Thomas?"

"This is she," Anne answered. It was a voice she didn't recognize and she felt expectant. Maybe one of her friends was fixing her up with a blind date.

"Hi, my name is Arthur Donegan." After a pause, he added, "I'm with the FBI and I'd like to get together for a coffee."

How disappointing. He was only calling about work. He must be doing the background check for Robert, the new American in the press release office around the corner from her. Robert had previously been a magazine writer and seemed competent and pleasant. Anne would be happy to tell the agent the little she knew about him so far. "Sure," she responded. "That'll be fine. When do you want to get together?"

As she waited for him to suggest a day, Anne recalled her own background check. Although the days of McCarthyism were over, the FBI remained worried that left-leaning American staff, in daily proximity to Soviet colleagues, might end up working against the United States. To guard against that happening, the FBI did an investigation of new American hires that left no stone unturned. How stunned Anne had been when she found out they'd even asked her sixth grade teacher in Oregon whether, as a student, she'd shown any interest in Russia.

Donegan's voice brought her back to the present. "What about next Tuesday at 5:30? At the Greek coffee shop at 56th and Third?"

Anne was just about to accept, when it struck her as odd that Donegan hadn't mentioned Robert. She commented, "You haven't said what this is about."

"I'd prefer to tell you in person when I see you."

She felt edgy. "I would really appreciate knowing now," she replied, trying to keep her tone courteous.

"You know what, it'll be better if we go over this when we meet for coffee."

Anne heard her voice become firm. "I'm sorry," she said, "but if you can't tell me now, I'm afraid there won't be a coffee."

There was a silence at the other end. Then, as though reading from a script, Donegan said, "It's about an investigation, perfectly empowered by law, into certain nationals working at the United Nations."

Her heart sank. Now she understood exactly what the call was about. They wanted her to watch the communist staff members around her and report any suspicious behavior.

Anne didn't respond right away. Finally she said, "Look, things may well be going on at the UN that shouldn't be happening. But I'm only a worker, and during my days I don't see those things. To help you, I'd have to go looking for them, and I don't have the nerves to do that."

"I'm disappointed. It would have been an opportunity for you to serve your country." Donegan cleared his throat. "And to prove your loyalty. Well, in case you change your mind, I'll give you my phone number." After he'd done so, he said, "Thank you for your time this evening."

Before she could respond, he hung up.

Anne's hands shook as she replaced the receiver. His phrase "perfectly empowered by law" struck her as strange and convoluted. Then her own part in the conversation came back to her. In trying to explain her position, she'd said she was merely "a worker". Bad word choice. It must have made her sound like a communist.

Her head was throbbing. She didn't want to get drawn into the Cold War by either side. She had to tell someone about this unsettling phone call. But who?

She slept fitfully that night. The next morning, as soon as she passed through the revolving door, she strode purposefully across the checkered lobby to the UN Security office at the back of the building. She entered a small anteroom and waited at the counter. In a room beyond, she could see rows and rows of flickering closed-circuit TVs, monitored by two guards.

It was a while before the nearest officer looked in her direction. Without apparent interest, he rose and asked, "Can I help you?"

"I want to make a report," Anne said, trying to put forward a confidence she didn't feel.

"What kind of 'report'?"

Anne leaned over the counter so she could speak in a low voice and still be heard. "Someone who said he was an FBI agent called me last night, and asked me to," she paused with discomfort, "well, to...to work for them."

The officer looked at her quizzically. "Why have you come to tell us that?"

"It's against the contract I signed when I joined the UN."

The officer seemed unimpressed.

Anne stood up straight. "And it's against the United Nations Charter," she said emphatically.

The officer narrowed his eyes and looked more closely at Anne. Then he studied the blue grounds pass she wore on a chain. "I see where you're going with this," he said. "I'll make a note of it."

She felt a sense of relief. "Thank you so much."

Once back in the lobby, she was heading toward the escalator when Fouad caught up with her. "Morning, Anne. Hey, you have an odd look on your face. What's up?"

She told him about the phone call the evening before and that she'd just reported it to Security.

"You what?" Fouad put his hand to his forehead and groaned. "Oh, Anne, what were you thinking? Are you that naïve?"

She looked puzzled.

He stared at her in astonishment. "You don't know? Anne, UN Security is run by the FBI."

She shook her head. "You're wrong. They're UN staff, the same as we are."

Fouad's face contracted. "Well, sure, the guards are from all over the world, like in every UN office. But the people who make the decisions? It's the FBI. How could you not know that?"

23

FLAGGING TROUBLE

Juanita knocked on Duarte's door and then respectfully opened it. His voice carried into the outer office. "What is it, Juanita?"

"Señor Duarte, Copenhagen asked us to send them flags of the five new Member States. They want to fly them on 24 October for United Nations Day. But the Flag Unit says they don't have any extras."

"Well then," Duarte responded, "tell Copenhagen we simply can't do it."

"That's just it, Señor Duarte. I did tell them."

"And…?"

"They said they found an excellent seamstress who'll sew the flags for them, if we can prepare half-scale drawings and get them in Friday's pouch."

Juanita backed out of Duarte's office as he emerged through the doorway with a thoughtful look on his face. "In that case, we'll have to accommodate them. Who here has artistic talent?"

Juanita, Benedetta and Jürgen, who was standing beside Benedetta's desk, all turned to look at Anne.

"Do you, Anne?" Duarte asked.

She was flustered. "I draw a little bit, and do some calligraphy," she said, "but I wouldn't really say I have artistic talent, that is, I…"

"Good, then it's settled," Duarte said, wheeling around and heading back to his office. Over his shoulder, he added, "And remember, have them ready for Friday's pouch." His door shut behind him like a decisive punctuation mark ending his sentence.

Juanita, Benedetta and Jürgen burst out laughing.

"It's not funny," Anne protested. "Have you seen those new flags?"

The others shook their heads.

"Cape Verde, Comoros and Suriname shouldn't be too hard. They're just geometric, mainly with bands of color," Anne said. "But Mozambique has the communist symbols of a hammer and sickle, made out of a tank tread and a rifle with a bayonet. And the flag of Papua New Guinea has a phoenix with very feathery wings. It will be a nightmare to draw."

Her mouth turned downward with such a look of dejection that despite her reproach, the others laughed again. "Cheer up, Anne," Jürgen said encouragingly. "It will be an adventure."

She scowled at him. He took the hint and withdrew to his office.

"Juanita," Anne asked, "where can I get paper big enough for the drawings?"

The merriment left Juanita's eyes. "Oh, that will be a special order. Let's get it in right now."

*   *   *   *   *

The way Duarte put his keys down on Anne's desk told everyone in the office he was displeased. "Anne, you have to be more careful. My wife went to three different art supply stores before she could find the right kind of paper. I'll ask you kindly not to make any more mistakes. It can't be that hard to draw a mere bird."

Color flared on Anne's cheeks. "It's not like it's a robin," she muttered under her breath, loudly enough for Juanita to give her a warning look. Mustering a more polite tone, Anne said, "I'll get it right this time, Señor Duarte. And please thank your wife for me. What level of the garage is your car parked on?"

"My wife says she left it on Level 2, about six rows from the elevator under the General Assembly building. It's a green Buick Skylark and has a New York license plate, *JAS 152*."

Anne jotted the number on a slip of paper. "Thank you, Señor Duarte," she said, as she rose from her desk. Nodding to Juanita and Benedetta, she said, "I'll be back in a little while."

In the elevator, Anne fingered the keys thoughtfully. She had to make a grid so she could more accurately position the feathers and tail of Papua

New Guinea's phoenix. Yesterday she'd made so many attempts that her eraser wore right through her last sheet of paper.

Exiting at Level 2, she stepped into the cool mustiness of the underground garage. The green Skylark should stand out easily among the rows and rows of glossy black diplomatic cars spread out before her.

But Anne was taken aback at the gloominess. The dim overhead bulbs were sparse, and massive support pillars blocked a clear view in any direction. An eerie rumble echoed above her head. It must be a car driving across Level 1. Whether from the chill in the air or the creepiness of the place, Anne shivered.

Some ten minutes later, she was feeling even more unnerved. Several times she had crisscrossed the area around the sixth row but hadn't spotted the Skylark. And there wasn't anyone else walking around the garage whom she could ask for help. The place was totally deserted.

She began heading toward the far wall. She would start there and work her way back to the elevator. She wished Señora Duarte had given a more exact description of where she'd parked the car, but it was too late for that now.

Anne skirted several small cinder block structures with doors, some marked with warning signs for high-voltage electricity. As she passed one, a lightbulb overhead flickered and then went out, making that section even darker. Cables and debris were strewn about, forcing her to step carefully. She wrapped her arms around herself to fend off the cool air and her growing anxiety.

Finally she reached the far wall. Level 2 was much bigger than it first appeared.

She'd just finished scanning the third row – fruitlessly – when she heard a car door quietly opening nearby. At last, someone who might be able to help her. She began walking in that direction, but then stopped. She'd been in the garage at least 20 minutes, and during that time, she hadn't heard any cars drive in. If someone was now getting out of a car, that meant they'd been sitting in it for a while.

Maybe there was a good explanation, but she felt wary enough to hang back. Instead of continuing toward the sound, she slipped behind one of the large support pillars and waited. Her ears strained in the silence, but she heard nothing. Her unease grew.

A whining scrape to her right alerted Anne that a door in a nearby cinder block structure was opening. She heard soft voices and then the metallic scratch of a cigarette lighter striking a flame. It was so close that she saw the flash of illumination reflect off a dark car window. Then it went out.

From the area where the car door had opened, she heard another cigarette lighter flaring up.

Definitely something wasn't right. Her whole body felt clammy. If someone was holding a clandestine meeting in this isolated corner of the garage, it was the last place Anne wanted to be. She pressed her hands against the cold cement of the pillar and tried to steady her breath.

Quiet footsteps told her the men were approaching each other. She heard the words, "*¿Alguien te vio?*" Did anyone see you?

"No."

Anne softly exhaled her relief. That must mean that when she first began searching the garage, she'd been far enough away that the person waiting in the car hadn't spotted her.

One of the men asked, "Do you have everything?"

"I'm missing one piece, but otherwise everything is here. It's all in the trunk. It's packaged and addressed, ready to mail out from the UN Post Office."

"Why is one piece missing? Which one?"

Anne struggled to make out their next words. As she was turning slightly to hear more clearly, she sensed something move behind her. She whirled around.

A dark shadow closed in and a gloved hand clamped roughly over her mouth. Another hand forcefully bent her right arm against her back. "Don't move," a harsh voice whispered in her ear.

24

RENDEZVOUS GONE WRONG

The man slowly turned Anne's face toward his. When she saw him, she flinched. He was a head taller and wore a black knit ski mask that left only his green eyes showing.

For several agonizing moments, they searched each other's eyes. Anne's body was trembling uncontrollably, when suddenly her emotions shifted. His look was bright and forceful, but it wasn't cruel.

It was the man who ended the taut silence. He said softly, with a hint of surprise, "You're just a girl." He paused and then added, "You're not with them, are you."

Within the limited range that his tight grip allowed, Anne slowly shook her head.

He studied her even more intently. "My team needs me, so I'm going to take a chance. I'm going to take my hand off your mouth. But don't even think of crying out. Do you understand me?" He roughly lifted Anne's arm higher on her back until she winced in pain. With wide eyes, she nodded.

Cautiously, as though still unsure of her, the man slowly removed his gloved hand from her mouth. She pressed her lips tightly together to show him she had no intention of shouting.

"I've got to go. Kneel here. And don't make a sound, no matter what happens."

Without turning around, he signaled to someone behind him. Lowering to a crouch, he began weaving noiselessly between the dark parked cars, circling to the left of where the conversation in Spanish was continuing.

Anne followed his orders and was lowering herself to the ground when an almost imperceptible sound made her head whip to the right. In the shadowy recesses of the garage, she could make out two other men in ski masks cautiously moving forward. She guessed that this team – whoever they were – intended to close in on the rendezvous from both the left and right. Instinctively, she felt glad they were there.

Her attention reverted to the conversation. The voices were growing louder. There seemed to be a disagreement. Two of the men moved back and began talking separately. Then all became quiet. Too quiet. The tension was palpable.

Anne's nerves were strained to the breaking point. She pulled in her arms and legs, trying to make herself smaller.

A loud clatter broke the silence. One of the men in ski masks circling to Anne's right must have tripped on some of the debris she herself had avoided earlier.

"*¿Qué fue eso?*" What was that? someone shouted. "You set a trap for me?"

A gunshot reverberated through the vast space. Anne's eyes swung to the right in time to see one of the men in ski masks crumple to the ground.

Hearing a commotion on the other side of the pillar, Anne looked forward just as a dark figure ran leftwards across her line of vision. "*¡Estafadores!*" Double-crossers! he cursed. He tore open the door of his car and its engine roared to life. He threw it into reverse and with squealing tires, careened out of the parking space and raced toward the ramp up to the street exit.

The other man in a ski mask to Anne's right leaped up from between two cars and raised a gun. "I'll get his tire!"

"Let him go!" Anne recognized the voice of her former captor. "It's these men we want!"

Pounding footsteps echoed off the cold concrete. Anne heard the nearby door grind open. For a second she hesitated, then threw her lot in with the pursuers. "They're going through the door," she called out, "the one over here!"

The leader of the team changed his direction and ran toward the doorway. As he disappeared through the opening, he yelled at Anne, "Go help my buddy!"

The second man of the team dove in after him.

Terrified, Anne stood unmoving, braced against the support pillar.

A soft groan from the man who was down brought her back to reality. She forced herself to make her way over to him.

He was sitting slumped against the front of a car. He'd removed his ski mask and it lay on the ground beside him. Bright crimson blood was spreading out from his leg. At the sight of it, Anne began to sway. Daunted, she whispered, "I don't know what to do."

His pallid face turned upward to look at her. "It's not a deep wound," he said through clenched teeth. "Quickly, though, take off your scarf and make a tourniquet."

Her voice wavered. "I don't know how."

"It's not hard. I'll walk you through it. I'm feeling too weak or I'd do it myself."

Anne removed the scarf from around her neck and with trembling hands, followed the man's instructions. Looking away as much as she could, she circled the scarf around the man's leg above the wound. She slowly tightened it until he said, "Okay, that's good right there. Now make a knot that won't loosen."

Once the tourniquet was in place, she sat down beside him on the ground. Squeamishly, she drew her skirt in close to avoid the pool of blood. "Does it hurt a lot? I wish I had some water to give you."

The man bit his lower lip, which made Anne think he was in more pain than he would admit. He said, "The main thing is that we slowed the bleeding. When my buddies get back, they'll take me to a doctor." He looked at her speculatively. "Who are you, and what are you doing here?"

For the first time since Anne heard the car door open, she remembered the art paper she'd come for. "My boss asked me to get something from his car."

"He picked a hell of a time to send you on an errand."

"I don't think he knew how deserted it would be. I guess everyone must be at the morning Security Council meeting. Maybe that's why those guys set their rendezvous for now."

The man beside Anne shifted on the ground, as though trying to find a more comfortable position. Absentmindedly, he nodded his assent.

Anne was puzzled. "Who are they? And who are you?"

"We're U.S. Postal Inspectors."

She was incredulous. "With guns?"

The man was staring at the large amount of blood on the garage floor and he looked alarmed. Distractedly, he said, "Yes, when we're tracking contraband being sent through the U.S. mail." He fingered his leg below the scarf. "You need to tighten the tourniquet."

Anne reached over and picked at the knot until it came undone. Then she carefully pulled the scarf more snuggly around his leg. She made a new knot as gently as she could, but all the same, the man winced.

She argued, "But our post office here is a UN Post Office, not an American one."

"That's better," said the man, still looking down at his leg. "The UN Post Office is independent, but mail from here feeds into the U.S. system. Once we figured out that the contraband was entering the mail at this location, we got the UN's permission to move in."

Anne paused, and then asked, "And who are those men?" Her throat tightened as she thought of them.

The postal inspector leaned his head back against the hood and closed his eyes. "We've been after them for a while, but we don't know their exact identities. They're..." His eyes flew open. "Damn! I shouldn't be telling you any of this."

Just then, the nearby door scraped open. Light footsteps were approaching. Both Anne and the man next to her stiffened. He was now on full alert. Gingerly, he lifted his gun off the floor and pointed it forward. Anne instinctively pulled in her legs, ready to jump up and run.

The footsteps came closer.

"It's us, Parker," said the voice Anne knew. "They slipped out of our grip."

The man on the ground beside Anne swore.

The third inspector approached. "It's my fault," he said. "I can't believe I tripped on that empty gas can." He stared down at his partner. "And look at you, Parker. You took the hit because of my carelessness."

As the two men drew closer, they removed their ski masks. The leader, his green eyes now filled with concern, squatted down in front of his wounded friend. "Don't worry, Parker, we'll get you looked at. At least you've got a good tourniquet there from…

He turned to stare at Anne, as though for the first time remembering she was there. "Miss, what the hell are you doing down here?"

"My boss sent me to get something from his car. His wife said she parked it on this Level, near the General Assembly elevator, but I couldn't find it anywhere. And then those men came, and then you…" She began shaking violently.

He took her arm. "Steady there. We'll help you find it, and then make sure you get out of here safely. What kind of car are you looking for?"

"It's green, with New York plates."

"Is it a Skylark?"

Anne nodded, surprised.

"There's a green Skylark parked on Level 1. We saw it when we were checking the cars up there, before we took our positions here."

"It's not even on this Level?" Anne asked in disbelief. "It's on Level 1? I could have grabbed the paper and left, without going through any of this?" Her eyes, which had stayed dry throughout the morning's ordeal, welled up with tears.

"Miss, did those men see you?"

It took Anne a moment to get control of her emotions. Finally, she replied, "I don't think so."

"This is very important, Miss." His voice became more insistent. "Are you sure?"

25

A FAMOUS WATERCOLOR

Anne stood in front of an oil painting called *Dusk at La Baie des Anges, Nice* and took in its various shades of deep blues. Two tall palm trees playfully framed the well-dressed figures on the esplanade who looked out across the bay at the Mediterranean-style houses climbing the opposite hill. Anne couldn't say exactly why, but she liked the painting very much.

"I think Detective Royce would like it, too," she mused. In fact, she was nurturing a slight hope that she might bump into him there at the Metropolitan Museum. Earlier, he'd mentioned he was becoming interested in artists who painted southern French landscapes.

However, Anne hadn't planted herself in front of the Raoul Dufy painting only to be there if Royce happened to enter that gallery. Part of her appreciation of the canvas was because it reminded her of another Dufy painting she'd seen up close, and under very dramatic circumstances.

It happened on the Sunday of the previous week. She'd been outside her apartment door, juggling a tennis racquet and a can of balls in one hand, while with the other she fumbled with her key. As the lock clicked into place, her telephone rang.

Anne turned her back on the jarring sound and started down the stairs. She was already late and they only had the court for an hour. But when she reached the floor below hers and the phone continued to ring, she hesitated. What if it was one of her tennis partners, wanting to change their plans?

She rushed back upstairs, two steps at a time. It took her a moment to unlock the door, and still the phone kept ringing. Someone really wanted to talk to her.

"Hello?" she said, with a question in her voice.

To her great surprise, it was Duarte. He had never once called her at home.

"Anne, Anne," he said hurriedly, "You must come to the office right away."

"But Señor Duarte," Anne protested. "I have a tennis date. We planned it weeks ago."

He raised his voice. "Well, cancel it. Come immediately!"

The phone went dead in her hand.

Annoyed, she changed from her tennis whites into a skirt and blouse.

Thirty minutes later, she arrived, breathless, at the UN. Duarte was waiting for her at their office door. "Come in, Anne, come in." He grabbed her arm and pulled her inside.

She was taken aback by his appearance. Sweat beaded on his normally relaxed forehead. Creases of anxiety formed around his mouth. His shirt was rumpled, his tie askew.

She waited for his explanation.

"Anne, there's a coup taking place right now in Cyprus. The situation is terribly dangerous. No one knows where Archbishop Makarios is, or even whether he's alive. And without the President, we're afraid the Greek Cypriots and Turkish Cypriots will start committing atrocities against each other, like in the 1960s."

Anne's eyes widened in alarm. "Oh God!" she exclaimed. "What do you want me to do?"

"You know Cyprus better than anyone else in the office. That's why I called you." Duarte picked up a handful of papers and thrust them at her. "We must monitor all the news dispatches and radio broadcasts coming from the field, especially the UN Information Centres. Their local media may have updates that haven't reached Headquarters another way."

For several long hours, Anne and Duarte checked many different news sources, but there was no word of Makarios. The tension was palpable in the dispatches coming from the Mediterranean. Each report told of scattered outbursts of violence in different parts of Cyprus. Armed men were now roaming the streets in most towns and villages. No full-scale hostilities had erupted, but the growing threat of an explosive civil war hung ominously over the island.

Anne felt tired and discouraged. And worried.

Then, in the early afternoon, they received an urgent cable from UNIC Athens. It read: "Shortwave radio picked up broadcast from Paphos, west coast Cyprus. Speaker identified self as President. Although static, we convinced its Makarios. He denounced coup. Appealed to all Cypriots to support government. Begged ethnic Greeks and Turks not to take up arms against each other."

Anne and Duarte turned their own shortwave radio to the frequency Athens gave them. As the receiver sputtered to life, they heard a voice speaking Greek. "It's Makarios!" Anne cried out. "I know that's his voice."

"Quick, quick, my dear," Duarte said. "Go up immediately to the Secretary-General's office and hand them this cable. I'll call and tell them you're on your way."

When the elevator reached the 38th floor, a security guard was standing in front of the opening doors. "They're waiting for you. Go straight to the SG's conference room at the end of that corridor."

Anne hurried down the hallway until she reached the conference room. The secretary on duty wordlessly waved her through.

As she entered, Anne's eyes sought out the Secretary-General's top aide, Andreas Lindhofer. She was sure he would be with Waldheim at that important moment. She knew the urbane, competent Austrian from delivering the *Press Analysis*, and it would be reassuring to see him there in such unfamiliar surroundings.

She spotted Lindhofer standing across the room and started toward him. He motioned that she should present the cable directly to Waldheim himself.

Anne shyly approached the Secretary-General. Without glancing at her, he impatiently grabbed the printout. Lindhofer thanked Anne and gestured for her to stand near the wall. She sensed he might want to give her further instructions before she returned to continue monitoring the dispatches.

As Anne waited, Waldheim and Lindhofer bent their heads over the printout and read it aloud, sentence by sentence. When they got to the end, they began an intense discussion in German. Anne wondered whether she should tell them she understood the language, but thought better of interrupting.

She felt electrified to be in the presence of these two important men at such a historic moment. Anne tried not to stare, but she'd never seen the Secretary-General so close up. His long, lanky body and stiff movements suggested a modern-day Ichabod Crane. She had to admit that his stern, craggy face was unattractive. She'd heard that he himself was so sensitive about his looks that on official trips, he always took the same UN photographer who knew to align each shot from a more flattering angle. And yet, Anne mused, Waldheim was the world's top diplomat. That inevitably gave him an aura of power.

The two men seemed to have completely forgotten Anne was there. While she quietly waited, she began to look about the room, which was furnished with understated elegance. On an end table, she saw a dark blue Sèvres porcelain vase with gold female figurine handles. She thought it must be a gift from France. On the opposite wall, she spotted an abstract bronze sculpture. It reminded her of a boat with delicate sails. This must be the Robert Cronbach she'd heard was in the UN collection.

Turning slightly, Anne was startled to see that she was standing next to one of the most notable treasures in the room. It was the watercolor by Raoul Dufy called *United Nations Headquarters, New York*.

Delighted to be so close to this famous painting, she took in every detail. The predominant coloring came from shades of slightly differing blues, offset here and there by light ochre. Her eyes lit up with admiration at the way Dufy rendered the tall UN Secretariat Building. The confident horizontal lines he had swept across the structure suggested its many stories, without detracting from its upward thrust. In his depiction, the building had a translucent quality, as did the cluster of skyscrapers forming the backdrop. Anyone looking at the painting would feel the vibrancy of the United Nations in its New York setting.

Anne would have stood much longer studying the painting, but a movement caught her eye. Turning her gaze back into the room, she saw Lindhofer indicate that she should leave. Silently, she withdrew.

Now in the Metropolitan Museum, standing before *Dusk at La Baie des Anges*, Anne could see that Dufy had used a similar palette of blues and ochre, although in this painting the colors were denser. As she stepped closer to study it, she felt a warm hand on her shoulder. She turned and looked up into eyes the color of the sky in the Dufy painting. It was Detective Royce, and he was smiling.

26

AN INEXPLICABLE DISAPPEARANCE

The apartment door opened only as far as the tarnished brass chain would allow. Looking from the outside through the narrow crack, Anne could barely make out the diminutive form of Dr. Ruzhinsky. "It's me," Anne said, in a voice she hoped sounded reassuring.

There was a clink as the chain was lifted from its holder. The door swung wide. Dr. Ruzhinsky said, "Come in, my dear, come in. The doorman announced you, but I had to make sure it was really you."

The elderly psychiatrist slid the chain back into place with shaking hands. She turned to Anne and breathed out, "Thank God you're here."

"Over the phone, you sounded very upset. I came as soon as I could."

"Thank you for that, my dear. Come, I have some tea ready for you."

As they made their way down the narrow hallway, the stringent odor of Russian chai reached Anne even before they entered the kitchen. There, a fragile china teapot, two delicate porcelain cups and a bowl of marmalade were set out on the tiny lace-covered table.

"Please, be so good, have a seat," said Dr. Ruzhinsky.

After the older woman herself sat down, she pressed a palm to her chest. A shadow of concern fell over Anne's face. "Is your heart all right, Dr. Ruzhinsky? Do you need your medication?"

"My heart is pounding so, but it's too soon to take more medicine." Looking up at the metal wall clock, she added, "Please tell me when it becomes 6:30. Then it will be safe for me to take another dose."

Anne asked, "Will it upset you too much to talk about it now?"

"I must," answered her boss. Her deep, intelligent eyes were filled with anxiety. "I must get to the bottom of this. Something has happened to her and she may need our help."

"Who, Dr. Ruzhinsky?"

"The Asian girl. She didn't come back."

"The Asian girl?" Anne asked deferentially.

"The student Professor Bernstein sent to see me."

"Dr. Ruzhinsky, maybe it would help if you started at the beginning."

"Well then. A girl phoned me this morning. She told me she was a Malaysian student at Columbia University working on a psychology thesis, and that Professor Bernstein suggested she come interview me on her topic. She…"

Anne prompted, "And Professor Bernstein is…?"

"From Paris, from Paris," Dr. Ruzhinsky said impatiently. "He was the dear friend of my late husband. When Professor Bernstein left for Free France, he tried to get my husband to go with him, but…" Her voice trailed off and tears welled up in her eyes.

"And now Professor Bernstein teaches at Columbia," Anne finished. She felt a wave of compassion. Her boss's husband had remained behind in Paris, where he was killed by the Nazis. "And did the Malaysian student come?"

"Yes, yes," Dr. Ruzhinsky said, getting agitated again. "She came at 4:00 o'clock precisely. She wore a long silk blouse over a patterned skirt in a beautiful red, with a matching shawl."

"And did you talk about her thesis?"

"I gave her tea in the living room and we chatted about this and that, but I never found out what her topic was. Instead, she wanted to talk to me about my library. She walked over to my bookcases saying, 'I really must see every volume in your wonderful collection.'"

Anne felt tension rising within her. "Let's go into your living room," she suggested, "and you can show me where she was looking."

"All right, my dear," answered Dr. Ruzhinsky. Bracing herself against the arms of her chair, she painfully raised her frail body to standing.

When they reached the living room, Anne stepped to the middle bookcase. Its shelves were filled with volumes on the Russian Revolution, the history of the Bolshevik and Menshevik movements, and European social democratic thought. Anne asked hopefully, "Was she looking mostly at your psychology books?"

"No, no," Dr. Ruzhinsky replied, "she looked at everything. As a matter of fact, she stood for a long time right where you are now."

Anne's heart sank. In a thin voice she asked, "Then what happened?"

"She asked me if she could have another cup of tea. I said, 'of course'. As I was going back to the kitchen, she told me she had to go out, just for a moment, to move her car."

"Car?" Anne asked. It was unusual for any student to have a car in New York City, let alone a foreign student.

Dr. Ruzhinsky's voice raised in pitch. "And she has not come back! That was more than two hours ago. I'm so worried that something terrible has happened to that lovely girl."

Anne thought for a minute and then suggested, "Why don't we call the police and see if they can tell us anything. What's her name?"

"That's just it," Dr. Ruzhinsky exclaimed. "I don't know her name. I couldn't understand it when she told me."

"In that case," Anne said, "why don't you call Professor Bernstein and ask him?"

"That's exactly what I'll do. I'm very glad you suggested it, my dear. I've been so upset that I haven't been thinking straight. I'll call him right away."

The psychiatrist moved over to her telephone table. Its small warped drawer opened reluctantly and she pulled out a tiny address book. Her arthritic fingers painstakingly dialed the number.

After several rings, she spoke into the receiver, "Bonjour, cher ami. C'est Galina." A rapid conversation in French ensued. Because of Dr. Ruzhinsky's thick Russian accent, Anne had trouble following her words, but she could hear greater and greater agitation in her voice.

When finally the elderly woman replaced the receiver, her face was pale.

Anne looked at her watch. "Dr. Ruzhinsky, it's 6:30. I'll run get your medication. Please sit down and try to calm yourself until I get back."

Anne rushed down the hallway and returned with a small dark bottle and a spoon. "Here, quick," she said, as she poured a dose.

After the color returned to her boss's face, Anne asked, "What did Professor Bernstein say?"

Dr. Ruzhinsky's voice wavered. "He knows no Malaysian student. He didn't tell anyone to come see me. Oh, what can it mean? What can it mean?"

Anne understood all too well what it meant. Her head began to spin. This was again her doing.

27

REMORSE

Anne stared down at the worn living room carpet without seeing it. She had to come up with something reassuring to say. Finally, she told the elderly woman, "I'm sure there's a logical explanation. It's just that right now we can't think what it is."

Dr. Ruzhinsky nodded thoughtfully and Anne was relieved to see that her pupils were now less dilated. Trying to sound unworried, Anne asked, "Would you like me to spend the night with you, so you won't feel so anxious?"

"No, no, my dear, I'll be all right. I'll call my son after he finishes work, and he or his wife will come to me." Reaching for Anne's hand, she gave it a grateful pat. "I've kept you too long, my dear. You must go home. It will be late for your dinner."

Anne felt reluctant to leave, but she rose from the sofa and followed Dr. Ruzhinsky back to the foyer. After walking through the apartment doorway, she turned around and said, "Please promise me you'll call your son."

"I will. And thank you for coming to me and listening to my worries. Goodbye, my dear. Be well."

Anne mumbled a "goodnight" that she hoped sounded normal to the older woman.

As the rickety elevator slowly descended, Anne twisted her hands in discomfort. "I'm responsible for this," she lamented to herself.

When she reached the lobby, she was so filled with remorse that she was unable to make eye contact with the kindly doorman as he wished her a pleasant evening. Instead, with a lowered gaze, she only nodded in return and stepped out onto East 97th Street as quickly as she could.

With leaden feet, she walked slowly until she reached First Avenue. She'd already run out of money for the month and didn't have enough for bus fare. Yet despite the chill in the air, she would have wanted to walk back to her apartment anyway. She needed time to reflect. There was no doubt in her mind that this latest disquieting incident was connected to her UN job application. It devastated her to think that her act of carelessness had once more placed her elderly friend at risk.

Again she berated herself for having wanted a higher-level job so much that on her application, she'd called Dr. Ruzhinsky's family memoir a "book on the Russian Revolution". She was convinced the KGB had sent the Malaysian girl to find out more about the manuscript. For Anne, it was the only possible explanation.

As she continued down First Avenue, Anne put one foot mechanically in front of the other. Any other time, she would have glanced around to make sure no one was following her, but that evening she was preoccupied by an urgent question.

What exactly had the girl done while Dr. Ruzhinsky was in the kitchen making more tea? Had she taken something? Hidden a bug? Planted forged documents that would discredit Dr. Ruzhinsky? Any one of those possible scenarios was cause for worry. When Anne returned the following Saturday to do more typing, she'd have to find an excuse to pull some books off the shelves to look behind and between them. Yet she wasn't sure what a bug even looked like. And a forged document would be almost impossible to spot if it were tucked in the pages of one of her boss's many volumes. Anne's shoulders sagged at the hopelessness of the situation.

A young man softly whistled his appreciation as he passed her on the sidewalk. She didn't hear it. She was struggling with herself as to whether she should finally tell Dr. Ruzhinsky the whole story. It seemed unfair to keep the obvious explanation from the elderly woman. Telling her would allow her to take specific precautions. But because of her heart condition, Anne still hesitated.

Once inside her apartment, Anne immediately locked the door and slumped onto the sofa. There she sat for over an hour, her head in her hands. There was one part of the story that didn't make sense. If the KGB were that afraid Dr. Ruzhinsky would publish damaging details about Lenin, it would be easy enough simply to do away with her. That very afternoon, the Malaysian girl could have put something in her tea or caused her to have a bad fall. Was the KGB merely curious? Or were they just biding their time?

Up to now, what Anne had put on her application was the one piece of information she'd held back from Patterson. Well aware how scornfully he would react, she'd been hoping time would prove it wasn't necessary for him to know. Now it was clear she had to tell him.

Anne was too distraught to move to her bed in the next room. Instead, she lay down, still clothed, on the sofa. She doubted she'd be able to fall asleep that night wherever she was. Yet despite her agitation, she eventually drifted off.

Several hours later, she sat bolt upright. Her temples pounding, she realized she'd had a nightmare. Images and phrases were swirling around in her head. She had to will her thoughts to calm down. Something important had happened in the dream, and she needed to recall what it was.

Slowly a scene came into focus. While waiting for an elevator at the UN, she was overhearing a low conversation in Russian around the corner. What caught her attention was that one man asked the same question twice: "What does she know about him? What does she know about *him*?"

His interlocutor answered, "That's what we have to find out."

Anne stiffened. At the hospital, Royce and Patterson had asked whether there was any information she had come across at the United Nations that the Soviets might not want brought to light. At the time, it never occurred to her that in fact she might know something, but not because she worked at the UN. What if the Russian man in her nightmare was asking, "What does she know about Lenin?"

What Anne herself knew about Lenin was in fact minimal, but whoever read her job application would have no way of knowing that. If the KGB thought she'd learned damning information about Lenin while working for Dr. Ruzhinsky, might they want to keep Anne from doing anything with it?

Cold sweat made Anne's clothes cling to her body as she tried to bring into focus what happened next in the nightmare. She was sure one of the men had said something more. Then she remembered. The first Russian had slyly asked the other, "Do we have to be completely sure before we act?"

Anne stifled a scream. The next scene in the dream came back vividly. A speeding taxi was jumping the curb and hurtling straight at her.

28

PROSPERITY

Anne held the phone a few inches away from her ear. Mr. Ajiboye, the Division Director, could be intense even over everyday issues. That afternoon, the pitch of his voice told her the matter was serious. "I need to speak to your boss. At once."

"Sir, he's at a meeting in the Indonesian Lounge with a delegation from Mozambique. They're inquiring…"

"I didn't ask you where he is or what he's doing, Miss Thomas. I told you I need to speak to him. Your only role is to get him on the phone immediately."

To deliver the Director's message, Anne would have to hurry down the long corridor, turn left just before the Delegates Lounge, and continue down another corridor before arriving at the Indonesian Lounge. That meant her boss wouldn't be calling Mr. Ajiboye back "immediately", but Anne didn't want to tell him that. Instead she replied, "I'll inform Señor Duarte right away."

Slightly out of breath, Anne stopped at the threshold of the Indonesian Lounge, an area normally off-limits to secretaries. Anne's few weeks at Headquarters had taught her that clerical workers were expected to adhere to their place near the bottom of the UN's rigid hierarchy. So she stood there patiently until she caught her boss's eye. In response to his raised eyebrow, Anne said across the space that separated them, "Mr. Ajiboye wants to talk to you. He says it's urgent."

Looking anxious, Duarte rose quickly from the sofa, made his excuses to the Mozambicans and hurried to the entryway. As he passed Anne, he said, "Bring the delegates refills on their coffee and tell them I shouldn't be long."

Anne returned with the coffees as quickly as possible. As she walked into the Lounge, she stared in awe at the graceful Balinese statue of *Prosperity* which presided over the room. Made of highly polished wood, the statue depicted an exaggeratedly slim woman who gracefully carried on her head an intricate basket of rice. Anne had been on duty at the press conference the day that *Prosperity* – along with a companion statue of *Peace* – was presented by the Indonesian government. She knew they were both very valuable.

While Anne was carefully placing each cup onto the glass table, one of the diplomats said, "Thank you, Miss. I'm the new Permanent Representative. Could you talk with us until your boss returns? We have many questions."

Anne felt it would be presumptuous of her to remain, but the Mozambicans, with encouraging smiles, insisted. Not wanting to offend them, she sat down hesitantly at the place on the sofa they indicated to her. She didn't think Señor Duarte would be happy to see her there when he returned.

The ambassador addressed Anne as though she were an equal. "We are here today, Miss, because we're hoping to introduce new UN radio programs in our country. Before decolonization, we were restricted in what we learned of the outside world. Now that we're independent, we feel it will be good for our people to hear news stories from many different regions. What can you tell us about other UN radio programs in our area?"

Anne felt flattered to be asked and began to speak about what she knew. "I think the UN radio programs in Tanzania might be especially good models for you because…"

As she was talking, Anne looked away so as not to appear too forward. Her gaze fell again on the statue of *Prosperity*. The statue brought a sense of serenity to the room, a serenity Anne very much needed while talking to a real ambassador for the first time in her life.

But as she continued to look at the statue, something made Anne lose her train of thought. The morning sun streaming through the windows to their right was highlighting a seam in the wood between the statue's front and back. But that couldn't be. At the donation ceremony, the Indonesian representative had proudly announced that *Prosperity* had been carved out of a single piece of wood. Anne was perplexed. Surely he wouldn't have been misinformed on this point.

After a long pause during which she remained silent, the Mozambican ambassador prompted, "You were telling us about the broadcasts in Tanzania. Is something wrong?"

Anne had totally lost the thread of what she'd been saying about the radio programs. Her thoughts had flown off in a totally different direction. She couldn't tell the diplomats the shock of what was starting to dawn on her, that the priceless statue of *Prosperity* may have been replaced by a fake.

Duarte's reappearance ended her dilemma. When he saw her on the sofa, his face took on a look of exasperation. "Anne, you were supposed to get more coffee for these delegates and then return to the office."

The Mozambican ambassador began to speak. "It was I who asked…"

Duarte appeared not to hear him. Pointing upward, he said to Anne, "Have you forgotten? You're expected on the 37th floor to take dictation for Under-Secretary-General Gavrez in…" He checked his watch. "Five minutes."

Anne leaped up from the sofa. "I didn't know that."

"Of course you did," Duarte countered. "Jürgen told me he gave you the message first thing this morning."

Anne felt whiplashed. Her boss's reprimand eradicated the happiness she'd been feeling because of the Mozambicans' kind attention. Then to find out that for some reason, Jürgen had intentionally caused her trouble by lying that he'd told her of Gavrez's summons. As if that weren't bad enough, now she had to go take dictation again from that brooding, overbearing man. And underneath it all, she was deeply shaken by what she now suspected about the statue.

Flushed with distress, she excused herself and hurried back toward the office to collect her steno pad.

As Anne drew near the Cypriot amphora, she remembered Patterson's instruction to avert her eyes from the fake. Then it hit her. If she was right about *Prosperity*, now two priceless UN artifacts had been stolen.

Patterson had cautioned Anne that she could be in danger if the amphora had been trafficked. If other UN art pieces were also being smuggled out of the building, was she even more at risk? But how could she know, if she had no idea what might be connecting her to the first theft? Patterson's earlier warning rang in her ears. "There may be people involved in this that you do not want to cross."

29

RESTRICTIONS

Anne called out to her friend, "Peggy, I have to go on an errand now. You can make a photocopy if you'd like, and then just put *The Economist* back on my desk."

Peggy looked up from the article she'd been reading. "Thanks, I'll do that. But where're you going?"

Anne pointed to three stacks of stuffed manila envelopes on the side table. "Juanita and I need to carry those up to the Pouch Office so they'll go out this afternoon."

Peggy glanced over at Juanita, who was typing at a rapid-fire pace. "No need to bother her," she said. "I'll help you carry the envelopes before I head back to my office, and we can chat on the way."

As she spoke, Peggy walked over to the envelope piles. She picked one up and then looked dubiously at the other two stacks. "Maybe all three of us will need to go. These are heavy."

Anne hoisted the remaining piles in her arms. "It's okay, I've carried this many before."

Juanita jumped up and hurried to open the door for them. "*Muchas gracias*, Peggy," she said. "I can really use the time."

As Anne and Peggy passed through the double glass doors into the main section of the Secretariat Building, Peggy said in a low voice, "Look, there are the Red Chinese." She tilted her head toward an area outside the Security Council Chamber.

Anne looked in that direction and spotted a cluster of people standing and conversing. All seven of them wore identical dark navy pants topped by jackets with the stand-up collar popularized by Chairman Mao.

"Yes," Anne said. "And see, two of them are women."

"Women?" Peggy's eyebrows rose. "I didn't think any UN delegations had women. Are you sure?"

"Look closely. Their hair is cut short and they're wearing the same clothes as the men, but they're definitely women."

Peggy studied the Chinese diplomats and then said softly, "You're right." She shook her head. "I'll bet that makes some of the other countries' diplomats uncomfortable. They're used to this being a men's club."

By this time Anne and Peggy had entered the elevator. As they exited at the 12th floor and started down the hallway, two men approached them from the opposite direction. The men walked slowly, their heads almost touching. Their voices were so soft that Anne couldn't make out what language they were speaking. She looked quizzically at Peggy. "Later," Peggy whispered.

When they reached the door to the Pouch Office, Anne paused. The three middle-aged men who worked there had rough edges, and she didn't enjoy being the target of their crude glances and comments. After mentally preparing herself for whatever they'd come up with today, Anne banged the door open with her hip.

She and Peggy entered and dropped the envelopes onto a long table with a loud thud. The men looked up in unison and one gave a low whistle. "*Two* beautiful babes today," he smirked.

Peggy preened and gave him a playful smile. Anne silently chastised herself. She should've known better than to bring Peggy with her to an all-male office. It wasn't like these guys were datable, even without the wedding rings they wore. Exasperated, she said to the man who'd whistled, "Stop it. You're at the United Nations."

"Okay, okay," he mumbled. "Just wanted to give you pretty girls a compliment."

"Instead of a compliment," Anne said in her most businesslike voice, "what I need is a receipt for these envelopes. They have to go out in this afternoon's pouches."

"Yes, ma'am," another answered with mock seriousness. "Whatever you say."

While Anne waited for him to fill out the form, she caught Peggy winking at the other men and shot her a dirty look. When Anne finally had the receipt, she grabbed Peggy's arm. "Come on, we've disrupted these gentlemen long enough."

Once back out in the hallway, Anne turned to Peggy. "You're hopeless," she complained.

"Clearly those poor lads have a dull job. What's wrong with bringing them a little glamour?" Peggy struck a sexy pose and grinned.

Anne laughed despite herself. "I guess I'll have to accept you as you are." Then she became serious. "But now you can tell me about those two men we saw before. They were talking to each other in such an odd way. What was going on?"

"Oh that," said Peggy. "I haven't seen those two before, but they must be Russians. Or other East Europeans. It's not only the Americans they're wary of. Their own people watch them pretty closely, waiting for them to make a misstep. So they don't have real conversations with each other in their offices, which are probably bugged. They don't talk much in the elevators either, where they might be overheard. Instead, they walk up and down the hallways, like we just saw, or go out to the UN Garden. And they always whisper like that."

Anne frowned. "Then I guess they can never really relax. Not at work, anyway. But maybe sometimes they go away for the weekend, to someplace where they don't have to be so cautious."

"They can't go that far," Peggy replied. "Not more than 50 miles from Columbus Circle here in New York City."

"What? The Soviets limit their own nationals that much?"

Peggy shook her head. "Not the Soviets. The Americans. The US gives them restricted visas. To the Cubans, too."

"But how would the Americans know if they went farther than 50 miles?" Anne asked.

"It's your government," Peggy answered. "What do you think?"

"Well, the United States is diligent," Anne said, thinking of Rick and Stewart going through her desk. After a pause, she said, "Maybe you can answer another question for me. Is it true the Soviet UN staff turn their paychecks over to their government's Permanent Mission here? And that the Mission redistributes the money according to each person's KGB rank?"

"I've heard that, too," Peggy said. "It would certainly keep them in line. But it may be just a rumor." Then she asked, "By the way, has anyone suggested you should work in Moscow for Pan Am or as a journalist?"

"No. Why would they?"

Peggy continued, "You know what that means, right?"

"What working for Pan Am or as a journalist in Moscow 'means'? Does it mean something different than how it sounds?"

Peggy playfully pushed Anne's shoulder. "Sometimes you're so naïve."

Anne visibly bristled. "Well, the last thing I want to be is *naïve*."

Peggy said quickly, "Please, I was just teasing. But you should know that when the Soviets want to recruit a young person, that's what they suggest."

It wasn't the mundane answer Anne had been expecting. "That's important to know. I'm sorry I overreacted."

"Not a problem," Peggy said. With a mischievous grin, she added, "It gives balance to my life to have an innocent friend."

It was Anne's turn to give her friend's shoulder a playful push. "Stop it, Peggy," she laughed.

They walked a while in silence until something else came to Anne's mind. "You know how I sometimes do typing for that Russian psychiatrist?"

Peggy nodded.

"The next two Saturdays I won't be able to help her. Would you like to fill in for me?"

"Of course," Peggy answered. "She sounds intriguing, and I'm always looking for occasions to practice my Russian with native speakers. Plus, I can use the extra money. Thanks for thinking of me."

By this time, they'd returned to the second floor. Peggy veered off toward the high-rise elevators to go back to her office, while Anne walked down the hallway to hers. Along the way, she considered what Peggy had told her about the communists working at the UN. The Cold War's impact on the organization's staff penetrated even more deeply than she'd realized.

30

OFF TO LIMA

Anne walked past the wall where delegates and staff were craning to read the long strips of breaking news that Benedetta had just hung up. Rounding the corner, she headed for the large room where the press officers worked. If the press release on the morning's Security Council meeting was ready, she'd be able to send copies that afternoon in the diplomatic pouches.

As she stepped into the office, loud laughter on all sides drowned out her question. "What's going on?" she asked, trying to be heard over the commotion.

Bertram replied, "I'm telling them about the trap Robert set for Anatoly last Friday."

Bertram, a British press officer, had fine sandy hair, pale skin, and light brown eyes that peered out watchfully from behind wire-rimmed glasses. His frame was slight, and he had first appeared to Anne to be mild-mannered. That's why his moments of abrupt anger had come as a surprise.

"What kind of trap?" Anne asked warily. Just as Yevgeni was evidently watching her, it seemed that Anatoly was supposed to report to his KGB higher-ups about Robert, the American press officer.

"You know Robert's been covering the Law of the Sea Conference for our office, right?"

Anne nodded.

"Well, he asked all of us not to tell Anatoly he would be going to Lima for the next round. So, no one said a word. Then Friday afternoon, Robert gathered up his things and walked to the office door. He waved to everyone and said, 'See you in two weeks.'"

"And?" Anne asked.

Oliver, an Australian, continued the story. "You should have seen the panicked look on Anatoly's face. 'Robert,' he said, 'you go somewhere?' 'Yes,' Robert answered casually, 'I'm going to Lima for the sea law conference.'"

Bertram interrupted Oliver. "Now Anatoly was looking desperate. He jumped up from his desk and practically shouted, 'Robert, you go to Lima?' 'Yes,' Robert said and walked out the door."

"Then what happened?" Anne asked.

"Anatoly grabbed his phone and called someone. He was speaking Russian, and said *Robert* and *Lima* several times. He didn't even try to hide that he was phoning in the information. He did it right in front of everyone."

The other press officers burst out laughing again.

Anne looked at them with disbelief. "Guys, this isn't funny. Do you know what kind of trouble this could make for Anatoly?"

The laughter stopped abruptly. Bertram said with irritation, "If he gets into trouble, that's his own fault. He's been serving two bosses, and maybe it's time for him to choose between them."

"But they could yank him back to Moscow, and who knows what would happen to him there," Anne said hotly.

"What's it to you?" Oliver shot back. "I think you're a little too sympathetic to them, like people say."

"What's that supposed to mean?"

"You know, that you're a little too prone to see things their way."

Anne opened her mouth to defend herself, but stopped when she saw two other press officers nodding. She groaned inwardly. *Is that what they think?* Then she'd have to tread carefully. Speaking more calmly than she felt, she responded, "Of course that's not true. It's just I don't think we should interfere with how other staff members deal with their own home countries."

Bertram looked at Anne appraisingly. "If I were you, I'd be careful how much understanding you express toward Anatoly, or any of them for that matter. And that goes for Benedetta, too."

Anne was at a complete loss. "Benedetta? What on earth does Benedetta have to do with this?"

Bertram turned around and headed back to his desk, and the others did the same. Anne knew that was her signal to leave. She didn't dare break the strained silence to ask about the press release. Juanita would have to come instead.

As Anne turned to go, she happened to glance at Anatoly's desk. The top was completely bare. "Where's Anatoly today?" she blurted out.

The others looked over, as though noticing his empty desk for the first time. "Hey," Oliver said. "All his stuff is gone."

At that moment, Eleanor, a secretary from the Division Director's office, came through the door. "Hello, everyone," she said. "I've come to collect a few things from Anatoly's desk."

"Why?" Bertram asked, looking uncomfortable.

Eleanor tilted her head in surprise. "You don't know? His mother became seriously ill over the weekend and he had to fly to Moscow immediately. He may not be coming back for some time."

The room fell silent. Anne dropped her eyes, afraid to meet the glances of the press officers. Her warning had turned out to be true. Even more, the press officers would think she understood the Soviet system all too well.

31

THE RAMBLE

Anne stared out the cafeteria windows at the crumbling ruins of the mental hospital on Roosevelt Island. She absentmindedly swirled the last remaining coffee in her cup. It wasn't like Peggy to be late. Maybe her boss had some work that couldn't wait? Anne took a last tepid sip and was standing up when she saw Peggy coming toward her.

A welcoming smile was spreading across Anne's face when something checked it. Uneasiness washed over her. There was a haunted look in Peggy's eyes, and she wasn't walking with her usual flirtatious self-assurance. As soon as Peggy drew close, Anne quietly asked, "What's wrong?"

Peggy darted a look at the people sitting at nearby tables and mouthed, "Not here."

Anne nodded. "Okay, let's find a quieter place."

She linked her arm through Peggy's as they walked toward the exit. Anne kept up a steady stream of mindless chatter to cover up the fact that her friend wasn't saying a word.

Anne led the way down the escalator to an isolated corridor in the First Basement, away from the meeting rooms on that level. There she and Peggy sat down on one of the leather sofas that were a ubiquitous fixture of the building's 1950s decor. After assuring herself that no one was nearby, Anne looked into her friend's face and said gently, "Now, please tell me what happened."

Peggy's words came haltingly. "This morning, I had enough time to walk from my apartment through Central Park. I entered at 79th Street and Central Park West and was strolling through the Ramble…" She held up a hand. "I know, I know. You, and some other friends, have warned me not to go to that part of the park. It *is* dark and secluded, but I truly love the greenery there. It makes me feel like I'm back in Ireland. And the sun was so bright today that I thought it would be safe."

Anne began to fear the worst. Had someone attacked Peggy along one of the Ramble's narrow twisting paths? Looking down, for the first time she saw light smudges of dirt on Peggy's skirt, and a run in one of her stockings. "Oh, Peggy, what happened?"

"That's when I saw them."

Anne wasn't used to seeing fear on Peggy's face and it unnerved her. "Who, Peggy? Who?"

"They shouldn't have been in Central Park. Not together."

Anne was having trouble grasping what Peggy was trying to say, but she could tell it was serious. She asked as patiently as she could, "Who was in the park together?"

Peggy turned to look directly at her. "I can't tell you. Otherwise you'll be in danger, too."

Anne's whole body went on alert. Peggy wasn't someone who exaggerated. Whatever danger she was afraid of must be real. Very real. Anne didn't want Peggy to become any more agitated than she already was, so she replied, "It's okay if you don't tell me who they were. But what were they doing?"

Peggy spoke in such a low voice that Anne could barely make out her words. "He gave him an envelope."

"Oh, God," Anne breathed out. Now she understood. Peggy had witnessed a hand-off. And it must have been between two people from the UN, or Peggy wouldn't mind telling her who they were. No wonder Peggy was terrified. If the men knew she'd seen them in that compromising situation, to keep her from talking they might...

Anne wouldn't let herself finish that thought. She took her friend's hands in hers. "Did they see you, Peggy?"

"I don't think the two of them saw me. As soon as I realized what was going on, I dropped behind a large boulder and crouched there while they were talking. But that's when I noticed the lookout standing a little off to one side. He was glancing in my general direction, and that made me afraid he'd spotted me."

"Did you recognize him as well?"

"I don't know his name, but he's a young Soviet who stopped by once to see Mr. Ipatov, my boss. You can't forget him. He's got a square head that sits oddly on his neck, and very close-cropped hair."

Yevgeni? Yevgeni as a lookout for an important handoff? Even Anne could have told the KGB that wasn't a wise idea. "What happened next?"

"A gay couple appeared on the path coming from the other direction. They got close to the two men before the lookout spotted them. Then he shouted out in Russian. The man receiving the envelope cursed at him and took off toward the north, with the lookout running behind him. The other man hesitated a minute. I don't think he understood Russian. But when he caught sight of the couple, he plunged into the bushes. He was looking straight ahead as he rushed by the boulder where I was hiding, but I saw his face clearly." Peggy was now trembling. "It was definitely who I thought it was."

Anne swore softly. It wouldn't have surprised Peggy to see a Soviet engaging in a clandestine Cold War encounter. It was the involvement of this other man that seemed to upset her. Now, more than ever, Anne wanted to know who he was, but Peggy had been adamant that she wouldn't tell. So Anne restrained herself and merely asked, "What did you do after that?"

"I stayed in my hiding place for almost an hour. Finally I thought it was safe to stand up. But I was too scared to go back to my apartment and be alone there, so I came to work."

Well, maybe one good thing would come from this whole mess, Anne mused to herself. If indeed Yevgeni had been the lookout who botched his job, she wasn't likely to be bothered by him anymore. He'd disappear from New York as fast as Anatoly. But there was still Peggy's predicament to consider. "Peggy," Anne ventured cautiously, "do you think you'll be safe? If there's any chance the lookout saw you, should you consider going back to Ireland, at least for a while?"

"Anne, Georgi Markov was killed in London on the Waterloo Bridge in broad daylight. It only took a pellet filled with ricin, shot into his leg from an umbrella. I wouldn't be any safer in Ireland than in New York."

"I've worried about the same thing, if I tried to get away from here."

Peggy looked surprised. "Have you seen something, too? Are you in some kind of danger?"

Inwardly, Anne berated herself for her careless words. Up to then, she'd been meticulous about following Patterson's instructions to keep all her friends in the dark about her own worrisome situation. "No, no." She tried to sound casual. "It's just I'd been thinking about what could happen to any of us."

Peggy lifted her gaze and stiffened. Anne whirled around to look behind her. There, sitting on another sofa only 20 feet away, was a man bending over some papers. Anne had checked the area when they first sat down, but then she'd become so absorbed in what Peggy was saying that she forgot to watch their surroundings. How long had he been there?

Peggy and Anne exchanged anxious looks, not needing to put into words their fear that they'd been overheard.

Was it because their conversation stopped abruptly that the man began putting his papers in his briefcase? As he rose from the sofa, Anne wasn't positive, but she thought it might be the man she'd seen sitting with Yevgeni in the Delegates Lounge, the day of the Israeli-Palestinian meeting. She strained to try to make out his features, but he walked too quickly in the opposite direction and disappeared around the corner. The soft soles of his shoes had made no sound at all.

32

FIRE DRILL

Anne was so engrossed in her typing that she didn't look up when the office door swung open. A heavily accented Greek voice called out, "Adolfo, hello, hello!"

Duarte interrupted the instructions he was giving Juanita and rushed to greet his visitor. "Georgios! When did you arrive? I didn't expect you until next week."

Georgios? Was it possible? Anne spun around. The visitor was indeed her thesis adviser from her junior year abroad in Geneva!

Professor Christopoulos engulfed Duarte in an affectionate bear hug, while Duarte thumped his stout friend enthusiastically on the back. Then the two men drew apart, their faces beaming, each with his hands on the other's shoulders. "This is a pleasure indeed," Duarte exclaimed.

While the old friends chatted, Anne looked expectantly at her mentor and waited for the right moment to greet him. When finally there was a pause in the stream of lively conversation, Christopoulos gazed around the office. He spotted Anne and his deep-set chestnut eyes widened in recognition.

Yet instead of the warm greeting she was anticipating, his face darkened. His voice thundered at her, "Why in heaven's name are you here, sitting at a typewriter?"

The happy smile ebbed from Anne's face. "Señ…Señor Duarte is my boss," she stammered. "I … I … work here."

"As a secretary?" Christopoulos demanded, his voice rising. "I spent a year painstakingly grooming a thesis student who is now working as a secretary?"

"It was the only job the UN offered me, and…"

Christopoulos cut her off. "I don't want to hear excuses. What a waste of my time and effort." Angrily, he turned his back on her.

Duarte, looking perturbed, quickly ushered Christopoulos into his office and closed the door behind them.

Tears formed in Anne's eyes. She murmured, "Being a secretary at the UN is nothing to be ashamed of. Our work does make a contribution."

Juanita said with compassion, "Of course it does, Anne. This just shows he has high regard for you. And he probably doesn't understand the system here. It's like the airlines, where men are pilots and women are stewardesses."

Anne breathed out, "But I owe him so much, and now he's lost faith in me." She rolled back in her chair and slowly stood up. "I think I'll take the news bulletin up to the 38th floor now, instead of waiting until 11:00. I need to collect myself before he comes out of Señor Duarte's office."

Her officemates nodded understandingly.

On the Secretary-General's floor, Anne left the bulletin with one of his assistants and was returning to the elevators when, high overhead, a bell began to clang. "Oh no," Anne said out loud. "A fire drill? Now?"

She quickened her pace, hoping to disappear into an elevator before the exercise began. It was too late. A security officer at the front desk called out, "Hold it, Miss. No one can use the elevators now that the drill has begun. You'll have to go into the fire tower with everyone else."

Anne saw there was no point arguing. It could be a blessing in disguise, she told herself. With the delay, maybe Christopoulos would be gone by the time she got back to the office. She might as well spend the next fifteen minutes in a dark airshaft, which would match the gloom she was feeling.

With resignation, she retraced her steps and joined the flow of people heading toward the south end of the building. A thickset Fire Safety Officer stood beside the door into the fire tower. Staff members designated as fire wardens for the floor diligently herded their groups in his direction.

The staff filed through the doorway and began spilling down the concrete stairs of the fire tower. Enclosed by brick walls dark with grime, the tower felt eerie and forlorn. But people laughed and jostled good-na-turedly as they crammed together into the small space.

The Fire Safety Officer called for everyone's attention. With a New York accent, he said, "Okay, folks. I'm sure you think you know all this already, but you need to listen up. This is an older building. Your quick thinking could be the difference between life and death."

He paused until there was complete silence. "Now as you know, the UN location here has a special international status. So the New York fire department, and even the police, can't come onto these premises without the UN's permission. We try to keep any delay to a minimum. But you gotta remember that firemen won't be able to arrive instantly if a fire breaks out."

One man, who'd been chatting up the young woman standing next to him, fell silent mid-sentence.

Nodding at him, the officer said, "I'm glad you're taking this more seriously." Gesturing at the dirty walls, he resumed. "Now this fire tower goes all the way from the top of the building down to the ground floor. The air you're feeling is coming from an opening in the roof, two floors above us. This tower is an entirely separate edifice, with its own self-sup-porting walls. This is a good thing for you," he said in a pedantic voice. "If you can make your way into this tower, even if a blaze is raging in the building, you'll be protected. All you gotta do is go down the stairs, without pushing or shoving, and then exit out from the First Basement."

Ruefully, a woman glanced down at her fashionable high heels. "If I'm going to walk down 39 floors, I'll have to start wearing different shoes."

"We hope it won't come to that," the officer continued. "That's why I'm going to demonstrate how to operate our fire extinguishers." He affectionately patted the huge stainless-steel cylinder affixed to the wall on his left. "The models mounted along your corridors aren't as heavy as this one. You can lift them off the hooks and take them where a fire is starting. Calmly remove the pin and point the nozzle at the base of the fire, not the top of the flames."

Now he had everyone's full attention.

"You're not likely to need these bigger units, but in case burning debris gets into the fire tower or the north stairwell, you'll want to know how they work. The principle is the same as for the smaller ones. Pull the pin and aim at the base of the fire. But be careful of the air currents in this shaft. You don't want fire retardant chemicals blowing into your eyes."

A hand went up. "What would happen if they did?"

"I'm glad you asked that question," the officer said. "The chemicals probably wouldn't do lasting damage, but they could temporarily blind you." Looking around at the group, he asked, "Now, who would like to demonstrate using one of the small extinguishers?"

A sharp-faced American, whom Anne had occasionally seen on the floor, stepped forward. There was something oddly intense about him as he took the small red unit from the officer.

The officer instructed him, "So first pull out the pin. Then point the nozzle downward … everyone stand back … and press the lever."

White particles and mist blasted from the nozzle with a deafening rush. Although most of the staff had been through this exercise before, they gasped and jumped back. An acrid smell permeated the air. The nervousness of everyone crowded into the fire tower was tangible. It felt too much like a real emergency.

"Okay, that's enough," the officer called out.

The American released the lever and the spurt stopped immediately. The tension was broken and the gathered staff laughed with relief.

"All right, if there're no more questions, you can all go back to work."

As Anne was moving slowly toward the exit, she saw the man who'd demonstrated the extinguisher pushing almost imperceptibly through the crowd until he reached her. "You're a fellow American," he said.

Warily, she nodded.

"We haven't met in person, but I think you'll recall my name. Arthur Donegan."

Anne was startled. She clearly remembered his phone call about helping the FBI, but she had no idea he worked in the building, let alone on a floor where he would often see her.

He said, "The offer still stands." Giving her a penetrating look, he added, "And after the accident, maybe now you have better reasons for accepting."

Not giving her a chance to answer, Donegan again pushed subtly through the crowd and disappeared.

33

A TELLING ACCENT

Anne was crossing 55th Street on her way home from work when she spotted Royce stepping off the curb opposite her. Her heart started beating faster. He caught sight of her and his face lit up.

He waited for her to reach his side of the street and then greeted her warmly. "What a pleasure to run into you like this."

"Yes, it is."

He looked around. Then, pointing to the coffee shop on the corner behind them, he asked "Do you have time to duck inside for an early dinner and a chat?" He smiled down at her. "But then again, an attractive girl like you probably already has evening plans."

"I don't have plans, and I'd enjoy having a bite with you."

Royce took her elbow and ushered her into the coffee shop. The waitress waved them to a table toward the back.

After they were seated, Anne thought to herself, We two always seem to eat at formica tables. Yet the coffee shop furnishings, although worn, were cheerful.

They chatted easily as they waited for their orders. She enjoyed watching his changing expressions as he spoke. He was telling her about an exhibit of Scythian artifacts he'd just seen at the Metropolitan Museum. "I liked it so much," he said, "that I'll go back again." He took a sip of coffee. "I think you, too, Anne, would really appreciate it."

She wished they could go to the exhibit together. She wondered if she dared ask outright, but didn't have the confidence, so instead she merely hinted. "Everything you've recommended so far has turned out well worth seeing, so I'll definitely go."

To her disappointment, he didn't follow up with an invitation. But perhaps he was distracted because at that moment, the waitress was setting down her salad and his spinach pie.

"Bon appetit," Royce said to her. Then, with animation, he continued, "My favorite object in the show is a small gold amulet of a crouching stag. The stylized rendering of the antlers and the muscularity of the body are miraculous."

As she watched him speak, in the background Anne picked up the soft sounds of Russian coming from a nearby table. Normally that would immediately have interested her and she would have tried to follow the conversation, to practice her Russian, but today she was too caught up in Royce's enthusiasm.

He signaled to the waitress that he'd like a refill on his coffee, and then resumed his story. Anne smiled to herself. A couple of vowels he said had a Russian ring to them. She mused that it was probably the effect of his overhearing that same Russian conversation. It reminded her of a train trip back to Oregon she'd once taken. Hearing more relaxed West Coast accents the further west she went, the carefully precise English she spoke at the UN slipped away until she found herself naturally speaking in the pronunciation of her childhood. The same thing must be happening to Royce.

Anne stiffened. What was she saying! That Russian might be his mother tongue? She listened carefully as he described some other objects in the Scythian exhibit. Once again she heard a vowel that sounded unmistakably Russian.

Only now did she recall that at least twice before, some of his vowels had caught her attention. On those occasions, however, she'd been so fascinated by what he was telling her that she hadn't given it any thought.

She tried to contribute to their conversation, but she felt an uncontrollable panic rising up in her. Was he not an American, but actually a Soviet?

She had to put her doubts to a test. But how?

Anne noticed that Royce's now empty plate was sitting very close to the edge of their table. That gave her an idea.

"Осторожно! Тарелка сейчас упадёт!" she called out urgently. (Watch out! The plate's going to fall!)

The minute she spoke the Russian words, his hand shot out to steady the plate.

They both froze.

Slowly, Royce brought his eyes to her face. They had a hardened look she'd never seen before. Then it was gone. Breaking into a charming grin, he said, "You see, I, too, am a student of Russian. I, too, enjoy reading Pushkin in the original."

Anne tried to control the shaking in her voice. "It is a lovely language, isn't it?" Without willing it, she began to ease her chair away from the table. She stammered, "I'm so sorry, but I really must be going home now. I still get a little tired at the end of each day."

Royce was sliding his chair back from the table as well. In his most solicitous voice, he said, "I apologize for overtiring you with so much conversation. Let me make it up to you by walking you to your apartment." As he was speaking, Royce's hand rose to his shirt pocket and he carefully extracted a thick pen.

Anne's eyes widened. "That really won't be necessary," she heard herself tell him. "I'll be fine walking there by myself." Warily, she stepped backward.

Like a panther slowly and methodically stalking its prey, Royce was easing around the table. "No, I really must insist."

Anne's eyes darted frantically around the coffee shop. She spotted a stranger, standing at a nearby table, who was gathering up his things. She quickly stepped over and grabbed the startled man's arm. "It's really not a problem," she said to Royce. "This is my neighbor, George. He lives on my block. He and I can walk back together."

Already Royce's hand was shooting out toward Anne. Instinctively, she darted behind the other man. The tip of Royce's pen missed Anne and planted in the stranger's arm.

Royce spun around. Rushing for the door, he banged into a table and upended it, sending plates and cutlery crashing to the floor. Several patrons cried out in alarm. He violently threw aside a chair that was in his way and bolted out the door.

The stranger moaned. Anne tore her eyes away from the door to look at him. As she stared open-mouthed in horror, he slipped from her grasp and fell to the ground.

34

THE ROOF

Clutching the bag containing her ballet clothes, Anne exited the high-rise elevator, hurried around the corner, and pushed open a heavy door on her left. She always felt taken aback when she left the plush furnishings of the 37th floor and entered the north stairwell, with its grimy walls and dirty concrete stairs.

The stairwell was open from the First Basement all the way to the 40th floor. As Anne climbed upward, she could hear distant footsteps on other floors echoing through the vast, eerie space. Unseen people on unknown errands.

Because she was late, she took the steps two at a time. That morning Anne had again been called to take dictation from Gavrez. After her terrifying encounter with Royce, she was now constantly on edge. She hadn't needed the ordeal of spending time in Gavrez's office on top of that. His whole bearing toward her was becoming even more belittling and harsh, and she'd left his office feeling unnerved. All she could hope was that the noontime ballet class would help distract her, if only for an hour.

Anne passed the landing of the 38th floor. There the exit door was locked and was monitored by a large overhead camera, since it was the floor of the Secretary-General's suite. She continued sprinting up the stairs until finally she reached the 40th floor, where UN staff had been given space for their various clubs. She darted across the small dark landing and tiptoed into the dance studio to the right.

She nodded apologetically to the instructor, who was already leading the other dancers through their stretches. She entered the narrow changing room and quickly swapped her dress for a leotard and tights. Then she quietly took a place at the long barre beside the mirror.

Too soon, the strains of recorded music faded out. Class was over. While the other dancers rushed to change, Anne stayed back to apologize to the teacher for her late arrival.

By the time she'd dressed again in her work outfit, the other ballet students had left and the modern dance class was underway. Anne moved noiselessly to the studio door and eased it open.

As she left the studio, she was startled to feel a strong, fresh breeze blow across her face. After gently closing the door behind her, she turned to her right to find out where the gusts of air were coming from.

What she saw delighted her. For the first time since she'd started coming to the 40th floor, the exit door to the outside was open. From the landing where she was standing, she was looking directly out onto the main roof of the UN Building. As her eyes adjusted to the blazing sunlight, she was able to see through the spaces in the nine-foot-tall metal latticework wall enclosing the roof. The view was breathtaking.

Anne walked to the exit door and cautiously poked her head outside. Looking around, she didn't see anyone who might stop her. With an intake of breath, she stepped through the doorway.

As she emerged onto the cement roof, the full force of the wind came over her with a rush, making her feel invigorated and free. Everywhere she looked, she saw dazzling sunshine and bright blue sky. It was magical, mesmerizing.

After pausing to take in the beauty of the moment, she turned to study the layout of where she was. The structure housing the 40th floor clubrooms took up only a small part of the roof's overall footprint, leaving a wide-open space at its south end. Anne realized that if she walked in that direction, beyond the small clubroom building she'd be able to look out at the city skyline on one side and the East River on the other, all from the same spot. It was a view she absolutely had to see.

As she headed toward the open space, passing between the clubroom building to her right and the metal latticework to her left, she noticed that a segment of that wall had broken off. The open gap, about five feet wide, was covered by orange mesh netting. As she drew closer, she became queasy. The flimsy netting was the only thing between her and a forty-floor drop.

Involuntarily, she edged closer to the clubroom building and put out a hand to steady herself against it. As she looked far down at the miniaturized cars on the streets of the borough of Queens across the river, her stomach churned. She realized how truly high off the ground she was.

The way the mesh netting was buckling and flapping in the unremitting wind seemed menacing, as though it might snap off at any moment. Bracing herself against the building, Anne tried to recapture the sense of elation she'd felt when she first stepped out onto the roof. She still wanted to see the view from the south of the building. But now she wasn't sure she dared risk being buffeted by the powerful wind as she walked past the gap.

She was still stuck in indecision when she heard a shout. "You there! What the hell are you doing out here?"

She whirled around and saw a security officer barging through the exit door. He was clearly angry. She called back, "The door was open, and I thought I'd take a quick look." Trying to win him over to her side, she added, "It's so beautiful out here."

It was obvious that line was going nowhere with the guard. Struggling to keep her balance in the wind, Anne headed back toward him.

The guard, standing legs akimbo and arms across his chest, glared at her as she approached. He waited until she passed back over the threshold and then followed her inside. "Do you have any idea how dangerous it is out there?" He pointed to the large sign on the door saying *No Exit*. "What do you think this sign is for?"

Anne mumbled an apology while he clanged the heavy door shut and immediately set the bolt. She blinked her eyes trying to adjust to the sudden darkness. After the brightness of the day and the crisp air outside, the landing felt dank and oppressive.

Anne's heels made a forlorn sound as she wordlessly crossed the cement landing and headed down the stairs to the elevator on the 37th floor. The sharp wind, the unnerving gap in the metalwork, and the guard's angry reprimand had left her feeling disoriented. Far from clearing her mind, Anne's hour away from work had left her feeling even more unsettled.

35

TAKING STOCK

Smoke from five cigarettes pooled under the acoustic tile ceiling. Frank Pritchard, a sober man in his fifties, sat erect and commanding in a leather chair. His desk top was pristine, holding only a phone, an inbox and a yellow legal pad. Four other men, on folding chairs, were arrayed in a semicircle around his desk.

In a gravelly voice, Frank asked the agent sitting directly across from him, "Bernie, do you have anything on the four new pizzerias that are about to open?"

"The mob's already visited all of them. According to my informant, every owner signed on, except the Romanian guy setting up *Nicu's*. He said he'd buy his cheese from them, but not the dough. Told them he's gotta use his grandfather's recipe because Romanian pizza crust is famous for being extra thin and crunchy. Said his customers will expect it that way."

"Brave man," Frank said, blowing out smoke as he spoke. "How did that go over?"

"After a talk in the family, they decided to let him get away with it. So long as he doesn't tell the other pizzerias."

"He's running a big risk, but maybe that's because he's not from here." Frank reached over to scribble a brief note on his yellow legal pad. "Have somebody check his shop from time to time at night, okay? I want to know if his windows get broken." Looking over at the man to his left, he asked, "What about the cop at 56th Street and Sixth Avenue?"

"Yeah, that cop. He's still shaking down the stonemasons every day for bribes before he lets them through to the building site."

"Ties to the mafia?"

"I'm not sure. There've been some shady characters stopping by to say a word to him, then quickly moving on. I recognized one of them from that prostitution ring operating out of *Gorgeous Girls*. You know, the peep show in Times Square."

Frank was thoughtful for a moment. "Don't do anything for now. Just keep him under watch. I'm only interested in little fish if they lead us to bigger fish." He made another jot on the yellow pad and then asked, "Bob, what's happening with the girl over at the UN?"

Patterson roused himself and answered, "Nada."

"Nothing?"

"Nothing that would say the taxi hit her on purpose. Or that she's in danger now. She tells me Soviets are whispering in the corridors. The East German is peeking over everyone's shoulder. Nothing really to go on." Patterson tapped cigarette ash into his empty paper coffee cup. "Since Yevgeni was yanked home, and then Royce, nobody's trailed her. The bug someone put on her office phone's still there, but no one's been listening in."

"What do you make of it?"

Patterson slowly exhaled before answering. For a moment, the only sounds were the efficient whir of the ceiling fan and muffled traffic noise from the street below. "For sure, things are going on at the UN, but I haven't found a link to her. And I doubt Royce invited her to have dinner so he could kill her in a coffee shop full of witnesses. Probably he tried to stab her with that pen tip so she wouldn't be able to blow his cover."

"That reminds me," Frank said. "What happened to the guy who got the pen instead of her?"

"They finally released him from the hospital two days ago. Looks like he won't have lasting nerve damage."

"At least that's good news." Frank leaned forward in his chair. "Any chance she's working both sides of the street?"

Patterson answered, "That's still a possibility. But since she knows we're watching her closely now, that would be a risky move on her part." He added, "There's the other question of the missing amphora and the Indonesian statue. I don't know if there's some connection. Anyway, I told her to stay away from the fakes and she said she would."

"And Rick and Stewart?"

"They don't like her. It gets to them that she's not patriotic, and she has a couple of friends they don't approve of. But after searching her desk and watching her for a while, they haven't come up with anything."

From under half-closed eyelids, another agent spoke. "I think the KGB sent Prince Charming to try to recruit her, not kill her. Since he failed at that, maybe they've lost interest in her."

Patterson nodded. "That could be."

Frank tapped his pen softly and methodically on the edge of his desk and then spoke. "Look, I don't want to waste manpower on a dead end. I'm going to keep the place across the street from her building, but from now on, let's not staff it around the clock. Just have the guys trust their gut and randomly drop in for an hour or so and then leave."

Patterson shrugged. "Okay with me. And on the street?"

"I don't think we need to follow her on the street anymore. We've got people in the UN area. They'll pick her up on their radar when she's in the vicinity."

Patterson studied his scuffed shoes for a moment and then raised his eyes to meet Frank's. "What if we're wrong? And they notice she's not as protected?"

Frank answered coolly, "Remember what I said before? I'm only interested in little fish if they lead us to bigger fish. If someone's seriously after her, she'll draw them out where we can see them."

"Like bait?"

"Like bait."

36

THE REPLACEMENT

Anne's face clouded over as she put the phone back down. "Benedetta, I've got to take dictation from Señor Gavrez again this morning. It's such an ordeal. And I hate that hazel smell of his Benson & Hedges cigarettes. It clings to me the rest of the day."

Benedetta wrinkled her nose. "You don't have to tell me. Your clothes reek of it when you come back."

Anne sighed. "Well, there's no way I can get out of it. I'll bolster myself with some coffee before I go. Can I bring you one?"

Benedetta shook her head. "I'm fine, thanks. But could you stop by the newsstand? I got here so early that some of the magazines weren't in yet. *Jeune Afrique* is missing, and also *Der Spiegel*, and maybe some others."

"Sure thing."

As Anne neared the ground floor newsstand, a man she didn't know was approaching from the opposite direction. His walk was calm and athletic. As the distance between them narrowed, she saw he had light brown hair, an aquiline nose, and a well-defined mouth which hinted at a strong personality. His high, flat cheekbones gave him the look of someone who belonged more on windswept plains than in an urban office building. *What an attractive man*, she thought to herself.

He came up to the newsstand just as the clerk behind the counter was holding out a stack of magazines, which Anne took in both hands. An unfamiliar voice commented, "You have quite an armload. It looks like you're planning to spend the whole day reading."

His accent, although almost imperceptible, was Russian. Anne stiffened.

She was saved from having to respond by the counterman. "Just a minute, Miss," he said, "I think I have one more for you. I'll look in the storage area."

The Soviet, now standing directly beside Anne, asked the cashier, "Miss, could I have Marlboros, please?"

The cashier grabbed a pack from a high shelf and placed it on the counter.

The newcomer seemed to take an especially long time fumbling in his pocket to pay for the cigarettes. As his fingers searched, he asked Anne, "So what *are* you going to do with all those magazines?"

She glanced over at him and saw humor in his Arctic blue eyes, slightly crinkled above an amused smile.

"My office prepares the Secretary-General's daily *Press Analysis*," she answered in a tone that was not particularly friendly.

"And you read so many different magazines? In so many different languages?"

"I'm not the only one who reads them. My colleagues do, too." Would the counterman never return?

"Your work sounds interesting," the Soviet continued. "I'd like to have coffee with you one day to hear more about it." Extending his hand, he added, "My name's Andrei."

With Yevgeni gone, Anne had been enjoying her freedom from his unwelcome pestering, but she had suspected that sooner or later a new Soviet would come along to keep an eye on her. It was dawning on her that this was the replacement. She was not going to make it easy for him. She pretended not to notice the hand held out in her direction. Instead, she continued to stare at the spot where the counterman had disappeared.

Andrei laughed pleasantly. "I'm not a pushy person," he said sociably. "But I think you'll find I'm good company, at least compared to others who may have tried to oblige you to have coffee in the past."

He knows I know, Anne thought. Still not looking at him, she said, "Unfortunately, my office keeps me very busy. I rarely go for coffee with anyone besides my officemates."

She caught Andrei's smile out of the corner of her eye. Unruffled, he said, "Nonetheless, at some point you may find it useful to have a channel for clearing up any, shall we say, misunderstandings that might arise. My surname is Drozdovsky. I just started in the Centre Against Apartheid, should you ever wish to contact me." Pointing to the magazines Anne held, he added, "You might actually enjoy an occasional diversion from spending so many hours absorbed in the world's woes."

At long last, the counterman re-emerged with the missing magazine. Anne took it gratefully.

Nodding at her full arms, Andrei said, "I won't try to shake your hand, since it's otherwise occupied, but have a nice day." With that, he headed for the high-rise elevators.

Well, he's definitely less abrasive than Yevgeni, Anne thought to herself. And he appears to have some sense of how absurd all of this is. Unaccountably, she was smiling.

37

CHAMOMILE TEA

Three days later, Anne walked into the office and was putting down her handbag when Benedetta spoke with concern. "Oh, Anne, what's wrong with your eyes?"

Anne peered at her through red, swollen lids. "I think it's an infection, the kind little kids get. Does it really look that bad?"

Benedetta nodded.

Anne said, "Then if we're not too busy, I'd better go to the Medical Service."

"I think you should," Juanita responded. "We can manage here without you for the time being."

"It's on the fifth floor, right?"

"Yes," Juanita replied. With a grin she added, "Just know that if you get the Turkish doctor, regardless of what's wrong with you, he'll prescribe yoghurt."

"And if you get the Soviet doctor," Benedetta chimed in, "she recommends chamomile tea for everything."

When Anne returned 45 minutes later, Juanita and Benedetta looked up expectantly. Anne lifted her hand and dangled two teabags by their labels. "Guess which doctor I saw?"

All three secretaries laughed. Anne continued, "I'm supposed to drink a cup of chamomile tea and then put the cold teabags over my eyes and lie down for a while. Okay if I do that now?"

"Of course," answered Juanita.

Anne walked toward the escalator. As she approached its glass enclosure she noticed, standing nearby, three men wearing the navy jumpsuits of UN Movers.

When Anne first started working at the organization, she was surprised to see how many movers were on the fulltime payroll. Special events led to a frequent shift of furnishings on the main floors. In addition, office spaces were continually being reconfigured. The building had been designed to apportion two, three or four windows to the offices of staff in the "professional" category. A high-level official like Gavrez might have even five. As departments gained or lost posts, walls were constantly being moved to create offices with the right number of windows, and that kept the construction teams and movers busy.

Drawing closer to the escalator door, Anne saw one of the movers nudge a taller colleague and then tip his head in her direction. When the second mover caught sight of Anne, he looked at her with open admiration.

Oh dear, Anne thought. This wasn't the first time. Now it was clear the young mover had a crush on her. He was attractive in a rugged sort of way and appeared to be a nice person. Yet the smitten look he was giving her, with the other movers watching, made her feel terribly self-conscious. She looked straight ahead and walked stiffly to the escalator steps. Once she reached them, she climbed rapidly to get out of the men's sight.

In the cafeteria, Anne paid for a cup of hot water, dropped in the teabags and immediately headed back downstairs.

By the time she returned to the second floor, thankfully the movers had left the area. She descended the few steps to the main corridor and walked a short distance to the ladies room nearest the Security Council Chamber. Just outside its entrance, the architects, for privacy's sake, had constructed a parallel partition wall which shielded the restroom door from the corridor.

Anne passed behind the partition and entered the ladies room. It was the only place she knew where she could lie down. Inside, to the left was an open space with sinks and stalls. To the right, hidden behind a wall, was a dimly lit area furnished with two upholstered armchairs and a sofa.

Anne was in luck. The sofa was unoccupied. She sat down and began sipping her tea. Then she reclined and placed a cold teabag over each eye. They felt surprisingly soothing and she soon fell asleep.

She'd been out for a while when something drew her to the surface. Where was she? She sensed the clammy teabags on her closed eyes and then remembered lying down on the sofa to follow the doctor's advice.

What had awakened Anne were the soft voices of two women conversing on the other side of the wall. "I don't like it," one said.

"You worry too much," a husky voice answered. "He knows what he's doing."

"But bringing in the Dutchman is adding one more risk. I don't know why he keeps taking these chances. He's getting so reckless that one of us could get caught."

The other woman laughed cynically. "This is the UN. No one stays in trouble here for very long. But trust me, he's untouchable. If he needs to, he'll find a scapegoat."

The conversation was troubling Anne, all the more because she thought she recognized one of the voices, but she was too groggy to place it. She told herself to make the effort to get up and go around the wall to see who was there. But she was still so tired. She'd do it in a minute. They'd mentioned a Dutchman. She'd think about that later, because it seemed important.

Anne didn't realize she'd fallen back asleep until she awoke with a start. There were no more voices coming from the other side of the wall. She jumped up from the sofa and quietly walked into the bathroom area. It was totally empty. She'd missed her chance. And what was worse, she couldn't recall anymore what it was the women had said that seemed important to her at the time.

Well, she'd been away from her duties long enough. Checking in the mirror, she was relieved to see that the redness and swelling were gone from her eyes. She smoothed her dress and hurriedly returned to the office. Hopefully the details of the conversation she'd overheard would come back to her later.

Eager to make up for the time she'd lost, Anne was pounding furiously on her typewriter when her phone rang. The voice on the other end told her it was the call she'd been expecting since the week before. What a disrupted day. "Hello, Andrei," she said. "How are you?"

"I'm well, Anne. And you?"

"I'm fine, thank you." She could hardly imagine a more stilted conversation.

He continued, "And have you made a dent in that impressive mountain of magazines you walked away with, or are you still poring over them?"

She smiled. "We finished them the day you saw me, but we have another set to deal with today."

"You know, when you have a lot of reading to do, it's a good idea to rest your eyes from time to time. Would you be free for coffee sometime this afternoon?"

Anne didn't answer right away. She hadn't yet decided how she was going to respond to his invitations. She wanted to talk to Patterson first. Maybe he would advise her to be on good terms, so as not to call any further attention to herself. But at that moment, her inclination was to keep her distance.

"In this very long pause," Andrei commented, "I can hear you thinking, Anne."

She laughed.

"Listen," he said. "I don't want to make you uncomfortable over the idea of having coffee with me today. I can ask you again later on."

Anne's relief could be heard in her voice. "I appreciate that, Andrei. Thank you."

"Not at all," he replied cordially. "And have a lovely rest of the day."

"Thanks, and you, too."

She'd postponed meeting with Andrei for now, but she knew the Soviets' thoroughness. He would call again.

38

FORMALITIES

Afternoon sun streamed through the enormous floor-to-ceiling windows of the Delegates Lounge. It brightened the room's brown furnishings and lit up the neon green details in China's massive tapestry of the Great Wall. Andrei sat back comfortably and said to Anne, "So you see, having coffee with me is not all that bad."

It was Andrei's quiet self-assurance, Anne thought, more than his well-defined features, that made him so attractive. "It's a definite improvement over some encounters I've had in the past," she replied.

He grinned and took a sip of his straight espresso. "What do you think of China's new gift?" he asked, nodding up at the tapestry.

"It's very big and very bright. It's going to take me a while to get used to it. Do you know, it's 30 feet long, and it's made with 50,000 yards of wool and 500,000 knots. And it weighs 600 pounds!"

Andrei looked puzzled. "How do you know all that?"

"I typed the press release for the UN Information Centres the day it was presented."

"So your job keeps you well-informed not only of major political events, but also important matters like the thread count of art donated to the UN." As Anne's face fell, he hastened to reassure her. "No, no, I'm certainly not mocking you. On the contrary, I admire how interested you are in everything."

Anne's hurt expression dissolved.

"Speaking of the arts," Andrei continued, "do you like American jazz? I myself am a true aficionado."

Anne tilted her head in surprise.

He put into words her unspoken question. "You're wondering how I had access to jazz at home? My government doesn't censor Western music as much as you might be thinking. It takes some looking, but one can find recordings of all the American greats. Miles Davis, for example. I have all his LPs, although they're very worn from overplaying."

Anne responded, "I went to a concert he gave last year at City Center. He's up in years now, but he still plays beautifully, and with such feeling."

"I envy you that experience. I'd love to hear him in person. So you do like jazz, at least a little. Is there anyone else you listen to?"

For a moment, the simple gold wedding band on Andrei's right hand caught the sunlight. She knew he would be married. Soviets couldn't be approved by their government to come to the UN unless they were. But although she barely knew Andrei, she didn't think he would have entered into a marriage of convenience just to qualify for a post abroad. He seemed to have more depth than that.

She answered, "I have records by Yusef Lateef, John McLaughlin and Jean-Luc Ponty."

Andrei burst out laughing. "How on earth did you become interested in such wildly different jazz artists?"

Flustered, Anne looked down at the table. "I briefly dated some men," she confessed, "who liked one or the other of them, so I got LPs to try to like them, too."

Andrei laughed again. "I hope your dates appreciated your efforts. But something tells me you never actually came to love those musicians."

"I tried my best, but…" She shrugged. "What artists do you like?"

"I'm afraid my tastes aren't as eclectic as yours. Besides Miles Davis, I enjoy Oscar Peterson, Ella Fitzgerald and Herbie Hancock. They sound more harmonious to my ears which, you must remember, grew up listening to Russian classical music."

Anne held her cappuccino in both hands and savored its froth. As the afternoon meetings were adjourning, the Lounge was slowly filling up. At nearby tables, other quiet conversations were taking place, punctuated by the occasional clink of heavy white china cups on saucers.

"So, Anne," Andrei said, "we do have a formality to get out of the way, and then we can resume talking about music." He took another sip of espresso. "First, I might tell you I think you're very bright, but that unfortunately you may not find at the UN the career you deserve. And then," he continued, "I could tell you that someone of your intelligence and talents might want to consider working for, say, Pan Am, or as a journalist, in Moscow. With your language abilities, I'm sure you would do well in either of those fields."

Anne looked closely at Andrei and felt reassured by the amusement she read in his friendly blue eyes. Keeping her tone light, she answered, "Thank you for your compliments, and your interest in my career. I'm sure that working for Pan Am or as a journalist would be rewarding. But even though my job here is modest, I enjoy it very much. So I plan to stay at the UN for the foreseeable future."

Andrei nodded. "A very reasonable answer," he said. "And now that we've covered the ground in an appropriate way, let's return to our more interesting conversation about music. Since we've established that you don't really like avant garde jazz, what kind of music do you like?"

Anne answered his smile with one of hers.

39

AN UNEXPECTED RETURN

Anne looked around her cramped apartment and sighed. She'd finished dinner and didn't know how to spend the rest of the evening. She'd have to find something absorbing to read because anxiety was getting the better of her. The recent days had been quiet. Too quiet. The calm felt ominous.

Despite its being early autumn, the evening was warm. Behind the safety gates, her windows were open. A pleasant breeze fanned wisps of her hair as she tipped her head to one side to scan the volumes in her bookcase. She wondered, though, how she'd possibly be able to concentrate with the infernally loud music coming from her next-door neighbor's. She liked Jethro Tull well enough, but not at 100 decibels.

After a moment's thought, she zeroed in on Richard Brautigan's *A Confederate General from Big Sur*. It might be just the thing. Although she'd read it several times, tears still rolled down her cheeks when she read that Lee Mellon finally stopped the incessant croaking of nearby frogs by shouting "Campbell's Soup!" at the top of his lungs. She pulled down the slim volume and began thumbing its familiar pages.

It was then that she sensed she wasn't alone.

She whirled around. Across the room, a man stood in front of the closed apartment door.

"Detective Royce!" she cried out. "Or whoever you really are. Everyone thinks you left New York."

He nodded, self-satisfied. "That's what they're supposed to think."

As he spoke, Royce started walking slowly toward Anne. Her mind was in complete turmoil. What had happened to the 24-hour close surveillance Patterson promised her? Royce shouldn't have gotten anywhere near her building, let alone inside her apartment. She could only stammer, "What ... what do you want?"

"What you really want to know," he replied, "is what happened to the FBI. I'm afraid, sweetheart, they gave up on you. There's no one across the street, and there hasn't been for a while."

She'd been betrayed. For a moment she couldn't speak. Then she repeated, "What do you want?"

"We have some unfinished business, you and I," Royce said, stopping a foot away and locking his eyes on hers. "Who told you?"

"What do you mean?"

"Anne, you're smart, but not that smart. Who tipped you off?"

"What are you talking about?"

"Before you blew my cover, I'm certain the FBI didn't think I was anything but a regular cop, so Patterson didn't tell you about me. But someone did." He took hold of her shoulders and shook her. "I need to know who."

"In the coffee shop, I heard your accent. It wasn't the first time, but it finally registered."

He glared down at her. "Come on, Anne. You can do better than that."

"You can believe me or not, but it's the truth."

Watching his face, now steely and impenetrable, Anne had trouble fathoming that it was the same man who'd brightened her life in the hospital, and then during their seemingly accidental encounters after that. She said, more to herself than to him, "You seemed so sincere. I was actually starting to fall for you."

Royce's look changed. His hands slid down slowly from her shoulders. Pulling her close, he said, "There's still time to do something about that."

She felt him hardening as he pressed his body firmly against hers. Her tension turned to despair. She'd already understood that after Royce finished grilling her, he'd kill her. Now she knew he would rape her first.

That damn music. It was getting louder. Even if she managed to scream, no one would hear her. Worse, she couldn't think straight, now when she most needed to. All that came to her was the cop's advice the day the kid tried to come through her window. "Don't fight. Otherwise you'll end up hurt. Or dead."

I've got to keep him talking, keep him from getting angrier, she said to herself. Straining to suppress her fear, Anne mustered what she hoped was a friendly tone. "Could we sit on the sofa and talk things over?"

"Sorry, hon," he answered. "We're way past that."

Royce roughly grabbed her chin and forced her to look up at him. The harshness in his eyes terrified her. To escape his penetrating gaze, she turned her head. As she did, she thought she saw a glint out on the fire escape. Was someone there? If so, it could be back-up for Royce, and then stalling wouldn't matter. But if it were one of Patterson's men, maybe she had a chance.

Then it hit her. There was something odd about Royce's still being in New York. If Soviets blew their cover at the UN, they were whisked back to Moscow and never returned. She'd seen that with Anatoly, and then Yevgeni. So why was Royce still here? There could only be one explanation.

Looking directly into his face, she said quietly, "The FBI knows you're not with the KGB."

The slight flicker in his eyes encouraged her that her hunch was correct. She felt his hold on her loosen almost imperceptibly. That allowed her to turn slightly to the right. As she'd hoped, Royce unconsciously moved with her, so that his back was now to the window. Over his shoulder, Anne again saw a glint. She prayed with all her heart that it was the FBI.

Royce seemed momentarily at a loss. Then he tightened his grip. "You're bluffing."

"And if I'm not?" she asked, surprised at her own calm voice. "I can answer that question for you. If I'm not, even if you kill me now, without the KGB to get you out of the country, it's only a matter of time before you're caught."

She'd gone too far. "You bitch," Royce spit out, and threw her to the floor. There was an agonizing pause and then his body slammed down onto hers. Stunned by the impact, she lay pinned under his weight, her eyes clenched shut, feeling utterly defeated.

The loud music next door had become the soundtrack to a nightmare. Royce, silent, remained on top of Anne, crushing her to the ground. She was immobilized with fear, knowing that when he made his next move, it would be vicious.

Then she felt warmth on her left hand. Slowly opening her eyes, she raised her hand and saw blood.

There was a cracking noise and the sound of grating metal. The safety gate at the right window crashed to the floor and two men climbed into the room.

Patterson rolled Royce's body off Anne and gave it a kick. "Damn," he muttered. "Damn! How did I miss that shot? I wanted this bastard alive."

Anne pulled herself to a sitting position. Blood from the bullet hole in Royce's back was spreading across the floor. Recoiling, she quickly moved as far from the body as she could.

When Anne finally caught her breath, she glared furiously up at Patterson. "Forget Royce! What about me? You left me totally unprotected. What the hell happened to the 24-hour close surveillance? You promised!"

He couldn't meet her eyes. Then she got it. She stared at him with disbelief. "This was on purpose," she accused him. "You let me be bait!"

Patterson grabbed some paper towels from the sink and handed them to her. She squeamishly wiped the blood off her fingers and then tossed the towels on the floor. She drew her knees to her chest and began rocking back and forth, shaking uncontrollably.

He said flatly, "It wasn't my idea." Under her hard gaze, he added, "My higher-ups had started to wonder about a lot of things. Was there really a threat to you? Were you holding back information? Were you playing on both sides? And you weren't telling me enough to answer those questions."

"So you just happened to wander by? Did it take me nearly getting killed for you to resolve your doubts?"

"I don't know anything more than before," Patterson responded with irritation. "I needed Royce alive to get any idea of what the Soviets are up to."

"It wasn't the Soviets."

Patterson looked at her quizzically. "What do you mean, 'it wasn't the Soviets'?"

"I got a hunch, and to stall for time, I told Royce the FBI knew he wasn't working with the KGB. The way he reacted, I'm sure I'm right."

Patterson frowned. "That's a big leap."

"Remember when the press officers didn't tell Anatoly that Robert was going to Lima? After Anatoly alerted his KGB bosses in front of everyone, he instantly disappeared. And when Yevgeni botched the hand-off in Central Park, he vanished, too. The Soviets don't leave people here who mess up."

Patterson looked unconvinced.

Anne continued, "If Royce were KGB, after he failed to kill me in the coffee shop, he would have been yanked back to Moscow."

"If you're right," Patterson said, "it's not helpful. It means we're back to Square One." Reaching down a hand, he hauled Anne to her feet. "We'll have a team here in about 30 minutes to take the body and clean things up." Pointing at her bloodied dress, he added, "Give that to the boys when they leave. You won't be wearing it again."

Anne looked down at her dress and shuddered.

WHITE BUSES

Royce's intrusion and his death haunted Anne day and night over the next few days. She stopped walking the thirty blocks from her apartment to the UN. Instead she got on a bus, but sat down only after she'd carefully scrutinized all the other passengers.

Then one morning she woke up and again felt ready to start walking to work. As she left her apartment building, she took in a deep, full breath. The reality was sinking in that Royce was gone. Really gone. Jürgen was still around, and Andrei, too, but she found herself daring to hope that any actual danger to her life might finally now be over.

As she reached 53rd Street, she saw the Secretary-General emerge from Sutton Place and stride energetically down First Avenue. A security guard followed some paces behind, obviously struggling to keep up with his long-legged boss. Anne smiled at his efforts.

She knew Waldheim was coming from the neo-classical townhouse on the East River that had recently been donated as the Secretary-General's official residence. Thinking of her own tilted, drafty apartment, Anne mused that it must be nice to live so sumptuously.

When Waldheim reached the north gate to the UN Garden, the security officer there greeted him deferentially. Anne, trailing a respectful distance behind, entered through the same gate. The Secretary-General continued his brisk walk, veering left toward the river on the most direct path to the lower entrance of the building.

Anne didn't want it to look as though she were following him, like some kind of UN groupie, so she took the path closer to First Avenue. As she strolled among the rows of stately oak trees, she glanced over at the street and noticed two unmarked white buses pulling up in front of the UN. They came to a stop right outside the public entrance. How odd. Visitors wouldn't be admitted for another hour.

The bus doors opened and out spilled the passengers, engaged in lively chatter with each other. Although a distance away, Anne could hear they were speaking Russian. In fact, she recognized several Soviet staff members from her department.

The two guards at the public entrance didn't seem surprised by this mass arrival. They merely gave a cursory glance at each blue UN pass as it was held up to their view, and waved the steady stream of people through the gates.

Anne continued on her way. After entering the building, she headed for the newsstand to collect the periodicals for her office. As she approached it, she was surprised to see Andrei coming into the building through the main doors. Apparently he hadn't arrived on the unmarked buses with the other Soviet staff. Spotting Anne, he waved.

He joined her at the newsstand and picked up copies of *Pravda* and the New York Russian newspaper, *Novaya Russkaya Gazeta*. Smiling, he said, "You have nice color in your cheeks this morning, Anne."

"I walked to work and, just for fun, I tried to keep up with Waldheim as he came from his residence. He sets quite a fast pace." Curious to know why Andrei hadn't arrived on one of the buses, she asked, "And how do you get to work?"

"I take the subway from my apartment in Brooklyn. It doesn't take long, usually about a half hour."

By this time, Anne's arms were loaded down with publications. She said, "The stack is heavy today, so I should be going. Have a great day."

He smiled again. "And you the same."

Anne was heading for the escalator when she heard a cheerful, "Hello, Anne." It was Peggy.

"Hi there," Anne said. "You're in early this morning."

"Only because I ran out of Irish Breakfast Tea and have to get some from our import shop. I can't start my day properly with your wretched Lipton."

"Well, aren't you the snob," Anne teased. Then she looked at her friend closely. "Peggy, are you okay? Do you think you're safe after what happened in the park?"

Peggy glanced around before answering. "I honestly don't know, Anne. No one's been treating me any differently in the office, as far as I can tell. That would be a good sign, wouldn't it?"

"Yes, Peggy, I think so," Anne said, hoping she was right. "Do be careful, though."

"I will. Since that day, I haven't been going out in the evening, much as I miss the theatre."

"That sounds wise, at least for the time being." Anne admired how her friend was keeping her equilibrium after such an alarming experience. Then it occurred to her that Peggy might be able to explain the strange scene she'd just witnessed outside the UN. "Peggy, do you know why the Soviets arrive together on buses in the morning?"

"All of them live in a complex in Riverdale, a little north of Manhattan. Mr. Ipatov told me they have their own apartment buildings, schools, theatres, shops, and even their own medical service. It's a complete world in itself."

Anne frowned. "Do *all* the Soviets live there?"

"I think so. Except from what Mr. Ipatov said, it seems like a few very important ones get to live where they want."

Like Brooklyn, Anne said to herself. Was Andrei that important? The thought was unsettling.

When Anne reached her office, she dropped the newspapers and magazines onto her desk with a satisfying thump and began sorting through them. At that moment, Juanita walked through the door. She greeted Anne and headed for her desk. "What's this?" she asked, holding up a piece of paper.

Anne looked down and saw, poking out from under the periodicals, the same paper. Together they read it aloud: "Worldwide Day of Solidarity against Staff Cost-of-living Freeze".

"¡No me digas!" exclaimed Juanita. "When the General Assembly voted to suspend this year's cost-of-living increase, I knew our Staff Union was discussing how to fight back. But I never dreamed they'd call a strike."

Anne read a little further in the announcement. "It'll be this Thursday. We're supposed to wear white and march around the traffic circle in front of the building. I might be too afraid to do that. What if we get fired?"

Juanita smiled. "Don't forget, the department heads won't get their cost-of-living increase either if the budget plan goes through. Even though the big bosses won't be walking around the circle with us, they may be glad we're there."

Anne still looked doubtful.

"You worry too much, Anne," said Juanita. "At lunchtime we'll go shopping for pretty white blouses, and then you'll want to go."

"Oh, Juanita, I wish I had your sunny disposition. Maybe I'll join in. But right now, that's only a *maybe*."

41

STAFF STRIKE

J uanita looked up at the wall clock. "Girls, it's time."

The three secretaries, wearing their new white blouses, rose from their desks. Juanita stopped in Duarte's doorway to tell him, "We're going now." Then they headed out the door.

All along the hallway, staff members dressed in white were emerging from their offices and heading for the ground floor. Juanita, Benedetta and Anne hadn't made signs, but many of their colleagues had:

> **No to UNpaid staff!**
> **Don't UNdercut staff!**
> **UNfreeze our pay!**

The atmosphere felt festive, as more and more people joined the river of staff that moved across the ground floor lobby, through the revolving doors and out into the traffic circle. But at the same time, there was an undercurrent of anxiety. Nothing like this had ever happened before at the UN, and no one knew how senior officials, or the most powerful Member States, would react.

Still, the three secretaries had made their decision. Without hesitation, they melded into the growing crowd circling the broad reflecting pool at the center of the traffic circle. As people continued to arrive, the pace slowed. Even when it seemed there was no more room, staff still poured out of the building and entered the demonstration. UN-accredited photojournalists were everywhere, eagerly snapping photos.

"There must be a thousand people out here," Benedetta exclaimed over the noise of the chatter around them.

"I think even more than that," Juanita called back.

As Anne was being gently jostled this way and that by the throng of staff, she peered up at the tall UN Building. The reflected sunlight made it impossible to see through the green tinted glass. Yet she was sure high officials must be watching the demonstration carefully, and maybe even jotting down the names of their own employees.

Juanita touched Anne's arm and pointed. The President of the Staff Union was standing at a microphone on a raised platform off to one side. He was holding up his arms for silence. Slowly the noisy conversations of the strikers ebbed away.

Everyone listened attentively as the President reviewed the situation. "I know all of you will agree," he said, "that management needs to do more, much more, to speak up against the unfairness of the General Assembly decision. Senior UN leadership needs to convince the Member States to roll back this unjust measure before irrevocable damage is done to the core principles of international civil service."

As she listened to his statement, Anne felt both exhilarated and worried. Where would this end?

After about an hour, small groups of staff began to break off the edges of the crowd and drift back into the building. Anne and her office-mates decided it was time for them to leave, too. They were approaching the revolving doors when Juanita exclaimed, "Anne, what happened to your blouse?"

"What do you mean?"

"Look, there's a rip in the sleeve." Juanita pinched the fabric and gently pulled it around so Anne could see. "Actually, it looks more like a cut. Did you catch it on something sharp?"

Anne was puzzled. "To do that much damage, I think I would have felt it. Oh, it really is ruined, isn't it," she lamented.

Juanita responded cheerily, "Oh, don't worry. You can shorten both sleeves and the blouse will be pretty again. And then you can wear it in hot weather, too."

Anne tugged the sleeve to where she could see it better. It did look as though the fabric had been cut.

Benedetta suggested going to the cafeteria to pick up coffees before they returned to the office, and the others agreed. They would be even later getting back to their desks, but surely Señor Duarte would understand that it was an exceptional day.

As Anne stood behind Juanita and Benedetta in the cashier's line, she opened her handbag to take out her wallet. Inside she found a small slip of paper. Curious, she unfolded it to see what it was. Her hands began to tremble. Typed on the paper were the words, "This time it was just a sleeve. Next time it could be more serious."

Royce was gone, but the danger wasn't.

42

NORWAY'S GIFT

Anne stood, in hushed awe, in the doorway of the Security Council Chamber. This was the first time she'd seen it devoid of the usual crowd of diplomats milling about or seated for an official meeting. Without the presence of another human being, the austere beauty of the room struck her full force.

She'd just delivered a phone message to Duarte, who'd been having drinks with a friend in the nearby South Lounge. When her boss heard the name of the caller, he jumped to his feet, quickly excused himself and hurried back to the office.

Anne would have followed right after him, but she happened to glance down the hallway leading from the Lounge to the back of the building. Off to the left, she noticed that the large doors to the Security Council Chamber were wide open. She couldn't resist walking toward them. Whenever she covered a Council meeting for the Information Centres, she sat up in the third-floor mezzanine. She had always wondered how the Chamber would look from its main floor. Curiosity propelled her forward.

Now, standing in the doorway, her eyes took in every aspect of the room, from the soft beige carpet underfoot to the delicate ceiling details. The famous horseshoe-shaped table fascinated her. Over its long history, so many distinguished ambassadors had sat there, and even world leaders on important occasions.

Surrounded by the horseshoe table was a small rectangular table. Press officers and verbatim record teams sat there to be sure they were able to hear every word of the statements being made.

At a distance from the horseshoe table, spread out along both the right and left walls, were several rows of red seats for delegates who were not Council members. Toward the back, more such seats were installed on flooring which sloped gradually upward until it reached a second tier. That section, in which each place had a writing board, was reserved for journalists. Rising still higher was the mezzanine used by the public and by staff members like Anne.

She knew the Chamber was the gift of Norway, and that most of the building materials and furnishings had been provided by that country. She once overheard a UN Guide describe the blue and gold tapestry used for the wall covering. Its woven design portrayed the anchor of faith, the growing wheat of hope, and the heart of charity. The heavy floor-to-ceiling curtains, which blocked the view of the East River, were made of the same cloth.

Anne hesitated at the doorway. Did she really dare go in? She looked behind her to make sure no one was watching and then slipped into the Chamber. As she passed over the threshold, her fingers admiringly traced the delicate inlays of the glossy wooden doors.

Once inside, she stared up at the interpretation booths set high within the walls on either side. Again and again, she'd heard the interpreters convert charged words from one language into another at an impossibly quick pace. Looking at the small, tilted windows, she felt deep respect for the men and women who sat behind them and followed every action at the table below.

Stepping further into the room, Anne was drawn toward the large mural set against the light-colored marble wall behind the Council President's seat. To her, it seemed to be about 30 feet wide and 20 feet tall. Coming closer, she was surprised to see it wasn't a mural after all, but actually an enormous oil painting on canvas.

Its bottom third was grim. There the Norwegian artist had portrayed – in dark shades of rust, verdigris and steel – the sufferings of war, slavery and displacement. The painting brightened as figures moved upward into a lighter, more colorful world, filled with scenes of cooperation, harmony and freedom. In the very middle of the painting was a large phoenix rising from its ashes.

While she was taking in the various images, Anne heard a sound behind her. Turning, she saw a man leaning casually against the wall just inside the doorway, wearing a satisfied smile.

It was Andrei.

Anne froze. While she'd been exploring the Chamber, she'd felt sure she was the only person there. It unnerved her to realize she hadn't been alone after all.

Andrei detached himself from the wall and strolled leisurely toward her. As he approached, she demanded, "What are you doing here?"

"I was in the South Lounge enjoying a coffee, when you delivered a message to that distinguished looking man. He's your boss?"

Anne nodded her confirmation.

"I rose to say hello to you before you headed back to your office, but then I saw you start down this hallway. The look on your face intrigued me, so I followed you here."

"You shouldn't have," Anne spluttered. "That...that's spying!"

As soon as the words were out, her hand flew to her mouth. What an absurd thing to say to someone undoubtedly working for the KGB.

The corners of Andrei's eyes creased with amusement as he replied, "That's an appraisal which I cannot dispute."

Anne's forehead knit in displeasure. "How long have you been standing there?"

"Long enough to see your happiness as you look at everything in this Chamber. It must be a special place for you."

"I think it's special for everyone, isn't it?"

Andrei shook his head. "No, not at all. I'm sure many people come into this Chamber every day and don't notice any of its beauty. It's just a place where they fight with words, where they try to carry their own side's point of view and outmaneuver their opponents. They could be in any large room and it would feel the same to them."

"I don't agree," Anne argued. "I'm sure everyone who participates in a meeting here is very aware how impressive this room is. How could it be otherwise?"

Andrei smiled again. "You think that, Anne, because you have faith in mankind. I like that in you." He paused. "But if I could offer any advice, I would caution you about where exactly you place your trust, or I fear the world will disappoint you. Especially here."

Anne bristled. There it was again, the idea that she was naïve. "I'm fully aware of this organization's seamy side," she shot back. "I saw it as soon as I arrived here. There are staff, even at the highest levels, who are abusing their positions in all kinds of ways. They're only using the UN for their own ambitions, and they don't care at all about its goals." More softly, she added, "Sometimes I wonder why I stay."

She'd never before voiced her doubts out loud. Hearing them put into words, she suddenly felt deeply conflicted.

Andrei said, "Seeing what's wrong with this place doesn't mean you have to leave it, Anne. It does mean, though, that you need to develop the right kind of cynicism."

His look was caring, and Anne faltered when she tried to reply.

"Never mind," he reassured her. "What I said doesn't require an answer."

During the pause that followed, Anne looked upward and then frowned. Andrei followed her eyes to the ceiling. "What's wrong?"

"Do you see the way the outer rim of the ceiling drops down, creating a recess above?"

"Yes," Andrei answered. "It's a pleasing effect."

She nodded. "That's why I'm disappointed. It seems to me that the lowered floor inside the horseshoe table was supposed to mirror the recess in the ceiling. I think it was a mistake for them to fill in the floor when the Chamber was renovated."

"Fill it in?" Andrei asked. "I don't understand."

"If you look at old photos, the floor inside the table used to be pitched about two feet below the main floor."

"Now that you mention it, I do remember seeing that." Andrei glanced from the ceiling to the floor several times. "I agree with you. Now the floor looks flat and uninteresting. It's a pity." Seeing the dejection in her face, he added, "But the Chamber is still a wonderful place. Let's not lose this special moment. When again will we have an opportunity to enjoy it in such tranquility?"

For the next minutes, there was absolute peace in the room. Without talking, Andrei and Anne slowly circled the Chamber. They looked at it carefully from all angles, as though memorizing every feature.

Abruptly, the calm was broken. Two conference officers barged briskly through the doorway. One carried a tall stack of documents, which she placed on a nearby desk. The other walked to the ends of the horseshoe table and snapped brown embossed nameplates into holders there.

"Looks like it's time for us to go," Andrei said to Anne.

As they emerged into the hallway, he took her hand. At first she thought he was going to shake it, but instead he merely held it. She felt a gentle warmth coming off his palm. "Anne, please remember what I said."

Before she could respond, he had released her hand and was walking away.

ANNE'S QUESTIONABLE COMPANY

At the close of the workday, Anne exited the UN premises through the main gate. Crossing First Avenue always brought back the nightmare of the taxi accident, especially when traffic was moving fast, as it was today. The message in her handbag had further set her on edge. She hung back on the sidewalk until several other UN staff reached the curb. Then she fell into step with them until they arrived at the other side of the street. Once there, she started walking uptown on her way to the Duane Reade at 72nd Street.

As Anne approached 45th Street, she saw the metal booth outside the Permanent Mission of Turkey. She could see through the booth's small window that a policeman was on duty inside. Ever since the Kurdistan Workers' Party set off bombs at the Turkish Consulates in Paris and Strasbourg, the police feared the next target might be the Turkish premises in New York. Before Anne joined the UN, she had no idea there was so much potential for crime and violence in its vicinity.

On the next block, Anne drew near a cluster of foreign tourists who were pointing across at the UN. She wove through them and was continuing up First Avenue when someone behind her put a firm hand on her arm. She cried out. Without turning to look at her would-be assailant, she wrenched her arm free and began running uptown.

"Miss, Miss," a man's voice called after her, "I only want that you take our picture."

Still running, Anne glanced over her shoulder. A bewildered tourist was standing on the sidewalk holding out his camera. She immediately realized her panic was unfounded, and yet she couldn't stop. The fear his grip had set off was too great. It took another block before she finally slowed to a walk.

At last, she passed through the pharmacy doors and made her way to the shampoo section. Facing the shelves, she was stepping back to survey the different brands when she bumped into someone behind her. She started to cry out again, but this time caught herself. Instead, she turned around carefully. The words "I'm so sorry" were on her lips, but she stopped mid-sentence.

"Stewart," she said instead.

"Hello, Anne," he replied. "You're a dangerous person to stand behind in a pharmacy." The words were humorous, but he wasn't smiling. Neither was Anne.

"This isn't an accidental meeting, is it," she muttered.

"I'm not saying I followed you here, but I do want to talk to you."

She tried to hide her nervousness. "What about?"

"I still have some questions about you," Stewart continued. "Rick and I genuinely care about our country. If there's anything going on at the UN that would damage the United States, we're committed to doing what we can to stop it. And that's why we need more clarity about you, and what you're up to."

"We've already gone over this," she protested. "You even searched my desk from top to bottom, and you yourselves said you didn't find anything."

Stewart studied her attentively. "That's right. We didn't. But you still make us uncomfortable."

"Stewart, you've got to be more specific than that."

"Well, it's partly the company you're keeping."

"What's that supposed to mean?"

He stalled. "Go ahead and get your shampoo. I'll wait."

Sullenly, Anne picked up a green bottle of Prell and then looked back questioningly at him.

"What else are you here to buy?" he asked.

"Toothpaste. Or is that also suspect?"

"Toothpaste is in Aisle 8. I'll walk you over there." He took Anne's arm and ushered her in that direction, away from two women who were approaching the shampoos. Once the women were out of earshot, Stewart said, "Let's start with the representatives of the liberation movements that come to your floor to read the news. It's come to our attention that you spend a lot of time talking with them. Especially the guys from Polisario."

"Oh, for heaven's sake. The Polisario representatives chat with all the girls."

"They may chat with the other girls, Anne, but that's just flirting. With you, they're talking about liberating the Spanish Sahara."

"You're well informed."

"It's my job to be."

"Stewart, I majored in political science. If they want to explain their position to me, I'll listen. But I know it's only one side of what's happening. And it's not like I'm passing around petitions on behalf of Polisario. Or inventing pro-Polisario entries for the Secretary-General's *Press Analysis*."

He ignored her sarcasm. "And your admirer Fouad?"

"Fouad's just a friend, and I don't tell him anything important. We only chat and hang out together."

"But you must be aware of his views on the Middle East and the Palestine Liberation Organization. I don't think you can pretend he's on the same page as the U.S. Government. Which, I might remind you, is your government, despite your scant interest in helping it."

The conversation wasn't going well.

Stewart continued, "And then there's Peggy."

She sighed. "What about Peggy?"

"How well do you really know her?"

Anne's shoulders tensed. Peggy had her share of faults, and Anne felt wary about where this new tack might be leading. "We met in Russian class. Well, you probably already know that. She's lively and likes to go on outings, as do I."

"She's awfully cozy with her Soviet bosses in the Outer Space office. That place is crawling with Commies. Shouldn't you be a little more concerned that she fits in so well there?"

"Practically every UN office has at least one Russian or other East European. You can't get away from them. And if they're your bosses, of course you're going to try to get along. Peggy's friendly with everyone. Maybe a little too friendly for her own good, but that's just how she is."

"You're thinking of her latest love interest?"

Anne felt trapped by his question. Peggy had started an affair with a representative of an international aid organization. He was an effective advocate, working for a good cause. To Anne, though, he was also clearly a womanizer and the affair had no future. "Okay, sometimes Peggy lacks judgment," she admitted.

"That's what we think, too," Stewart commented. "So why would Anne Thomas want to be friends with someone who 'lacks judgment'? We have to ask ourselves that."

"Listen," Anne said wearily. "I'm sure you'll continue to be suspicious of me. I'm sure the Soviets will continue to be suspicious of me. And nothing I say to explain myself seems to have any effect."

"I'm glad you mentioned the Soviets. That brings to mind Andrei."

Anne felt her face get warm.

Stewart appeared to notice her discomfort. "It seems like you and Andrei are getting along almost too well. From what we saw, you always gave Yevgeni the cold shoulder. But look how often you're in the Delegates Lounge having coffee with Andrei. I'm sure other people must be noticing, too."

She glanced over her shoulder apprehensively. "Should you even be asking me about this in public?"

Stewart's voice was patronizing. "Anne, Anne, this is New York City. No New Yorker pays attention to anyone but himself." Turning to eye the shoppers around them, he added, "But if the KGB should happen to overhear us? Well, maybe they should know our side is careful about these kinds of things."

"Okay. I meet with Andrei to keep things clear, for them to know I'm not working for or against them. And do you really think that if I were on their side, I'd make contact in a fishbowl like the Delegates Lounge?"

Stewart shrugged. "Why not?"

Anne's eyes flashed. "I can assure you that especially after the taxi accident, I have every reason to want to stay out of trouble."

"I'm glad to hear that," he said, sounding unconvinced. "Let's just keep it that way. Got your toothpaste?"

She held up a box of Crest.

"Why don't you go ahead and check out. I've got to pick up some aftershave."

She turned to head toward the cashier, but stopped when she heard Stewart's voice. "Anne, I'm serious when I say that you need to be more careful about the company you keep."

44

A PAINTED LADY

Juanita studied Anne intently as she walked through the office door. "Is everything okay?"

Anne dropped her steno pad onto her desk but remained standing. "I don't know why Señor Gavrez keeps calling me to take dictation. His two secretaries are right outside his office, and they don't seem to do a thing." She looked down at the floor. "He dictates so fast that I can barely keep up, and then orders me to bring back the typed pages in an hour." Anne sounded like she was on the verge of tears.

Juanita knew about Gavrez through her Latin American grapevine, but the stories her friends told her were about his many affairs, his lavish lifestyle, and his ambitions. She hadn't heard anything that would explain why he was giving Anne such a hard time. Shaking her head, Juanita said, "You're not even in his department. It doesn't make sense."

"It can't be because he likes my work. I get so rattled that I make lots of mistakes, which he doesn't hesitate to point out to me."

Juanita was as confused as Anne. She studied Anne carefully. Could Gavrez possibly be interested in her? The thought had occurred to Juanita once before, but at the time she quickly dismissed it.

From everything Juanita knew about Gavrez, he was drawn to flamboyantly beautiful women, and that description didn't fit Anne. Juanita liked Anne – a lot – but she felt her friend didn't make as much of her looks as she could. Juanita had tried to nudge her toward wearing more make-up and more stylish clothes, but Anne's casual West Coast roots ran deep. Still, as Juanita looked at her now, she saw a quality that might be attractive to Gavrez. If not, she had no other explanation for what was going on.

Still looking dejected, Anne said, "I'm going across the hall to the ladies room to freshen up. I'll be back in a minute."

"Of course," Juanita answered. "Take as much time as you need."

While Anne stood in front of the sink, she allowed her face and body to fully show the anxiety she was otherwise constantly trying to hide. With male eyes on her seemingly everywhere she went in the building, it was a relief to be in a place where she could drop her guard, if just for a moment. It was barely a month since the taxi accident, but she could no longer remember what "normal" felt like.

Anne remained at the sink for several minutes, mindlessly letting the water run over her hands. She was brought back to the present when she heard the restroom door open. From the corner of her eye, she saw a slender, Latin-appearing woman enter and ease up to the sink on her right, between her and the restroom door.

Glancing in the long horizontal mirror stretched out before them, Anne couldn't help but admire the woman's well-tailored suit, fine jewelry, perfectly styled hair, and especially her flattering make-up.

Anne mused that, to a woman so attentive to her appearance, she herself must look plain and nondescript. For that reason, she was surprised to notice that the woman was studying her with keen interest.

The woman made no move to use the sink or mirror, but instead kept her eyes locked on Anne. In the silence between them, Anne felt a rising tension. A strangely knowing smile started to spread over the woman's face. As her lips parted, Anne flinched. One of her front teeth was chipped at a harsh angle, incongruous with her otherwise polished appearance. It made her face look almost sinister.

Under the woman's unbroken stare, Anne was growing increasingly uneasy. Something wasn't right. Maybe even seriously wrong. Anne needed to leave. Now. She eased away from the sink and began heading for the door.

She wasn't fast enough. The woman moved quickly between her and the exit, blocking her way. "It's not time for you to go yet."

The voice was deep. It was a man! The shock made Anne's legs start buckling beneath her.

Her sense of being safe in a ladies room had been shattered. She was trapped in that small space with a man who didn't belong there, a man who seemed to have intruded so he could confront her in some way. She opened her mouth to scream, but the warning look in his eyes made her stop.

Anne desperately longed for someone, anyone, to walk in. But so much of her part of the building was taken up by meeting rooms that there were few offices. That meant only a handful of women used this restroom. There was a good chance no one would enter it any time soon.

With mounting agitation, Anne demanded, "Who are you? What do you want?" She tried to make her voice sound firm, but even she could hear the fear in it.

"Stay away from what doesn't concern you," the man replied. His eyes bore into hers. "Am I making myself clear?"

Trembling, Anne was struggling to control her panic when the restroom door opened with a bang. Two middle-aged women rounded the corner.

Anne saw her chance. She bolted past the man and around the two startled women and burst out into the hallway.

Expecting the man to emerge right after her, she frantically looked in both directions. To her left, at the end of the hallway, three press officers were passing through the glass doors which led to the open area on the floor. Anne quickly rushed after them. Once through the doors, she hurried to the escalator. Before she entered it, she whipped her head around. The man hadn't yet come into the hallway. Relieved, she began climbing the escalator as fast as she could, dodging around the people above her. She'd go to the bank on the fourth floor and hide there.

In her hurry, Anne didn't notice Jürgen off to one side, coming up the stairs from the Security Council Chamber. His eyes followed her attentively as she rushed by.

45

UPPER WEST SIDE

Just after 10:00 p.m., Anne got off the No. 1 train at 110th Street. She climbed the foul-smelling stairs and exited the subway station at the northeast corner. Once above ground, she began walking up Broadway as she'd been instructed.

Supposedly she was being covered, but that did nothing to ease her taut nerves. The neighborhood brought back memories, and not good ones. Before she dropped out, Anne had spent a year at Columbia Law. Leaving the Law Library late every night had terrified her, because students were sometimes mugged as they walked across the dark campus. She felt that same fear now.

Three blocks north of the subway station, Anne spotted a garbage truck stopped on a diagonal at the curb. The angle at which it was parked shielded a dark van from the view of anyone driving uptown. Anne checked the van's license plate. It was the right one.

A man lighting a cigarette in a doorframe gave her a subtle nod to let her know no one was following her and that she could approach the van. The van door slid open just as she came up alongside. Two hands reached out and helped her quickly get in.

Even as the door was being slammed shut, the van was already in motion. It shot forward and quickly spun to the right at what must have been the street corner. It continued at full speed until the driver hit the brakes and made another sharp turn. Then the van's pace became more leisurely.

"You're on time for once," Patterson said.

As he spoke, Anne noticed how completely soundproof the back of the van was. It was also very dark. Only gradually did she perceive that there was a man sitting beside Patterson.

"Anne, this is Marco Capaccio. He's one of our linguists."

Capaccio said, "Hello, Anne. I hope I can help."

Patterson continued, "Marco is going to play some recordings of men from different Latin American countries repeating what that guy said to you in the ladies room. I don't think the man is someone who's usually in the UN Building. I doubt he'd take the chance of being recognized by you again. But if we can figure out his nationality, that may give us a trail to whoever he's working with."

"Anne," Capaccio began, "you'll only be able to listen to a few of these recordings before your ear will lose its capacity to discriminate, so we're going to be as targeted as possible. In your message to Patterson, you wondered if the man could be Cuban. That's the first accent I'll play for you. You said he was young, so this speaker is a Cuban in his twenties."

Capaccio clicked his tape recorder and an accented voice spoke the words, "Stay away from what doesn't concern you. Am I making myself clear?"

Anne shivered as she remembered her shock in the restroom. "Could you play that again?" she asked.

"Stay away from what doesn't concern you. Am I making myself clear?"

Anne shook her head. "No, that's not it."

Capaccio popped out the cassette and inserted a different one. Again Anne heard, "Stay away from what doesn't concern you. Am I making myself clear?"

"Once more, please?" After a pause, Anne said, "No, not that one either."

"Okay," said Capaccio. "By the way, that speaker was from Bolivia. What about this one?"

After Anne heard a few words, she commented, "That's an Ecuadorian."

Patterson leaned forward. "What makes you say that?"

"That's how Antonio Gavrez talks."

Patterson asked, "Who's he?"

"The UN's former mediator in Cyprus. We were both on the island at the same time. Now he's an Under-Secretary-General at Headquarters." She sighed. "He's pretty important."

"Are you thinking that could have been him in the ladies room?"

"Oh no," she replied. "He's much taller and more muscular. It's just that I recognized the accent." Turning to Capaccio, she asked, "Can you play some other ones for me?"

The process repeated with nine more recordings, but none of them matched the accent Anne recalled.

Patterson became impatient. "Anne, you're at the UN, day in and day out. Surely you can recognize an accent you must hear all the time."

Her voice rose. "It's not as easy as you think. There are 144 Member States, and many of them have several national languages and dialects, and…"

"Bob," Capaccio broke in, "it *is* much harder than you imagine."

"You're the expert," Patterson said grudgingly. "But we're wasting time and resources on a case that's going nowhere. I was hoping this would finally give us a real lead."

Capaccio asked, "Can I make a suggestion?"

Patterson nodded. "Sure."

Turning to Anne, Capaccio said, "Here's what I want you to do. Over the next few days, listen closely any time anyone is speaking near you. There may be a lot of Member States, but only about two dozen of them use Spanish. If you're still able to recall how that accent sounded, you should pick up on it before long."

"All right, I can do that." Anne opened her handbag. "There's one more thing," she said. She pulled out the note and handed it to Patterson. "Here, read this."

He took the piece of paper and struck a match so he could read it. He groaned. "Where the hell did this come from?"

"Someone slipped it into my handbag during the staff strike. After they made a cut in my blouse." Anne's voice quavered. "First this note and then the guy in the ladies room. Bob, I'm getting scared."

"They're obviously *trying* to scare you," Patterson replied. "They're showing up in places where you thought you were safe – in a ladies room, or in a crowd with your friends." He folded the note and put it in his pocket. "When I get back to the office, I'll get this analyzed. We'll just have to keep taking things one step at a time."

Anne sighed. "That's not very reassuring. But I guess there's no other choice."

The van began to slow. Patterson said, "Okay, Anne, that's enough for this evening. You'll be getting out at 79th Street and First Avenue. It's late, so there'll be a man walking a dog behind you until you get to 74th Street and your apartment."

"Thank you." Anne had felt secure inside the van and cringed at the thought of being alone again.

The van came to a sudden stop. Patterson quietly eased the door open and motioned for Anne to descend. As she stepped out, she was screened from the sidewalk by a garbage truck.

She whispered through the closing door, "How many garbage trucks do you have?"

Just before the door shut, she heard Patterson reply, "As many as we need."

The night air was bracing. Anne took off at a quick pace down First Avenue. She didn't turn around when she heard footsteps a short distance behind her and the jangling of a leash.

46

THE POUCH UNIT

"Juanita, this is NOT a good idea," Anne protested.

She and Juanita rarely argued, but this time they had dug in on opposite sides and neither was budging.

Juanita planted her fists on her hips. "It's one little package, among the thousands that go out in the diplomatic pouches every day. No one will think anything of it, and it will make Ishwari so happy. She's desperately lonely now that she's posted to the Information Centre in New Delhi."

Anne was incredulous. "How can Ishwari be lonely? She's Indian, for heaven's sake, and the UNIC is in India."

"Ishwari isn't from New Delhi, she's from Bombay. And it's New York City she misses, not her home town. Sending her the black push-up bras from Bloomingdale's will cheer her up. I'd do it myself, but I've got to finish this rush for Tokyo."

"No, and no again," Anne said. "I can't believe you're even suggesting this. It's not worth the risk of getting caught. You know the rules. UN diplomatic pouches can only be used for official business."

"Oh, Anne," Juanita countered, "I'm sure other things come and go in those pouches all the time. Even if we were caught – and we won't be – no one's going to be upset about some bras."

"What makes you so sure we won't get caught? Just look at it." Anne pointed at the puffy envelope. "That doesn't look like a set of documents to me. Someone will get suspicious, either here in the Pouch Unit or in Delhi, and they'll open it. Can you imagine how much trouble we'll be in?"

"Listen, I've already promised Ishwari we would do it, and we can't disappoint her now. She needs them by Friday, for an important reception at the Foreign Ministry." Juanita glanced up at the wall clock. "The package has to get to the Pouch Unit by 4:15 if we want to catch this afternoon's run to the airport. Lighten up."

Normally, for Juanita to say an Americanism like "lighten up" would have made Anne grin, but today she was not amused. "If Señor Duarte knew what…"

As if summoned by his name, their boss opened his door and called out, "Juanita, I need to add a few more paragraphs to the Tokyo memo."

Juanita rose from her desk. As she was disappearing into Duarte's office, she looked meaningfully at the clock and then at the envelope on her desk.

For the next half hour, Anne willed the hands of the clock to move more slowly, but by 4:00, Juanita still hadn't reemerged. "Drat," Anne muttered, "this is Ishwari and Juanita's stupid idea, but I'm the one stuck carrying it out."

With obvious distaste, she grabbed the envelope and headed for the service elevator.

To drop an envelope off directly at the Pouch Unit meant winding through several long, windowless corridors in the Third Basement. Anne felt sympathy for the dozens of men who every morning entered the same UN gates as the delegates and office workers, but then left the diplomatic world above ground to spend eight hours in the building's somber basements. Still, neither Anne nor her officemates liked taking their turn to deliver outgoing mail to the pouches. Any young woman who stepped into that all-male world was met by a barrage of whistles and leers.

Today was no different. Anne walked with her eyes straight ahead as she made her way along the Third Basement's main corridor to the Pouch Unit and pushed open the heavy double doors. "Hey, beautiful," sang out the supervisor. Looking her up and down, he came forward until only inches separated them.

Instinctively Anne stepped back, but the supervisor merely closed the gap. He was so near that she could smell his tuna fish lunch on his breath. He took her package and then dawdled as he read aloud each word on the label. He seemed to enjoy his power to keep her standing there. She was impatient to go, but had to stay until he finished registering her mail.

While she waited, over the blare of stale rock music and the rumbling of cloth hampers, she started to overhear a conversation coming from behind a partition of shelves. "This large one needs special handling," a voice said. "The boss says me and you personally gotta take it to the truck."

Special handling? Anne had sent out her share of packages in the diplomatic pouches, but no one ever told her there were some that got "special handling". Trying to tune out the repeated banging of the doors, she strained to catch what the reply would be. She managed to hear a second voice say, "Lucky for us. Every time we get one that needs special handling, it means more money in our pockets."

"Shut up," the first man said. "Watch your big mouth."

It was an odd exchange. She looked at the supervisor to see if he also had overheard, but he was too engrossed in checking out her breasts. She jabbed a finger at his logsheet and complained, "Haven't you finished yet?"

He shrugged and bent back over his clipboard. When he finished logging in her envelope, he handed it to a man passing by. "Rush this to the Loading Dock. The next truck to the airport is about to leave."

As Anne was turning to go, she saw two men emerge from behind the shelving and head in the direction of the Loading Dock. Neither looked familiar. They were struggling to push forward an unwieldy canvas bag on a dolly. Whatever it contained was at least four feet high and awkwardly shaped. As the men passed by her, she strained to read the number on the bag's tag. She thought it said *7509*.

Exiting the Pouch Unit, this time Anne was oblivious to the catcalls that came once the men saw her from behind. As she walked back down the long corridor and then pushed the button for the service elevator, she was ruminating over the shipment that needed "special handling". Why would it lead to extra pay? The UN didn't give any bonuses, as far as she knew. And what was that large, misshapen object in the pouch bag? Here she'd been thinking her package looked suspicious.

Anne was still lost in thought when the doors of the service elevator opened. The operator asked impatiently, "Well, are you getting in or not?"

Anne shook her head and started walking back to the Pouch Unit. How many times had Patterson criticized her for not being aware enough of suspicious activity that must be going on all around her? This time, she was going to follow up.

When she re-opened the double doors, the supervisor immediately spotted her. "Well, well, look who's back." He winked at her. "I guess you want to flirt a little more."

Ignoring his comment, she said in a businesslike way, "I think I made a mistake with the envelope I just brought. I need to check what you wrote down on the logsheet."

The supervisor reached for his clipboard. "How come?"

She lied, "I think I may have put the wrong name for the recipient."

The supervisor stood to Anne's left, holding the logsheet for her to see. She pretended to look for her own entry in the column labeled "Outgoing", but instead her eyes darted over the page searching for the sender of pouch bag *7509*. Finally she spotted the number, but maddeningly, the supervisor's thumb covered the name next to it.

"Well?" he drawled.

Anne glanced at him and then back at the log sheet. His thumb was still in the way. She hesitated a moment, and then jerked hard on the clipboard, freeing it from his hand. "Hey, what are you doing?" he cried, massaging his thumb.

Anne again found the number and quickly looked at the next column. Her breath stopped.

47

PARK BENCH

Anne leaned on the bench's rough boards and basked in the warm afternoon sun. Against the distant hum of traffic, she gazed across the vast expanse of Sheep Meadow and watched the people drawn to Central Park by the unseasonably high temperatures. Frisbees flew through the air, lovers lay entwined on blankets, and laughing children chased each other, while parents called for them not to go too far.

Anne enjoyed the scene a little longer, and then bent forward toward the small, bedraggled dog prancing at her feet. Its owner was an unkempt man sitting at the other end of the bench. His clothes were threadbare and he looked none too clean. "May I pat your little dog?" Anne asked.

The man kept one hand firmly on his wire shopping cart, which was overstuffed with odd belongings. He waved the other hand holding the leash and replied, "Sure, go ahead."

Anne jolted. It was Patterson's voice. She said, "I knew I was supposed to sit on this bench, but I didn't expect you'd be dressed like that. You should have warned me."

"What difference does it make?" he asked. "So what's the big urgency?"

Anne scrunched the uneven fur of the dog, which made satisfied grunts. "I'll get right to the point. Tuesday afternoon, I took a package down to the Pouch Unit. While I was there, I overheard two men conversing. One said they might get a bonus for taking care of a bag that needed 'special handling'. That caught my attention."

"Why?"

"Everyone at the UN is on straight salary. There are no bonuses. I checked."

Patterson asked, "Did you recognize the men? Could one of them have been the same guy who frightened you in the ladies room?"

"No, these men were taller and heavyset."

"Keep playing with the dog. How big was the bag?" Patterson asked.

"It was at least four feet high, and whatever was inside seemed almost cone-shaped."

"That doesn't sound like a bag full of documents. But still, without more details…"

"Let me finish," Anne said impatiently. "I saw the number on the bag and checked it against the supervisor's logsheet." Despite the soothing sunshine, her whole body tensed. "The sender was *A. Gavrez.*"

"Gavrez. I've heard that name before. Oh yeah, you mentioned him in the van. The big honcho who was in Cyprus the same time you were."

"That's him. What I haven't told you is that recently he's been calling me to his office to take dictation, even though I'm not in his department."

"Is that unusual?"

"Very."

Patterson absentmindedly cracked each of his knuckles. "By any chance could that pouch bag have held the Nigerian statue of *Anyanwu?*"

"That tall bronze Sun Goddess near the Delegates Lounge? I guess it could have. But that statue looks really heavy."

"The real one is heavy. The one there now is a copy."

"Oh my God!" Anne exclaimed. Her loud voice startled the little dog, which jumped to its feet and started yapping. "Shhh, shhh," Anne said, trying to calm it with gentle pats. "How did you find out?"

Patterson fixed his eyes on the ground. "Keep your voice down. We heard it from a Nigerian. That statue is a source of national pride for his country. He could tell immediately that the present one is slightly inferior to the original."

Anne distractedly stroked the little dog, which was again lying contentedly on its back.

Patterson asked, "Did you see on the logsheet where the bag was going?"

Anne slapped her palm to her forehead, a Russian gesture she had unconsciously picked up from Dr. Ruzhinsky. "Oh no! It never occurred to me."

Patterson sputtered, "How could you miss a lead like that? You were looking straight at the logsheet. It must have been right there."

"I'm so sorry."

Just then, with a rumble of wheels, two rollerbladers careened down the path, causing the little dog to yelp and take cover under the bench.

Patterson muttered, "Well, you can at least check the schedule and find out which pouches go out Tuesday afternoon."

"I know New Delhi is one. That's why I went to the Pouch Unit that day. But I wouldn't expect a big market there for Nigerian statues."

Patterson shook his head. "Don't be so sure. A wealthy Indian might want it. Or someone international could pick up the statue and then take it out of the country. But I think our best bet will be to focus on pouches going to Europe, like . . ."

"For Europe, the UN has offices in Madrid, Paris, London, Brussels, Vienna, Rome, Geneva…"

"Good. Check all of those and let me know. But I want to get back to this Gavrez fellow. What can you tell me about him? Because he was in Cyprus, can we assume he would recognize the value of the amphora?"

"He might. I think he bought some Cypriot artifacts while he was in Nicosia. We didn't work together there, but the day his secretary introduced me, as a new arrival, I saw a few in his office. By then I'd spent enough time in antiquities museums on the island to know they were expensive pieces, not something the UN would buy to furnish a field office."

Finally she succeeded in coaxing the little dog to come out from under the bench and sit again at her feet.

Patterson said, "If Gavrez is such a big fish, his UN salary must be pretty high. I can't really think he'd be looking for more money through dealing in stolen art. Probably there's a practical reason why his name was on the logsheet. And anyway, we're just guessing it might have been the *Anyanwu*."

"You're wrong about his salary," Anne responded. "UN officials, even the top ones, aren't paid as much as you might think. The US Government keeps a pretty tight lid on the organization's budget. But, according to Juanita, Gavrez has a lot of family money."

"Do you know anything about his lifestyle?"

"From what I've heard, he spends a fair amount on fast cars and fast women."

Patterson thought for a moment. "It may not get us anywhere, but I'm going to put two of our people out at the airport as baggage handlers and have them watch the outgoing diplomatic pouches. Still, if Gavrez – or anyone else – is using the pouches to smuggle art from the UN collection, with the prices they can get for only a few pieces, they wouldn't have to do deals very often."

"Isn't it illegal for the United States, as the UN's host country, to inspect diplomatic pouches?"

Patterson kept silent. Anne knew from experience that was an answer.

"One more thing," he added. "Try to find out from Juanita why Gavrez keeps calling you for dictation.

"I can answer that already. She's as puzzled as I am."

"Then we'll just have to see what develops."

By this time the sun was beginning to set. Looking at the darkening sky, he said, "You should start heading home."

Anne straightened up and began buttoning her jacket, unsettling the little dog who'd been leaning peacefully against her leg. It whined in protest. Patterson scooped it up as he told Anne, "A little ways down the path you'll see a business type in a tweed jacket with a copy of *The Financial Times*. He'll follow you until you get to First Avenue."

Anne rose from the bench and quietly melded into the flow of people heading toward the nearest park exit.

48

EVACUATION

"Look!" Anne called out. "That small plane is flying too low over the East River. We're on the second floor, and it's almost level with us."

Benedetta nodded. "It *is* low. It looks like it's following the river northwards. Do you think it's sightseers?

"Could be," Juanita commented. "Anyway, now it's gone."

They returned to their work and soon forgot about the plane.

Moments later, however, the roar of a small engine could be heard over the din of their typing. Their heads swung to the windows in time to see the red, silver and blue Cessna pass by again.

Once it was out of view, they resumed their work, but this time with lingering uneasiness.

The sound of bells broke through their rhythmic strokes. An officious voice came over the loudspeaker: "Attention all staff. *Attention tous les fonctionnaires.*"

The three typewriters fell silent.

The announcement continued, "The Secretary-General has declared a total evacuation of the building. All staff should proceed at once to the UN's North Garden. More information will follow." The message was repeated in French.

Worried, Anne asked, "Juanita, can you find out from your grapevine what's happening?"

Juanita was already dialing. She spoke a few words into the phone and then listened. At the same time, she lifted her jacket from the back of her chair and motioned to Benedetta and Anne to do the same.

After Juanita replaced the receiver, she quickly stood up. "Come on, girls," she ordered. "This is for real. I'll tell you about it on our way out."

When the three of them reached the double glass doors at the end of their corridor, they saw diplomats hurrying out from the Security Council Chamber to join the flow of staff leaving nearby offices. There was a low hum of conversation, as everyone speculated on the reason for the evacuation.

While Juanita led the way down the packed escalator, she whispered to Anne and Benedetta, "It's the plane we saw. My friend in Security says the pilot has been flying up the East River, turning around north of the UN, flying down First Avenue to the southern end of the UN, and then repeating the loop. The police are trying to make radio contact with him, but he hasn't responded."

Anne started to feel queasy. Benedetta's face looked drawn.

By this time, they'd reached the First Basement and were enmeshed in the crush of staff making slow headway toward the exit out into the Garden. There were no signs of panic in the crowd, but the tension was pervasive.

The three secretaries emerged into the bright sunlight of the Garden, where hundreds of people were already congregating. Other staff, who'd exited out the Public Lobby one level above, were streaming down the broad granite steps to join them.

The throaty sound of the Cessna caused everyone to look skyward. "See that plane? It's flying almost directly over us!"

Anne raised her eyes and saw a flash of metal as the plane headed upriver.

Benedetta was upset. "But why are we in the Garden? If the plane hits the building, the debris will fall on us. Or maybe the pilot will even crash land it right here!"

Juanita put a comforting arm around her. "My friend from Security is standing over there. Come, we'll ask her for an update. I'm sure it'll turn out okay."

The three young women were starting in that direction when Anne felt a tap on her shoulder. Turning around, she exclaimed, "Peggy!"

"Anne, I'm so happy to see you. If I have to fall behind on my afternoon work, at least I can have a nice chat with you." Peggy's face was cheerful, without a trace of worry.

"You don't think this will end badly?" Anne asked.

"There's no reason to be afraid. I just got the whole story from Sidney. You know, the handsome guard from Jamaica." Peggy batted her eyelashes. "The pilot's not out to do the UN any harm. That's the building he's after," she said, pointing north to the Alcoa Building on 49th Street. "He's a frustrated author and he's threatening to crash his plane into his editors' office unless they agree to publish his latest book." She smiled. "So you see, it pays to flirt with the guards, because when you need to know something, they'll tell you."

Anne laughed. "Today, at least, I'm glad you're flirtatious so you can fill me in." She frowned. "But otherwise, I think you know Sidney's not someone you should be spending time with."

"Oh, pooh, Anne. You really don't believe in fun, do you." She grabbed Anne's arm affectionately and said, "Come on. Here we are in the sunshine, in one of our favorite places, with all the time we could want for a nice stroll."

Peggy's lightheartedness was infectious, and Anne felt her shoulders relaxing. She noticed the tension was also easing in those standing around them. It seemed the longer the pilot continued to fly past the UN without doing any damage, the more the evacuees were starting to feel reassured.

Peggy and Anne moved to the edge of the crowd and headed to the far path leading between the two rows of oak trees. Peggy was in the midst of telling Anne about a quirky French movie she'd seen, when Anne spotted Andrei walking toward them. Seeing him from a distance, she was struck again by the easy confidence of his walk.

Peggy, too, had seen Andrei. She perked up and flashed him a bright smile across the space that separated them. At the same time, she nudged Anne with her elbow, "Look who's coming this way. Isn't he dreamy?"

Rattled, Anne blurted out, "How do you know Andrei?"

Peggy turned and looked closely at Anne. "Aha. I can tell you're interested in him. Well, I don't blame you. He *is* one of the handsomest men at the UN."

"Shhh, Peggy, someone will hear you. And besides being the very wrong nationality, he's married."

"What you mean is that he came to New York with a wife. But all East Europeans do. That doesn't mean he's 'married'. Not in my book, anyway." Her smile for Andrei grew brighter.

"Peggy!" Anne protested. She wanted to change the subject, but her curiosity outweighed her discomfort and she couldn't help repeating her question. "How do you know him?"

Andrei was getting closer to them, but he was still out of earshot.

"He's a great chum of my boss, Mr. Ipatov. He drops by all the time to see him. Then the two of them go whispering up and down the corridor, like all the communists who have something to…"

Peggy interrupted herself. In a honey-laden voice she said, "Andrei, what an unexpected pleasure to run into you on this sunny day." Her look was coy.

He nodded courteously first to Peggy and then to Anne. "*Dobryy den*, Peggy. *Dobryy den*, Anne."

Was it Anne's imagination, or was there something significant in the way Andrei and Peggy made eye contact with each other? Anne glanced surreptitiously at Peggy and then at him, but the moment was gone. He was already wishing them a good afternoon and continuing on his way.

Peggy and Anne resumed their stroll. As they walked, Anne absent-mindedly studied the thick, glossy ivy lining the path on either side. She was feeling off balance, and it wasn't only because of the evacuation. For a reason she couldn't pin down, their brief encounter with Andrei had disconcerted her.

When they were approaching a wooden bench, Peggy said, "I have a sandwich that I didn't eat at lunchtime. Let's sit here and I'll share half with you."

Glad for the distraction, Anne replied, "That'll be nice."

Once they were seated, Peggy pulled the sandwich out of her canvas tote. As she was unwrapping it, Anne asked, "So how's work going with Dr. Ruzhinsky?"

Peggy looked up quickly. "You aren't upset, are you? It was so kind of you to suggest that I substitute for you while you were tied up. I never dreamed Dr. Ruzhinsky would ask me to stay on and replace you. I feel so uncomfortable about the whole thing."

Anne stared off in the distance as she answered, "Really, it's fine. The last weeks I'd been finding it hard to work full time here and still keep up with her work. Twice I was very late with some typing she'd told me was urgent. So I'm sure this new arrangement is better for everyone, myself included."

But that wasn't really how Anne felt. Dr. Ruzhinsky's preference for her friend had hurt her deeply. True, since the taxi accident, Anne had been distracted and hadn't given the psychiatrist's typing the attention it deserved. But she rather depended on the extra income. And more important, she'd become very fond of the elderly woman. She thoroughly enjoyed the time they spent chatting over cups of pungent Russian tea, and it was hard to give up those special conversations. But she didn't blame Peggy. Peggy undoubtedly had done her best mainly because Anne had recommended her.

Peggy smiled warmly at Anne and handed her a half sandwich. "I'm so relieved to hear that. I didn't want it to affect our friendship."

Unable to meet her eyes, Anne changed the subject. "Delicious sandwich, Peggy. What did you put in it?"

Peggy smoothed out her yellow miniskirt with an air of satisfaction. Just then, two debonair middle-aged men walked by and Peggy gave them a playful smile. As she did, Anne covertly studied her friend's profile. Her heart started pounding. How could she have not noticed it before. Peggy's features would be at home on any street in Moscow.

Who was Peggy, really? Anne thought back to all the times Peggy had filled her in about the Soviets at the UN. How did she know so much about them? And she was doing extraordinarily well in Russian class. Was her story of what happened in Central Park only a ruse? Stewart had hinted that Peggy might be in league with the KGB. Was she coordinating with Andrei? Was that why a special look had passed between them just now?

Then Anne was overwhelmed by an even more distressing thought. Had she unwittingly introduced a KGB agent directly into Dr. Ruzhinsky's home?

49

FOUAD'S OBSERVATIONS

Fouad poked his head through the office door. "Hi, Juanita. Hi, Benedetta. Will it be all right if I steal Anne for a coffee?" Looking at Anne, he added, "That is, if you want to."

"Yes, I do."

Anne was happy to see Fouad. He'd just returned from a mission with his boss to the Spanish Sahara and she was eager to hear about it. He, too, was clerical staff, but at a higher level. Anne envied him because he got to travel on official visits to parts of the world she could only read about. Fortunately for her, Fouad was an excellent raconteur. Hearing him tell, in his own perceptive way, what he'd seen was almost as good as going on the mission herself.

Rising from her desk, Anne said to her officemates, "Don't worry. It won't take me long to finish typing the noon briefing after I get back."

Fouad and Anne chatted animatedly as they rode the escalator up to the cafeteria. After pouring their coffees from the massive urns, they settled into chairs along the windowed façade overlooking the East River.

Fouad was pleased to find in Anne an avid listener, and he recounted in detail what he'd observed while in the Sahara. With Spain's General Franco hovering near death, the situation in the territory was precarious. "Now that Madrid's grip over the Sahara is weakening," he told her, "we saw definite signs that Morocco or Mauritania, or both, may try to claim the territory. In fact, tens of thousands of Moroccan civilians are amassing at the border, prepared to march into the Sahara at any moment."

When the conversation finally hit a lull, they both leaned back in their chairs to enjoy the expansive view. Under the clear autumn sky, patterns of sparkling sunlight reflected off the East River, while barges lying low in the water floated steadily upstream and down.

Fouad broke the silence. "Oh, by the way, I've been meaning to tell you something."

"What's that?" Anne asked lazily, without taking her eyes off the river.

"The evening before I left on mission, I went inside the Security Council Chamber and Benedetta was there, kissing that German fellow."

Anne jerked upright and her eyes flew to Fouad's face. "What German fellow?"

"The creepy one from your office."

"That can't be, Fouad. Not Benedetta. She has more sense than to get involved with an East German agent." Anne spoke calmly, but she was unnerved. By now she had no doubt that Jürgen, behind his gentlemanly façade, was a committed spy with a mission. Definitely not someone you would want any of your friends to get close to. As much to reassure herself as to convince Fouad, she added, "And besides, Benedetta is Catholic and Jürgen's married."

"Listen, Anne," Fouad replied. "I know what Benedetta looks like, and I know what that German looks like. When I turned on the lights, I clearly saw them standing with their arms around each other in the middle of a kiss."

Anne's discomfort became acute. If this was true, then Jürgen must be cultivating a relationship with Benedetta to use her in some way. And Anne feared Benedetta had led too sheltered a life to recognize his insincerity. She and Benedetta were friends, but not close friends. It would be awkward to try to warn her.

For a moment, neither of them spoke. Then Anne asked, "Did Benedetta – or whoever it was – see you?"

"I don't think so. I was so embarrassed to catch them there that I quickly flipped off the lights and got out. They were just turning their heads toward me when it went dark."

Anne perked up. "Oh, so you only saw their profiles? Wouldn't it be hard to recognize them if you didn't see their faces full on?"

"I was certain it was them. I mean, a person's appearance is more than their face." But now Fouad sounded less sure. "Well, maybe it wasn't them. It all happened very fast."

"That explains it," Anne said, a little too brightly. "You saw them from the side and that's why you mistook them. It really was someone else."

She had planned to stay longer with Fouad in the cafeteria but now, despite her confident words, she felt too unsettled. Glancing at her watch, she said, "I should get back to the office. I don't want there to be extra work for...the others." In her discomfort, she couldn't quite bring herself to say Benedetta's name.

After Anne returned to her desk, she resettled herself quickly at her typewriter to make up for the time she'd been away. Partway through her typing, though, she stopped and looked over at Benedetta. Seeing Benedetta engrossed in her work, with her usual studious concentration, reassured Anne. She didn't know Benedetta as well as she knew Juanita, but she knew her well enough to be sure she wouldn't be so reckless as to fall for Jürgen.

50

RETURN ADDRESS

Anne stood in front of the two empty desks and impatiently tapped her foot. In her hands was a thick document. Gavrez had told her to type the report as quickly as possible and bring it immediately to his office. Yet she'd been waiting more than ten minutes and his secretaries were nowhere in sight. And the office reeked with the sickening hazel odor of his Benson & Hedges cigarettes.

Gavrez couldn't have picked a worse morning to take Anne away from her regular duties. She, Juanita and Benedetta had a large mailing to get into the afternoon pouches and they were seriously behind schedule. Even Duarte, who seemed in awe of Gavrez, had muttered with irritation when Anne told him she'd been called upstairs again.

After Gavrez had finished dictating, he told Anne he would be at a meeting the rest of the morning, and that she should give the report to his secretaries. However, it seemed they were taking advantage of his absence to enjoy themselves elsewhere in the building. From what Anne had seen, neither of them did much work anyway. They seemed to be in Gavrez's office as decorations. Haughty decorations at that.

Should Anne just leave the report? She was in a hurry to go back downstairs, but the report covered some sensitive developments. The last thing she wanted was for Gavrez to lose his temper because he thought she hadn't handled its confidentiality with sufficient care.

While Anne was debating what to do, a messenger walked through the door. She stepped slightly to one side so he could dump the mail into the inbox. As the envelopes cascaded into the wooden tray, a hand-written return address caught Anne's eye. She thought she saw *134 Morningside Avenue.*

Anne waited until the messenger left and then looked again at the small envelope, which was now slightly covered by other mail. She'd seen the return address correctly.

How odd. Anne knew that neighborhood. It was on the Upper West Side, just east of Columbia Law School, and was dangerous. Because Morningside started at 110th Street, the address would probably be around 125th Street, a main thoroughfare through Harlem. That was where her esteemed law professor, Wolfgang Friedmann, was murdered in 1972. Who on earth would be writing to a distinguished UN diplomat from such a rough part of the city?

Another ten minutes passed and still the secretaries hadn't returned. Anne had waited long enough. She grabbed a manila envelope from a shelf and inserted the report. She wrote *Personal and Confidential* on the envelope, sealed it, and slid it under Gavrez's locked door. If he got angry about her returning the report that way, so be it.

Finally free to return to her office, Anne was at the door when she stopped. She'd seen that despite Gavrez's polished exterior, he could be callously aggressive in pursuing his own interests at the UN. Now evidence was gathering that he might also have a shadowy life beyond the walls of the organization. First there was his name as the sender for the oddly shaped pouch bag. And now this envelope sent from a part of New York City known for crime. Anne was still angry with herself for not looking to see the destination of his pouch shipment. Maybe the envelope could give her another chance to find out what he might be up to.

But it was more than curiosity. A desire for revenge was brewing in Anne. Gavrez had been browbeating her week after week, keeping her in a state of tension. If he were involved in any kind of misstep, she'd like nothing better than to tarnish his reputation and knock him off his pedestal.

She decided to act. She'd take the envelope to Patterson to have it carefully opened. Once the FBI had seen what was inside, she'd figure out some way to get it back into Gavrez's inbox, hopefully before anyone realized it was missing.

She worried, though, that when she pulled the envelope out, her fingerprints would get on it. That could be a problem when she tried to return it to Gavrez's office later. Then she got an idea. Anne tore a routing slip off the pad on the secretary's desk. After folding it, she used it to gently extricate the envelope from the pile without touching it. She looked nervously over her shoulder at the office door. She had no idea what she'd say if the secretaries came back at that moment.

Because her fingers were shaking, it took Anne a while to insert the small envelope into a larger one. Finally she was done.

Anne walked quickly to the door and cautiously opened it. No one was in the hallway. She slipped out and headed toward the stairwell beyond the elevators. She would walk down to the 27th floor. There she could catch a mid-rise elevator, to avoid those used by Gavrez and his secretaries. She was sure guilt was written all over her face. They might remember that later if they realized the envelope hadn't arrived when expected.

She'd just passed the elevator bank and was disappearing into the stairwell when she heard the bell announcing the arrival of an elevator. Anne recognized the two languid voices that emerged. She'd missed crossing paths with Gavrez's secretaries by a fraction of a second.

51

ANNE'S TURN

Anne stood in front of the mirror above her kitchen sink. Gazing at herself, she tucked a few stray strands of hair up under the dark Greek sailor's cap Fouad had loaned her. She looked at her face from either side. *Good enough*, she thought to herself. She added her old wire-rimmed glasses, the unisex ones with perfectly round lenses, and again surveyed the result. Then she put Fouad's navy blazer over her black turtleneck and slipped into his loafers. They were surprisingly comfortable.

She gave herself a mischievous grin in the mirror and said, "Two can play this game." Since Patterson had surprised her at their meeting in Central Park by dressing like someone homeless, she'd surprise him today by showing up disguised as a young man.

Anne picked up a plastic shopping bag, headed downstairs and stepped out onto First Avenue. As she walked past the Czech glass shop, she admired her reflection in its window. *Not bad at all*, she congratulated herself.

However, after walking two blocks, she realized she'd made a serious miscalculation. "Damn," she muttered. "I don't know how to walk like a guy."

Anne thought of turning back and changing her clothes, but she was already late. So with great concentration, she strode stiffly down the street, trying her best to keep her hips from swinging. How do men do it? she wondered. The best thing, she decided, would be to follow behind a man and copy him. Just then a middle-aged shopper emerged from the Duane Reade on the corner. He'll do nicely, she thought.

Falling into step behind the stranger, Anne tried to swing her arms in the same manly way he did, while keeping her hips pointed forward. It was hard work. To herself she said, "This is consciousness-raising. I never thought before how differently men and women walk. But I'll never do a stupid thing like this again."

Anne was focused so intently on mimicking the man that before she realized it, she'd overshot 58th Street by two blocks. She'd have to turn and head back the other way. But she didn't want to stop in her tracks, wheel around, and immediately walk in the opposite direction. The last thing she wanted, dressed that way, was to call attention to herself.

She slowed her pace while trying to think of something that would make her change of direction less abrupt. Absentmindedly, she put her hand in the pocket of Fouad's jacket. There her fingers found what felt like an empty candy bar wrapper. Perfect.

Anne walked over to a garbage bin at the corner of 56th Street and tossed in the wrapper. As it landed on top of the other refuse, she noticed it was from a bar of Lindt white chocolate. Now she knew what she could buy Fouad to thank him for lending her his clothes.

From there, Anne casually headed back to 58th Street. By now she felt she'd cracked the code of how to walk like a man. She turned the corner less self-consciously and continued west on 58th Street until she came to the Paris Theatre.

A dozen people waited in line in front of the ticket booth. Anne spotted a custodian with a wide broom who was sweeping up discarded ticket stubs, popcorn containers and cigarette butts from the sidewalk. She was approaching him, but then stopped. "Oh no," she moaned to herself. "I forgot I have a high-pitched voice. Why did I ever think this was a good idea?" Deepening her tone as much as possible, she stepped closer to him and asked, "Can you tell me if this film has been selling out?"

Speaking so loudly that he could be heard by everyone in the line, the custodian berated Anne. "Why are ya asking me? What d'ya think the box office is for?" Under his breath he said, "For God's sake, Anne, what the hell are you doing?"

She whispered, "You disguised yourself in the park, and that jerk dressed like a woman in the ladies room. It's my turn."

Through clenched teeth, Patterson shot back, "Then make this the first time and the last." More audibly, he complained, "Well, why are ya standing there? Ask at the box office." He turned on his heels and again began plying his broom.

Anne got in line. By the time she reached the window, her courage had fled. Instead of trying to speak, she held up one finger and then silently nodded thank-you as the cashier pushed the ticket toward her.

Once inside, Anne walked up to the concession stand. She felt more comfortable speaking there. The noise of the popcorn maker would drown out the femininity in her voice. The popcorn smelled good, so she bought some. *And if I don't like how Patterson talks to me*, she thought, *I'll throw the container on the sidewalk after the movie and he'll have to sweep it up.*

Entering the dark theatre, Anne made her way to the left and took a seat against the wall in the back row. Right after the opening credits of the film hit the screen, Patterson slipped in beside her.

With her eyes fixed forward, Anne reached into her shopping bag and pulled out a manila envelope. Softly she told Patterson, "I went to drop off a report I typed for Gavrez, but he wasn't in his office, and neither were his secretaries. While I was waiting, a messenger came with their mail, and I caught a glimpse of the small envelope that's inside this bigger one. The return address is handwritten, not typed, and it says, *134 Morningside Avenue*." She added with a hint of pride, "I was really careful not to touch the envelope with my hands. I didn't leave even one fingerprint."

She allowed herself to glance at Patterson's profile. She expected to see approval there, but instead he looked puzzled. "Why did you worry about your fingerprints? Fingerprints don't mean a thing if you don't have a registry of prints to check them against. You get the silliest notions sometimes."

Anne recalled the care she'd used to draw the envelope out of the inbox. She felt utterly foolish.

Patterson shifted in his seat. "134 Morningside," he mused. "That's got to be around 125th Street. Not the kind of neighborhood I'd expect Gavrez to frequent, if he's as high society as you say. Ring any bells for you? You were at Columbia."

"It's close to where Wolfgang Friedmann was murdered in 1972. He was my professor."

Someone several rows in front of them half turned and hissed, "Shhhhhh."

"I remember that case," Patterson said. "Truly tragic. Those kids killed him because he wouldn't hand over his watch." Lowering his voice, he continued, "Of course we'll check, but do you know if Columbia has any offices on Morningside?"

"I doubt it," Anne answered. "No university staff would want to be walking around that area. It's too dangerous."

"Well anyway, we'll open this in the lab and see if it leads anywhere."

Still feeling subdued, Anne replied, "Look, maybe it will turn out to be a dead end, but I thought it might be worth looking into."

"Anything else?"

"No, that's it," Anne answered.

"Then I'll leave now." Looking up at the subtitles, Patterson added, "This isn't my kind of movie."

"I'll watch it to the end, if you don't mind," Anne replied. "After all, I had to pay for my ticket."

"I'll see to it that the government reimburses you." Patterson's voice was thick with sarcasm. The popcorn container was definitely going onto the sidewalk when Anne left.

THE GREY LADY

Anne stepped onto the escalator and rode to the third floor. This was the press floor and it was usually a lively place. The Secretary-General's Spokesman had his office there, as did dozens of journalists from all over the world who covered developments at the UN.

After exiting through the glass doors, Anne walked down the hallway into the main "Bullpen" area. In this large open space, several rows of tables were arranged edge-to-edge and furnished with typewriters. Although journalists had their own small offices on the floor, many would gather in the area when an important UN news story was breaking. Watching the in-house TV mounted on the wall, they would use the typewriters on the tables to compose their stories on the spot. The blaring TV and clacking typewriters created a pleasant ruckus.

Today, however, the area was quiet. Anne went directly to one wall and began collecting pages of UN press releases. These were set out in the shelves of the large metal documents rack affectionately known as *The Grey Lady*. Each page of each release was separate, so it always took a while to assemble enough sets of every story.

As Anne was gathering her copies, she heard a friendly "*Bonjour.*"

Looking up, Anne saw an African of about her age and height, with intelligent eyes and a close-cropped beard. He gave her a warm smile. Holding out his hand, he introduced himself. "*Je m'appelle Pierre Djebou.*" Continuing in French, he added, "Actually, that's not my real name, but it's what's printed on my press pass." He lifted up, for Anne's inspection, the white card he was wearing on a chain.

She read, "Pierre Djebou, *La Nouvelle Tribune*." Puzzled, she asked him, "Why isn't that your real name? Is it the byline you use when you write articles for your paper?"

"No, it's the name I use when I'm bringing you a message from Monsieur P."

His words so startled Anne that the press releases she'd been collecting fell from her hands and swirled out in all directions over the grey linoleum floor. With a reddening face, she dropped to her knees to retrieve them. Pierre helped her.

Once they were both back on their feet, she clutched her now-rumpled pages and stammered, "I beg your pardon?"

"I said I use that name when I'm bringing you a message from Monsieur P. He asked me to give you an update about the envelope."

A look of wariness came into Anne's face.

"Don't be alarmed," Pierre continued. "Monsieur P. said I could convince you I'm telling the truth by giving you the reason he sent me, instead of meeting you somewhere himself."

Her eyebrows lifted. "And what might that be?"

"He said that after the outfit you wore the last time, he was afraid of what you'd think of next."

Anne burst out laughing. "In that case, I'm very curious to hear his message. But first, can you tell me how you fit in with all this? I've never seen you before, and I know most of the journalists here."

"Actually, this is my first visit to New York, and it's a very short one. I'll be flying back to Cotonou tonight. So while I'm known to Monsieur P., I'm unknown in this building, which makes me an ideal person to contact you. And I've always wanted to see the inside of the United Nations."

"So you're from Dahomey," Anne said. Then she caught herself, "Well, as of last month, your country has been renamed Benin, hasn't it?"

"Just so." He smiled patiently. "May I continue with the message?"

"Please do."

"While we talk, let's both pick up some more press releases." He reached into the shelves for the pages on that morning's General Assembly meeting. "The envelope contained only a small key."

"Interesting," Anne responded. "Did Monsieur P. and his friends figure out what the key was for?"

"A locker at Port Authority Bus Terminal."

Anne tried to contain her excitement. "And did they open it?"

Just then, two journalists approached *The Grey Lady* and began taking out pages of the same Assembly press release. Anne knew the men by sight and nodded to them. One of the journalists looked carefully at Pierre as though trying to place him. Casually, Pierre allowed the man to get a glimpse of his press pass, while he continued talking to Anne in French. "Mademoiselle, if you could explain, in a little more detail, how the UN Information Centre system works, that would be very helpful to me."

Finally, the two journalists moved on and Pierre resumed his report. "Yes, they opened the locker. And you, especially, will be intrigued to hear what was in it. But please keep looking at the press releases while I tell you."

Anne turned away from him and focused on the shelves of *The Grey Lady*. He said, "The locker contained a small bronze sculpture of a tambourine player. It may once have been part of the collection of Cypriot art that Luigi di Cesnola donated to the Metropolitan Museum in the 1800s."

Anne whistled silently. "Then it would be worth a lot, either to a private collector or to a major museum." She sighed. "I wish I could see it."

"Monsieur P. knew you'd say that. But they had to return it quickly to the locker before anyone noticed it was missing."

She felt a chill of anxiety. "I guess this means now I'll have to get the envelope back into the inbox where I first saw it. I don't know how I'm going to do that."

Pierre put a reassuring hand on her arm. "Don't worry. Early this morning – before I enjoyed a coffee and then came looking for you – the envelope found its way into a sack of mail waiting to be opened by the Messenger Unit on another floor. By now," he looked at his watch, "I'm sure it's been redelivered, with no one the wiser."

Anne gave him a grateful smile. Then she asked, "Was it Van der Waals who identified the sculpture?"

"No. Monsieur P. said to tell you he prefers not to talk to the same experts more than once about an open case. Just to be on the safe side."

Anne nodded, although she knew how riveted Van der Waals would be if he found out that another piece from the Cesnola Collection might actually be in New York.

"I need to be off now," Pierre said. "If you ever come to Cotonou, do look me up. But don't ask for me at *La Nouvelle Tribune*," he added with a grin. "They might be surprised to find out they have a journalist named Djebou working for them."

53

BOMBED OUT

Anne picked up the *New York Times* from the pile of newspapers on her desk. Blazoned across the top of the front page, in the large font the *Times* used for its most important stories, was the headline, "F.A.L.N. BOMB EXPLODES AT PORT AUTHORITY".

Anne slowly lowered herself into her chair. "Oh, please not," she whispered. Reluctantly, she began to read the article.

The accompanying black-and-white photo of the bus terminal showed rows of molten metal lockers, a few with twisted doors still attached. Debris was scattered everywhere and smoke hung in the air.

"I feel so sorry for the injured people," Anne said to herself, "but I'm desperate to know if someone collected the bronze statue from the locker before the blast. It will be such a pity if, after so many centuries, the statue was destroyed because Puerto Rican separatists chose that moment to set off a bomb."

In any event, although the FALN blast was important to Anne and to the American public, it wasn't the kind of international news that would make it into the Secretary-General's *Press Analysis* that day. So Anne dragged her eyes away from the story and looked to see what else was reported on the front page.

Her phone rang. An unknown female voice at the other end said cheerily, "Good morning, Anne. It's Ebba Inez. How are you?"

Ebba Inez? Who was she? Anne started to ask the caller, but then thought better of it. Instead, she merely responded, "I'm fine, Ebba, and how are you?"

"Actually I'm disappointed," the young woman said. "I'm not going to be able to have lunch with you today after all."

"That's too bad," Anne said, playing along until she got a better idea where the conversation was going. "What's come up?"

"You heard about the bomb that went off yesterday at Port Authority? Well, it seems like everything was destroyed there, and now my mom won't let me take the bus into the city today."

Anne didn't know if it had been intentional, but it seemed as though the unknown caller had put slight emphasis on the words "everything was destroyed." She thought for a moment. It seemed to her that this "Ebba" might be an intermediary for Patterson, letting Anne know the statue had been destroyed in the blast. If so, it was disheartening news.

The conversation was definitely odd. But knowing her phone was bugged, Anne continued to play along. "Yes, what happened at Port Authority was tragic. So many people were hurt. I can see why your mom wants to make sure you're safe."

"I'm glad you understand. And you know, my mom is also a little afraid of my being followed. She says a lot of unsavory types hang out at the bus terminal watching for someone they can try to pick up. She says most of the time they don't succeed, but still, it makes her anxious."

The caller again seemed to have given emphasis to some of her words, this time "try to pick up" and "don't succeed". Anne guessed she was saying that whoever was supposed to pick up the statue didn't succeed before the bomb went off.

There was a pause. It appeared the caller had finished her message, so Anne decided to bring the conversation to an end. "Well, Ebba, I'm disappointed we can't get together today. But later on, once your mom's okay with you making the trip, let's try again."

"Anne, really, thank you so much for understanding. And I'll be in touch with you later. Bye now."

"Goodbye," Anne replied and hung up her phone. Now she was really imagining things, or the caller had highlighted the words "in touch with you later". Anne still had unanswered questions, so she hoped that meant Patterson would set up a meeting with her soon.

She was grateful, in the meantime, to get the update, discouraging though the news was. If she'd understood correctly, not only had the statue been destroyed, but Patterson and his men had lost the opportunity of seeing who would come for it.

Discovering the key had seemed so promising. Yet in the end, it had led only to a bombed-out locker.

54

A SMALL BOX

As they left Russian class, Peggy asked Anne, "Do you have time to stop off with me at the import shop and then walk in the Garden?"

Anne hesitated. Since the day of the evacuation, she'd become increasingly wary of Peggy. She shared her concerns with Patterson, who promised to do some checking and get back to her. In the meantime, when Anne was in Peggy's company, she tried to act as though nothing had changed. "Okay," she answered, although even to herself her voice sounded a little flat.

As they were nearing the shop, Anne spotted her officemates approaching from the opposite direction. "Look," she said, "here come Juanita and Benedetta."

All four reached the entrance at the same time. Juanita said, "Hi, Peggy. You haven't stopped by recently to read our *Economist*. I've missed seeing you."

Peggy smiled, obviously pleased by Juanita's friendliness. As Peggy was responding, Anne noticed that Benedetta, with a slight frown, was studying Peggy carefully. Again that day, Peggy was wearing a tight top and miniskirt. Often her clothing was inappropriate for the UN, but Anne had become so used to it that she didn't pay much attention. That is, except when she noticed that others were a little put off, as Benedetta appeared to be now.

Trying to ease the awkward moment, Anne urged them all inside. "Let's go do our shopping, and we can chat after we've finished."

The others nodded. Entering, they scattered in different directions. Peggy picked up more Irish Breakfast Tea. Juanita found a small, brightly colored woven bag from Guatemala. She said, "Perfect for make-up, and a reminder of home." Benedetta, too, got something from her country.

Smiling, she approached the cashier with a bottle of Italian Frantoio olive oil. Anne was the only one who was disappointed. The shop was out of the brand of Lebanese tahini that Fouad had urged her to try.

As they were waiting to pay, Anne noticed a display of tiny gold foil boxes. Inside each box were four exquisite-looking pieces of Godiva chocolate imported from Belgium. "How precious!" she exclaimed.

Juanita winked at her. "A perfect gift for that special someone."

"Now Juanita," said Anne, frowning. "You know that Fouad and I are just friends." She gave her a teasing look. "But, I could buy one to give to Otto Koether and say it's from you."

Juanita blushed. "Oh Anne, don't even joke about it," she pleaded.

While Juanita and Anne were bantering with each other, Benedetta picked up a Godiva box and held it thoughtfully in her hand. After a pause she said, "I'm going to get one."

"Ohhhhh," said Juanita, Anne and Peggy in a single voice. "Who's the lucky man?"

Benedetta, looking mysterious, didn't answer.

After paying, the four women strolled together down the hallway until it was time to part near the escalator. After they said their goodbyes, Juanita and Benedetta started back upstairs to the office. Anne and Peggy, who still had another half hour of their lunch break, continued in the direction of the UN Garden.

After a few steps, Anne turned around to call out to her officemates that she wouldn't be in the Garden for very long. As she did so, she caught Benedetta staring at Peggy. Why did she look so apprehensive?

55

THE UNVEILING

"Anne," her boss said, "I have a small job for you."

"I'll be happy to help, Señor Duarte," she replied. "What would you like me to do?"

"The Press Unit is short an officer this morning, and they need someone to draft a press release on the unveiling of a new statue. It's nothing technical or political," he assured her. "I think you can manage it."

Anne beamed. Finally she was getting the chance to write something of her own, instead of merely typing what other people wrote.

"Where should I go?" she asked eagerly. "And at what time?"

"It will be at 10:00 in the UN Garden."

Looking up at the clock, Anne said, "Then I'll leave in fifteen minutes. Is there anything I should know beforehand?"

Duarte handed her a paper. "Here's the fact sheet."

Anne quickly scanned it. The gift was from the German Democratic Republic, that is, East Germany. It was an eight-foot stone statue called *The Rising Man*. Sculpted by the East German artist Fritz Cremers, it was intended to symbolize the liberation of subjugated people from colonial oppression. Anne smiled. That was one of the communist countries' favorite themes, since all the colonial powers happened to be NATO countries. This assignment, she thought to herself, may be a little more political than Señor Duarte anticipates.

A few minutes later, Anne walked through the glass doors into the Garden. In her anticipation over the assignment, all her sensations were heightened. She was keenly aware of the satisfying crunch of brown leaves under her feet and the crispness of the autumn wind blowing off the East River.

She walked up to the small crowd gathering around a cloth-draped monolith at the north end of the Garden. The statue seemed to be mounted on a substantial base, because the top was at least eleven feet off the ground. The East German ambassador was already there, with some members of his delegation. Anne also recognized diplomats from other Soviet bloc countries, as well as a number of African representatives and the ambassador of Cuba. There didn't appear to be many Western diplomats present.

There was a bustle as two security officers came into view, leading the way for the Secretary-General. Waldheim walked up to the East German ambassador and took a position at his side.

The ambassador began his remarks. Thankfully he spoke slowly, enabling Anne to jot down every word on her steno pad. After paying tribute to the sculptor, he proudly proclaimed, "This statue represents my country's unwavering solidarity with all subjugated peoples who are valiantly endeavoring to throw off the unjust shackles of rapacious colonialism, so as to take their rightful place in the brotherly community of all peace-loving nations." The assembled onlookers clapped enthusiastically.

Then with a flourish, a worker stationed on a wobbly ladder behind the statue lifted off the blue cloth. The crowd murmured its approval. "Wonderful!" "Impressive!" "Extraordinary!"

Anne was disappointed. The statue didn't look anything like what she'd expected. She was used to the bulky forms of East European communist art – the overly muscled men and women, with heroic poses and gazes fixed far in the distance. There was no drama to this statue, no noble light shining in his eyes, no look of determination as he asserted his freedom. Instead, with his drooping head and protruding belly, he looked more like a man struggling to wake up after a night out drinking beer with his buddies.

Still, she would have to find some positive things to say about the statue. She studied it carefully, thinking she could at least write approvingly about the oversized feet, which she rather liked. And anyway, the point of the gift was not its artistic merit, but its source and symbolism.

Waldheim expressed his appreciation on behalf of the UN, and then the ceremony was over. After Anne checked her notes to make sure she had enough material, she looked around to see who else had come for the unveiling.

Of course Jürgen was there, speaking with two men she didn't know. They were near enough for her to hear they were speaking German. Were they two of the other five East Germans who joined the UN when Jürgen did?

Anne glanced at the men's feet, the reliable way to tell East Germans from their Western counterparts. Seeing the sophisticated cut of the smooth leather shoes on the one, and the drab, uncomfortable-looking shoes on the other, she immediately knew one was from West Germany and the other, from the East.

At that moment, Jürgen noticed Anne was gazing in his direction. Excusing himself from his companions, he walked toward her. "Hello, young lady," he said, making a gentlemanly bow. "What brings you to our fair garden today?"

"Señor Duarte asked me to draft the press release on the presentation of the statue." She tried not to show her proud feelings to Jürgen, but her excitement was obvious.

He responded with exaggerated enthusiasm. "This is wonderful, Anne. This is a *very* important assignment." Then, looking slightly amused, he asked, "And what does our lovely temporary press officer in fact think of the statue?"

Normally she would have concealed her true thoughts from him, but for some reason this time she spoke honestly. In a low voice she confessed, "I don't really like it. I thought it would be more noble and inspiring."

Now Jürgen appeared truly amused. "Then I'll let you in on a secret. Just between us, this isn't the statue that was supposed to be presented to the UN today."

Anne looked at him with surprise.

"No," he continued, "our Erich" – Anne knew he meant East Germany's communist leader Honecker – "liked the original statue so much that he didn't want it to leave the country. So last-minute, he decided to keep it."

"You're serious?"

"Ah yes, dear Anne." Jürgen gave her a conspiratorial smile. "He did exactly that. He asked the sculptor to substitute another statue from his atelier, and this is the one Cremers provided." He nodded up at the bulky figure lurking above them.

"Really?" Anne exclaimed.

"Absolutely," Jürgen replied. "Otherwise you would indeed have seen all the nobility and inspiration that you were hoping for."

For just one moment, Anne thought she caught a glimpse of the more genuine man who dwelt behind the artificial façade that Jürgen maintained most of the time. But that moment quickly passed. Once again his tone became patronizing. "And now I must not keep our talented young writer from drafting what I know will be an exceptional press release."

With another courtly bow, Jürgen returned to the men with whom he'd been speaking.

On her way back to the office, Anne was puzzled. Since Jürgen's arrival at the UN, she felt he'd been making every effort to get on her good side, trying in his own way, she thought, even to be a bit seductive. But recently, although he'd certainly been friendly, it felt as though he were no longer trying to draw her closer to him. *What had brought about the change?* she wondered.

It wouldn't be long before she found out.

56

CIRCUMSTANTIAL EVIDENCE

Jürgen burst, red faced, into the office. Staring straight ahead, he strode past the secretaries' desks without acknowledging any of them. Anne heard him mutter in German under his breath, "Soviets and Americans are all alike."

He stormed into his office and slammed the door behind him.

The secretaries looked at each other. Over the weeks Jürgen had been part of their office, they'd never once seen him angry. And Soviets and Americans being "all alike"? That was an opinion Anne had never heard voiced during the Cold War.

However, the three of them had no time to speculate over what might have happened. Duarte was leaving that afternoon to visit several Information Centres in Africa and they were swamped with assembling his flight documents and briefing notes.

An hour later, Juanita had just taken all the completed paperwork into Duarte's office when Jürgen's door opened. As he walked over to Anne's desk, she was relieved to see that his face was back to its normal color and that he again appeared calm.

Anne conscientiously typed the memo he'd given her and then took it to his office. These days she was becoming increasingly comfortable with him, so she spoke more directly than she would have in the past. "I couldn't help overhearing you say that Soviets and Americans are alike. I'm wondering what you meant. Most people believe they're polar opposites."

Jürgen smiled. "I guess it would sound odd to you, especially since you're one of them."

Anne looked even more puzzled.

He continued, "I went to see our Assistant Secretary-General, Mr. Kulikov. I made a perfectly reasonable proposal, but he immediately dismissed it without even giving me a chance to explain. And that," Jürgen frowned, "is the way officials behave when they're from one of the super-powers. Whether they're Soviets or Americans, they feel totally superior to those of us from smaller countries."

"Oh," Anne replied. "That's a new way of looking at things. I'll think about it." She handed him the paper. "Anyway, here's your memo."

Jürgen took it and began reading. After a few lines, he looked up at her. "I'm afraid you've made a spelling mistake," he commented, motion-ing for her to come around to his side of the desk.

Standing next to his chair, Anne looked at the word he was point-ing to. "Oh, *connexion*," she said. "You're probably thinking it should be spelled the American way, with a 'ct'. But here at the UN we have to use British spelling. That's why I put an 'x' instead."

"Really? The British use an 'x'? Well, I'm sure you must be right, but if you don't mind, I'll check my *Fowler's* dictionary." As Jürgen spoke, he pulled open his top desk drawer.

Anne's eyes widened. There in the drawer, behind the dictionary, was a gold foil box just big enough to hold four Godiva chocolates.

Jürgen glanced up and saw the unsettled look on her face. "Please don't be upset, Anne," he reassured her. "I'm not trying to find fault. I just want to check the spelling for myself. That's how I make my English better."

He slowly drew his finger down one page of the dictionary and then stopped at a word. "Well, young lady, you're absolutely right. As always, I should add."

It took a moment for Anne to become calm enough to speak. Finally she said, with effort, "Then if the memo meets with your approval, you can sign it and I'll send it out."

Leaving his office, Anne was relieved to see that Benedetta and Juanita were away from their desks. She didn't know how she could have looked Benedetta in the eye.

Anne slumped into her chair and tried to settle her racing thoughts. She recalled her conversation in the cafeteria with Fouad. Slowly she shook her head. "Fouad was right," she whispered to herself. "He was right."

57

ANDREI'S QUESTIONS

Anne walked quickly toward the Delegates Lounge. Unexpectedly, Andrei had called and asked her to have coffee with him in 15 minutes. Up until then, Anne's conversations with Andrei had felt casual and relaxed, but this time, his voice over the phone sounded strained. That bothered Anne, and although it was a busy afternoon, she agreed to meet him.

By the time she reached the Lounge, Andrei was seated at a table off to one side. Waiting at her place was a cappuccino with extra milk, the way she liked it. Yet as they greeted each other the Russian way, with three kisses on each other's cheeks, Anne felt a stiffness in his manner.

While she was taking her first sip of the scalding hot cappuccino, Anne noticed a file folder on the table to the left of Andrei's espresso. Normally he didn't bring any papers to their get-togethers, and that added to her unease.

To put off finding out what was amiss, she immediately asked if he'd been to any jazz concerts recently. Of course he had, and that meant that the first few minutes of their conversation were taken up with Andrei's description of hearing Ella Fitzgerald the previous Friday.

Anne asked a few questions about the performance. But she could stall only for so long, and then Andrei took control of the conversation. She expected he'd begin with his usual questions about how she'd spent her weekend or whether she'd attended the latest Security Council meeting, but today he took a different tack.

"So, Anne, it seems you have a new neighbor in your apartment building."

She looked genuinely surprised. "No, as far as I know, no one has moved in recently."

"I believe you're wrong," Andrei said steadily. "There's now an eligible young man living there, which must be nice for you."

Anne had no idea where the conversation was going, but it was making her uncomfortable. She replied, "No, I don't think we have anyone new."

He gave a half smile, which she thought held a hint of sadness. "Anne, there's now a tenant who's a slim young man, about your height."

Andrei picked up the folder. Opening it, he took out some documents and wordlessly passed them across the table to her. The paper on top was the first page of a press release. Anne looked up at him questioningly. He motioned for her to go to the second page. Turning to it, she froze. In the center of the page was a photo of a young man in a black turtleneck and wearing a Greek sailor's cap. He was walking past the Czech glass shop next door to her apartment building.

Anne tried not to show any reaction, but inwardly her thoughts were in total upheaval. It was unmistakably a picture of her, the afternoon she put on Fouad's clothes to meet Patterson at the Paris Theatre.

"Let's not play games with each other, Anne," Andrei said. "I'll be straight with you, and I expect you to be straight with me. Look at the next page."

Reluctantly, Anne flipped over the picture. Underneath was a photo of her from behind, right at the moment she was tossing the chocolate wrapper into the trash bin at 56th Street.

He said, "Our man waited a long time, but no one ever came to collect the wrapper. So finally he retrieved it himself." Andrei's look became intense. "So if you were supposed to get a message to someone, now you'll have to do it a different way. But maybe," he drew the next words out slowly, "you should consider not sending any messages at all."

"Oh, Andrei," Anne exclaimed. "I can honestly tell you the wrapper wasn't a message. It was only some trash I found in the pocket of the jacket I borrowed. It was just a silly disguise I wore to make a friend laugh when I met him at the movies."

Andrei looked genuinely conflicted. "Anne, I shouldn't say this much, but already before this, some of your behavior has appeared, well, problematic. Based on your and my conversations, I've said I believed you were staying outside of anything that would create awkwardness for my side.

But when I was shown these photos, there was nothing I could say to explain them away. Nothing."

Anne's shoulders sagged. She was furious with herself for having dressed like that to meet Patterson, but it was too late. After having been so careful about everything she said and did in front of the Soviets, now her whole profile with them had been upended. She put her hand to her forehead and stared unseeing at the table. Thank God, at least the man following her waited to see if someone would come to retrieve the wrapper. Otherwise he would have followed her to her meeting with Patterson, and things would be even worse.

"I'm sure you understand that because of this, everything is now on a different footing," Andrei continued. "I also believe you're smart enough to understand that it will do no good if you report our conversation. You know as well as I do that if I'm sent home, another will come in my place. My country has its quota of staff positions in the UN Secretariat, so there will always be someone. If I were you, I would tell whomever you're helping that you have to stop. Immediately." His eyes were troubled as he added, "My disappointment in you isn't just professional, Anne. I trusted you…as a friend."

Andrei's clenched jaw told Anne there would be no going back to their easy camaraderie of the past weeks. She felt acutely the loss of a friendship she hadn't even realized she had.

After several minutes of strained silence, she pushed her unfinished cappuccino back from the edge of the table and slowly stood up, as did Andrei. His face was now impenetrable. They gave each other perfunctory kisses on the cheek.

With downcast eyes, Anne turned to walk back to her office.

58

BENEDETTA'S DISTRESS

Returning from a late lunch, Anne pushed open the office door. Stepping inside, she saw immediately that something was wrong. Benedetta was sitting bent over her desk with her head down on her folded arms, and she was sobbing. Juanita stood beside her, gently patting her shoulder.

Juanita turned quickly at the sound of Anne's entrance. She silently motioned for her to go back out the door.

It was too late. Benedetta lifted up her tear-stained face. Wisps of wet hair stuck to her temples and dark make-up was smudged around each eye.

Anne had never seen Benedetta look so distraught, and her heart went out to her. "What's wrong, Benedetta?"

She was unprepared for the answer. "Anne, you of all people must know what happened. It's that friend of yours who did it."

"I'm sorry, I don't know what you mean."

Juanita quietly nodded toward Jürgen's closed door. Anne shook her head. "I don't understand."

Juanita said carefully, "Jürgen and Benedetta are no longer...special friends."

Benedetta's voice was full of reproach. "Anne, you knew Jürgen and I were in a relationship, and yet you purposely introduced him to that... that Peggy. And now he's broken off with me, and I'm sure it's because she's been flirting with him. He's just another conquest for her."

Anne hedged. "Benedetta, did you think I knew you were having a relationship with Jürgen because Fouad saw you together in the Council Chamber? He did tell me, but I couldn't quite believe it. It didn't sound like you. I mean, with Jürgen married and all."

"Oh Anne, you know communists can't come work for the UN if they're single, so they marry anyone at all, just to get out. But for Jürgen it isn't a real marriage."

Anne said, "Well, I can assure you I never did anything to bring Peggy and him together. One day in the cafeteria, I was saving a table while she was in the cashier's line. Jürgen stopped to say hello to me, and when Peggy showed up, they introduced themselves to each other."

Juanita was more emphatically signaling Anne to leave the office, but Anne tried once more to reassure Benedetta. "If you've seen Jürgen and Peggy chatting together, I'm sure it doesn't mean anything. She talks to me about men a lot, probably too much," Anne said. "If something were going on between them, she would have told me. As it is, I happen to know she's very interested in someone else." But now doubt was growing in Anne's own mind. If Peggy in fact was working with the Soviets, maybe she did have some kind of relationship with Jürgen.

Benedetta shook her head. "Of course you want to cover for her. She's your friend. But I know what she's up to. She doesn't really care for him, but I do. He's the first man I've truly loved. How will I ever get him back?" She started crying again.

Juanita said, "Anne, I know you mean well, but you're not helping. Please leave for a little while. Benedetta needs some time by herself."

Benedetta said, "Yes, Anne, leave me alone. You're only making things worse."

Murmuring "I'm so, so sorry," Anne walked slowly back out the door. Tears of frustration stung her eyes. How was she ever going to mend things with Benedetta?

59

SORTING CLIPPINGS

An uneasy calm slowly returned to the office. It was difficult, though, for Juanita and Anne to see Benedetta looking so pale and unhappy. Jürgen was very businesslike with all of them, and spent most of each day in his office with the door closed. Understandably, now he gave work only to Juanita or Anne, and that very sparingly.

Although Benedetta was still obviously brokenhearted, Anne was relieved that she no longer seemed to feel that Anne was complicit. At least she never said anything more about it. For her part, Anne tried to be kind in small ways, and especially to lighten Benedetta's workload whenever she could.

So it was that one afternoon, when a messenger brought three large envelopes full of clippings from the Information Centres, Anne rose up immediately. "I'll take care of these," she said. "I can see you're both busy."

It was true that Juanita's fingers were flying over her typewriter. But Benedetta appeared unable to focus, and her keystrokes were slow and uneven.

Anne actually enjoyed sorting the clippings. Every week, each Information Centre sent to Headquarters articles about the United Nations from local newspapers and magazines. Anne's office sorted them and decided to which UN officials they should be forwarded. The job left Anne's fingers blackened with newsprint, but it was fascinating to see how differently the media in various countries portrayed the organization.

She was halfway through the second envelope, from UNIC Athens, when she stopped short. In her hand was a photo of four men in World War II uniforms. The dateline was *May 22, 1943, Podgorica, Yugoslavia*. A tall man in a Nazi uniform, standing second from the left, was identified as Kurt Waldheim. The others with him were listed as

Italian Commander Escola Roncagli, German Colonel Hans Herbert Macholtz, and General Artur Phelps of the 7th SS-Division. As best Anne could read the accompanying story in Greek, it seemed to report that Waldheim was present when the Jews of Salonika were being transported to Auschwitz.

"Wait a minute," she exclaimed out loud. "The Secretary-General has always said he was wounded early in the war and spent the rest of it recovering in Vienna." Frowning, she scrutinized the lanky man with the prominent nose in the photo. She had closely studied Waldheim in person the afternoon she waited in his conference room for further instructions. "This is clearly him."

Juanita glanced at the clipping Anne was holding out to her. "Oh, those," Juanita said, waving her hand dismissively. "We get a lot of them."

Anne looked stunned. "You mean people know about this? Why hasn't anyone said anything?"

Juanita shrugged.

Anne read further. "I picked up some Greek while I was in Cyprus, and if I'm right, it says that after the war, Yugoslavia reported Waldheim to the UN War Crimes Commission, which added him to their list of potential war criminals." Her eyes widened. "The Americans and Soviets had that list, and the British and French, too. Why would they still support him to be appointed Secretary-General?"

Juanita kept typing.

Anne said, more to herself than to the others, "I guess it suited the permanent members to have a Secretary-General who doesn't want the public to know about his past."

Anne studied the clipping a while longer, still digesting its revelation. "What should I do with it?" she finally asked.

"Just throw it in the wastebasket," Juanita said, without looking up.

Anne sighed as she tossed the clipping, and then opened the next envelope, from UNIC Quito. As she was shaking its contents out onto her desk, a long *Últimas Noticias* article on the Law of the Sea Conference flipped over and a story on its back caught her eye. It included a photo showing a large warehouse behind a barricade manned by six police officers. Before them stood a dapper, silver-haired man, gesturing angrily.

Across the warehouse in tall letters was the name *Mondo de Agronomía*. In the article itself, the name "Gavrez" appeared several times.

"Juanita?"

Juanita looked up and saw the clipping in Anne's hand. Firmly she said, "In the wastebasket, Anne."

"No, no, this is a different one." She got up and walked to Juanita's desk. "Look."

Juanita took the clipping. "¡*Qué lástima!*" she exclaimed. What a pity!

Anne asked. "Does it have something to do with Under-Secretary-General Gavrez?"

"It certainly does," Juanita answered. "*Mondo de Agronomía* is his family's company. A very old and established one. Probably the most important enterprise in Ecuador, maybe all of South America. And now they're in such big trouble."

"Why are the police there? And who is the tall, silver-haired man?"

Juanita silently read a few more lines. Then she explained, "All their food distribution warehouses are in foreclosure. That man is the uncle of our Señor Gavrez." She read further. "They must have had very serious problems for the banks to move against them. Everyone in Ecuador is afraid of the Gavrez family and its power."

"Do you think this will blow over?" Anne asked.

Juanita shook her head doubtfully. "The article says their debt is more than $105 million."

Benedetta surprised Anne by joining the conversation. "But our Señor Gavrez doesn't have to worry because he has his UN salary."

Juanita countered, "I think he would have trouble living only on his UN earnings. He has very expensive tastes."

"I've heard that rumor," Anne said, "but is it really true?"

"According to my grapevine, he won't drive any car but a Bugatti, and his penthouse here is one of the most expensive apartments in the city. Not to mention his ladies. No, this may be a bigger blow for our Señor Gavrez than for anyone else in the family."

60

JAPANESE PEACE BELL

For some reason, Professor Bulgakova ended Russian class almost ten minutes early. Most of the students were happy to have a longer lunch, but Anne didn't feel like eating just yet. Instead, she decided to use the extra time to visit the exhibit on the upcoming Habitat conference in Vancouver. The exhibit featured photos of indigenous architecture from all over the world, and Juanita had told her she absolutely must see it.

After taking the escalator up to the ground floor, Anne walked from the tall Secretariat Building through a revolving door into the wide corridor leading to the Public Lobby. To her left, outside the expansive windows, was an arch-roofed wooden temple from which hung the Japanese Peace Bell. Over three feet long, the oblong bell was cast of heavy metal, the color of verdigris, and imprinted with intricate Japanese characters.

Tranquility emanated from the carefully laid out plantings and pathways of the Japanese-style garden. Anne paused to drink in more of its harmony. As she did, she noticed that a tour group of about 40 people was approaching. Most UN guides wore their national costumes, and the young woman leading the group was wearing a turquoise kimono.

Anne had been told the bell was smelted from coins collected by children, but there must be more to the story. Since the guide appeared to be Japanese, her description to the tourists might be especially insightful. Curious to hear what she would say, Anne decided to mingle with the visitors and eavesdrop.

As she moved to meld with the crowd, Anne glanced up and down the corridor to see if anyone there might notice her intrusion. Nobody seemed to be paying attention to her. Yet inexplicably, the hair at the nape of her neck began to rise and she felt instantly alert. She looked around once more, trying to figure out what had made her apprehensive.

Two slightly built men were approaching from the far north end of the corridor. She didn't recognize either one, but the closer they came, the more unnerved she felt. Instinctively, she edged closer to the tourists.

What was it about the men that seemed threatening? It had something to do with how they moved, and the cocky way each held his head. Then it struck her. One of them might be the same man who, disguised as a woman, had menaced her in the ladies room.

For some time after that encounter, Anne feared the man would accost her again. But when he never reappeared, she figured Patterson was right in concluding the man probably had come to the UN only that day. Gradually, she'd stopped worrying about him. But now her sixth sense told her he might be back.

At all costs, Anne didn't want another encounter with him. To conceal herself, she quickly threaded her way among the tourists. At that moment, surrealistically, the tour guide's calm voice began wafting over the group. "Dear guests," she said, "the Peace Bell was donated by the UN Association of Japan in 1954."

The men were coming closer. They appeared engrossed in conversation and Anne couldn't tell if they'd spotted her. She moved deeper into the group.

The guide explained, "The inspiration for the Peace Bell came from Chiyogi Nakagawa. He was drafted during World War II and fought in the calamitous Burma campaign. When he finally returned home, he discovered that the bell of his family temple had been melted down to make weapons. You can imagine his sorrow."

As the crowd murmured in sympathy, Anne looked around anxiously to see if the men had come abreast of the tour. She didn't spot them.

The guide's narrative continued. "Nakagawa had seen enough of war. He decided to make a new bell for the temple, using foreign coins and his own sword. It was so well received that he decided to launch a campaign to create this one for the United Nations. It's made from coins donated by children from over 60 countries, and even by the Pope. It also contains melted–down military medals, sword guards, bullets and weapons."

Surging forward to get a better look, the group pressed in upon itself, making Anne's cover more impenetrable to anyone on the outside. Feeling safely hidden, she turned and looked more steadily through a slight gap in the crowd. Just then, two men walked by.

She exhaled audibly. She'd been mistaken. These two diplomats were taller, and each had very different features from the man who'd threatened her. Her unease had been the product of her anxious, overworked mind.

Now, with relief, she listened more freely to the guide, who was saying with deep feeling, "And so the important symbolism of this gift is that first a bell was turned into weapons, and then weapons were turned into a bell."

Out of the corner of her eye, Anne suddenly saw two other men drawing near, and their pace was slowing. Instantly she recognized the one man's sharp features and the calculating look in his eyes. She stifled a gasp. She hadn't been wrong after all.

As the men approached, they carefully scanned the crowd of tourists. Had they spotted her before, and were they searching for her now? Anne pivoted to face forward and bent her knees slightly, to better hide herself. Sweat beaded on her forehead.

By this time, the guide seemed ready to lead the group to the next point of interest. As the tourists moved along, they would inevitably spread out, and Anne would be exposed.

Peering through the crowd, she saw the men had stopped directly alongside the visitors. With their heads close together, they were having a muted discussion. As they spoke, the lips of one man parted, exposing a chipped front tooth.

Anne shrank back, brushing against a middle-aged woman standing beside her. The woman turned in her direction and concern washed over her motherly face. "What's wrong, dear? You look so pale."

Anne thought quickly. "I'm very shy," she said. "There's one more thing I'd like to know, but I can't bring myself to interrupt the guide. Would you be able to ask a question for me?"

"Oh, honey," cooed the woman. "If that's all that's bothering you, of course I can. What would you like to know?"

"Could you ask the guide about the shrine?"

The woman nodded and spoke up with a clear voice. "Excuse me, Miss Akahori, but could you tell us about the shrine?"

Anne rewarded the woman with a grateful smile.

The guide seemed pleased by this show of interest. "Actually, this is a *temple*, not a *shrine*. Since the late 1800s, temples have been for Buddhism, and shrines, for Shintoism. Temples have large bells, like this one, which are struck from the outside with a wooden rod. Shrines have bells with a ball inside and are sounded by tugging on a rope."

While the guide spoke, Anne nervously looked around for the men. They had now split up and were each slowly circling in opposite directions around the outside of the group, looking intently into the crowd. Anne's legs were trembling so much that she thought they'd buckle under her.

A sharp voice rang out. "Excuse me, sir. What are you doing here?" Miss Akahori demanded. "This is an official UN guided tour, organized only for those who have bought tickets. I ask you kindly to move on."

Anne saw one man start to protest, but then apparently change his mind. He exchanged a sullen look with his partner and they both withdrew. Moments later, they disappeared into the revolving door through which Anne had entered the corridor.

Anne's whole body went limp with relief.

"And now, if you're ready to continue," the guide said, "let's proceed down the corridor. Next we will view an exhibit about the upcoming UN Conference on Human Settlements in Vancouver."

To be on the safe side, Anne clung to the group a little longer. When the tour at last reached the Habitat exhibit, she eased herself away. Willing herself to walk normally in case anyone was watching her, she headed across the Public Lobby until she reached the stairs.

Her feet barely grazed each step as she rushed down. Touching bottom, she hurried to the public ladies room. She entered, dashed into an open stall, and slammed the door behind her. There she stood unmoving, her eyes wide with fear.

61

AT A CROSSROADS

T he air in the damp stairwell was stale, and Patterson's Winston made it worse. Still, Anne was grateful he'd responded quickly to her request for an urgent meeting, even if it had to take place in a narrow, airless space off the back of a garage in Queens.

"Well, Anne, now we know that man still has access to the building and that he hasn't forgotten you. And that he's got a partner."

She nodded nervously.

"This means we've come to a place where a decision has to be made." He paused and then added, "By you."

Patterson studied her with some concern. Dark rings circled her eyes. She'd lost weight. She fidgeted first with her handbag and then her necklace. The tension she was under was clearly taking a toll.

"We've talked about this before," he continued, "but we could send you back to your home town in Oregon. We'd make sure you had discreet surveillance."

Anne shook her head.

Patterson drew deeply on his cigarette, then slowly blew out a stream of musty smoke. "Okay, so you haven't changed your mind. I had to ask."

"You say I'd have surveillance, but for how long? What if eventually the FBI concludes again that I'm no longer in danger and decides not to waste any more taxpayers' money? Royce almost got me with a pen in a coffee shop. If anyone wants to attack me, I won't be any safer in Lincoln City than here." Anne bit her lower lip. "And anyway, I have nothing, and no one, to go back to."

"What about a bigger city? We could get you a new identity. A nose job, if you want."

"A nose job?" Anne gave Patterson a sharp look of annoyance.

He held up his hands in propitiation. "Sorry, I didn't mean there's anything wrong with your nose. I just thought girls liked to do things to their faces. That is, I…it…oh, hell, never mind."

Both of them fell silent. The grinding of tools and the radio music coming from the adjoining garage sounded even louder.

Finally Anne spoke. "What would I do somewhere else? I don't have a high-level job at the UN, but it's the only way I know to use what I studied in college." She adjusted the plastic bag she was sitting on to protect her clothes from the grime. "Despite everything that's happened, I want to stay."

Patterson blew out another long stream of smoke. "I can't think when I last met anyone as stubborn as you. And I have to protect you. Which you're not making easy."

Another long silence pervaded the stairwell.

This time it was Patterson who broke it. "Okay. I won't mention leaving again, but we have to do something. With those guys in the picture, the situation's more serious."

Anne breathed out, "I know."

Patterson opened his jacket and reached into an interior pocket. He placed a Beretta 950 BS on the step between him and Anne and slowly slid it over to her. "You're going to have to carry one of these."

She drew back. "I couldn't."

"It has a manageable recoil for a woman. I'll teach you how to use it."

"If I pulled out a gun because someone was threatening me, they'd have it out of my hands in a second. And then they'd use it against me. No."

Wordlessly, Patterson returned the revolver to his pocket. Reaching into another pocket, he pulled out a piece of gold-colored metal with four holes and passed it to her.

"Brass knuckles," she said approvingly. She bounced them lightly in her upturned palm to feel their weight, and smiled.

"Do you know how to use them?"

"When I was hitchhiking in Europe, I traveled for a while with a Swedish girl who had some. She showed me how." Anne opened her handbag and dropped the brass knuckles inside.

Patterson's face broke into a grin. "Let this go on record as the day I suggested something to you, and you agreed."

Anne laughed and, for a brief moment, looked almost carefree.

Patterson laughed as well but then grew sober. "Listen, we'll back you up all we can. I've tried to convince you to get out. But you should know that by staying in, you're helping us." He looked at her intently. "Something's going on at the UN that shouldn't be. By not running away, you may be the one person who'll be able to get us the break we need. Don't think that's unappreciated."

"Thank you."

Patterson stubbed out his Winston and heaved himself to his feet with a grunt. "Okay, time to get you home. Walk through that door into the garage and one of the mechanics will drop you off a couple blocks from your apartment. We'll shadow you from there until you're inside."

Anne got up and stepped gingerly through the warped metal doorframe.

Patterson's brow furrowed with uneasiness as he watched her disappear.

62

HEATED WORDS

Anne stole a glance at the wall clock in the language classroom. It was already five minutes past three. Usually Anne never worried about being late to a Security Council meeting, but today Bulgakova was finishing her grammar explanation with agonizing slowness.

Anne shifted uncomfortably in her chair. She was particularly anxious to get to this afternoon's meeting on time. The agenda was the situation in the Middle East, and given the outbreak of violence the day before, the session was expected to be a fiery one. To cover the meeting, a press officer, probably Bertram, would be sitting at the rectangular table inside the larger horseshoe table. But the session was considered so important that Anne had been told to sit up in the mezzanine and take more thorough notes than usual, in case Bertram couldn't keep up.

Anne wanted to slip out before class was over, but she resisted the impulse. Bulgakova was considered the strictest of the Russian teachers. That made sense to Anne, since her husband was the top Soviet ambassador and a committed hardliner. His dour, set expression left no doubt as to his inflexible character. To be married to him, Bulgakova would have to be equally strong, and indeed she permitted no laxity in the classroom.

Another four minutes passed. Finally, with relief, Anne heard the long hoped for Russian words, "*Studenty, urok okonchen.*" Students, the lesson has ended.

With her books already in one hand, Anne sprang to her feet and hurried out the door. Her other hand clutched her wallet, which she'd brought along hoping she could grab a quick coffee before the meeting. There would be no time for that now.

She ran to the escalator which would take her up to the Council mezzanine. "Excuse me, excuse me," she called out to two men on the steps above her. "I need to get to a meeting right away."

Seeing her flustered face, the men quickly moved out of her way and she sprinted up the steps. At last she arrived, breathing hard, on the third floor. She yanked open the door to the Council Chamber and quickly went inside. The Council President for the month, the representative of Indonesia, was striking his gavel to declare the meeting open.

The mezzanine was unusually crowded with staff and public visitors who'd come to observe the proceedings. Just below, in the section reserved for the media, every seat was filled by a journalist or news photographer. That confirmed to Anne that the session was going to be an important one. There was a feeling of expectancy throughout the Chamber, especially on the main floor, where the ambassadors of the fifteen Security Council member states had all taken their designated places around the horseshoe table.

Near the top of the mezzanine, on the left, Anne spotted an empty seat. She murmured her apologies as she brushed against people's knees along the row until she reached it. She sat down and quickly flung her Russian books and wallet underneath. She grabbed an earpiece from its cradle in the armrest and hooked it over her ear. Then she flipped open her steno pad, ready to write down as much of each speech as she could.

The Council President gave the floor to the Egyptian ambassador, who was seated on the left side of the horseshoe table at the very end. Even before starting to speak, El-Mahmoun's face was flushed. Anne suspected that some representatives who addressed the Security Council portrayed more emotion than they actually felt, in an attempt to sway the Council members and the public. But that day El-Mahmoun's anger looked real. Glowering at the Israeli delegate sitting at the other end of the table, 12 feet across from him, he began his statement.

Speaking in Arabic, he said, "I find myself compelled to ask for the floor because I can hardly be expected to remain silent in the face of such a mockery of the truth as that to which the Council has been subjected by the Israeli representative's letter of this morning. Israel should be the last Member of this august organization to talk about respect for international law. No other Member has ever been so often condemned by the United Nations for the breach of exactly that law."

He continued, his voice rising higher. "Yesterday, by attacking six villages in brotherly Lebanon, Israel has committed a premeditated and obvious act of aggression. Israel, which owes its existence to violence and terror, can live only through violence and terror. But Israel has miscalculated the stern resolve of the Arab countries. We will undertake whatever actions are necessary to ensure that the Zionists pay in full for their heinous crimes!"

With these words, El-Mahmoun pounded the table so hard that the glass pitcher in front of him overturned, scattering water and ice in every direction. The Costa Rican representative, sitting two seats away, drew back in alarm as water spread quickly in his direction, but the Egyptian was oblivious to the chaos he'd caused.

Listening through her earpiece, Anne was startled to hear the English interpreter forcefully pound the desk in his booth, and then the clatter of his pitcher overturning and ice scattering. That's how engaged the interpreter was in faithfully conveying El-Mahmoun's anger.

A conference officer jumped to her feet and ran over to the Egyptian with paper towels, but he waved her away. Raising his voice still louder, he shouted, "The Zionist occupiers' disregard for the resolutions of this Council is in complete defiance of the UN Charter. We will never renounce our support for the Palestinian freedom fighters. It is a law of history that national liberation movements cannot be put down by force!"

Applause erupted on the main floor from the seats reserved for delegates who were not members of the Security Council. Some people in the mezzanine clapped as well. The Council President repeatedly banged his gavel for order, but it was several minutes before calm returned to the Chamber.

The President squared his shoulders. "Before I call on the representative of Israel, I wish to remind everyone in this Chamber that you are attending an official meeting of the United Nations Security Council. As its President, I must insist on appropriate comportment at all times." Nodding in the direction of the Israeli ambassador, he said, "Sir, you have the floor."

Ambassador Yavets, who usually appeared calm in all circumstances, stared menacingly at his Egyptian counterpart. In a strong voice he declared, "The Egyptian ambassador referred to terrorism in the Middle East. Indeed, terrorism in the region goes way back. The Arab Governments, Egypt foremost among them, having failed to stifle the Jewish State at birth by military invasion, decided to pursue warfare against it by terrorist incursions that would sow bloodshed and destruction in the midst of Israel's civilian population."

Looking one by one at each of the Council members, Yavets exclaimed, "This Council must hold the Arab States responsible for allowing their territory to be used by murderous organizations which are waging an open campaign of barbaric atrocities against innocent Israelis in many parts of the world." His voice reaching a crescendo, he exclaimed, "For its part, the Government of Israel will give no quarter to the ruthless killers of the innocent. It will pursue them and strike at them until mankind is free of their bloodthirsty savagery!"

These last words were too much for El-Mahmoun. He jumped to his feet and sprang into the opening between the two ends of the horseshoe table. There he stood, waving his fist at Yavets. A gasp went up in the Chamber as Yavets rose and rushed toward El-Mahmoun. Before anyone could stop them, the two ambassadors were fiercely grappling with each other.

As other delegates leaped from their seats, more pitchers overturned, sending water flying in all directions, even onto the press writers' table at the center. Several chairs toppled to the ground. A startled conference officer dropped the entire stack of documents he was distributing.

The President banged his gavel, but the pandemonium continued. Someone shouted, "The TV cameras, the TV cameras…cut the cameras!"

The security guards, as dumbfounded as everyone else, suddenly remembered their duty to keep order. From their posts beside the exit doors, they began running toward the struggle at the Council table. But before they could reach the two diplomats, the Soviet and French ambassadors hurried up to the battling men.

Ambassador Bulgakov threw his muscular arms around the Egyptian representative and yanked him back. El-Mahmoun's hand flung out, knocking Bulgakov's glasses to the ground, where a wayward foot shattered them with a sickening crunch. The French delegate came around to face Yavets and forcefully pushed him back toward his seat. He shoved him down into it and held his hands firmly on the Israeli's shoulders, as Yavets struggled to rise again.

Security officers now entered the mezzanine where Anne, open-mouthed, was gaping at the astonishing scene on the main floor. "Listen up, people," one guard ordered. "We have to evacuate the Chamber immediately."

"But, but…" exclaimed a news photographer sitting in the section below Anne. "I need a few more pictures!"

"NOW," said another guard. "You've got to turn in your camera anyway. We have instructions to confiscate all film."

He walked over to the photographer and held out his hand. Reluctantly, the man placed his camera on the upturned palm. The guard told him, "You can retrieve it from the Spokesman's office later. Come with me now, all of you."

The guard guided the journalists to the left end of the tier below Anne, where a few steps led down to the exit for that level. She watched the grumbling newsmen descend and then pass through the doorway one by one. "How can they make us lose a big story like this?" a journalist protested. "Yeah, isn't the UN supposed to be promoting freedom of the press?" asked another.

Ignoring the journalists' angry complaints, the guard turned his attention to the mezzanine. "Hey, you folks up there. Get moving."

Anne snapped her steno pad shut and stood up. As her row began to empty, she took a last look over her shoulder. Chairs, documents, briefcases, pens, microphones, pitchers, glasses and ice were strewn all over the floor below. Deeply shaken, she followed the others out the rear exit.

63

AN INTERMINABLE WAIT

Back in the office, Anne briefed her boss. "El-Mahmoun and Yavets became angrier and angrier, but no one expected they'd actually start fighting with each other. Señor Duarte, it was absolute chaos. I don't know how long it's going to take them to clean up the mess. The Council Chamber is in shambles."

Duarte stroked his chin. "But Anne, this is neither here nor there. We still have to get a summary of the diplomats' statements to the Information Centres. Of course, it goes without saying that we won't include anything about the fight." He thought for a moment and then said, "Go ask Bertram which of your notes he'd like to see first, so you can prioritize your typing. And be quick about it. We want the cable on this meeting to go out as soon as possible. The UNICs need to get it to their local press in time for the morning editions."

Anne dutifully walked around the corner to the press officers' room. "Bertram," she called out, "Señor Duarte said I should ask you which of my notes…"

She stopped mid-sentence. Bertram was scowling as he looked down at his drenched clothes. "I'm not doing anything until I get myself dried off. Be a good girl and go get me some paper towels."

As Anne feared, the evening did not proceed smoothly. Every time she peeked in at the doorway to see how Bertram's draft was coming along, she saw him rip a sheet of paper out of his typewriter, crumple it, and toss it onto the growing pile on the floor next to his chair. "It's going to be a long night," she sighed to herself.

By 10:00 p.m., Duarte had lost all patience. "Anne, what's holding up that press release? I'm going to insist that Bertram finish it right now."

"Señor Duarte, I really wouldn't do that if I were you. Bertram's in one of his moods. If he gets any angrier, it will only take longer."

"Well, I simply can't stay here indefinitely. My wife has been keeping my dinner warm already for three hours. Three hours!" Looking at her carefully, he asked, "Anne, could I trust you to proofread the press release very thoroughly? You would have to make sure it includes nothing that would tarnish the UN's image before you send it out."

"I can do that," Anne replied. Somehow her boss was oblivious to the fact that her dinner had been delayed by three hours, too. But tired and hungry though she was, she'd rather have the extra burden on her shoulders than her boss pacing back and forth beside her desk waiting for her to finish. "You can count on me, Señor Duarte. I'll give it my full attention."

Rewarding her with a grateful look, Duarte lifted his coat and hat off the coat rack and walked out the door.

Anne typed for a few moments and then stopped. She rose from her desk and carefully locked both office doors.

64

A WRONG MOMENT

The maintenance supervisor, hands on his hips, carefully surveyed the Security Council Chamber. Nodding his head in approval, he said to his cleaning crew, "Well done, men. Let's go."

Three janitors pushed rolling canvas hampers toward the door. The hampers were filled with water-soaked documents, shards of glass from shattered pitchers, broken chairs, bashed in microphones and other debris.

It had taken them until late that evening to get the Chamber back in order after the afternoon's chaos. Now at the horseshoe table, all the damaged green blotters had been replaced. For every ambassador, sharpened pencils and new notepads again stood at the ready, as well as fresh blue booklets of the UN Charter and yellow copies of the Council's rules of procedure.

Turning around for a last look, the supervisor shook his head, still amazed at the disarray that had greeted him and his crew when they arrived for their evening shift. Then he flipped off the ceiling lights.

After the last man exited the room, the supervisor closed the door behind them. On the outside wall, he dimmed the lights in the corridor. Then he and his men trundled the hampers up the hallway toward the service elevator. The squeaking of the wheels slowly diminished until it could no longer be heard.

Dark silence pervaded the Council Chamber as the minutes passed.

About an hour later, the door opened again, this time very slowly. A faint ray of light spread briefly across the main floor. Then the Chamber was again plunged into total darkness.

Male voices spoke softly and a dim light appeared. The light moved toward the center of the room.

Moments later, there was a creak, like the sound of something springing open on a hinge, and then the rustling of thick paper.

More discussion followed, still in low voices.

All at once, the Chamber door was thrown wide open. A silhouette was faintly framed in the doorway. A tense female voice called out, "Are you there? Are you there with someone?"

A man muttered, "What the hell?!"

The woman's voice again echoed through the Chamber. "Jürgen? Jürgen, are you there? Are you with someone?" She sounded anguished. "Are you there with … Peggy?"

There was a sharp click and bright overhead light flooded the Chamber. The woman had flipped the main light switch. Her whole tone changed. Sounding bewildered, she asked, "What's happening here?" She had moved deeper into the Chamber, but now her voice receded back toward the door. "What…what are you doing? Why is the…" Her words trailed off.

Rapid footsteps crossed the plush carpet and the Chamber once again went black.

"Stop," the woman protested, "you're hurting me."

A man replied through the darkness, "I'm sorry, Miss. I don't know who you are, or why you're here, but you've come at a very wrong moment."

In a trembling voice, she said, "I … I only came to look for a friend. I …I didn't think anyone else would be here."

"Well, you did not think correctly. That is a problem for us. And," he added somberly, "for you."

"Please, please don't hurt me," she pleaded. "I won't tell anyone. I didn't see anything. Really, I didn't."

Another man spoke. "I'm afraid, Miss, that it's too late. We have no choice."

There was a sharp intake of the woman's breath. "Please, I beg you…"

The men began whispering among themselves, while the woman cried softly.

Finally one man spoke with authority, "Do it now. And please, no blood. I find gore very distasteful."

There were sounds of scuffling. The woman's voice rose from a whimper to loud sobbing.

After a dull thud, something crumpled to the floor.

Then all was silent.

65

WHAT WAS FORGOTTEN

It wasn't until after midnight that Anne finally finished the cable. Bertram was long gone. She'd taken extra time to go over every word meticulously until she was certain Señor Duarte would not disapprove.

Her floor was deserted as she walked with the green cable pages to take an elevator upstairs to deliver them to the Cable Office. After the night duty officer there assured her the transmittal would go out immediately, her job was done. Finally, she could go home. She returned to the office, wearily put on her coat, turned off the lights and closed the door behind her.

As she passed through the dim hallway toward the escalator, Anne glanced toward the Security Council Chamber. She shook her head, recalling the chaos of that afternoon's Middle East meeting.

At the ground floor lobby, she signed out in the logbook. The guard gave her a sympathetic look. "It's pretty late," he said in a kind voice. "I'll activate the taxi sign for you." Seeing Anne flinch, he added, "I know, I remember what happened. Tonight, you go stand with the officer in his guardhouse until the cab comes to a complete stop."

Anne swung through the revolving door and recoiled as the cold night air stung her face. She tugged the collar of her coat up around her ears. Trudging toward the street exit, she was oblivious to the shimmering beads of water arcing out from the fountain, still brightly lit against the dark sky.

She was about to go through the gate when she realized her handbag felt light. Too light. She stopped, unclasped it and peered inside. Her wallet was missing.

Then she remembered. She'd tossed it, and her Russian books, under the seat in the mezzanine just as the Council President was banging his gavel to start the afternoon's meeting. In the confusion that followed, she'd evacuated the Chamber without them. Were they still there?

All she'd been thinking of was getting home and collapsing onto her bed for an all-too-brief sleep. Now she'd have to go back into the building. Both her taxi fare and her housekeys were in the wallet.

She whirled around and hurried back toward the building entrance. On her way, she passed a group of night-shift translators. "Hey," one of them laughed, "aren't you heading the wrong way?"

"I know," she moaned, "I left something important."

Once back inside, she explained to the guard, "I can't believe it, but I forgot my wallet. So please turn off the taxi sign for now, if no one else wants it."

"Will do," he replied, "but you'll have to log in again."

One more delay. Sighing, she picked up the pen. Already a number of staff members had logged out after her earlier signature. She signed in below their names.

Now that the last stragglers seemed to have left, the building felt totally deserted. Anne thought of asking the guard whether someone might accompany her to the Council Chamber, but she guessed that the few officers on duty overnight couldn't be spared from their essential posts. And actually, she felt safer with the building almost totally empty than during regular hours, when people who might do her harm could blend in with the crowd.

She patted her handbag for reassurance, thinking of the brass knuckles inside it, and began walking back through the lobby toward the escalator. The echo of her heels across the empty expanse had a mournful ring.

66

WHAT LIES BENEATH

Anne arrived at the entrance to the third-floor mezzanine of the Council Chamber. She eased open the polished wooden door and let it close softly behind her.

Standing still, she allowed her eyes to adjust to the darkness. She had hoped there would be some light on the main floor, seeping in from the corridors, but either those fixtures had been turned off or the doors were flush to the carpet. The Chamber was pitch black.

She pulled a pocket flashlight out of her handbag. Although it would be easier to find her books and wallet with the ceiling lights on, she didn't want to be spotted on Security's closed-circuit TV screens. Probably the guards wouldn't be watching closely at that hour, and she wasn't doing anything wrong. But it was already late, and she didn't want to be delayed by a lot of questions.

She switched on her flashlight. By its faint beam, she made her way to the left side of the mezzanine. She couldn't remember exactly where she'd been sitting that afternoon, but she guessed it was somewhere in the second row from the top. She entered that row and, moving toward its end, reached under several seats until her fingers touched the cold metal spiral of her Russian notebook. Relieved, she dropped to her knees and retrieved her things.

After climbing back to the top of the mezzanine, Anne was approaching the door when she turned around. There she was, completely alone in the Security Council Chamber, the most important room in the world. She recalled the one time she'd been on the main floor, the day Andrei followed her inside. She remembered the awe and elation she'd felt, standing where so much history had taken place.

That day, she'd hung back near the wall because she knew she didn't really belong there. Now, with no one else around, she was seized with a strong longing to actually sit at the iconic horseshoe table, around which so many pivotal, landmark decisions had been taken.

She placed her books and wallet on the nearest seat and listened. All was quiet. She decided to do it.

The weak beam from her flashlight was just enough for her to discern each step leading down from the mezzanine to the middle tier of seats reserved for the press. There she moved gingerly from row to row, taking care not to bang into the wooden writing boards attached to each seat.

At the bottom of the press section, Anne came to a solid wood barrier. Cautiously, she swung first her left leg over it, and then her right. Once on the other side, she found herself in the sloping section of red seats reserved for diplomats who were not Council members. Slowly she negotiated each step, until finally she reached the main floor.

Anne stopped and waited. All was still quiet. She approached the table.

She was reaching out to touch it when the flashlight slipped out of her hand. As it struck the floor, Anne heard a hollow sound.

She paused, wondering if her ears had betrayed her. Then she remembered her conversation with Andrei, here in the Chamber, about the space inside the table which had been brought up to floor level during the renovations. All this time, she'd assumed the cavity had been filled in with cement, but maybe that wasn't true. She tapped with her right heel near the place where the flashlight had dropped. Again, she heard the same empty sound.

Curious, she knelt down and with the butt of her flashlight, she struck several different spots in the area. Outside the circular footprint of the horseshoe table, the floor sounded solid. But inside the table, it was unmistakably hollow.

Wondering if she could see where the two areas of the floor met, Anne stood up and began sweeping her flashlight slowly back and forth over the carpet. Her beam highlighted something on the ground. It was moving!

Frightened, she jumped back. She stood transfixed, watching the object slowly undulating. Then she realized it wasn't actually moving. Rather, it was shimmering in the faint light of the flashlight.

She moved closer and tentatively stretched out her hand. The object felt soft to her touch. It was a small piece of cloth lying on the carpet.

Anne tried to pick it up, but it didn't come loose. She tugged harder, but it remained stuck. Oddly, it seemed somehow to be inserted into the floor.

She began pressing into the carpet around the cloth. After a moment, her fingers slipped down through a slit in the carpet and touched wood. There she felt a slight indent. Might the cloth be caught in the seam between the two areas of flooring?

Anne set her flashlight down on the carpet, pointing in her direction. Fitting her fingers into the small gap, she began testing to see if there was any give to the wood. At first there was none. Bracing herself, she pulled a little harder. With a creak, a section of the flooring hinged upward as though spring-loaded. It rose so forcefully that Anne fell back. About three feet above the floor, it clicked into place.

Anne recovered her balance and crawled forward to investigate. With the lid now secured above ground, she could detect the outline of an open space below. So it was true. The original dropped floor had never been filled in.

But why would there be a piece of fabric sticking out? She took hold of the cloth, which she expected now would come free. Instead, it seemed to be attached to something inside the hollow space.

Anne reached for her flashlight and shined the beam downward. It picked up something stretched out horizontally not far from her. She slowly followed its contours with her light until she came to a long, narrow cylinder that was lighter in color. Puzzled, she leaned forward to get a better look.

She froze in horror. It was the flesh of a lifeless human arm.

Anne fought back the scream rising in her throat. Trembling uncontrollably, she grasped her flashlight with both hands and directed it along the mass until she reached its end. It was the body of a woman lying face up, the dark eyes fixed open.

Anne sprang to her feet and recoiled backward. She clenched her eyes tightly, trying to shut out what she'd seen. Her thoughts raced wildly. It wasn't possible. How could the room she revered so much be hiding something as hideous as a corpse. She gasped for breath.

For several minutes, she was unable to move from the spot where she stood. Her eyes were still closed, but it was as if they were open, so vivid to her was the image of the dead body.

Then it dawned on her that whoever had hidden the corpse might return at any moment to remove it, before it began to decompose. She forced her eyes open. She had to lower the flooring back into place and leave immediately.

With trepidation, she inched back to the yawning hole. Her legs unsteady, she knelt beside it to release the catch. As she did so, inadvertently she looked down.

This time she saw the cloth more clearly. It was purple, with gold threads running through it. Shock tore through her. "No, no, no," she mouthed silently. The shimmery fabric which had drawn her to the seam in the floor was the edge of a skirt. A skirt she knew well. A skirt she'd admired the day she returned to work after the taxi accident.

A wave of nausea swept over her. She shined the beam directly into the dead woman's face. The rich brown eyes, locked in a faraway stare, were so familiar to her, as were the smooth olive skin and long wavy hair.

Her heart hammered in her chest. Who would have done such a thing? Who could possibly want to kill Benedetta? Tears of grief welled up in Anne's eyes.

There was something she had to do. She steeled herself and reached down into the opening to close Benedetta's eyes. It was the least she could do for her. Unnerved by the feel of the cold flesh, she quickly snatched back her hand.

Her other hand, holding the flashlight, shook. As the beam wavered, it picked up something lying near the body. Training her light in that direction, Anne spotted a thin rectangular package, about two feet wide, wrapped in brown paper. In one corner, she noticed a sizeable tear. She focused her light on that spot.

Through the hole in the paper, she saw something that looked like the edge of a painting. She could just make out a light blue background surrounding several yellowish cubes which were outlined in black and daubed with small, regularly spaced black dots.

Anne knew exactly what she was looking at. It was the Dufy watercolor she'd studied so intently the day she waited in Waldheim's conference room. That afternoon, she thought she'd never see the painting again. She'd been wrong.

A cold chill overtook Anne's body. She had to get out at once. Urgently she lowered the heavy flooring back down. Once the wood fitted securely into place, she stroked the tufts of carpet around its edges so the area would look undisturbed.

She was rising to her feet when she heard the thump of a heavy object hitting the floor in the corridor outside the Chamber. Someone was coming already for the body.

Panic-stricken, Anne clicked off her flashlight and spun around. As she did, the flashlight fell from her hand and dropped to the floor. She didn't have time to feel around for it. Instead, she flicked out her foot. It connected with the flashlight and sent it skidding noiselessly toward the seats near the door. Hopefully it wouldn't be spotted there.

As quickly as the dark would allow, Anne hurried back up the shallow slope toward the higher tiers. Her outstretched hands had just touched the wood barrier in front of the journalists' section when the door began to swing open. As faint light from the hallway spread into the Chamber, she flung herself over the barrier. Behind it, she flattened her body onto the floor and held her breath.

67

A NARROW MARGIN

Anne lay on the ground without moving. From the pattern of light, she could tell the door was still open. She heard something bang into it softly, first once, then twice.

Cautiously she lifted her head only enough to see over the barrier. She could make out, but barely, that a man was propping open the door with his foot, as he and another man maneuvered a long object into the Chamber. Before she could distinguish what it was, they managed to get it fully inside. The door swung shut, and the Chamber again went black.

A flashlight snapped on. By its weak beam, Anne saw they'd brought in a squared-off leather sofa, the kind scattered all over the building. After propping their flashlight on the armrest of a seat near the door, the men started carrying the sofa toward the center of the Chamber. As they came abreast of her hiding place, Anne quickly dropped her head.

The noise of the spring release and creaking wood followed. They were raising the flooring.

Struggling to identify every sound, Anne thought she heard the men moving the sofa cushions in some way.

Then she understood. They'd probably hollowed out the sofa to hide Benedetta's body inside so they could transport it unseen out of the Chamber.

After some shuffling noises, Anne heard the cushions being put back into place. A moment later, she caught the sound of the wood flooring being lowered back down.

The men were now talking to each other. At first they spoke too softly for Anne to make out their words, but by their voices, she could tell they were moving back toward the door. Just when she expected them to reach it, she heard one ask, "What's this?"

"A flashlight? Did the girl have one when she came in? I didn't see it, did you?"

Sweat formed on Anne's forehead.

The other man replied, "That's odd. It feels warm. We've been gone a while. If the girl dropped it, shouldn't it be cold by now?"

"Give it to me," said the first man. "See, it's a cheap one. It just overheated. Put it in your pocket and we'll show it to the boss later."

"If we tell the boss, he's gonna ask if we searched the Chamber. You know how thorough he is. Leaves nothing to chance."

"All right, all right. But let's make it fast. I don't want to be caught with a dead body when Security brings the dog to sniff for bombs. There's a meeting this morning, so they'll be here soon. And keep your light on low," he cautioned. "Before long, the guards monitoring the closed-circuit TV will start watching more closely."

Judging from the sweeping rays, Anne guessed the men had begun searching the rows of seats against the wall next to the door. She allowed herself to hope that looking there would be enough to satisfy the men and then they'd leave.

Yet after they'd investigated the area, one said, "Let's look over there."

The beam pivoted and was now facing in Anne's direction. Her whole body shuddered.

"Why? The flashlight was dropped here, not there. We've done our job. We've looked. Let's get out of here."

"I'm gonna check over there all the same."

Anne pressed her body to the floor and willed it not to move. The man began methodically scanning the diplomats' section right below her. His beam started at the far end of the section. With agonizing slowness, it passed by each seat until it reached the opposite wall. Then it began its return, searching the next higher row of seats, and then the next.

An impatient whisper broke the silence. "Okay, okay, you've checked enough. Let's get the damn sofa into the corridor so we can leave the building."

"Don't be in such a rush," retorted the other man. "It'll only take a minute more for me to finish."

To Anne's horror, the nearness of his voice told her that he'd begun walking up the center aisle toward the journalists' tier. The light from the flashlight began moving across the top of the wood barrier between the two sections. Her chest was heaving. If the man looked over the barrier, he was bound to see her.

Then she remembered. At the meeting that afternoon, when the guard ushered the journalists out of the media tier, she'd noticed that at the side, they walked down two or three steps to get to the exit for that section. She recalled that the barrier wall changed directions at that point. The angle it formed might be enough to hide her from the men, if only she could get there fast enough.

Rising noiselessly onto her hands and knees, Anne began crawling backward. It was a race against time, but she had no choice except to move with excruciating slowness. Finally her foot felt the edge of the first step. Carefully, she lowered herself down onto it, then onto the step below, and then the next. Leaning against the wood barrier, she drew her arms and legs in close to her body. There she waited, barely breathing.

The sound of cloth brushing against wood, and the slight burst of light, told Anne the man had climbed over into the journalists' section. The flashlight beam moved to the wall farthest from her and slowly searched every seat in that area. Then the beam came closer, sweeping over the next group of seats.

The light grew still brighter. Anne could actually hear the man's breath. Terrified, she compacted her body even more tightly.

"Come on. We're wasting time." The voice coming from below was full of tension. "There's no one here, I tell you."

"Hey, I'll finish looking at the end of this row, and then we'll go."

Abruptly, the light moved toward Anne's hiding place with such speed that a sharp intake of breath escaped from her throat.

The beam froze.

"Enough already, we've gotta go," the other man protested.

"Shhh," came the answer. "I heard something. Right over there."

Anne's heart was pounding so forcefully that she was afraid the man would hear it. He was now only about fifteen feet away. His light traveled up into the higher rows on her side of the section and then back down.

"Idiot!" muttered his partner. "I'm taking that damn flashlight."

Anne heard him approach the barrier and climb over it. The beam shot up to the ceiling. There was the sound of scuffling and the light swung wildly in all directions.

Anne knew this was probably her only chance. Her body was shaking violently, but she managed to rise to a crouch. The men, still struggling with each other for the flashlight, were at the center of the section and not looking in her direction. Bending low and keeping close to the wall, she climbed cautiously, one row at a time.

The scuffling below continued as she stole up the steps. At last, she made it to the top of the section. Behind the highest row of seats there, she carefully stretched out and once again pressed her body low to the floor.

At the bottom of the tier, the men were still arguing. "Give me that thing. Let's settle this once and for all."

One of them violently seized the flashlight. Anne could see his shadowed face, lit from below, as he walked purposefully to the exact spot where she'd been hiding only moments before. Moving the beam all around the area, he crowed, "See? There's no one here."

"Okay, okay, maybe not there. But I know I heard something."

The other voice rose higher in anger. "I've had enough. The guards watching the screens will change shifts at any moment. You can keep looking if you want, but I'm leaving. If we're caught, the boss won't lift a finger to rescue us. He said so."

For once, his partner didn't argue. "All right, let's go."

The light swung around and receded toward the main floor, as the men retreated back over the barrier.

Anne heard them grunt as they lifted the sofa and carried it to the exit. They managed to maneuver it out of the Chamber without light from the corridor shining on them for very long.

The door closed softly. Anne was left in complete darkness.

68

CHASING A LEAD

Slowly Anne rolled over onto her back. Her breath came in gasps. Utterly exhausted, she lay on the ground as the minutes passed.

All at once, she lurched upright. She wasn't out of danger. She had to get out of the Chamber without being seen.

The most direct route would be to leave through one of the doors on the main floor. The two men made it sound like they would bolt as soon as they got the sofa into the corridor. But if, for any reason, they were still there when she came through the door...

She shivered at the thought. She had no doubt what would happen to her if they saw she'd been in the Chamber. The better course, although slower, would be to retrace her steps back to the top, and exit from the third floor mezzanine. As she did, she could grab her books and wallet on the way out. If there was any trace left of a murder having taken place in the Chamber, she didn't want her belongings, with her name in them, being found later on.

Anne quietly rose to her feet. She was lightheaded and had to wait, impatiently, until she felt steadier. Then cautiously, she slipped over the railing that separated the journalists' section from the upper mezzanine. From there, feeling her way in the dark, she made the slow ascent.

As she climbed carefully upward, a comforting thought came to her. She wasn't in this alone. First thing in the morning, she'd contact Patterson. If there was ever a time she needed his help, it was now.

She stopped short. Without knowing who the men were, what could Patterson do? All Anne could tell him was that Benedetta had been murdered and that for a while her body had been concealed in a hollow space under the Chamber floor. And that the Dufy watercolor had been hidden there as well. Yet that information, by itself, was almost worthless. She was sure that by the time Patterson could get someone to investigate the space, the trail would be completely cold.

A thought that Anne had been pushing into the background kept coming forward in her mind. Finally she let it in. The men had said that once they put the sofa in the corridor, they could go. That meant someone else would have to have come, and fairly soon, to remove it before the body started to give off a stench. If Anne could steel her nerves and hide somewhere in the hallway to see who showed up, then she'd have something concrete to tell Patterson.

When at last she reached the top, she picked up her books and wallet and continued to the exit. There, she opened the door narrowly to listen. Hearing nothing, she slipped out. She stayed close to the dark wall and moved quietly down the hallway.

Soon she reached the edge of the open space where the escalator carved through the floor going in both directions. Before she could talk herself out of it, she broke away from the obscurity of the wall and quickly passed through the glass doors.

The escalator was still turned off at that early hour. As quietly as possible, she descended the stalled metal steps. There was nowhere to hide within the glass enclosure if anyone should walk by.

On the second floor – her floor – she pushed through the doors and darted to the shadowy safety of the nearest wall. There she waited to accustom her eyes to the gloom, and to listen. After assuring herself that the area was empty, she went down the few steps to the main corridor.

From there, she moved cautiously until she reached the parallel partition outside the ladies room where she'd rested that day with the chamomile teabags. It was behind the partition that Anne now stationed herself. All remained quiet.

As she leaned against the partition, Anne's eyelids began to droop and she had to force them open again and again. She was just starting to think she might have made a mistake when, from the far end of the corridor, she heard the ding of an elevator. Two voices reached her ears. She listened intently to the conversation as the speakers came closer.

"It's supposed to be in the north hallway outside the Security Council Chamber. Near the main doors."

Anne dropped low to the floor and peered around the edge of the partition. Two men in dark clothes were approaching, each carrying a large dolly. They rounded the corner toward the Council entrance and disappeared from her view. She heard the dollies fall to the ground and the sound of the sofa being loaded onto them. "It's heavy," said one of the men.

A squeaking of wheels told Anne the dollies were in motion. After a moment, the first man came back around the corner, guiding the sofa. She caught a full view of his face and recognized the tall young mover who had a crush on her.

What a disappointment. Anne felt certain he wouldn't be mixed up with murder or art theft. She didn't know how the men who hid Benedetta's body had gotten a work order processed so early in the morning, but evidently removing the sofa was being handled as a regular UN moving job.

As the men pushed their dollies toward the elevator, she saw the extra sag under the sofa and cringed. Where would they take it? As though hearing her question, Anne's admirer asked, "What are we supposed to be doing with this, anyway?"

His older partner said, "I know we gotta take it down to the Third Basement, but I'm not sure what's happening after that. Wait a minute and I'll check the work order."

He stopped and pulled a folded paper from his breast pocket. "Ah. We're taking it to the Loading Dock. A van will pick it up from there to take it for repairs."

"Repairs?" asked the younger mover. He stepped back to stare at the sofa. "It looks okay to me."

"You never know with these diplomats," said his partner. "They can be picky about the smallest details. Let's just get this job done. After that, we've got to move the whole UNDP Communications Office into the new DC-1 building. That's going to be a headache, let me tell you. And after being called in this early, I don't want to work any more overtime today than I have to."

He returned the work order to his pocket and they resumed pushing the sofa toward the elevator.

The Loading Dock. Anne knew her way around the Third Basement fairly well from taking envelopes down to the Pouch Unit. If she descended the service stairwell just beyond the restroom, it should eventually bring her out into the corridor that led to the dock. If she hurried, she might get there before the movers. Then she could watch to see who picked up the sofa, and hopefully get the van's license number. It was risky, but she had to try.

Bolting from her hiding place, Anne ran to the stairwell door and plunged through it.

In the corridor she had just left, behind a support pillar on the opposite side, a cigarette lighter flared. A moment later, a wisp of hazel-flavored smoke curled slowly toward the ceiling.

69

REFLECTIONS

Standing at the windows of his office on the 37th floor, Gavrez looked out across the East River to the borough of Queens, which was slowly awakening. A reddish-yellow glow tinged the horizon line. The lights on one building after another came on as he watched. He raised a Benson & Hedges to his lips and drew the smoke in slowly and fully. He held it deep in his lungs for an extra moment before releasing its hazel aroma back into the air.

When the ash grew long, Gavrez turned toward his desk. Still standing, he reached over and tapped the cigarette on the edge of his marble and bronze ashtray. Drawing in another deep inhalation, he slowly rounded the corner of the desk and eased himself into his custom-made leather chair. He raised his left foot, clad in impeccable black Gucci, up onto the desk and followed it with his right. He had a problem to solve.

Anne Thomas.

His thoughts went back to the first time he'd seen her, in Cyprus. He was working in the well-appointed office which he'd insisted be built for him before he accepted the assignment of UN Mediator. The talking points he was writing would be critical to the success of the next round of negotiations. Pausing to come up with just the right word, he'd lifted his eyes to the expanse of parched earth leading to the main UN office, housed in drab army barracks built when the island was a British colony. A willowy young woman was walking toward the far entrance. She was looking around, taking in her surroundings with an expression of delight and expectancy. It was a look Gavrez rarely saw, surrounded as he usually was by cool beauties who only showed that kind of anticipation when they sensed they were about to receive an expensive gift.

The girl was not bad looking. She was not well-dressed. An American, probably. She wore no makeup or jewelry, and her hair was nondescript. But something about her was not displeasing. And her figure was actually rather good, if you looked through her unfashionable clothes the right way. He wondered what it would be like to have sex with a girl like that. She wouldn't be a very experienced lover, he didn't think. Not like the kind of woman he usually bedded.

Gavrez forgot about the girl almost immediately, as he plunged into the next round of inter-communal talks between the Greek- and Turkish-Cypriots. Waldheim had imprudently announced that he intended to get the two sides to sign a peace agreement before the end of his term. To say so publicly showed his ignorance of the political realities in Cyprus, where neither leader could afford to be seen as accepting an agreement imposed from outside the country.

The Secretary-General's gaffe had created a major setback for Gavrez. It had taken intense effort over several months – of flattery combined with astute political maneuvering – to get the two parties to agree to resume the talks. Now he was meticulously studying their positions so that no further miscalculation would derail his carefully constructed strategy for the negotiations.

The UN's second mediator in Cyprus had been, like Gavrez, an Ecuadorian. Galo Plaza Lasso had credibly handled the negotiations from 1964 to 1965, but in the end, he was unable to bridge the gap between the two Cypriot communities. Gavrez believed time was now on his side, and that he himself could achieve what had eluded his illustrious countryman. If agreement wasn't reached now, it wouldn't be because Gavrez had left a stone unturned.

One day, during a break in the talks, he was pouring over documents spread across his desk when his secretary knocked on the door. "Señor Gavrez, the Spokesman sent his new secretary, Anne Thomas, to pay her respects."

At first, Gavrez had been irritated by the interruption. Yet when he looked up, he was pleasantly surprised when he recognized the girl he'd seen from his window. He was even more pleased, although he couldn't say why, by the shy smile she gave him and the warm feel of the hand which she extended for him to shake. He felt himself smiling back. It wasn't his usual smile, so much so that his secretary looked quizzically from him to Anne, and then back at him.

He caught himself and immediately became businesslike. "It's a pleasure to meet you, Miss Thomas. But now you must excuse me. I have a demanding amount of work to take care of today."

The smile left the girl's face. She murmured an apology for having disturbed him and moved gracefully to the door. Once he was sure his secretary's back was turned, Gavrez looked attentively at Anne's retreating figure. There was definitely something interesting about her.

After that encounter, their paths crossed from time to time in the UN compound, but without any real conversation. Gavrez was always hurrying from one meeting to another, or studying and thinking alone in his office.

In their spare time, UN staff scattered all over Cyprus, drawn to its breathtaking beaches and picturesque ruins of civilizations which, over its long history, had left their traces – Phoenicians, Assyrians, Egyptians, Persians, Greeks, Romans, Jews, Byzantines, Arabs, European Crusaders and Ottomans. There were so many possibilities for losing oneself on the island that only once had Gavrez seen Anne outside the UN compound. It was on a Sunday afternoon at the trendy resort town of Famagusta, on the east coast.

At an upscale restaurant overlooking the water, Gavrez was having lunch with an arrestingly beautiful French model who was in Cyprus for a fashion shoot. Juliette and Gavrez were bantering flirtatiously with each other when he noticed a waiter seating Anne at a nearby table. She was with a tall blond man he recognized as the Civilian Affairs Officer of the Swedish peacekeeping battalion. He felt oddly displeased to see them together.

This time Anne was more stylish. She wore a white sundress with thin stripes of primary colors which complemented the tones of her skin. Snatches of what they were saying wafted over to Gavrez. Anne told the CAO about the wonderful artifacts she'd been discovering in the local museums, and the Swede shared with her his own discoveries. It was the way she was smiling and laughing with the Swede that annoyed Gavrez. They were having a real conversation, unlike his with Juliette.

The more Gavrez watched Anne and her companion out of the corner of his eye, the more his exchanges with Juliette lost their vitality, until finally the two of them finished their meal in silence.

Shortly afterward, the negotiations gained significant traction, and over the next few weeks, Gavrez put all his energies into moving the talks forward. Anne never crossed his mind.

It was at a full staff meeting during one of his rare free afternoons that he again saw her. He hadn't been paying any attention to the Administrative Officer's lengthy explanation of the new UN benefits system. He'd deal with that later. Rather, his thoughts drifted to what he would do that evening. Juliette had returned to Paris. He'd grown tired of his affair with the Finnish ambassador's wife and his dalliance with the wife of the president of the second largest Cypriot bank. And by now he was fully bored with his secretary, who'd been his fallback when he didn't want to bother with the foreplay of wining and dining a woman.

The staff meeting ended and he hung back so the Admin Officer wouldn't try to engage him in meaningless chatter as he left. The room was clearing quickly. It was when Gavrez finally rose to his feet that he saw he was alone with the American girl, who was still gathering up her papers.

He passed close by her. The floral perfume she was wearing was light and fresh. As he took in her scent and the soft curve of her neck, an idea quickly formed in his mind. "I want you to come to my place at 9:00 this evening," he told her.

She looked up at him with puzzled eyes.

Scrutinizing her, he added, "And for God's sake, wear something sexier."

She fumbled out the words, "Is...is it a party?"

"No, it will just be the two of us," he answered over his shoulder as he walked out.

That evening, he contemplated his wine collection. At first, he brought out one of his better bottles, but then he guessed she wouldn't know the difference, so he selected a medium one.

He took care in how he dressed. He thought the black shirt, unbuttoned some but not too much, would make the right impression. He knew he was doing Anne an honor by paying attention to her at all, but he wanted to awaken in her more than admiration.

Once he was satisfied with what he saw in the mirror, he surveyed his living room. He repositioned a throw pillow on the sofa to make it look more casual. From his large bookcase, he pulled out a photographic history of Cyprus. He opened it to what looked like an interesting page and added a bookmark to give the impression he'd been reading it. Then he stretched out on the sofa to enjoy a cigarette.

It was at 9:45 that he started to have an edgy feeling. Most women arrived at his place on the dot, as though they couldn't wait to feel his hands caress their bodies. Usually he didn't drink before his date arrived, but now he poured himself a Christian Drouin Calvados and threw it back in one gulp.

At 10:15, he sensed the evening wasn't going according to his plan.

By 10:30, he was seething. He grabbed the UNFICYP directory and dialed her number. The phone rang endlessly. Twenty, thirty times. Finally she picked up.

"Why the hell aren't you here?" he demanded.

There was a long silence.

"Señor Gavrez, I…I know I…should have called…and I very much appreciate…your invitation." Her voice was shaking. "But I can't…can't accept…I can't come."

He exploded. "What do you mean, you can't come? Do you have any idea who I am?"

From when he was sixteen and succeeded in seducing his reluctant piano teacher, no woman had rebuffed his advances. Ever. Through gritted teeth, he told Anne, "I only have to say the word, and your UN career will be over. Take a cab here immediately."

"Señor Gavrez…I'm so sorry…but…I can't."

He let out an oath and slammed down the receiver. Before he could stop himself, one of his favorite Lladró figurines had sailed across the room and lay in pieces at the foot of the opposite wall.

He would have made good on his threat right away, but the next day, a surprise call came from Waldheim himself, offering Gavrez the position of Under-Secretary-General for Political Affairs. It was an unheard-of opportunity for someone his age. Within 48 hours, he was on a plane back to New York.

He had only seen Anne twice after she returned to UN Headquarters some months later. The first time, he caught sight of her entering an elevator as the doors were closing. Reminded of her existence, he promised himself that once he was fully settled in his new functions, he would say what was necessary to the right people to demolish her career. But for the time being, he gave her no further thought.

No further thought, that is, until the day he saw her standing behind the Cypriot amphora, studying it carefully. She was looking directly at what he knew to be the only flaw in the reproduction. And she was frowning.

He was irate. Lunching in Famagusta the previous year, he'd overheard her talk about getting acquainted with Cypriot artifacts. This insignificant girl was the one person at the UN who might recognize it wasn't the real amphora. If she reported her suspicions to someone, his whole operation could be at risk. By now he was too well known on the black market for dealing in stolen art. If any of his contacts were offered the right amount of money, they might talk.

Was she onto the fake or not? He had to find out. Or frighten her enough that she wouldn't dare say anything to anyone.

His first idea for intimidating her had backfired. The fool cab driver was only supposed to scare her, not send her to the hospital. When she came back to work, he knew he'd have to try a different approach. That's when he began summoning her for dictation. And had one of his men cut the sleeve of her blouse, and later accost her in the ladies room.

To his satisfaction, he saw he was gradually wearing her down. Each time she entered his office, she looked more demoralized. He became confident that soon her spirit would be so broken that she'd pose no threat to him.

In the meantime, the nervous tension within him grew. Was she an obstacle to his ambitions or not? For a man who liked to hold all the cards, the uncertainty was agonizing.

Early that morning, in the darkened second floor corridor, he'd finally gotten his answer.

And only by chance. He was signing out in the logbook of the deserted UN Lobby when a name above his own caught his eye. An *A. Thomas* from a 2nd floor office had logged in after midnight and hadn't yet signed out. That was worth checking. Gavrez told the guard he'd forgotten something and would be back shortly.

But instead of taking an elevator to his office, Gavrez continued on, out of the guard's view, until he reached the darkened escalator. Quietly he began climbing the immobilized steps up to the second floor, where he knew Anne's office was. He'd almost reached the top of the flight when he heard light footsteps descending the escalator from the floor above. He stopped where he was, his head concealed, and waited until the person passed through the glass doors on the second floor.

He held back another moment, and then climbed the last remaining steps and exited through the same doors. The dim figure ahead of him turned to the left and began moving noiselessly down the wide corridor. He headed in the same direction, trailing a safe distance behind.

There in the corridor, while the movers rolled away the sofa, he watched as she hid behind the partition and then dashed for the stairs to the Third Basement. He'd seen all he needed to see.

Now, sitting at his desk, Gavrez snapped open his engraved gold lighter and stared at the steady orange flame for several minutes.

Then, with an emphatic flick, he brought the lid down heavily onto the flame, abruptly extinguishing it.

He had made his decision.

70

THE LOADING DOCK

The faint light in the stairwell was just enough for Anne to make out the steps of each of the four flights leading downward. Despite her lack of sleep, the need to reach the Loading Dock in time gave her a rush of adrenaline. She hurtled down the stairs and soon reached a door marked *Third Basement*.

She turned the knob and cautiously eased the heavy metal door outward. The lighting there was also dim, and she struggled to recognize where she was. This wasn't the stairwell she usually took to that level and it had brought her into a different corridor than the one she'd been expecting.

The Third Basement was an immense underground labyrinth that stretched for blocks underneath the UN property, from 42nd Street all the way to 46th. Trying to orient herself, Anne guessed that the Loading Dock must be to her right. Clutching her books to her chest, she sprinted in that direction.

After continuing for some moments down the long hallway, she arrived abruptly at a dead-end. She'd reached the doors of the Publishing Section, where the daily mountain of UN documents were printed in-house.

Forcing herself to remain calm, she quickly retraced her steps until she was back at the door through which she'd entered. Yet the best way to proceed still wasn't clear. She could go down the hallway in the exact opposite direction from the one she'd just taken. But shortly ahead of where she stood, another corridor branched off to the right.

Time was getting short. Anne had to make the right choice between the two options. Her head pounded under the sense of pressure. She knew the Loading Dock was located at the very south of the complex. From a service road near the East River, trucks entered a long underground drive-through that ran the entire width of the UN premises. The trucks, travelling westward, would stop midpoint at the dock to load or unload. Then they would continue out to an exit tunnel at First Avenue and 42nd Street.

But from where Anne had entered the Third Basement, she simply couldn't envisage where the south end of the property was. She mentally pictured her descent down the service stairwell from the second floor and tried to count the number of times she'd changed direction as she hurried from landing to landing. It was no use. She was too flustered to figure it out. She'd have to guess.

Taking off at a run, Anne turned the corner and headed down the corridor to her right. She rushed straight on until the hallway turned left. She was about to follow it around when she heard jangling keys. She stopped short and stood completely still.

She heard a key fitting into a lock and then the sound of a door swinging open. Someone must be starting work in the Locksmith's Office. She'd noticed that it was across from the stairwell when she first entered the Third Basement. Anne chafed at the delay. She'd already lost time by going in the wrong direction. And now this. But there was nothing she could do except wait.

She allowed enough time for the locksmith to be well inside and then stepped silently around the corner. She walked cautiously down the long hallway. Since he'd already arrived, other workers might also be coming soon.

In a few moments, Anne came to a sign for the Loading Dock, with an arrow pointing in the direction she was heading. Finally, she was going the right way.

After hurrying a short distance, she reached the metal door to the dock. Approaching it, she brought her face to its small glass window and looked through.

Instantly she jumped back. The two movers, carrying their dollies, were striding toward the door and about to reach it.

Anne hurried back down the hallway and disappeared into the first small corridor she came to. Listening carefully, she heard the movers push through the door and walk in her direction. "Well, that's done," said one.

"Let's go to the cafeteria and get a coffee, a strong one, and then head over to the DC-1 building."

Anne waited, motionless, in the shadows as they passed by. She delayed a minute longer, until she gauged they must be far down the hallway. Then she left her hiding place and ran softly back to the Loading Dock door.

This time when Anne peered through the window, she saw no one. She tugged open the heavy door. To her right was a high stack of corrugated boxes that she could hide behind until she got her bearings. With a few short steps, she reached its shelter.

Hearing no voices or movement, Anne was about to come out from behind the boxes when a motor springing to life broke the silence. With a squeal of tires, a grey van shot into view on her right as it picked up speed in the direction of the First Avenue exit. Throwing off all caution, Anne leaped forward and ran to the edge of the dock. She had to see the license plate. She had to.

It was too late. The van was already so far away that she couldn't even make out if it had a New York plate. She saw the right turn signal blink in the distance and then the van disappeared into the exit tunnel.

She turned slowly away from the edge of the dock. After all the risks she'd taken, to get so close and then fail. Making no attempt to hide herself, she stumbled over to a stool and collapsed onto it in a daze.

Minutes passed.

Then with a jolt, she became aware of where she was. She had to leave the Loading Dock before she was discovered there. She jumped to her feet and let herself out through the metal door.

As Anne trudged back up the stairs, her first thought was to head to her office and start the workday as though nothing had happened. But exhaustion and shock were overtaking her body and mind. She realized she would be incapable of functioning that day. She'd go home and call in sick.

When she reached the door to the main floor, she brushed off her clothes and smoothed her hair as best she could. She crossed the black-and-white terrazzo with what she hoped was a steady stride. Thankfully, an unfamiliar guard was on duty at the staff entrance. With a shaking hand, she signed out in the logbook using a false name.

The sun was not yet fully up. The early morning air was bracing as she passed through the gate onto First Avenue. She again pulled her coat collar up around her neck and chin, but this time to conceal her face. She didn't want to be recognized by any staff heading toward the UN to start work. She didn't trust herself to be able to speak.

After a walk that seemed endless, Anne wearily put her key into the front door lock of her building. She lifted one heavy foot after the other up the four flights of stairs and entered her apartment.

Without taking off her shoes, she collapsed across the bed.

71

THE NEXT 24 HOURS

A feeling of discomfort awakened Anne. As she stirred on the bed, she became aware of the shoe still on one foot. With her other foot, she stabbed at it a few times until it dropped to the floor. She rolled over onto her side and despite the bright sunshine streaming into her apartment, fell again into a deep sleep.

The insistent ringing of the telephone brought her back to the surface. She hoped it would just stop. But after too many jarring rings, she rose on unsteady feet and made her way into the other room. After some fumbling, she picked up the receiver.

"Anne!" It was Juanita and she sounded agitated. "Aren't you coming to work? It's almost 11:00."

"Oh, Juanita, I'm so sorry," Anne mumbled apologetically. "I wasn't feeling well when I woke up, and I guess I fell back asleep."

"You do sound terrible. But you should have called. It's really busy this morning. And for some reason Benedetta isn't here, and she hasn't phoned either."

At the thought of Benedetta, Anne winced. It was an effort for her to muster an even tone. "I'm so sorry, Juanita," she said. "Really I am. But I can't make it today. Could you maybe get someone from the Director's office to fill in?"

"If you're not feeling well, of course you should stay home. And that's a good idea to call Mr. Ajiboye's office. I'll do that when I get off the phone with you. But will you be coming tomorrow?"

"Yes, I should be feeling better by then," Anne answered, trying to believe it herself.

"Okay, get some rest. We'll be fine here, don't worry. But call next time."

"I will," Anne said. "And I'm really sorry."

After she hung up, Anne stood, her eyes closed, swaying for a moment. Then she retraced her steps back to the bed and slipped under its covers.

In the late afternoon, pangs of hunger roused her. Peering out from swollen eyelids, she saw on the kitchen table some cold toast and congealed scrambled eggs left from breakfast the day before. Slowly she stood up and began walking to the table.

Partway there, Anne's grogginess lifted and she stopped abruptly. The wrenching image of Benedetta's corpse exploded into her awareness. A storm of grief hit her with overwhelming force. Her sobs came hard and fast, wracking her body. She stumbled backward and collapsed onto the sofa. There, with her arms encircling her body, she rocked back and forth while she wept.

At the UN the night before, she'd been so focused on what to do next that she hadn't completely felt the impact of Benedetta's murder. Now it stood clearly before her in its full horror. All the tears there had been no time to cry broke through, and she couldn't have stopped them even if she'd tried. It seemed impossible to Anne that someone as luminously beautiful as Benedetta could be gone from the world. It was senseless. And irrevocable.

At last Anne's tears were spent. She sat on the sofa, still holding herself. Her thoughts refused to line up in an orderly way. She was on new terrain, where life had become totally incomprehensible and there was no clear way forward.

Finally she realized that at very least, she needed to eat. She sat down at the table and mechanically chewed the lifeless toast and eggs.

Once the edge was off her hunger, Anne's head cleared a little, enough for her to realize she still had a pressing need for more rest. She returned to her bed and once more fell into a sound sleep.

72

A RELUCTANT RETURN

Anne awoke to a bird singing in the one tree that grew outside her back windows. A ray of light made a soft stripe across the blue-green carpet of her main room. She rolled over and checked the alarm clock. Seven thirty! She'd slept straight through to the next morning.

She'd told Juanita she would come to the office that day, but was it the right thing to do? Now she knew unmistakably that someone capable of murder had access to the UN Building.

Yet staying home seemed like a worse option. She knew that without the distraction of work, her thoughts would recycle endlessly around the gruesome discovery of Benedetta's body. And if she went to the office, she would avoid attracting attention to herself by being absent for too long. She remembered Patterson advising her over the past weeks that her safest course would be to go about her daily routine as though nothing were wrong.

She would marshal the strength to go. And on her way, she could drop off a message for him. She sat down immediately to write it.

Midway through the note, she paused. Early on, when Patterson was speculating about why the taxi struck her, he wondered out loud whether she might have been mistaken for someone else. Anne would never have considered herself as beautiful as Benedetta, yet they were somewhat similar. They were about the same height. They each had brown hair, and although hers was shorter, that might not be obvious to others. Was it possible that all along someone had wanted to kill Benedetta instead of her? But why?

Anne finished her message and folded it into a small square. After she washed and dressed, she felt stronger, and more certain she would be able to face the day. When she hit the street, the fresh morning air revived her even more.

After walking a few blocks, she entered a small deli and joined the line of waiting customers. When it was finally her turn, she asked the harried man behind the counter, "Could I please have a toasted sesame bagel?"

As he was handing her the wax paper bag, she pulled out a twenty. "I'm sorry," she said, "I don't have anything smaller." She added, "I know shopkeepers don't like to break a big bill for small purchases."

The man's hand stopped midair and his eyes flew to Anne's face. After studying her carefully, he gave an almost imperceptible nod. "Not a problem," he responded.

Anne lightly tapped the bottom of the twenty as she handed it to him. She was reassured to see him place the bill under the counter instead of in the cash register. Handing her the change, he repeated, "Not a problem."

Leaving the deli, she felt a wave of relief. When the morning rush eased, she trusted the counterman would retrieve the folded note under the bill and make sure it got to Patterson.

As Anne continued down First Avenue, she felt increasingly buoyed. Then all at once she saw the tall UN Building looming before her. She froze in place. How could she possibly enter it after what had happened there?

Her skin felt clammy and her feet would not go forward. People hurrying to work adjusted to the sudden obstacle in their path. Without breaking their pace, they flowed steadily around her on either side and then resumed their onward rush.

She felt a hand on her shoulder. "Anne, is everything okay?" It was Bertram. "You're very pale. Here, take my arm to steady yourself."

She reached out with gratitude for his extended arm. "I *am* feeling a little shaky," she admitted. "I haven't gotten enough sleep lately. But I think my head will clear between here and the office."

"Are you sure?" He looked doubtful. "Well, come on then, let's walk the rest of the way together."

As they approached the UN entrance, Anne was glad that Bertram's banal conversation helped hold at bay the images she didn't want to recall.

He supported her through the security checkpoint and then, once inside the building, they parted.

Anne felt agonized as soon as she stepped onto the escalator. It was the most direct route to her office on the second floor, but it would mean passing directly in front of the Security Council Chamber, the site of the murder. The escalator raised her upwards in small, steady jerks, ominously bringing her closer and closer to the Chamber. She started to tremble.

Steeling herself, Anne forced her eyes to look straight ahead. After she reached the top, she plunged through the glass doors as though she were bursting out of a suffocating subway car.

She hurried down the corridor to her office. When she entered, Juanita was already there, typing. Benedetta's chair was reproachful in its emptiness. It was all Anne could do not to start crying again.

"Hi, Juanita. Did you manage okay yesterday?" Anne hoped her voice sounded normal.

"Yes, it was fine. Mr. Ajiboye sent one of his secretaries down, and between the two of us, we got everything done, except the report I'm typing now. And two memos. Can you start on those?"

"Of course," Anne said, holding out her hand.

"But Benedetta never called yesterday, and she didn't answer when I phoned her apartment again this morning." Juanita's eyes were full of concern.

Anne hesitated before she responded, choosing her words carefully. "That's not like Benedetta. Did you try talking to any of her friends?"

"I think most of her friends are from the Italian community outside the UN," Juanita said. She nodded toward Jürgen's office. "He might know who they are, but I'd feel uncomfortable asking him now."

"And his door is closed," Anne remarked.

"He seemed very upset about something yesterday. And this morning when he arrived, he went straight into his office without even saying good morning." In a strained voice Juanita added, "It isn't like Benedetta not to check in. I'm worried that something's really wrong."

For once, Anne could speak truthfully. "Oh Juanita," she said. "I'm sure something terrible has happened."

73

IMPORTANT MESSAGE

It was afternoon, and Anne still hadn't heard from Patterson. Her shoulders sagged as she tried to concentrate on the report before her. Señor Duarte had asked her to check the information it contained about amending the pouch schedule. Her thoughts, however, were so scattered that she kept reading the first sentence over and over without any comprehension. She was desperate to talk to Patterson, to unburden herself of the horrific discovery of Benedetta's body.

Something brushed against her arm. She bolted in her seat and cried out. Duarte took a step backwards. "Good God, Anne. What's gotten into you? I only came to give you this insert for the report."

"I'm sorry, Señor Duarte." Anne tried to compose herself. "I didn't get much sleep last night and I'm feeling a little frazzled. Where does the insert go?"

He showed her and then returned to his office.

A little while later, the outer door swung open and someone quickly entered, startling Anne again. But the slim, olive-skinned young man who approached her desk was hardly frightening. With his smooth cheeks and guileless eyes, he appeared to be no more than a teenager. *I'm overreacting*, she chastised herself. *It's just a new messenger.*

The young man seemed in awe of Anne. Dropping his eyes, he said in a voice so soft that she could hardly hear his words, "A *Special* for the pretty lady."

As he spoke, he held out to her an ochre interoffice envelope. She signed the receipt and handed it to him. He smiled with appreciation, as though she'd given him a gift, and quietly left.

When Anne opened the envelope, she was surprised to see that it contained a batch of blue folders, the kind her office used every day to transmit the *Press Analysis* to the Secretary-General. Normally, those folders were given back to them whenever she or Benedetta delivered the *Analysis* to the 38th floor. Anne couldn't remember the folders ever coming back through the interoffice mail, and certainly not as a *Special*.

Puzzled, she carefully opened each folder. Finally, in one of them, she found a memo typed on UN letterhead. It was addressed to her from Walter Printemps, a name she'd never heard before. It read:

"An important meeting will be convened today at 4:00 p.m. on the fortieth floor for curatorial purposes. In this connection, your presence is respectfully requested. Others whose expertise is relevant will also be in attendance. Your prompt attention to this invitation will be most appreciated."

Anne was used to convoluted drafting by some UN staff, but this message was obscure even by United Nations standards. She checked her in-house phone directory and couldn't find any listing for a Walter Printemps.

She stared off into the distance, puzzling over what the memo might mean. Not a single idea came to her. Bringing her eyes back to the page, she noticed there was a "cc" at the bottom. The memo had been copied to "AVDW". Now she was even more confused.

Then she got it. Those were the initials of Adriaan van der Waals. Patterson was letting her know he'd received her message. In fact, it might be Patterson himself who would meet her on the 40th floor. A feeling of relief swept over her. It was already close to 4:00 p.m. Very soon she might be under his direct protection. He would know what to do next.

Anne sprang up from her chair so abruptly that Juanita looked up. "What is it?" she asked.

At first Anne wasn't sure what to say. Then she pointed to the hands on the wall clock, which showed 3:50. Patting her handbag, she replied, "I just realized I have to deposit a check before the Chemical Bank upstairs closes at 4:00." As an afterthought, she added, "I may be awhile. The lines are usually long right before they shut the doors."

"That'll be fine," Juanita said and returned to her typing.

After Anne got past the double glass doors, instead of heading up to the bank, she turned left into the waiting area for the high-rise elevators.

In front of the six doors, she saw a small group of ambassadors milling about. From covering Security Council meetings, she recognized the representatives of all five permanent members. She also spotted the ambassador of Israel standing somewhat apart, while the representatives of Egypt, Jordan, Lebanon and Syria conversed in a nearby cluster. If all of them were heading upstairs, Anne guessed that the Secretary-General must be convening a private discussion on the Middle East.

She swore under her breath. Protocol demanded that she wait to enter an elevator until all the diplomats had gone before her. Today that would be a long process. The Arabs would not step into the same elevator as the Israeli ambassador, which meant the "P5" would go in one car, the Arabs in a different one, and the Israeli in a third.

Finally, the doors closed on the last ambassador. When the next elevator arrived, Anne quickly stepped inside. As it rose higher and higher, her spirits began to lift with it. It wouldn't be long now.

When a soft ping announced she'd arrived at the 37th floor, she exited the elevator and turned the corner. Seeing no one in the hallway, she quietly opened the door to the somber stairwell and slipped inside.

These were the same three flights she climbed every week for ballet class, and she knew how to pace herself so as not to arrive at the top out of breath.

When Anne reached the last set of stairs, she shivered. The stairwell was cold and dank, and now that the day's classes were over, most of the lights had been turned off. The only bulb that was lit cast dark shadows against the dirty concrete walls.

As she was nearing the 40th floor landing, Anne made out the dim silhouette of a man facing away from her. Disappointment washed over her. It was not Patterson's reassuring bulky frame. This man had a slight build. It was Van der Waals. Coming closer, she noticed he was wearing the uniform of a security officer. She wondered why. She called out, "Adriaan?"

There was a pause, and then the slender man slowly turned around.

Anne's breath caught sharply in her throat and her legs began to buckle. It was not Van der Waals.

Under his pencil-thin mustache, the guard's mouth broadened into a twisted smile, revealing a chipped front tooth.

74

OUTNUMBERED

Anne opened her mouth to scream. No sound came out. There was time to get away if she whirled around and ran back down the stairs, but her legs wouldn't respond. Her feet were heavy weights, pinning her to the top step. Paralyzed, she stared at the man walking toward her. The twisted smile never left his face.

He reached her and roughly seized her arm. Over his shoulder, he called out, "*Señor, está aquí.*"

Anne heard the door of the dance studio open. The sound of one firm footstep, followed by another, echoed across the small space. In the dim light, she strained to discern the approaching form, but he stopped while still in the shadows and she couldn't make out his face.

Her thoughts spun in a wild panic. Sensing her desperation, the man beside her dug his fingers into her arm until she winced.

For more than a minute, no one moved.

At last, the man on the landing took a step forward, finally bringing his face into the light.

In a voice admitting defeat, Anne murmured, "Señor Gavrez."

"Yes, it is I, Miss Thomas. The Señor Gavrez who has reached the end of his patience."

Gavrez gestured to the guard. He jerked Anne up the last step and onto the landing.

Gavrez walked casually over to her until only a foot separated them. He was so close that she was forced to tip her head back to look up at him. The icy glare in his eyes was terrifying.

"You never knew your place," he reproached her. "Not in Cyprus, and not here. Have you any idea how insignificant you are? And do you not understand how important I am, and how important I'm going to be? I will be the next Secretary-General. The world needs me in that role."

Pulling himself up to his full height, Gavrez turned his head to the right, as though inviting her to admire his profile. Then facing her again, he said, "I should have dealt with you long before this. Like I dispensed with the Italian girl."

Anne's eyes widened in shock. "You killed Benedetta?"

"Of course I did. She gave me no choice. She made a mistake. A foolish mistake."

Anne tried to hold back the tears pooling in her eyes. "She was only 23."

"My dear," Gavrez explained, as though speaking to a small, ignorant child, "what does it matter how old she was? What matters is that she was in the way." His eyes hardened. "Just as you are now in the way."

"But how can that be? You yourself just said I'm insignificant."

"Insignificant, yes. But even insignificant people can cause trouble. The day I passed you near the amphora, I realized you were the one person who might be able to expose it as a fake. Surely even you understand I couldn't let that happen."

Anne's eyes dropped to the ground. She understood. She would not be leaving the 40th floor. Not alive, anyway.

Gavrez spoke calmly. "But still, I'm an honorable man. I'll make this easy for you."

He raised his hands and placed one on each of her shoulders. She cringed at his touch.

"All you have to do," he said coaxingly, "is walk outside onto the roof. I'll help you up onto the wall. From there, you simply let go. You won't feel pain until you hit the ground, and it will be over quickly. I'll take you there now."

Warily, she shook her head.

"It's the best course for you, Anne. I assure you that if you die at my hands, you'll suffer."

Keeping a hold on her shoulders, he took a step back. His eyes swept slowly and intently over her body. "There is one alternative," he mused. "If I were confident you wouldn't talk. If, in fact, I knew you wanted the best for me, wanted with all your heart to see me succeed…"

He searched her face for an answer to his unspoken question. His penetrating gaze unnerved her. Her eyes darted about in distress and she tried to draw away. He pulled her closer. With one hand, he lifted her chin and whispered, "Anne, do you want me to succeed?"

His changed tone threw Anne completely off guard. She felt whiplashed.

He became more insistent. "Anne, do you?"

Her hands flew to his chest and she shoved him with her full strength. "No!" she shouted.

Caught unaware, he stumbled backward. It looked as though he would fall to the ground, but at the last moment he recovered his balance. He stared at her with disbelief. Uncertainty clouded his face. For a moment, he looked almost vulnerable.

Breathing hard, Anne stood alert in front of him. Pushed to the extreme, something in her snapped and her fear gave way. Defiantly she told him, "I'm not intimidated by you anymore. You're not as powerful as you think you are."

Her taunt broke through his confusion. His eyes bored into hers. In one stride, he closed the gap between them and grabbed her. "You're a fool," he spat out. "You deserve what's going to happen to you."

Motioning with his head toward the door to the roof, he commanded the guard, "Open it."

The guard sprang to life. He hurried to the heavy metal door, unbolted it, and heaved it open.

A powerful blast of cold air off the East River rushed through the doorframe. Looking outside, Anne saw the cement roof and its surrounding wall of metal latticework. Involuntarily, she recoiled backward. As she did, she felt the shock of cold metal pressing between her shoulder blades. Someone was standing behind her.

She froze in place, panic-stricken, as the hopelessness of her situation sank in. She was outnumbered three-to-one.

Slowly she looked over her shoulder, expecting to see the guard's partner from that day near the Japanese Peace Bell. That's not who it was.

"Jürgen! What are you doing here?"

With his free hand, Jürgen took her arm in a firm grip, while his gun continued to press into her back. "I'm truly sorry, lovely Anne," he said in the courtly voice she knew so well.

"I don't get it. What's going on between Señor Gavrez and you communists, and why does it involve me?"

"It's personal, dear Anne. He," Jürgen nodded at Gavrez, "has been a friend ever since he learned I was facing, shall we say, financial unpleasantness, and kindly eased my way. And now it is Señor Gavrez who needs my help. You risk undermining his whole career. I can't allow that to happen."

Anne looked from one to the other and saw no leniency in either of their faces. In a barely audible voice, she said more to herself than to them, "Then this is the end."

75

CONFRONTATION

Gavrez and the guard began an animated conversation in Spanish. It was too fast for Anne to follow, but it gave her time to collect herself. Was there nothing she could do? Did she have the strength to break free from Jürgen and push him to the floor? If she caught him unaware, it might distract the others long enough for her to start down the stairs. But she would have to elude her pursuers for three flights until she got to the 37th floor, the first floor with an unlocked door leading back inside the building. She knew there was only the slightest chance of succeeding, but she had to try.

At that moment, Jürgen whispered close behind her, "I'm here to help. Trust me."

Anne felt that his gun was no longer pressing against her back. His other hand, still holding her arm, felt looser. Could she believe him?

She followed her instinct and rushed at Gavrez. Out of the corner of her eye, she saw Jürgen tackle the guard.

Gavrez wasn't expecting her sudden assault and once again he stumbled backward. At the same time, the guard whipped his gun from his holster. With surprising speed, he raised it high and struck Jürgen heavily on the side of his head. Jürgen staggered and started to collapse. As he was falling, he managed to lift his gun and fire it. The guard cried out. Clutching his abdomen, he toppled down the cold concrete stairs and lay moaning on the half-landing below. Then Jürgen passed out.

Distracted by the struggle between Jürgen and the guard, Anne lost the advantage her sudden lunge at Gavrez had given her. He regained his balance and leaped at her. Overcoming her resistance, he began dragging her to the open door. When he reached it, with a sudden surge of force, he threw her outside of the building. Her body skidded across the rough cement and slammed into the metal latticework.

Stunned by the impact, Anne lay immobile on the ground. Then she recovered. She quickly rolled over and braced herself against the lattice-work behind her. Just as Gavrez was approaching, she kicked out at his leg, knocking him to the ground.

She stumbled to her feet. The wind was whistling and blowing with force. She saw that the latticework was much higher than Gavrez's head, so she figured he wouldn't be able to heave her over it by himself. But there were other ways to kill her. She had to have a strategy.

She stopped too long to think. Gavrez sprang to his feet. He seized her around the chest and began dragging her along the walkway between the club building and the latticework. He must have spotted the gap several yards away, which was still covered only by flimsy construction netting. Clearly he intended to shove her off the side of the roof.

Her mind was racing. It came to her that her one chance would be to try to push him off the side instead. But for that, they'd both have to be in front of the opening. So while pretending to struggle, actually she allowed him to slowly bring her closer.

When at last they drew abreast of the gap, she concentrated all her strength and broke free of his grip.

With only a few feet between them, they stood facing each other, each measuring the other's resolve. His dark hair glittered in the stark sunlight and his eyes did not leave hers. Then he started to move.

A savage cry of self-preservation came unexpectedly from her throat. Anne lunged at him with full force and the two of them crashed to the ground.

At first each kept a lock grip on the other, but then Gavrez managed to flip his body over hers. From behind her, he braced himself against the building. Then with one foot, he shoved her toward the opening with all his might.

Anne's prone body tore across the concrete, painfully scraping her flesh. At the last moment, her arms and legs flung out. With both hands she managed to grab the metal strut on the left side of the gap. One of her feet slammed against the strut on the other side. Inches from the edge, her body came to a shuddering stop.

With a curse, Gavrez threw himself on top of her and started furiously beating her face with his open hand. Releasing her hold on the latticework, Anne grabbed Gavrez's hand and bit down hard. He cried out in pain and loosened his hold on her.

Pushing off with her free foot, Anne scrambled over Gavrez's body and made it to the side of the club building. He rose up and rushed at her. She braced herself against the building as he had done. When he got close enough, she shoved out her foot at him.

Gavrez wasn't expecting it. He hurtled backward and his legs crashed through the netting. Just in time, he managed to catch the strut on one side of the opening. There he hung, holding on with both hands, his legs dangling dangerously over the edge of the roof.

Anne heaved herself to her feet. The wind lashed her hair across her face. She stood partly bent over, panting, gathering the strength she knew she'd need to knock loose his hold and push him off the side of the building. She underestimated Gavrez. With a grunt, he pulled hard with both hands and hurled his whole body back onto the roof.

Rising to his feet, he charged at her with his own savage cry. At the last moment, Anne sidestepped his lunge. His right hand crashed into the wall of the building. There was a loud crack. His hand dangled limply from his wrist. He howled in pain.

The wind gusted more strongly, almost pushing them both back against the building. While Anne struggled for breath, his foot shot out, entangling her ankle, and brought her crashing to the ground. With his good hand, Gavrez grabbed her arm and began dragging her to the opening. The torn orange netting flapped ominously in the wind.

Once more the gap loomed before her. Panic-stricken, Anne grabbed Gavrez's wounded hand and yanked hard. He shouted in agony. Dropping his hold on her, he clutched his aching hand. She sprang to her feet.

They were now directly in front of the opening. They stood opposite each other once again, each one panting, each one looking for the other's weakness.

Out of the corner of her eye, Anne spotted a heavy metal pin holding the construction netting in place. With a quick move, she wrenched it out and held it high. Gavrez, who was starting to step closer, halted where he was.

"Stop right there!" Anne cried out. "If this hits your temple, it'll kill you." She looked directly at the throbbing vein on the side of his head and steadied her aim.

Gavrez briefly appeared uncertain. Then collecting himself, he said soothingly, "Anne, Anne, you don't have it in you to kill someone. And you know it'll only be worse for you if you try."

As he spoke, he began slowly inching forward.

Anne shouted, "I only have this one chance! I'm not going to miss!"

Gavrez stopped moving. He was clearly torn.

At that moment, the sound of hurried footsteps made them both look back at the open door. Patterson, disheveled and out-of-breath, ran out onto the roof. Taking in at a glance Anne's battered face and torn clothing, he swore.

The distraction gave Gavrez all the time he needed. He quickly stepped behind Anne. Flinging his injured arm across her waist, he pressed her body against his, while he grabbed her throat forcefully with his good hand. Turning both their bodies to face Patterson, he shouted, "Come any closer, my dumpy friend, and your girl goes over the side!"

Patterson froze in place.

Gavrez began slowly backing up to the opening, taking Anne with him. He tightened his grip on her throat. Gagging and choking, Anne desperately mustered one last bit of strength and jerked her right arm free. Swinging it across her chest and over her left shoulder, she struck his head with the metal pin as hard as she could. She missed his temple, but the blow was still enough to make him drop his arms and stagger toward the opening.

Anne raised her hand again, ready this time to hurl the pin. Gavrez recoiled and involuntarily took another step backward.

Instantly his bravado yielded to visible terror. For one agonizing moment, he teetered on the very edge of the opening. Then, his arms flailing wildly, he lost his footing. With a piercing cry, he plummeted over the side of the building.

There was a pause. Then, even forty floors above the ground, Anne and Patterson heard the sickening thud.

Anne slumped to the ground. Patterson ran over and dropped down beside her. He put her head against his shoulder and held her clumsily while she wept.

76

EXTINGUISHED

Anne and Patterson stayed on the ground. Cold air off the East River continued to blast through the metal latticework, but neither of them moved.

They remained huddled together on the cement for almost ten minutes. They would have stayed longer, but Jürgen appeared in the doorway. "We should go," he urged.

Patterson nodded. Gently he lifted Anne to her feet and half–carried her back into the building.

Jürgen, still weak from the blow to his head, moved awkwardly to shut the heavy door. The wind, pushing against it from the outside, fought back. Patterson propped Anne against the adjacent wall and went to help Jürgen. It took both men straining against the air pressure before the door finally settled into its frame with a loud grinding of metal against metal. Patterson clicked the bolt into place. After the fresh, stringent air out on the roof, the landing seemed all the more dark and dank.

Patterson turned back to Anne. He put his arm around her for support and then began leading her slowly forward.

Jürgen, ahead of them, reached the stairs first. But he had only gone down a few steps before he started to sway.

"Hold it, Jürgen," Patterson said.

He lowered Anne so she could sit on the edge of the landing, with her feet on the step below. Then he descended to Jürgen and put a hand on his shoulder. "Hey, it looks like you're having trouble. Do you think you got a concussion?"

Jürgen fumbled for words. "Pain… my head…"

Patterson took out a penlight and shined it in each of Jürgen's eyes. A look of worry came over Patterson's face. "Can you tell me what day it is?"

Jürgen seemed perplexed. "S… Saturday? Tues… day?"

Patterson's brow furrowed. "What's this?" he asked, holding the pen-light before Jürgen's eyes.

Jürgen stared at it and then said haltingly, "a… fork?"

"Damn it!" Turning toward Anne, Patterson said, "I have to leave you here for a few minutes. I've got to get Jürgen downstairs fast, and I can't help both of you at the same time. I think he has internal bleeding, and it'll get worse the longer he stays on his feet. Where can we get back into the building?"

The concern on Anne's face mirrored that on Patterson's. "Go to the 38th floor and stand under the large camera over the door. Wave your arms to get their attention and I'm sure they'll let you in." Looking at Jürgen, she added, "You'd better hurry. Don't worry about me. I'll be fine."

Patterson was already carefully guiding Jürgen down the steps, one at a time. He called over his shoulder to Anne, "I won't be long."

"Will schheeee be okay?" Jürgen asked, his speech now slurred. "All by…hershhelf?"

By then they'd reached the half-landing. With his foot, Patterson nudged the guard sprawled there. Blood had pooled beside his inert body. "This guy's not going to bother Anne, or anyone else," he reassured Jürgen.

Anne watched the two men slowly descend out of view, their voices gradually fading. Although she felt chilled sitting on the concrete, a profound peace was spreading over her. Gavrez, who had tormented her for so long, was gone.

She forced herself to breathe deeply to regain her strength. Gradually her limbs began to feel warmer and more connected to her body. She flexed her feet and stretched her legs. In a minute she should be able to get down the stairs unaided.

But not just yet.

Struggling against almost overwhelming fatigue, Anne looked around in the gloom. To stay awake, she tried to focus on the few objects in view. As she did, an odd movement caught her eye. Something wavered to her left, and then stopped. She scanned the dirty cement wall on that side. After a moment, she again saw something move, but only for a second. What was it?

She watched attentively. When the movement came again, she spotted it on the large stainless-steel fire extinguisher affixed to the wall. She stared at the extinguisher as though hypnotized, straining to decipher the strange blue object shimmering on its surface.

Below her, Anne heard voices. A metal door scraped open and then banged shut. She was sure that meant Security had let Patterson and Jürgen enter at the 38th floor. Reassured that they would quickly get help there, she turned her attention back to the extinguisher.

Finally, she realized what had caught her attention was a reflection of some sort. But the distortion from the rounded cylinder made it hard to tell what it was. Then it came into clearer view.

It was a man, in a security officer's uniform, creeping up behind her.

Anne's head spun around, just as the guard's partner emerged fully from the shadows. From the look on his face, it was clear he was enjoying her shock.

She was terrified. In her weakened state, she felt totally helpless to defend herself.

Before she could rise, with a few quick steps he closed the gap between them and reached down for her arm. Giving it a rough shake, he commanded, "On your feet."

Anne's legs were shaking so badly that she could hardly lift herself. Once fully upright, she couldn't stop her body from trembling, which seemed to amuse him. But as Anne continued to look at him, she saw the smirk ebb from his face, giving place to agitation. "Where is Señor Gavrez?" he demanded. "Where is he?"

Anne looked down at the floor and kept silent.

He jerked her arm so forcefully that her head snapped. In a subdued voice, she answered, "Señor Gavrez was out on the roof. He slipped."

"And?" The look on the man's face became fiery. "He is injured? He is…?"

Mustering a neutral tone, Anne said, "There was a gap in the wall. He fell over the side."

"You lie!" came a shout from below. Anne looked down the steps and was astonished to see the guard below sitting propped against the wall of the half-landing. Patterson had been too quick in thinking he was dead. A wild look came into his eyes. "He could not have slipped. You killed him!"

Anne measured her words carefully. "Patterson would not have killed him. He would have wanted to question him."

The two men stared at each other in disbelief. The loss of Gavrez was clearly devastating to them. The guard below murmured, "*Decidió todo para nosotros.*"

Anne whispered his words to herself. "He decided everything for us."

An agitated conversation in Spanish broke out between the two guards. At first she couldn't make out any words. Then she heard, "*Entonces la matamos.*"

"Oh God," she breathed out. They'd decided to kill her.

The man next to her drew out his gun and placed it directly against her temple. She flinched as the cold metal made contact with her skin. She could almost hear what the bullet would sound like, fired point-blank at her head.

Forcing herself to speak calmly, she said, "If you don't kill me, I'll ask the FBI to do everything they can to make sure you get light sentences."

The smirk returned to the guard's face. "If I kill you, there will be no sentences at all. The East German's mind is gone, and the other guy doesn't know who we are."

She answered back, "But you'll still need to get out of the building. Out of New York City, in fact." Pointing at the guard's injured partner, she added, "And he won't be able to get very far without help."

The man below spoke up. "She's right. We will need help getting out of the building."

"*We?*" The man beside Anne drew out the word. "*We?*" he repeated with disdain. Stepping to the edge of the landing, he stared down with a calculating look.

The wounded man's eyes widened in alarm. "No, no, do not think that. Please don't kill me," he pleaded. "Remember our mother. It would break her heart to lose her youngest son. I would not do it to you. If you have to go without me, then leave me here. I promise I won't talk."

Without a flicker of emotion, the older brother lifted his gun and methodically attached a silencer. Then with a steady arm, he took aim. He calmly pulled the trigger and sent a bullet into his brother's chest with a muted thud. The brother, a look of incomprehension on his face, toppled over onto the ground.

Anne gasped and turned away. At the sight of such cold barbarity, tears blurred her eyes so much that the outline of the extinguisher on the wall was hardly visible.

As though nothing had happened, the man resumed his conversation with her. "You speak the truth. I will need help to get out. I will need a hostage." Taking her arm in a tight grip, he gloated, "And I have one."

Anne didn't have to guess what would happen to her after he got out of the building and didn't need her anymore. Her eyes frantically searched the landing for something she could use to save herself. On the wall, she saw it.

Looking down the stairs, she said softly, "Your brother's still alive."

Startled, the guard let go of her arm. He edged forward and peered down at the half-landing. "It's not possible," he muttered. He dropped onto one step, and then the next, his head cocked to one side, examining the body below.

Anne had the opening she needed. She dashed to the wall and ripped the pin out of the extinguisher. As she seized the hose, the guard whirled around and shouted with rage. He bounded back up the stairs and rushed at her.

When his face was only two feet away, Anne resolutely pushed the lever. With a deafening blast, she sent a stream of chemical foam directly into his eyes.

77

BLIND FURY

The guard dropped to the ground, his face contorted in agony. "*¡Mis ojos!* I can't see!" Coughing and gagging, he frantically tried to clear the foam from his eyes.

Reeling from the loud blast of the extinguisher, Anne let go of the hose and put a hand to her heaving chest. During that long-ago drill, the fire safety officer had said the chemical foam would blind a person, but only temporarily. She knew she had to move. Immediately.

Anne spun around to run down the stairs. In her haste, she stepped on a patch of the slippery foam. Her legs flew out from under her and she fell with a crash onto the cement floor. She cried out, as pain from her ankle seared up her leg.

Hearing her voice, the guard instantly became alert. While he continued to blink his eyes to try to clear them, a determined look came over his face. He quietly rose onto his hands and knees and began stealthily crawling in her direction.

Anne sat slumped on the ground, stunned by the fall. After a moment, she reached to take her throbbing ankle in her hands. Even her own touch was excruciating.

She was so dazed that at first she didn't perceive the figure slowly approaching her. Steadily, he advanced on one leg and then the other, like a crocodile single-mindedly stalking its unaware prey.

All at once, Anne sensed movement in front of her and her head shot up. She shrank back in alarm. He was crawling very deliberately toward her. As he moved, he stretched one hand out ahead, tapping the air in front of him, feeling forward for her body. His unseeing face was taut with concentration.

Now only twelve feet separated them. As he came still closer, Anne tried to stand up, but her right leg gave way. The guard heard the sound of her crumpling back onto the floor and crawled ahead with greater certainty.

Her nerves near the breaking point, Anne put both palms down beside her hips. Trying not to make a sound, she lifted her hips slightly off the ground and carefully slid away from the guard's line of movement. But even so small an effort caused pain to rocket through her ankle. Despite herself, she moaned.

The guard, with a cunning look on his face, shifted his course to the left. Inexorably, he put one knee forward and then the other. Gripped by fear, Anne inched out of his path as quietly as she could.

The landing became eerily still.

The man paused, sensing she'd moved again. Then he corrected his course and continued crawling. She was barely able to slide out of his way in time. But she was getting ever closer to the back corner of the landing and soon would be trapped.

Desperate, she steeled herself for the pain, and then pushed backward with both legs. She managed to put a greater distance between the guard and her, buying a little time. But now her throat was starting to burn from the chemical fumes still hanging in the air. She fought the urge to cough, but the irritation in her throat was too great. In the small space of the landing, her cough, when it came, sounded like an explosion.

New keenness came into the guard's face and he moved toward Anne with assurance. Her breath came in sharp gasps, directing him straight to her. She was struggling to push herself out of his reach once again when her body slammed against the wall behind her.

In the same moment, the guard's arm shot out. With a triumphant shout, he clamped one hand around her leg. He'd grabbed the ankle that was injured, and Anne wailed in pain.

He launched his upper body toward Anne's, attempting to pin her to the ground. Urgently, she brought both her hands to his chest and pushed him with all her remaining strength. Caught off balance, he fell to one side. She quickly tugged on her leg and managed to drag it out from under his body.

The man righted himself and reached out for her, but she'd already struggled to her feet. In her terror, she was now oblivious to the pain in her leg. With determination, she started hobbling toward the stairs.

The guard rose onto his hands and knees and rapidly blinked his eyes. They seemed to be clearing.

He saw her.

In one movement, he leaped to his feet and rushed after her. He quickly caught up with her, seized her shoulder and spun her around.

As her body turned, Anne's arm brushed the extinguisher hose, dangling loose beside her. Frantic to try anything to save herself, she seized it and, raising her arm, encircled his neck and tugged hard.

The guard's hands flew to his neck. He tore at the hose, trying to loosen it, but Anne held tight. His face turned red and his eyes began to bulge. Desperately he thrashed about, straining to free himself. A gurgling sound came from his throat.

Suddenly other hands began prying Anne's fingers off the hose. She struggled fiercely to hold onto it, but couldn't maintain her grip. The hose relaxed around the guard's neck and he fell limply to the ground.

Anne slumped against the wall as Patterson dropped to his knees. Just before she fainted, she heard the snap of handcuffs.

78

RETREAT

An intense, acrid smell brought Anne to her senses. Prying open her eyes, she saw Patterson pull a small strip of moist paper away from her nostrils. "That's better," he muttered.

She was sitting on the ground, with her back against the wall. Patterson, bending over, put a hand under each of her armpits and cautiously lifted her a little higher up. "You took a while to come around," he said. "I was starting to worry. How're you feeling?"

She blinked a few times, as though bringing the world back into focus. Then she winced. "I did something to my ankle. It really hurts."

"Do you think you can put weight on it?"

She shook her head.

"Well, do you want to sit a little longer, or do you feel like moving?"

Anne looked around the gloomy landing and at the sullen guard handcuffed to the railing. She shivered. "I want to get out of this place."

"Let's go."

Patterson helped her stand up on her left leg and supported her as she slowly hopped to the edge of the landing. Looking behind them, Patterson said wryly, "I'm not even going to ask you what's with the foam."

Anne didn't have it in her to laugh, but she did smile.

He descended one step and held his hand out to her. "Steady now, just a little hop."

She looked doubtful for a moment, and then dropped carefully onto the step.

"Good enough," Patterson said. "Let's try the next one."

It was painstakingly slow, but finally they reached the 38th floor. "Don't even think of complaining," Patterson warned her. "That was much harder on me than it was on you."

This time, she laughed.

Without their having to knock, the heavy door swung open. The security officer stared with dismay at Anne's bruised and cut face.

Patterson said, "Let's carry her. She's at the end of her strength."

The officer asked, "Do you want her in the Secretary-General's waiting room, too?"

"Yes, that'll be best."

They locked hands together and Anne eased herself onto their joined arms. Gently they lifted her off the ground and started down the hallway.

As they approached the waiting room, the door opened and a wheelchair emerged. In it, Anne saw Jürgen slumped to one side, awake, but very pale. Pushing him was the Soviet doctor from the UN Medical Service who'd given Anne the chamomile teabags. "What's happening?" Anne asked her. "Is he going to be all right?"

The Soviet doctor gave Anne a severe look. "That's our concern, not yours," she snapped. Then after a pause, she added grudgingly, "But yes, he'll have no lasting deficit."

Turning to Patterson, Anne said softly, "But surely the UN Medical Service can't handle such a serious case."

He whispered back to her, "They're taking him to the Soviet medical facility in Riverdale. Better there than a New York hospital, where they'd ask questions. It was Andrei's idea, actually."

At the mention of Andrei's name, Anne became attentive. "What's Andrei got to do with this?"

"He's here," Patterson answered, "in the waiting room."

At that moment, the guard said to Patterson, "Why don't you go call a second doctor. I can take her the rest of the way."

Patterson nodded and they set Anne down onto her good foot. Then the officer took her fully in his arms and carried her into the waiting room. As he laid her down on the small sofa, Andrei, who was standing at the window, turned around. "*Bozhe moi*," he exclaimed, quickly walking over. "Patterson said you'd had a rough time, Anne, but I see it's much worse than I expected."

"I'll be okay," Anne said shyly. "But what are you doing here?"

By this time Patterson had entered the room. "After I asked the guard to call in a report to the Chief of Security, I found out that there are not one, but two bugs on the Chief's phone."

"Two?" Anne asked. Glancing around, she saw Rick and Stewart standing stiffly against the opposite wall.

"All three of them got here before the Chief," Patterson said.

Andrei continued to stare at Anne's battered face with concern in his eyes. Patterson caught his look. "She'll be fine, really," he said.

"I truly hope so," Andrei answered, still looking worried. To Anne, he said, "I wanted to see that you were okay before I left for Riverdale with Jürgen. But I should catch up with them now." As he was walking out, he gave her an encouraging smile. "You probably won't get back to work right away, but I'll see you when you return."

The security officer followed Andrei out into the hallway. Patterson approached Rick and Stewart. "Listen, since you're here, there's something you can do. There are two guards up in the north stairwell. One is in handcuffs. The other one's dead."

They nodded. Patterson continued, "I've asked Security to take care of the body lying on the back terrace. It's after hours, so hopefully no staff have seen it, but it should be moved fast." He added, "And let's make sure we all line up with whatever the UN concocts as the official story about this whole thing."

"Whose body is it?" Stewart asked.

"Gavrez."

Rick gave a low whistle. "Gavrez?"

Gesturing at Anne, Patterson replied, "It came all too close to its being her on the ground, instead of him."

Stewart looked contrite. "What can I say, Anne. I'm truly sorry. I was so focused on what the Soviets might be doing here against our government that I completely misunderstood what was going on."

She answered wearily, "It wasn't clear to any of us, until it was almost too late."

The two agents left the room. Once they were gone, Anne settled deeper into the sofa. Her eyelids flickered and then closed.

A moment later, one of the Secretary-General's secretaries noiselessly entered the room. She carried a small plastic bag of ice, which she placed over Anne's ankle. Then she dipped paper towels into the pitcher of water on a side table and gently sponged Anne's swollen face.

Patterson walked over to the window. Deep in thought, he stared out at the East River.

79

IN THE OPEN

Anne finished stirring the milk in her coffee and looked across the table. "It feels odd," she mused, "to meet you openly in public…"

"With neither of us in a disguise," Patterson said, finishing her sentence.

"Well, I *am* wearing some theatrical make-up," she said. "I still have a few last bruises to hide."

"All in all, you emerged in pretty good shape. Having that hard head of yours served you well up there."

She raised her hands. "Hold it right there. From you, that's close enough to being a compliment to make it unsettling. Totally out of character."

Patterson grinned.

Anne's gaze swept the small Greek coffee shop. They'd come between breakfast and lunch, so most of the tables were empty. And the young couple sitting closest to them were arguing so loudly that they weren't likely to hear anything but their own raised voices. Turning her attention back to Patterson, Anne asked, "So can I get the rest of my questions answered?"

"That depends. What are they?"

"Did you ever find out what was going on with Royce?"

"Yeah, we did. He was – and wasn't – working for the Soviets. Looks like they planted him in the US as a sleeper. He got himself hired as a police officer, but time was dragging on and the KGB still hadn't activated him. So when he was randomly sent to the hospital about your accident, he seems to have decided on his own to try to recruit you."

"Why would he do that?"

"Probably hoping to prove to his bosses he was ready for action. But after that backfired, he was hiding from them as well as from us. Until he showed up at your place."

"Don't remind me. I still have nightmares about that." Anne shuddered. After a moment, she said, "There's something else I've been wondering about. How did Gavrez know to use Van der Waal's initials in that memo to mislead me?"

"Your curator made a big mistake."

Seeing Anne's quizzical look, Patterson continued. "After Van der Waals identified the amphora as a fake, and a masterful one, he started making inquiries in Europe. Eventually a black market contact put him in touch with Gavrez, first indirectly and then directly."

"What did he want with Gavrez?"

"Van der Waals offered to use his connections in the art world to help Gavrez get higher prices for any other art he could steal. What he asked in return was for Gavrez to help him add more Cypriot artifacts to the Museum's collection."

"So that small bronze statue that got blown up at Port Authority was for him?"

"Yep."

"And I had such a high opinion of him." Her voice was full of disappointment. "Can I ask what will happen to him?"

"He can't get out of spending time in prison. Trafficking stolen art is a serious offense. But by special arrangement, he'll serve out his sentence quietly in the Netherlands."

Anne sighed. "He must be devastated to lose his job at the Met. He truly loved that Cypriot art collection."

"Really, Anne. His stupidity almost got you killed."

"I know," she said, shaking her head, "but I still can't help feeling sorry for him."

Anne slowly stirred her coffee, even though it no longer needed it. "I'm still having trouble sorting all this out. The whole time, I was trying to figure out why I was being dragged into what was going on between the Soviets and Americans. But all along, it was Gavrez. My life was in danger not because of the Cold War, but because of a piece of pottery."

"Let it go. It's over, and now you can get on with your life."

"You're right." After a long silence she added, "Anyway, I'm grateful it turned out to have nothing to do with Dr. Ruzhinsky. I was so worried about her."

Patterson nodded. "I'm glad we could clarify with our Soviet friends that her memoir is just for her family, and won't be published." He gave Anne a sharp look. "But you'll be more careful filling out any future applications?"

Flushing, Anne nodded. Then she said, "Not to change the subject, but how did you know to go up to the 40th floor?"

"For some reason, the message you left at the deli took a while to reach me. Once I finally got it, I called your office right away, but you didn't answer. Someone else did."

Anne shifted in her chair to avoid the glare of bright sunlight now pouring through the coffee shop's front window. "What did they say?"

"It was probably Juanita. She said you'd gone to the bank. But when I checked with our teller there…"

Anne looked startled. "You have someone working in the bank?"

Ignoring her, he resumed, "But when I checked with our teller, she said she hadn't seen you. That's when I started to worry. I wanted Rick or Stewart to look for you, but as luck would have it, neither of them was in the building. So I headed for the UN myself. But before leaving, I got one of our cleaning staff there…"

Anne interrupted again. "Those guys I remember. I had a run-in with them the night Rick and Stewart were going through my desk."

"Do you want to hear this story, or don't you?" Patterson asked with exasperation.

"Sorry."

"So I got one of our cleaning staff to go to your office. Fortunately, you'd left the damn memo on your desk. He read it to me as soon as I got to a pay phone across the street from the UN. That's when I rushed to the roof and…"

"...and found Gavrez gripping my neck, about to push me over the edge."

"Exactly." Patterson looked down ruefully at his rounded belly. "By the way, I don't think it was very nice of him to call me 'dumpy'."

Anne laughed out loud and it felt good. Then she asked, "Are you going to get a promotion because of your work on this case?"

"That's not what I requested," he replied. "I only begged them never again to assign me to work with an amateur."

Laughing, Anne dipped her fingers into her glass of water and flung the icy drops in his face.

"I deserved that," he said.

80

MUTUAL GOODBYES

With a barely visible limp, Anne walked the long, broad corridor from her office to the Delegates Lounge. Her feelings were mixed. In her hands was a wrapped package containing a leather briefcase she'd bought as a goodbye present for Andrei. She realized she would truly miss him. And who knew what kind of agent the Soviets would have watching her after he was gone.

Just as she reached the area where another corridor branched off toward the General Assembly, she saw a short, portly man rushing toward her. "Señorita Thomas, Señorita Thomas, please wait."

Anne stopped. As he got closer, she took note of his well-tailored suit and his distinguished white hair and mustache. His round face had a decent look, although at that moment it was tense with agitation. She had absolutely no idea who he was.

When the man reached her, he removed a pale silk handkerchief from his breast pocket and wiped his forehead before speaking. "Señorita Thomas, I am Carlos Moreno Marquez, Ambassador of Ecuador. I have heard what terrible things happened to you."

Anne looked disconcerted.

The ambassador continued, "No, no, it was in great confidence that I was told. But I had to know, because that scoundrel was from my country. He has brought such dishonor upon us. But Señorita Thomas, please, please believe me when I say that we other Ecuadorians are not like him. And I will do anything in my power to compensate you for the dreadful difficulties he caused you."

She was touched by his genuine concern and tried to reassure him. "Mr. Ambassador, I know he's not at all representative of your country or its people. In fact, I've had a wonderful association with Ecuador. When

I was writing a thesis on UN peacekeeping in Cyprus, Galo Plaza Lasso, the former mediator, generously shared with me his insights. I'll always be grateful to him."

At the mention of Plaza Lasso, a relieved smile illumined the ambassador's face. "Then, my dear," he said, taking Anne's hand warmly in both of his, "you have met the best of Ecuadorians. Please always recall him, instead of that abomination of a man who put you in such danger. I so deeply regret the day he used his family's influence to force his way into this organization, but I was unable to stop it. He was too well connected." He looked at Anne carefully. "So you are truly all right?"

"Truly I am."

Clearly relieved, Moreno Marquez said, "It would be my great pleasure if you would accept my invitation to have lunch with me and some members of my delegation at my official residence."

Anne smiled. "Mr. Ambassador, I would enjoy that very much."

"Splendid. I will have my secretary call you."

The two cordially shook hands and then continued on their separate ways.

As Anne rounded the corner into the Delegates Lounge, Andrei rose quickly from his chair. He had a cappuccino waiting at her place at the small table. He and Anne kissed cheeks three times, the Russian way.

"Here," she said, rather awkwardly, holding out the package. "A farewell gift."

After they sat down, Andrei unwrapped it and took out the briefcase. With irritation, he asked, "What is this, Anne? I know leather and this is a very expensive gift. Too expensive. I can't accept it."

"Please, I really want you to have it."

He looked unpersuaded. "Why?"

She smiled. "Of all the Soviets who've been assigned to monitor staff here, you've been by far the most pleasant and reasonable. And interesting. I know that when we talked, you had to probe for information, but I still always enjoyed our conversations."

Andrei was caught off guard. A moment passed before he said, "Okay, then I'll accept it. And I thank you sincerely. But now I wish I'd thought to bring a gift for you."

"It doesn't matter. And anyway, you're the one who's leaving and I'm the one who's staying." Sadness crept into her eyes and she couldn't meet his gaze.

"Anne," Andrei said. "After I left the Lounge that day, I realized I knew you well enough to trust you were telling me the truth about those photos. But after that, I couldn't have any more contact with you. Can you forgive me for not having believed you?"

"Of course I can," she replied. "I realized how misleading it looked." She was about to say more when she noticed two men walking toward them. "Look who's here," she laughed.

Andrei turned and saw Rick and Stewart approaching. He gestured to the two empty chairs at his and Anne's table.

As Rick sat down, he asked, "You don't mind the intrusion? A receptionist let us know you were here."

Andrei grinned. "I saw how she looked at me when I walked in. I've been expecting you."

Stewart sat back in his chair and sighed. "What a trio of fine agents we all turned out to be. This is your last day, right, Andrei? It's ours, too." Looking at Anne, he chided, "It's all your fault, you know. If you hadn't gotten mixed up with our art lover friend and his penchant for collecting, none of us would have looked so inept in our bosses' eyes."

Anne started to protest, and then realized he was teasing her. "I'm sad," she said, "that now all of you are going." After a pause, she asked hesitantly, "Could we talk a little about what happened, or is it off limits?"

Stewart scanned the nearby tables and then said, "I don't see the harm. The case is closed and each of us has been called back by our governments for incompetence. We might as well sort out the last pieces among ourselves."

Rick said, "For a long time, none of it made any sense to us. Finally we started to have suspicions that Gavrez was up to something. But if he were, we thought he must be working with you," he said, nodding to Andrei.

"We were starting to have doubts about him as well," Andrei responded, "only we assumed he was working with you. And your allies, because of the fake Dutch diplomat."

Rick, Stewart and Anne looked surprised. "Oh, come on," Andrei said. "We're all professionals. Of course we memorize the identifying features of most UN diplomats. So the day he showed up on this floor with the Netherlands delegation, we knew he was from the outside, checking on something. And we assumed it was information you wanted."

Anne looked around before telling Andrei in a low voice, "I don't know how much I should say, but he was brought in, as an expert in Cypriot antiquities, to see what might be odd about the amphora. And it turns out that the one there now is a fake."

Andrei smiled. "That's superfluous information, Anne. You must give us more credit than that."

She blushed.

At that moment Rick said, "Now our gathering is complete."

The others turned and saw Jürgen walking in their direction. Anne was relieved to see that good color had returned to his face, and his eyes looked alert and fully present. When he reached their table, he said, "Juanita told me you were here, Anne. May I join the conversation?"

Stewart stepped to an adjacent table and dragged over a fifth chair. As Jürgen settled into it, Anne blurted out, "Jürgen, I can't tell you how grateful I am for all you did for me."

He raised a hand dismissively.

"No, Jürgen. Literally, you saved my life." Sounding contrite, she added, "And from the beginning, I was always so curt and rude to you."

Jürgen responded, "No need to apologize, Anne. You read me correctly. You were right to be suspicious."

"Can I ask how you got involved with Gavrez?"

"I started to sense something was amiss when he kept summoning you to take dictation, especially when I saw how disturbed you were each time you returned. I knew you'd just come back from his office the day I saw you rushing for the escalator. You looked so upset that I decided to make contact with him."

"Without clearing it first, Jürgen," Andrei remarked. "Not a good idea."

Unperturbed, Jürgen continued, "Anyway, a little flattery, and a hint that I might defect if I had enough money, made Gavrez suggest that we work together. That suited me."

"Why was that?" Anne asked.

A dark cloud passed over Jürgen's face. "In the end, I also had a personal score to settle. That was when I learned he was responsible for Benedetta's murder. And I couldn't let the same thing happen to you." To Anne's questioning look, he responded, "How did I know about Benedetta? I had an audio set-up in the Security Council Chamber. If I seduced a Western girl, I planned to take her there so I could record any useful information she told me."

Then looking beseechingly at Anne, Jürgen said, "I want you to know that I didn't break off with Benedetta because she had no information to give me. I did it because I didn't want her to get hurt." Remorse filled his eyes. "But it had the exact opposite result. I'll carry that guilt with me for the rest of my life."

"I believe you," Anne said gently. "I truly do." After an awkward pause, she asked, "What will happen to you now?"

"I fly out tonight. I'm no use here anymore."

Everyone looked down at the table, lost in their own thoughts.

Suddenly Anne lifted her head. "Do you think the stolen art will ever be recovered?"

"You're mainly thinking of the amphora, aren't you," Rick replied. "I wish I could answer 'yes', but it's hard to say."

Looking at his watch, Andrei interrupted. "Sorry, it's time for me to go."

He rose to his feet and the others stood as well. By now, their habitual mistrust of each other had seeped back into the gathering, and they became more formal.

At the receptionists' area of the Lounge, they said their last goodbyes. Anne shook hands with Rick and Stewart, and then she and Jürgen exchanged kisses on both cheeks. When she and Andrei moved closer to give each other Russian kisses, he said to her quietly in his language, "I won't forget you, Anne. Against the odds, we did become friends."

Anne's throat locked and she could only nod. Then bringing a smile to her face that she didn't feel, she waved to the four men and started back down the long corridor to her office.

It felt as though many years had passed since she walked along the same corridor the day Gavrez spotted her looking at the amphora. As she drew closer to its display case, she realized there was no longer a need for her to stay away from it. Although it would make her sad to look at the fake, and to think that the real amphora might never be returned, she started slowly circling the case, just as she used to.

When she came halfway around, she stopped, transfixed. A reddish-brown patch of underlying clay showed through the amphora's ivory paint. It was faint, but unmistakable. The original amphora, which had come to mean so much to her, was back in its rightful place.

A broad smile lit up Anne's whole face. Looking back toward the Delegates Lounge, she saw four matching broad smiles.

Then wistfully, Anne watched as Rick, Stewart, Jürgen and Andrei, with a final wave, turned to go down the stairs and walk out of the United Nations building for the last time.

AUTHOR'S NOTES AND APOLOGIES

The author offers here notes about events which actually occurred, as well as a few apologies for instances where the truth was bent in the interests of telling a good story.

Page 5: The UN Peacekeeping Force in Cyprus (UNFICYP) was established in 1964 to stem violence between the Greek-Cypriot and Turkish-Cypriot populations spread throughout the island. The unfolding of the 1974 coup attempt occurred as narrated in the book.

Page 16: In 1973, West Germany and East Germany abandoned the idea that they would be able to join the UN as a unified country. Instead, they submitted separate applications and were individually admitted that year. Although prior to this some West Germans worked at the UN, it was only after the admission of the German Democratic Republic that East Germans became UN staff members. After reunification in 1990, both parts of Germany became a single UN Member State.

Page 38: During the UN's first decades, the staff cafeteria was on the fourth floor.

Page 39: This interpretation problem did occur, but in a different UN body than the Security Council.

Page 63: Cypriot police raided the home in Nicosia of an official with the UN High Commissioner for Refugees and removed "a large quantity of antiquities, including more than 30 Byzantine Church icons, scores of pieces of ancient pottery and Greek jars known as amphorae", according to the *New York Times*. However, the incident took place not in 1974, but in 1979.

Page 69: It's true that dynamite was left in the Meditation Room in 1974 and didn't explode.

Page 95: The Dufy painting is in the Secretary-General's conference room, but wasn't donated until 1979. The Cronbach sculpture is in the UN Public Lobby near the Chagall stained glass window. The Sèvres porcelain vase was donated by France, but to the Universal Postal Union rather than UN Headquarters.

Page 106: The Indonesian statues of *Peace* and *Prosperity* were donated not in 1974, but in 1954.

Page 109: At the time of this novel, the People's Republic of China was sometimes popularly referred to as "Red" China, to identify it as being under Communist leadership and to distinguish it from the Republic of China (Taiwan). The Republic of China was the original UN Member State until 1971, when the General Assembly voted to expel its representatives and that the People's Republic should thereafter represent China in the UN. During their early years at the UN, the representatives of the People's Republic did dress identically in "Mao suits" and tended to keep apart.

Page 141: The hillsides in the Chinese tapestry were an almost blinding neon green when it was donated in 1974, but have become muted through years of exposure to bright sunlight.

Page 151: This staff strike took place at UN Headquarters, but in a different year.

Page 159: The recessed floor inside the horseshoe table wasn't brought up to the main floor level until the Capital Master Plan renovation of the Chamber, completed in 2012. It's true, however, that the cavity was not filled in, but is merely covered by plywood so that the Council members, should they ever so decide, could authorize the restoration of this important architectural detail. In actuality, the cavity is less than two feet deep.

Page 171: In 1974 there were 144 UN Member States, in contrast to today's 193.

Page 173: Prior to its official name change to Mumbai in 1995, the city was known as Bombay.

Page 178: Because the actual *Anyanwu* statue is almost seven feet tall, the author had to shrink it to about four feet so that it would fit in a diplomatic pouch bag.

Page 181: The pilot circling the UN premises was an actual occurrence, but took place in 1979.

Page 194: The tragic killing of Professor Wolfgang Friedmann in 1972 is unfortunately a true story. Among his many books, *The Changing Structure of International Law* remains a classic.

Page 197: The change of the country's name from Dahomey to Benin occurred in 1975.

Page 200: While the Fuerzas Armadas Liberacion Nacional Puertoriquena (FALN) carried out several bombings in New York City, notably of Fraunces Tavern in 1974, the group never set off a bomb at Port Authority Bus Terminal.

Page 205: The East German statue was actually donated in 1975. The story of a swap circulated at the UN, but was never confirmed.

Page 216: Such photos and related articles were published over the years in various periodicals, but Waldheim's wartime record remained largely undisclosed until he ran, successfully, for President of Austria in 1986.

Page 227: With some editing, these are excerpts from actual statements made in Security Council meetings by Egyptian and Israeli ambassadors. For years the story circulated that one day they did actually come to blows in the Council Chamber, but if so, it was kept out of the verbatim records and the press. And it did happen once, during a Security Council meeting, that after an agitated diplomat accidentally knocked over his water pitcher, an interpreter then did the same, to give realism to his rendition of the statement.

Page 249: The DC-1 (UN Development Corporation) tower at 44th Street and First Avenue was in fact built in 1976.

To learn more about the UN art collection, see the author's article, "Purposes, Politicisation and Pitfalls of Diplomatic Gift-giving to the United Nations", *The Hague Journal of Diplomacy*, *16*(1), 110-119. doi: https://doi.org/10.1163/1871191X-BJA10065

9 798985 571905